Praise for *THE NANN*
MANAGI
by *(*

"*The Nanny's Handbook to Magic and Managing Difficult Dukes* is a whimsical, wonderfully romantic treasure trove of laugh-out-loud delights. Its spirited heroine, Emmeline Chase, proves a worthy successor indeed to Mary Poppins. I had such a fabulous time reading this book and can't wait for the next in the series!" –India Holton, *USA Today* bestselling author

"Amy Rose Bennet makes a graceful pirouette toward romantic fantasy and sticks the landing—*The Nanny's Handbook to Magic and Managing Difficult Dukes* was a delight from beginning to end! This *Mary Poppins*-inspired romance brims with wit and whimsy but never scrimps on emotional depth and sensuality. I loved Xavier and Emmeline and the whole cast of zany characters, and I can't wait until our next visit to the Parasol Academy!" –Susanna Craig, author of *The Lady Makes Her Mark*

"Ms. Bennett has crafted a clever and sensual page-turner that is magical from start to finish. Give me more!" –Minerva Spencer, award-winning author of *The Bellamy Sisters*

"A dizzyingly charming romance with a dash of mystery, a dollop of magic, and an enormous amount of heart. Whimsical, sexy, and utterly delightful—I loved this book!" –Alexandra Vasti, *USA Today* bestselling author of *Ne'er Duke Well*

"An enchanting, whimsical delight! Readers will be charmed by the winsome cast of characters, witty banter, and deep emotions that make *The Nanny's Handbook to Magic and Managing Difficult Dukes* a standout!" –Liana de la Rosa, *USA Today* bestselling author

The Nanny's Handbook to Magic and Managing Difficult Dukes

Amy Rose Bennett

KENSINGTON PUBLISHING CORP.

kensingtonbooks.com

Content warnings: kidnapping of a child, mild violence, characters with autism, mentions of infertility, sexual content, loss of a spouse, debt, incarceration.

KENSINGTON BOOKS are published by

Kensington Publishing Corp.
900 Third Avenue
New York, NY 10022

Copyright © 2025 by Amy Rose Bennett

All rights reserved. No part of this book may be reproduced in any form or by any means without the prior written consent of the Publisher, excepting brief quotes used in reviews.

Without limiting the author's and publisher's exclusive rights, any unauthorized use of this publication to train generative artificial intelligence (AI) technologies is expressly prohibited.

All Kensington titles, imprints, and distributed lines are available at special quantity discounts for bulk purchases for sales promotion, premiums, fundraising, educational, or institutional use.

This book is a work of fiction. Names, characters, businesses, organizations, places, events, and incidents either are the product of the author's imagination or are used fictitiously. Any resemblance to actual persons, living or dead, events, or locales is entirely coincidental.

To the extent that the image or images on the cover of this book depict a person or persons, such person or persons are merely models, and are not intended to portray any character or characters featured in the book.

Special book excerpts or customized printings can also be created to fit specific needs. For details, write or phone the office of the Kensington Sales Manager: Kensington Publishing Corp., 900 Third Avenue, New York, NY 10022. Attn. Sales Department. Phone: 1-800-221-2647.

KENSINGTON and the K with book logo Reg. US Pat. & TM Off.

ISBN: 978-1-4967-5442-4 (ebook)

ISBN: 978-1-4967-5441-7

First Kensington Trade Paperback Printing: October 2025

10 9 8 7 6 5 4 3 2 1

Printed in the United States of America

The authorized representative in the EU for product safety and compliance is eucomply OU, Parnu mnt 139b-14, Apt 123
Tallinn, Berlin 11317, hello@eucompliancepartner.com

To my darling husband and children, I love you all so very much.

I would slay dragons for you.

And to Taylor Swift . . . thank you for the gift of secret gardens.

The Parasol Nanny's Essential Tool Kit for the Healthful Raising and Protection of Children

Pockets

In times of need, the Parasol Nanny's pocket may supply a suitable object (magical or perfectly ordinary, but always practical) for a Nanny to use in the service of one's charges.

Parasols

A Nanny's parasol—or umbrella if the weather proves to be inclement—may be employed defensively during occasions of particular crisis. For example, when necessity compels one to disappear, or to discombobulate an assailant or kidnapper. (During a physical attack, a well-placed thwack, as per the Handbook's self-defense guidelines, may not go astray either.)

Spells

With the utmost discretion, certain pronouncements of a magical nature—Fae incantations—may be cast in the line of duty, especially when a charge's safety is at risk. Or, if one's Parasol Academy uniform is besmirched. A prim and proper appearance is paramount at all times.

Chapter 1

Concerning the Nanny's Plight; Spilled Tea, Dickens on Toast, Cucumber Sandwiches, and Jelly; A Teleportation Cock-Up of Magnificent Proportions; And an Unexpected Encounter with a Raven...

The Parasol Academy, Sloane Square, London
Spring 1851

At the age of five-and-twenty, Mrs. Emmeline Chase had come to the realization that, much like her unruly red hair—which seemed to do whatever it liked unless ruthlessly pinned into submission—she would never be *quite* the right amount of prim and proper to satisfy Polite Society. Indeed, even though Emmeline had just graduated from the Parasol Academy for Exceptional Nannies and Governesses, it was common knowledge within its ranks that she *sometimes* struggled to comply with the Academy's exacting standards of etiquette, despite her best efforts.

So when Emmeline spilled her half-finished cup of tea down her snow-white nanny's pinafore and, without thinking, exclaimed, "Blast and drat and dickens on toast," in the middle of the Academy's refectory, it really shouldn't have been a surprise to anyone. Nevertheless, there were more than a few censorious glares from teaching staff sent her way, along with a flurry of horrified gasps from fellow Academy graduates and the latest cohort of up-and-coming students. There was definitely a titter or two.

Her cheeks flaming, Emmeline blew out a frustrated sigh and blotted ineffectually at the unsightly brown splotch with a linen napkin.

"It's just because you're nervous," murmured her bookish, fiercely intelligent friend, Hermina "Mina" Davenport, who was seated beside her. "Everyone knows you're not your usual bright self. No one would blame you for spilling a bit of tea given the circumstances."

Of course, Mina's thick chestnut hair never misbehaved regardless of the circumstances, thought Emmeline. It was always as smooth and glossy as the polished surface of the elegant oak dining table at which they sat. A hurricane could hurtle through the Parasol Academy and Mina would still look completely unruffled. But Mina was so sweet and supportive, Emmeline couldn't begrudge how perfectly poised she was. Or how clever. She would always be grateful she had such a steadfast friend.

Emmeline drew a breath and offered Mina a smile. "I suppose you're right. Although, when it's time for me to leave, I fear my knees won't support me. They're already quivering like a barely set jelly."

In less than an hour she would be attending an interview for a nannying position—her first ever since she graduated from the Academy a fortnight ago. And Emmeline needed the job more than she needed a spotless pinafore, or hair that behaved, or knees that didn't knock together. Because if she *didn't* secure a permanent position with decent wages, she had no idea how she would be able to continue to pay off the turnkey at Newgate Prison where her father was currently incarcerated. This week's payment was already late . . .

Emmeline's situation might not have been so dire if her

ne'er-do-well late husband, Jeremy, hadn't frittered away everything they had, leaving her nothing. She also couldn't rely on her brother, Freddy, to come up with the money. After all, it was *his* fault that their father's antique clock store had fallen into bankruptcy in the first place.

The fact that Emmeline's father was in prison for unpaid debts was the only thing that Mina didn't know about Emmeline. No one at the Academy knew either. And Emmeline's secret had to remain exactly that. Secret. Because who would employ a nanny whose father was locked away in one of England's most notorious prisons?

"You didn't even touch your luncheon," said Mina, her clear hazel eyes soft with understanding.

Emmeline grimaced at the neat row of cucumber sandwiches on her porcelain plate. The Academy's cook obviously used a set square to cut each one into a perfect equilateral triangle. "I hate being so wasteful, but my stomach's full of rampaging butterflies at present."

Mina touched Emmeline's forearm. "You'll be fine. You're one of the bravest, smartest people I know, and I'm certain you will get this job."

Emmeline smiled back at her friend. "Thank you. I wish I had your confidence—"

"Mrs. Chase?"

Emmeline looked up to find the relatively new headmistress of the Parasol Academy, Mrs. Felicity Temple, standing right in front of their table.

Oh, double blast and drat and a bucketload of botheration as well. At least Emmeline remembered to swear in her head this time. Although, according to the *Parasol Academy Handbook*'s guidelines in Chapter 2, which pertained to nanny and governess etiquette, "botheration" and any of its variations were permitted, along with: oh my; oh dear; my goodness; good gracious; good heavens; heavens above; for mercy's sake; and on the odd occasion, by Jove, or by Jupiter. Unfortunately, "drat" was too close to "damn" so its use was discouraged.

Even though Mrs. Temple was only thirty years old (and styled herself "missus" because she was a headmistress, not because she was or had ever been married), there was an unmistakable air of authority about her. A marked steeliness in her bearing. In fact, up until six months ago, Mrs. Temple had been employed by none other than Her Majesty, Queen Victoria, in the Royal nursery, and everyone at the Academy was in complete awe of her.

Yet there was a soft gracefulness about Felicity Temple too. Her pale blond ringlets perfectly framed her heart-shaped face, and her petite frame was always immaculately attired in a haute couture gown. Indeed, there were occasional whispers in quiet corners of the Academy that Mrs. Temple might just be the *teeniest* bit vain given she always kept a rather ornate silver and crystal-encrusted hand mirror upon her office desk. Emmeline didn't believe such talk though. In her mind, the headmistress was the epitome of everything the Academy stood for: prim and proper and prepared for anything.

Right now, Emmeline feared she might have to prepare herself for a public drubbing of the verbal kind. She swallowed to moisten her dry mouth. "Yes, Mrs. Temple?" she ventured in a suitably polite tone. The refectory had grown as hushed as a church hall as there was a collective holding of breath.

"May I see you outside?" the headmistress asked quietly. But, to Emmeline's relief, there was no hard edge of disapproval in her voice, and the expression in her gray eyes was thoughtful, perhaps even compassionate. Perhaps she would simply express her disappointment and issue Emmeline with a stern reminder about the "rules."

Emmeline could but hope. She inclined her head in acquiescence. "Yes of course, Mrs. Temple."

As she put down her napkin, Mina gave her hand a reassuring squeeze and murmured, "Good luck."

Emmeline nodded her thanks as she pushed unsteadily to her feet. Truth to tell, she was grateful her knees *didn't* give out as she followed the headmistress into the deserted corridor outside the refectory.

When Mrs. Temple came to a halt by the door of the study hall, she gave Emmeline a smile. "I'm not going to reprimand you for using impolite language, if that's what you're concerned about, Mrs. Chase."

"Oh..." Emmeline pressed a hand to her stomach to help still the rioting butterflies within. "Thank you, Mrs. Temple. I assure you that I *do* know which particular exclamations are permitted as per the *Parasol Academy Handbook*."

"I know you do." Mrs. Temple gave her another reassuring smile. "Just like I know that you're nervous about your upcoming interview with Mr. Culpepper Esquire. I can practically see that you're quivering in your half boots. But you really shouldn't be so anxious. I'm confident that you'll do very well." Her smile widened. "As long as you remember *not* to say things like 'blast' and 'drat' and 'dickens on toast.' Especially in front of the Culpeppers' two young children."

"I promise I won't," said Emmeline. "And thank you for your understanding." She might not be perfect, but it seemed the Parasol Academy's headmistress didn't think she needed to be absolutely perfect all the time either.

"Now," said Mrs. Temple as she examined Emmeline's uniform, "let's see what we can do to remedy your attire so that you won't be late for your appointment." She withdrew a small feather duster from the pocket of her dove-gray silk skirts, then murmured, "*Unsmirchify,*" as she made a grand sweeping gesture down the front of Emmeline's pinafore.

A soft incandescent glow enveloped Emmeline's person for a brief moment, and a warm breeze, almost like a sigh, gently swirled around her, ruffling her clothes. When she looked down at herself, she could see that the tea stain had magically vanished; the white linen of her pinafore was spotless once more.

She smiled at the headmistress. "You're too kind, Mrs. Temple. Although"—she glanced toward the arched window at the end of the hall that revealed a bleak leaden sky—"I do hope my uniform can survive the trip to Bedford Square." She didn't have any spare coin to afford a hansom cab or even an omnibus fare at present, but she couldn't very well tell Mrs. Temple that.

"Of course, you have my permission to teleport to your interview," said Mrs. Temple. "It's official Academy business after all. There's a Metropolitan Police box at the northern end of Bedford Square you can make use of to conceal your arrival. Then it will be but a short walk to the Culpeppers' residence."

Emmeline nodded. Te-*ley*-porting, which harnessed the secret leyline magic of the Fae, was just one of the many magical tools a Parasol nanny or governess had at her disposal to discharge her professional duties. But one had to be discreet about it. Teleporting out in the open where members of the general public might see one mysteriously disappear or materialize as if from nowhere was frowned upon and one of the worst breaches of the Academy's rules. As per the guidelines in Chapter 1 of the *Parasol Academy Handbook*, strictly guarding the Academy's unconventional practices was of paramount importance, so cupboards and wardrobes and pantries and, on occasion, Metropolitan Police sentry boxes, were the preferred "vehicles."

Although, as Emmeline understood it, access to police boxes for the purpose of teleportation was a relatively new practice. The Academy had recently been granted a Royal Charter by Queen Victoria, so an "arrangement" with Scotland Yard had been established. Needless to say, Parasol nannies and governesses still had to be judicious with exercising such a privilege. Anyone who was careless with the Academy's secrets risked having their training cut short or even their Parasol nanny or governess accreditation revoked. Such an eventuality was something that Emmeline could ill afford.

Emmeline farewelled Mrs. Temple then hastened to the Academy's dormitory on the floor above. Once she'd donned her navy-blue cloak, her coal-scuttle bonnet, and had retrieved her Academy umbrella from the stand near the door, she was ready.

Well, as ready as I'll ever be, she thought. She checked her Academy-issued silver pocket watch, which kept perfect time, and noted she still had half an hour to make it to her interview. *If* she successfully teleported to Bedford Square without making a hash of it . . .

Tel-*ley*-porting was *always* a discombobulating experience. And when Emmeline lost her focus, that's when things tended to go spectacularly awry. That's when she ended up in places she wasn't supposed to be. That didn't happen often, thank goodness, but when it did (like that one time she'd ended up in the middle of the Thames and had to be rescued by the River Police), it proved to be all kinds of mortifying and inconvenient, to say the least.

But not today. She couldn't afford to lose her focus, today of all days.

Emmeline dug out her pewter leyport key from her pocket, then crossed the room with sure strides to the wardrobe she shared with Mina. Even though the door wasn't locked, she needed to use her key to open up the leyline portal. Without it, the wardrobe would be an ordinary closet, not a conduit for teleportation.

The wardrobe's interior was cloaked in deep shadow, but when Emmeline pushed all the clothing aside, a small but bright light glimmered at the very back like a beckoning candle flame at the end of a long dark tunnel. The key had sparked the leyline magic to life.

Emmeline inhaled a deep breath, bracing herself for the journey. The process was simple enough in theory. All she had to do was step inside the wardrobe and focus on the leylight while simultaneously picturing herself where she needed to be. She'd whisper the required Fae incantation to set the magic completely aflame and then she'd be on her way.

"Keep calm and nanny on," Emmeline murmured as she

hopped into the wardrobe, her eyes fastened on the flickering leylight flame. No sooner had she conjured up a mental image of Bedford Square and murmured, "*Vortexio*," when there was a sudden flare of blinding light. A familiar but also unsettling *whoosh* filled her head, and then a strange sensation of whirling weightlessness—like one was spinning around inside a Catherine wheel—engulfed her.

And then the movement and the rushing sound stopped, leaving Emmeline panting and slightly dizzy. Even though she'd closed her eyes at some point, she could sense that the intense white leylight had faded away.

Inhaling a bracing breath, she dared to crack open an eyelid... and when she discerned *exactly* where her derriere had landed, her stomach pitched and she uttered a string of curses a lot worse than *blast and drat and dickens on toast*.

She was not in a stone police box. She was not even in a wardrobe or cupboard.

She was on a roof. A roof!

Another wave of dizziness assailed Emmeline and she clutched at the rain-slick tiles beneath her gloved palms to stop herself accidentally plunging to a quick and untimely death.

Was she at least in Bedford Square?

There was only one way to find out. Emmeline forced herself to open her eyes and then she very carefully adjusted her seat so that she could peer down at the cherry-tree-lined square below. Belgrave Square according to the sign. *Not* Bedford Square.

Blooming hell with bells on. Had she said the wrong word in her head? Belgrave and Bedford both started with *B*. Had she conjured up the wrong mental image because Belgrave Square was close to the Parasol Academy in nearby Sloane Square? She must have.

What a monumental cock-up. What a complete henwit she'd been.

The mildly startled pigeon perched upon the row of chimney pots to Emmeline's right stared at her as if in complete agreement with everything she'd thought. A soft empathic coo was followed by a ruffling of its gray feathers, but then the bird took off, winging its way over the London rooftops to whatever its destination might be ... unlike Emmeline, who was well and truly stuck on a most precarious perch for a human—four stories up with no foreseeable way down.

Emmeline couldn't help but mutter, "Lucky blighter," as the pigeon became a mere speck against the cloud-shrouded sky. And then she fell to contemplating her options and her future, which hopefully wouldn't be short-lived.

One: Stay stuck on this roof forevermore. While Emmeline hadn't envisioned a future as a nanny weathervane, she reasoned that it was a slightly better fate than her next logical option...

Two: Fall and become a rather unfortunate splat on the cobblestone square far below. Emmeline shuddered. Although that particular outcome *would* be far from ideal, at least it would be over with quickly. But the drawback was that she'd never see her dear father, who rather depended on her, again. Or her brother for that matter. Or darling Mina. Becoming a "splat" wasn't a good choice in the big scheme of things.

Three: Call out and hope someone would be moved to rescue her. There did appear to be a Metropolitan Police box at the other end of the square, but Emmeline doubted her voice would carry that far. And the bobby might be anywhere.

What she needed was an impossibly long ladder. Even a long rope would do at a pinch. While Emmeline's training had equipped her with the ability to scale a tree or a wall should she need to rescue a trapped charge, or even a charge's far-too-curious cat, she'd still need a rope and possibly a grappling hook to lower herself to safety.

In certain circumstances, Emmeline could simply reach into

her uniform's magical "nanny pocket" to procure whatever she needed to manage a difficult situation. But as per Chapter 4, Section 2 of the *Parasol Academy Handbook*, she could only produce "necessary items" from said pocket, "while in service to a child in her care, or in certain situations, a child in need." Getting oneself stuck on a rooftop because you were distracted and failed to discreetly teleport from one location to another did not signify.

Emmeline blew out a heavy sigh and frowned at the toes of her kid half boots. Her fourth consideration was probably the most important of all. If she did survive this massive teleportation blunder, she hoped to God that Mrs. Temple didn't hear about it. She'd already been in enough trouble for one day.

"Remember, you're a Parasol Academy nanny, Emmeline Chase. You're prim, proper, and prepared for anything. Exactly like Mrs. Temple," she sternly reminded herself as she somehow shoved down her nerves, much like one would shove down a mouthful of castor oil. Her nerves had gotten her into this mess to begin with, so she had no time for them at the moment. "You will work out how to get down from here without breaking your neck. You will not sully your reputation or the Academy's by drawing undue attention to yourself. And you *will* secure that nannying job. Failure is *not* an option."

Emmeline examined the impressive townhouse she was presently seated upon. It was entirely on its own at one corner of the square. Craning her neck to look behind her, she spied two whitewashed wings that jutted off the main edifice. Each wing had numerous casement windows. Perhaps she could attract the attention of one of the townhouse's occupants. Well, if they looked outside.

Taking a deep breath and tightening her grip on the slate tiles, Emmeline carefully swung one of her legs over to the other side of the steeply sloped roof, then proceeded to inch herself along the ridgeline toward the row of chimney pots and the nearest wing. She supposed she could always lob her umbrella at one of the windows. She was a good shot, and surely that would arouse someone's notice.

There! A movement—a dark sort of fluttering—in one of the windows on the second floor caught Emmeline's attention. Someone was watching her, she was sure of it.

Emmeline made herself let go with one hand then waved madly. "Hulloooo," she called. "I say, hullooo!"

What the deuce? What on earth are you doing up there? sounded a voice in her head. An avian voice with a distinct rasp that reminded Emmeline of a distinguished gentleman who was fond of pipe-smoking. The sort of man who'd don a velvet banyan and prop his leather-slipper-clad feet upon a footstool with a brandy at his elbow and the latest copy of the *Times* spread out before him.

Emmeline dared to lean forward a little more as she squinted at the windowpane in question. *It's all rather complicated*, she replied to her all-but-invisible conversational partner. She suspected that he *was* a bird of some kind. Aside from dogs and horses, birds were the easiest animals for Parasol Academy graduates to communicate with by thought alone. Cats, on the other hand, were altogether too aloof and not likely to respond at all.

As you can see, I'm in a bit of a pickle, Emmeline continued in what she hoped was a friendly manner, not a panicky, Oh-Lord-I'm-going-to-die fashion. *Is there anyone inside the house that might be able to help me? If someone could summon a chimney sweep, I could climb down his ladder . . .*

I see . . . I suppose I could do that . . . As long as you're not up to anything nefarious . . . Suddenly the casement window swung open, and a rather magnificent raven appeared on the window ledge. Cocking his head, his dark inquisitive gaze met Emmeline's. *I hope you'll excuse my impertinence, but what is your name? It's not often that I come across someone like you. An an-*

imalis sussurator *or animal whisperer, so to speak. You are a rarity, indeed.*

Animal whisperer... Emmeline liked the sound of that. Not all Parasol Academy graduates could telepathically communicate with animals. The ability seemed to be a side effect of using Fae magic and you either developed it as a skill—like learning to play the pianoforte or speak another language—or you didn't. And like any other skill, once you had attained it, you possessed the ability for life. At least that's what Emmeline had learned during her Parasol Academy training.

Casting a smile at the raven—it wouldn't do to appear rude—she responded to his question. *My name is Mrs. Emmeline Chase and I'm...* She drew a fortifying breath. *I'm a nanny with certain singular talents.* She didn't think it would be wise to elaborate further on that score—disclosing she had magical abilities would certainly ruffle feathers in more ways than one—so instead she asked, *And to whom am I speaking?*

The raven puffed out his chest and his glossy black feathers gleamed like polished ebony. *Horatio Ravenscar, Esquire. At your service, madam. I shall summon my master. I shan't be long.* And then, with an elegant flap of his enormous wings, he disappeared.

Emmeline released a shaky sigh of relief. Things were looking up after all. Well, as long as Horatio Ravenscar's master wasn't an arrogant, snobbish pain-in-the-derriere who refused to help her. She didn't like playing the role of damsel-in-distress. And she really should curb her unruly tongue, even in her head. She was in Belgravia. Not Cheapside, where her father's store had been. Or Shoreditch, where Freddy's struggling music hall, the Oberon, was located.

But then, Horatio's master wasn't going to employ her. Mr. Culpepper of Barclays Bank would. All going well. If only she could get down from this infernal roof.

Chapter 2

In Which a Raven Turns into a Pirate; A Horological Design Is Ruined; A Sooty Smudge Ruffles Feathers; A Tin Solider Is Recovered; And the Duke Meets Archimedes...

"Nanny ahoy! Nanny ahoy!"

Xavier Mason, the seventh Duke of St Lawrence, jumped so violently in his seat that his fountain pen skittered over the intricate horological design he was working on, leaving an unsightly zigzagging line that bisected the middle of the page.

Damn.

Looking up from his ruined work, he frowned at his pet raven, who'd soared into his private study in a great flurry of midnight-black feathers. As Horatio landed on a pile of books at the end of Xavier's desk, the resultant breeze set a number of other pages flying, and Xavier emitted a disgruntled sigh.

Would he never get any peace and quiet? At this rate, his design for a veritable "King of Clocks"—a spectacular and incredibly accurate clock mechanism that would grace the top of St Stephen's Tower in the newly rebuilt Palace of Westminster—wouldn't be finished until the end of the century. Which meant he'd miss the deadline for submissions to the Astronomer Royal on the first of June, an eventuality altogether too frustrating for words. The horological competition to win the commission was fierce and as the clock was ticking—both literally and figuratively—he couldn't afford any more delays.

Xavier released a heavy sigh as he placed his fountain pen in its silver stand. "Nanny ahoy?" he repeated. "What on earth do you mean, Horatio? Is something amiss with Nanny Snodgrass?" *Again.*

The woman had only been working for Xavier for a fortnight—employed to care for his three young wards, Harry, Barry, and Gary, after the last nanny up and left in the middle of the night—and chaos *still* continued to reign in the nursery.

And elsewhere in St Lawrence House, if truth be told.

A headache began to beat at the back of Xavier's skull as he contemplated what might have gone wrong *this* time.

The raven bobbed up and down. "Nanny ahoy," he croaked again, then fluttered over to the window ledge behind Xavier. "At two o'clock. In the crow's nest." Horatio pecked at the glass pane with his glossy black beak. "All hands on deck. Fetch Jacob's ladder. Raise the mizzenmast. Sound the ship's bell."

"Nanny ahoy at two o'clock? In the crow's nest? Have you gone mad?" Xavier pushed out of his seat and then crossed to the window. "And why are you talking like a dashed pirate?"

Xavier peered out of the casement window in the direction Horatio had indicated. And then his mouth fell open. "Good God," he muttered as a great tide of incredulity flooded his brain. "There's a woman on my roof."

A petite copper-haired woman in a smart, dark blue gown and matching cloak and bonnet with an umbrella tucked beneath her arm, to be precise. Xavier pushed open the window. "I say, what in God's name are you doing up there?" he called out. "Are you all right?"

The woman lifted a gloved hand and waved. "I'm er . . . Well, good sir, to be perfectly frank, I'm more than a little embarrassed as well as more than a little stuck," she called back.

"And while I'm dreadfully sorry to be creating such a fuss and most likely putting you out . . . if you wouldn't mind . . . if you would be so kind, would you be able to fetch a chimney sweep? I'm going to need a ladder to climb down from here. Perhaps onto one of your balconies? Because I'd rather *not* fall and become an ignominious blob of strawberry jam on the pavement. Between you and me, that would be far too awkward for words."

Xavier scrubbed his own gloved hand through his hair. *An ignominious blob of strawberry jam?* Who said things like that? If he weren't so flabbergasted, he would have laughed. But then, what sort of person got themselves stuck on top of a four-story townhouse? Unless he'd fallen asleep at his desk and this was all a bizarre sort of dream? He *had* been having trouble sleeping lately.

Horatio gave Xavier a sharp little peck to the arm as though to remind him that he wasn't, in fact, asleep, and that he needed to do more than gape like a complete and utter berk. "All right," Xavier muttered at the raven. "There's no need to get tetchy with me. I'll help her."

He placed his gloved hands on the window ledge and leaned farther out. Damn it, it looked like rain, too. Xavier hated the rain. On a scale of duck to cat, he was firmly at the feline end. Nevertheless, he said, "We won't need to summon a chimney sweep. Behind that row of chimney pots at your back is a small rooftop terrace and a trapdoor leading down into the attic. If I help, do you think you'd be able to climb over to the other side, miss?"

She glanced over her shoulder then gave Xavier a decided nod. "Most definitely. And it's missus, by the way. Not miss. Mrs. Emmeline Chase."

Xavier inclined his head. "Mrs. Chase. How do you do? I'm the Duke of St Lawrence. I shall meet you up on the roof in a tick. Don't move until I get there."

"I promise I won't!" she called back.

If the woman fell... Xavier pushed down a rising tide of panic on Mrs. Chase's behalf. While he wasn't afraid of heights himself, not everyone was like him. Although, he suspected that Mrs. Chase wasn't quite like anyone else, either. He still had no idea how she'd come to arrive on his roof, but he supposed he would find out in due course.

In a handful of strides, he was across the room and scaling the stairs to the upper floors and the attic of St Lawrence House.

The door to the attic creaked open, revealing a crowded space that was dimly lit. It had been years since Xavier had been up here, and he hovered on the threshold for a moment. A cold gray light filtered through a small, high-set gable window illuminating trunks and crates and discarded furniture shrouded in holland cloths. In one dark corner stood a silently brooding walnut longcase clock with a cracked face. A clock that had once belonged to Xavier's father.

Unpleasant memories Xavier would rather not contemplate gathered like cobwebs at the corners of his mind, but he steadfastly pushed them away as he crossed the dusty wooden floor to the ladder that led up to the small trapdoor and thence, the roof. He was on a rescue mission and time was of the essence. He didn't have time to dwell on the past.

To his relief, when Xavier peered around the low brick wall crowned by a row of chimney pots, Mrs. Chase was still upon the roof, sitting astride the tiled ridge like she was riding a damned horse. Indeed, the woman's skirts were slightly rucked up and her neat black leather half boots, a sliver of fine white stocking, and the lacy hem of a pair of drawers were clearly visible.

Egad. Xavier swallowed and his cheeks heated as he momentarily averted his gaze. The poor woman was in a most precarious position. He should *not* be gawking at her like a green schoolboy who'd never glimpsed a woman's ankle before. Or even worse, a leering, lecherous old roué.

He certainly didn't want to be living up to the horrid moniker he'd been dubbed at Eton: Lord Weirdbrook instead of Lord Westbrook, the courtesy title bestowed upon him at birth.

Xavier could almost hear those long-ago taunts. *Look, Weirdbrook is staring again. Or maybe we should call him Mad Mason* . . . Xavier closed his eyes and reminded himself he was a thirty-year-old man now. And a duke. While he still had trouble gauging if he was looking too much or too little at someone, ogling women was not the sort of thing he did.

Especially a woman stranded on his roof. That was entirely inappropriate.

"I'm here, Mrs. Chase," he called out. "If you can carefully inch yourself toward me, I'll be able to reach out and hold you steady when you stand. Then I'll help you to climb around this wall of chimney pots to my side of the roof."

"I can manage that," she called back. She shuttled herself along and when she was close enough that Xavier could grasp her arm, she deftly climbed to her feet, using one of the chimney pots as a support. A moment later, she was beside him on the rooftop terrace, safe and sound. She'd been so swift and sure in her movements, so completely fearless, Xavier hadn't even had time to be afraid for her. Her physical dexterity was, in a word, remarkable.

Who *was* she? *What* was she?

Horatio had mentioned something about her being a nanny, but perhaps he'd simply adopted "nanny" as a new word to denote anyone of the opposite sex.

"Thank you, Your Grace," Mrs.-Chase-who-might-be-a-nanny said, drawing Xavier's attention away from his musings.

"That's quite all right . . ." As their gazes connected, Xavier's voice trailed off and a wash of bright color flooded Mrs. Chase's face.

Xavier was suddenly transfixed. Time almost seemed to stop, at least for him. Was that soot on the young woman's cheek?

His fingers twitched inside his silk-lined gloves. He had the odd urge to wipe the dark smudge away, but he clenched his fists and stopped himself. He might hate mess and disorder, he might loathe it when his clothes got wet or grubby or his fingers sticky, but others didn't mind sensations of that nature so much. It certainly wasn't his place to touch the woman's face in so intimate a fashion.

Then Xavier wondered why Mrs. Chase *had* blushed. Was she experiencing a degree of discomfiture because he was staring at her? Discerning what someone else was thinking was often a challenge for him. Perhaps she *was* ill at ease beneath his focused scrutiny. But for the life of him, he couldn't seem to look away.

Up this close, he realized Mrs. Chase had eyes the color of a midsummer sky and her copper-red curls were as bright as the glowing center of a candle flame. Aside from the sooty smudge, there was a fascinating dusting of freckles across her nose and cheeks. Xavier had to force himself not to count each tiny spot but instead, pay attention to what she'd begun to say.

"I've never met a duke before," she said, her voice as soft and melodious as a nightingale's. "But I do hope you can forgive me for not curtsying. I find that my legs are a trifle shaky, Your Grace."

"I..." Xavier met her gaze directly again. "Given the circumstances, of course I don't mind. Besides, I'm not the usual sort of duke."

"So you're an unusual duke?" Beneath the brim of her dark blue bonnet, Mrs. Chase arched a fine brow, and Xavier wondered if the glint in her eyes was one of mischief.

His mouth twitched with amusement. "Some certainly think so. I hope you won't consider me rude, but I suspect that you're rather unusual, too, Mrs. Chase. You never answered my earlier question about how you got stuck up here."

Mrs. Chase winced. The expression crossing her features

might have been one of embarrassment. "It's rather difficult to explain, I'm afraid. Let's just say . . ." She drew a quick breath. "Let's pretend a force of nature like the wind blew me up here. Or something like that. Would that suffice?"

"I see." Xavier crossed his arms over his chest. That was likely a tall tale, but now didn't seem like quite the right time to challenge the young woman.

If truth be told, he suddenly found himself tongue-tied, exactly like the awkward youth he used to be. Before he could think of something else to say—unless the topic was horology or politics or mathematics, he often struggled for the right words—a blustery gust of wind tore at Mrs. Chase's bonnet and skirts and at Xavier's shirtsleeves.

His *shirtsleeves*. Good Lord, he was only in his shirtsleeves, a black silk waistcoat, charcoal-gray trousers, and patent-leather shoes. He wasn't wearing a coat at all. Nor his usual black cravat. He'd forgotten entirely that he was underdressed when he'd charged out of his private study up to the roof like a knight-errant of old.

He opened his mouth to apologize, but then a squall of cold stinging rain hit, stealing his breath. But it also had the effect of stirring him to action.

"This way, Mrs. Chase!" Xavier caught the woman's gloved hand and they dashed toward the trapdoor leading down to the attic. Even though it probably went against the usual dictates of gentlemanly etiquette, he descended first just in case he needed to assist the young woman. He'd already witnessed that she was quite nimble on her feet, but nevertheless, if she tripped, he reasoned he could catch her.

He'd reached the floor, and Mrs. Chase was two-thirds of the way down the ladder when she did indeed miss her footing. He wasn't quite sure how it happened—whether the heel of her boot caught in her voluminous skirts, or her foot slipped on the rung because her legs were still "a trifle shaky," he couldn't have said—but all of a sudden she emitted a small cry, her umbrella that had been tucked beneath her arm went flying, and she tumbled backward, straight into Xavier's arms. Even though she was slight, the force of her fall caused Xavier to lose his balance, too, and they both went down, rolling sideways, tumbling over and over each other until they landed in an awkward jumble of limbs and navy-blue skirts upon the dusty floorboards. Xavier cracked his elbow on something—a nearby trunk perhaps—and only just bit back an ungentlemanly curse.

"Oh my God. I'm so sorry." Mrs. Chase was astride him, staring straight into his eyes, her pretty face only inches from his own. Like him, she was slightly breathless, her chest rising and falling in time with his.

"I . . . No harm done," Xavier lied. His elbow throbbed like the very dickens. "Are *you* all right?"

"I-I think so. Thank you for saving me. Again." She scrambled off him, then to Xavier's surprise, offered him a helping hand. "I'm most grateful."

Xavier placed his gloved hand in hers and then he climbed to his feet. "Think nothing of it, Mrs. Chase," he said, as he slammed the trapdoor shut to stop the rain pouring in. But he hadn't been quick enough to escape a decent dousing. As he ran a hand through his dripping disheveled hair, an involuntary shiver ran through his body. His clothes were uncomfortably damp—his shirtsleeves annoyingly so—and he had to tamp down the urge to peel everything off.

Instead, he satisfied himself with tugging down his waistcoat and adjusting his cuffs. He knew he often came across as quite exacting and distant, but for some reason he couldn't fathom, he didn't want to seem that way in front of Mrs. Chase. Was it customary to invite a woman who'd been stuck on your roof to take tea with you? He hardly knew.

While he'd been fussing with his attire and ruminating on the rules of etiquette, Mrs. Chase had retrieved her umbrella.

When she spoke, she put him out of his misery. "Righto, I've probably taken up too much of your time already, Your Grace. I'd best be on my way. I have an interview to get to." She pulled a small silver watch from a pocket in her skirt then winced. "Goodness, I fear I shall be very late."

Xavier escorted Mrs. Chase through the attic to the door. "An interview?"

"Yes, for a nannying position," she said as she carefully descended the stairs to the third floor. "I'm a nanny."

Ah, Horatio had been right, thought Xavier as they followed the gaslit hall, heading for the main staircase. But how had his raven known? More to the point, if Mrs. Chase was on her way to an interview, the fact that she'd been on his roof made even less sense. Her far-fetched explanation—that the wind had somehow magically deposited her there—was woefully inadequate, and Xavier liked to *know* how things worked. All the minutiae, all the tiny intricacies of what made something "tick" fascinated him. It's why he loved the science of horology so much. Mysteries—anything unexplained or loose threads of any kind—bothered him more than he could say.

Just like the mystery of why things kept going wrong in his household of late.

Xavier's wards created a great deal of the daily hullabaloo in St Lawrence House. They'd only arrived a month ago, but they had certainly made their presence felt. Like the time a firecracker had "mysteriously" ended up in the nursery stove. That was the incident that had sent the first nanny—a Miss Butterworth—packing. While no one had been hurt so far, the same couldn't be said for Xavier's own peace of mind. That had been blown to smithereens, just like his ability to sleep well and to concentrate.

Although, if he were perfectly honest with himself, Xavier would also own that he'd been struggling with maintaining a stable, uninterrupted routine even before his wards arrived on his doorstep. In actual fact, countless things had been going wrong at St Lawrence House for some months, and he was beginning to believe there might be an element of sabotage involved.

Boilers kept blowing valves. Rats and mice had invaded the walls. Pipes had mysteriously leaked, flooding the scullery and basement. The clocks in St Lawrence House were constantly slowing down or speeding up; in Xavier's opinion, there was nothing worse than the unsynchronized ticking and chiming of clocks. And then many of the staff at St Lawrence House—maids and footmen especially—kept leaving without notice for no discernible reason. None that Woodley, his butler, or the housekeeper, Mrs. Lambton, could fathom anyway. If bats were suddenly found roosting in the attic, or all the chimneys started belching giant clouds of smoke, Xavier wouldn't have been the least bit surprised.

As the closing date for the Westminster Palace clock submission drew closer, the pressure was mounting and the nagging, decidedly unpleasant thought that someone might be deliberately trying to upset the smooth running of his household wouldn't leave Xavier alone. Was someone like a rival horologist attempting to unsettle him so much that he wouldn't be able to work at all? Or worse, was there a concerted effort to discredit him? To paint him as disorganized or perhaps even mad? A man not to be taken seriously because he was so obsessed with clocks that his daily life and affairs in general were in complete disarray?

Could it be that someone might actually mean him harm? There had been that odd incident a few nights ago when he'd been followed...

Although, if there *was* some sort of elaborate conspiracy afoot, Xavier didn't think Mrs. Chase could be any part of that. He might not be experienced when it came to women, but she seemed quite lovely. He rather liked the spark of mischief in her eyes.

It was a pity Nanny Snodgrass wasn't more like her.

Xavier frowned. Nanny Snodgrass was altogether too serious. Harry, Barry, and Gary hadn't taken to her, and he wondered if that was part of the reason for the ongoing havoc in the nursery. He suspected that they—in particular, Harry—were testing her mettle. And perhaps they were simply bored. It had been raining for days and his wards were undoubtedly sick of being cooped up inside for so long. Xavier suspected that Nanny Snodgrass was the equivalent of a wet blanket soaked in the Thames during a rainstorm.

As Xavier led the nanny past the third-floor nursery, there was an almighty crash followed by a woman's ear-piercing scream.

Good Lord. What now?

The door flew open and one of Xavier's wards—the youngest and smallest—appeared in the hallway. Gary or Barry? To his own mortification, having spent only a minimal amount of time with his wards since they'd arrived (entering the nursery rather felt like visiting a topsy-turvy land where everyone spoke a foreign language and nothing made sense), Xavier was never quite sure which child was which. He really should try harder to learn their names. It was common courtesy after all.

When Gary—yes, it *was* Gary (really Gareth)—saw Xavier and Mrs. Chase, his eyes grew as round as saucers. "Oh, Cousin Xavier—" he began, but then he broke off as another scream burst forth.

Xavier frowned. "Gary, what in heaven's name is wrong?"

Before his ward could respond, the door swung open wider and a pale-faced Nanny Snodgrass rushed into the hall.

"Your Grace," she cried. "Your Grace! Miss Harriet is deliberately tormenting me."

"A nine-year-old girl is tormenting you?" Xavier repeated. "That sounds a tad dramatic."

"Well, she is! With a frog! She hid it in one of the toy boxes with malice aforethought, so I'd find it." The nanny pressed her trembling fingers against her throat. "I swear my heart almost stopped when it jumped on my hand. I thought the devil himself was coming for me." Her expression grew fierce with anger. "Something must be done to curb Miss Harriet's wicked ways."

"Wicked ways?" Mrs. Chase stepped forward. Her fine brows had plunged into a deep frown. "Children are *not* wicked. They can present with challenging behaviors at times, but I'm firmly of the opinion that one should never proclaim a child to be 'wicked.'" The younger woman shook her head as if she were quite disgusted with the nanny's declaration. Xavier was nothing but impressed by her self-assured manner and her willingness to be Harry's champion, even though she'd never met the child.

Nanny Snodgrass clearly thought otherwise. Her voice was laden with hoarfrost as she said, "I don't think anyone asked for your opinion, Miss . . ."

The young woman lifted her chin. "I'm Mrs. Emmeline Chase, a graduate of the Parasol Academy for Exceptional Nannies and Governesses. And no, you didn't ask for my opinion, but if you're going to make damaging assertions about a child's character, I'm going to feel compelled to intervene."

If Nanny Snodgrass were a porcupine, no doubt her spikes would be bristling. "Now see here, Mrs. Chase—"

"Mrs. Chase is right. Harry isn't wicked," piped up another small voice. Xavier's "middle" ward, Barry, thrust his head around the door. "It's not her fault if Archimedes—"

"Archimedes?" repeated Xavier. "Who or what is Archimedes?"

"My frog. A *Rana temporaria*, or common frog." Harriet emerged from the nursery, and in her hands she carried a rather handsome olive-green frog with a peppering of black spots along its back. It emitted a deep croak, as though it agreed with everything Harry had said.

Nanny Snodgrass squealed and jumped back. "Get that hideous thing away from me."

"Archimedes is *not* hideous," declared Harry, scowling at the nanny over the top of her spectacles. "And you can't blame him for wanting to explore the nursery. I can't keep him locked up in a dark box all day and night. That would be cruel."

"Harry, how long have you had Archimedes?" asked Xavier.

The girl turned and regarded him steadily. She really was quite fearless. "I found him in the garden three days ago. The last time we were allowed outside." She threw her nanny a baleful look.

"Three days?" shrieked Nanny Snodgrass. She clutched the doorjamb as though her knees were going to give out. "Miss Harriet, are you telling me that *thing* has been roaming the nursery for three whole days?"

"I don't see what all the fuss is about," replied Harry. "Archimedes is a friendly frog. He wouldn't harm a fly." She frowned. "Well, that isn't quite true, because he does like to eat flies. What I mean to say is, he wouldn't hurt anyone. Even *you*, Nanny Snodgrass."

Xavier bent down to Harriet's level so he could meet her eyes. "Under the circumstances, I think the best thing to do would be to get Archimedes an aquarium. While Horatio is well-fed and generally well-behaved, ravens do eat frogs and lizards on the odd occasion. It would be safer for everyone, don't you think?"

Harry considered him with large solemn eyes. "Very well, Cousin Xavier," she conceded after a moment. "I think your proposed solution is acceptable."

Xavier straightened. "What say you, Nanny Snodgrass?"

The woman gave a haughty sniff. "It is your home, and these

are your wards, Your Grace. So I will abide by your decree. But I hope Miss Harriet will keep the aquarium and its occupant in her own room. A nursery is *not* a place for a frog."

The three children and Nanny Snodgrass disappeared back into the nursery, and Xavier escorted Mrs. Chase downstairs to the grand entrance hall of St Lawrence House.

"Again, I'm so sorry for disrupting your day," said Mrs. Chase as they paused by the front door. One of the footmen had opened it to reveal rain scudding across Belgrave Square in a thick gray curtain. "It seems like you have a lot to contend with."

"Yes . . ." Xavier managed a tight smile. "My wards have only been with me a month, and I employed Nanny Snodgrass only a fortnight ago. I expect the children are still getting to know her, and vice versa." Of course, he was still getting to know them too. He really wished children came with some sort of guidebook or instruction manual.

Mrs. Chase made a low humming noise, a soft "mhmmm," which Xavier seemed to feel all the way to his fingertips. He was suddenly possessed by the absurd and completely inappropriate impulse to take off one of his gloves and reach out and touch the woman's coppery tresses to see if the strands had the same texture as silk. *How strange.*

She'd been looking outside, contemplating the rainy aspect, but then her gaze suddenly returned to his face. "Even though it's not my place to say, I did wonder if Nanny Snodgrass might not be quite right for your wards. They seem high-spirited and Miss Harriet, especially, seems quite intelligent. You mentioned she's nine?"

Xavier clasped his hands behind his back. "Yes, nine. *Almost* ten."

The nanny nodded. "She might even need a governess to keep her inquisitive mind occupied."

Xavier sighed. "I think you might be right."

Something like a look of sympathy crossed Mrs. Chase's

features. "I do need to be on my way, Your Grace, but before I go . . ." She reached into her pocket and pulled out a tiny tin soldier. "This belongs to your ward, Gareth. I-I found it . . . on the roof."

Xavier frowned as he took the toy. Horatio must have flown off with it and dropped it there. The soldier was slightly dented and a little of the red paint had been scraped off its uniform, exposing the tin beneath. Nevertheless, it was familiar; Xavier had seen Gary playing with a set of toy soldiers when he'd ventured into the nursery on the odd occasion. Apparently, the set had once belonged to the children's late father, a distant cousin of Xavier's. He shot the nanny a quizzical look. "How did you know it belonged to Gareth?"

"He was holding one just like it when he came rushing out of the nursery." Mrs. Chase shrugged a slender shoulder. "It seemed like a logical assumption to make."

Xavier's eyes met the nanny's. "And how did you know my ward's name is Gareth?"

Her lightly freckled cheeks turned pink and her bright blue gaze skittered away from his. "Oh, I thought you or someone else said his name. I apologize if I've overstepped."

"No, no. It's quite all right." Xavier studied the young woman's flushed countenance. When he quickly went over the conversation outside the nursery in his head, he'd only referred to Gareth as Gary. But it wasn't illogical to assume that Gary might be short for Gareth . . . And what did Mrs. Chase have to gain from lying about such a thing?

Of course, Xavier was staring again, so that might have set her to the blush rather than anything else.

What was it about this woman that had him so intrigued? She was a "missus," for one thing, so there must be—or had been at some point—a Mister Chase. Xavier estimated her age to be in the vicinity of twenty-something, so she was quite young for a widow.

"Well, if you ever need another nanny"—Mrs. Chase withdrew a business card from her pocket and passed it to Xavier—"ask for Mrs. Felicity Temple of the Parasol Academy. She'll be sure to recommend someone who's perfect for your wards."

Xavier glanced down at the cream and gold-embossed card in his hand and read:

The Parasol Academy
Bespoke Nanny and Governess Services
51 Sloane Square, Chelsea

Bespoke nanny and governess services? Xavier's interest was instantly piqued. He'd never heard of the Parasol Academy until today. And to think it was virtually around the corner from St Lawrence House! He turned the card over to read what was on the other side:

Come rain, hail, or shine, everything will be perfectly fine!
Whether your offspring are big or small, expert staff will be at your beck and call.
For all your child rearing and youth educational needs, in London or farther afield, contact the Headmistress of the Parasol Academy for Exceptional Nannies and Governesses, Mrs. F. Temple, for an obligation-free consultation.
(Confidentiality and the utmost discretion guaranteed.)

He looked up to thank Mrs. Chase, but like magic, she'd disappeared. "Good luck with your interview," he called into the rain, but the wind snatched his voice away.

And then of course, he didn't really mean it.

He shut the door. Curmudgeonly though it was, part of him hoped Mrs. Chase didn't get the job she was applying for. If Nanny Snodgrass didn't work out, Xavier rather thought he'd like to secure the young woman's nannying services himself.

Not only did she retrieve toy soldiers from roofs and stand up for others when she didn't need to, she'd made him smile, which was no mean feat. And even though his elbow still ached, his headache had miraculously dissipated.

If he was an unusual duke, he could safely say that Mrs. Emmeline Chase was a most unusual nanny.

Chapter 3

Concerning Quizzing Glasses, Sooty Smudges, a Police Box, and an Umbrella; And an Intriguing Offer from a Highly Ranked Individual . . .

"There's a leygram for you," said Mina as Emmeline entered their dormitory room. "It appeared on the rug by the door while you were out. I put it on your pillow."

"Oh?" Emmeline deposited her wet umbrella in the stand and tugged at the ribbons of her bonnet. She'd been out all morning running errands, if "running errands" meant trying to earn a little money by attending auctions and picking up bargains to sell to antique store owners for a small profit. It's how she'd been scraping by since her father had been incarcerated just before Christmas . . . with varying results. "I suspect we both know who it's from. The question is, will Mrs. Temple have good news or bad for me?"

Mina, who was sitting in the window seat with a book in hand, cast Emmeline a sympathetic smile. "I suppose there's only one way to find out. It's time to rip off the plaster and see what's there."

Equal measures of curiosity and trepidation sparking, Emmeline crossed to her narrow bed with its starched sheets and Academy-regulation counterpane of pale blue wool. Her interview with the Culpeppers yesterday had *not* gone as planned. Despite her best efforts—her second teleportation attempt between the police boxes in Belgrave Square and Bedford Square had been successful—she'd been terribly late. And her uniform hadn't been up to snuff after she'd landed on top of St Lawrence House and subsequently got caught in the rain. There'd even been a smudge of soot on her cheek!

But a tiny part of her hoped that she'd impressed Mr. and Mrs. Culpepper anyway.

The enigmatic Duke of St Lawrence certainly seemed to like her. Even though he'd been a *little* hard to read. And despite the fact she'd caused him no end of inconvenience. Good Lord, she'd even fallen on top of the poor man when she'd lost her blasted footing on the attic ladder! Every time Emmeline revisited that awkward moment, heat scorched her cheeks.

But he already had a nanny, so it wasn't likely that she'd encounter the nobleman again. Emmeline sighed. *More's the pity.* She'd quite liked him, too.

As soon as Emmeline picked up the missive from her pillow, the familiar buzz of magic—a faint electrical humming—made her fingertips tingle, even through her kid leather gloves. A te-*ley*-gram or *ley*gram was sent by magical means rather than by the British Electric Telegraph Company. Unlike regular telegrams, which relied upon the transmission of electrical signals over wires running along railway tracks or undersea cables to send messages, leygrams utilized the power generated by the Fae's ancient and mystical leylines. Whenever leygrams were sent, they would appear at one's door as if from nowhere. Emmeline didn't know precisely how it all worked. It just *was*. A bit like all the other magical methods employed by Parasol Academy members.

Apart from the magical thrum emanating from the paper, the sheet was covered in script that looked like gibberish. A leygram could only be deciphered by one who possessed an

Academy-issued pair of ley-spectacles, or a quizzing glass fitted with a ley-lens of deep azure blue.

Her pulse zipping through her veins like quicksilver, Emmeline dug out her own quizzing glass (she always kept it in her reticule or pocket as per the *Parasol Academy Handbook*'s Chapter 4: Guidelines for the Use and Handling of Accoutrements, Equipment, and Other Indispensable Paraphernalia) and read the contents of the message. And then she permitted herself a sigh.

"Mrs. Temple wants to see me in her office as soon as possible. But she hasn't said anything else." She looked up at Mina. "I have an awful feeling about this. If the Culpeppers haven't offered me the job . . ."

"You still have two more chances," said Mina firmly. "You have absolutely nothing to worry about."

All Academy graduates had three opportunities to secure a position. During their two-year-long course, and while they were in the process of applying for a post as a nanny or governess, they could board at the Sloane Square headquarters for a small fee of four shillings and three pence per week. Unless, like Emmeline, one was a "legacy" nanny or governess—because Emmeline's late mother had been a Parasol nanny before she'd wed, Emmeline's tuition and board hadn't cost her a thing.

However, if a graduate *failed* to secure a job after three interviews, she had to undertake three months of intensive remedial training, and that was *not* free, regardless of whether one was a legacy nanny or not. The boarding fee was not waived either. If Emmeline had to undertake remedial training, she didn't know how she'd manage. She wouldn't have time to go to auctions or markets to pick up bargains to obtain the funds needed to keep her father safe. Nor would she be able to afford to have him transferred to a smaller, more hospitable debtors' prison. That was an even more expensive enterprise.

She dropped the leygram on the bed and willed herself not to panic. Her mind was racing frantically, conjuring up all manner of worst-case scenarios when perhaps she had nothing to worry about at all. Mina's advice was sound. She'd best rip the plaster off and go and see Mrs. Temple.

Not knowing what would happen was always the worst bit.

Emmeline caught Mina's eye. "Do I look all right?" she asked, smoothing her uniform's wool skirts.

Mina put down her book and crossed the room to Emmeline. "Absolutely perfect. Except for this bit." The young woman reached out and repinned one of Emmeline's stray curls. She then fluffed up the lace flounces of Emmeline's nanny's cap. "There." She smiled. "You'll do. And chin up. The Culpeppers might want you to start working for them straightaway."

"I hope so," said Emmeline as she headed for the door.

But it turned out the Culpeppers *didn't* want her to work for them at all.

"Mrs. Chase," said Mrs. Temple in a kind but solemn tone that did not augur well, "There's no easy way to say this, but I'm afraid you didn't get the job."

"Oh." Emmeline's heart plummeted to the Aubusson rug on the floor beneath her booted feet, while her gaze fell to Mrs. Temple's silver and crystal-encrusted hand mirror which winked at her from a corner of the headmistress's desk. Clasping her gloved hands tightly together in front of her pinafore, Emmeline tried very hard not to let her disappointment show on her face. To keep the tears pricking at the back of her eyes at bay.

While she *had* been expecting a "no" from the Culpeppers, the news was still a blow.

It was at moments like this that a little voice at the back of Emmeline's mind would whisper that she was on the verge of becoming quite desperate. And not just any garden-variety sort of "desperate," but "Desperate" with a capital *D*.

Yes—"Desperate"—like a tragic heroine in one of her brother's pantomimes at the Oberon. The theatrical poster would proclaim:

Mrs. Emmeline Chase, Cheapside Widow, Is Desperate!

Mrs. Temple, who was seated behind her desk, was watching Emmeline, waiting for her to say something more than "oh" in response to the bad news. Drawing in a fortifying breath, Emmeline added in a voice that quivered only a little, "I'm so sorry to have disappointed you, Mrs. Temple. I do hope I haven't sullied the Academy's reputation. It was entirely my fault that I was running late and arrived at the Culpeppers' in a less than presentable state. The elements conspired against me. I got caught in a particularly heavy rain shower and I was in such a rush, I forgot to use the *Unsmirchify* incantation to repair my appearance." It wasn't a *complete* lie.

"Pfft." Mrs. Temple waved her hand with a vigor that sent her blond ringlets bouncing. "To be perfectly frank, Mr. Culpepper and his wife struck me as far too persnickety. In hindsight, I'm not sure you and the Culpeppers were the best fit. And as you know, we endeavor to provide a *bespoke* service."

"Yes . . . Yes, I do know," said Emmeline. "And I'm nothing but grateful that you're not miffed with me."

Mrs. Temple inclined her head and her lips curled in a gracious smile. "Occasional indecorous cursing aside, you are one of our best graduates to date, and I'm absolutely certain that I have something else for you. A situation that is far better suited to your personality and the needs of your potential employer." She leaned forward, her fair countenance alight with excitement. "Earlier today, I received a visit from a highly ranked individual— the Duke of St Lawrence, in fact—who needs a nanny straightaway. Not only that, but he said that he would like to interview *you* for the post, if you were not otherwise employed. He actually asked for you by name, Mrs. Chase! What say you to that?"

Emmeline's mouth dropped open and her heart did a little jig. It looked like Nanny Snodgrass had not worked out after all. It might have seemed mean-spirited, but she couldn't say she was sorry. "I-I would say that I would be most interested. Exceedingly so."

The headmistress nodded her approval. "Having such an elevated client will be excellent for the Academy's reputation. The Queen will no doubt be pleased too."

The Academy's Royal Charter had been granted less than a year ago after there'd been an attempt on the Queen's life—the fifth attempt in only a handful of years. A man named Robert Pate had viciously struck Her Majesty with his cane as she'd quit Cambridge House in Piccadilly in her carriage. Quite shockingly, three of the Royal children had been present during the attack, along with Mrs. Temple, who'd thrown herself in front of her charges to defend them. The Queen had been so impressed with the young woman's selflessness and bravery, she'd issued the Parasol Academy's Royal Charter the very next week when she'd recovered from her ordeal.

What *wasn't* known by the public—or even the Crown—was that the Parasol Academy had another Royal Charter, which had been issued when the training college had first been founded by Mrs. Temple's great-grandmother, Verity Truelove, ninety years ago. A secret charter, not from the earthly realm, but the Fae Realm that had been granted by Good Queen Maeve to help combat her evil sister Mab's practice of abducting human children and leaving changelings in their place. It was why Parasol Academy nannies and governesses were equipped with magical abilities to aid in the protection of children.

The students didn't know exactly how the Academy's founder had managed to secure such untold support from a Fae queen—and Mrs. Temple always remained tight-lipped on the subject—but Emmeline did wonder if there might be Fae blood in the headmistress's family. It would certainly account for the woman's petite stature and ethereal air. And her almost preternatural insight.

Mrs. Temple was aiming one of her thoughtful, far too perceptive looks at Emmeline right now. "You know, Mrs. Chase, I'm still trying to fathom how the Duke of St Lawrence knew about you."

Emmeline shrugged, barely resisting the urge to squirm like a naughty child who'd been caught with a hand in the sweetmeat jar. "I could not say." She didn't want to keep secrets. She didn't want to lie, but admitting she'd mistakenly teleported herself onto the duke's roof wouldn't do her any favors.

Although Emmeline would readily own that she did *not* regret meeting the Duke of St Lawrence yesterday. Truth to tell, he was the most curious man she'd ever met. After she'd quit St Lawrence House, she'd found that her thoughts kept drifting toward the nobleman at odd moments. Like now, and it was all kinds of bothersome. But she really *couldn't* stop thinking about his starkly handsome features. His fierce arctic-blue eyes and his storm of black hair. And then there was his rich cultured voice. It was the most beautiful baritone Emmeline had ever heard. Listening to the Duke of St Lawrence speak had been the auditory equivalent of wallowing in melted chocolate. He was a peculiar mixture of hot and cold, and Emmeline was nothing but intrigued.

While her face still flamed at the way they'd met, it hadn't been quite so awkward at the end. And even though the man's manner had been quite unusual—he had the most disconcertingly direct gaze Emmeline had ever come across—she couldn't help but think he might be a good employer. He'd gone out of his way to personally help her yesterday when he hadn't been obliged to. And he'd been kind to his ward, Harriet, about the whole frog incident. He might have come across as a little stuffy at times, but he certainly wasn't an arrogant pain-in-the-derriere. Oddly, it was the upper-middle-class banker, Mr. Culpepper, who'd turned out to be the prig.

Mrs. Temple was speaking again, so Emmeline forced her thoughts away from her encounter with the duke so she could pay attention.

"Just so you know," said Mrs. Temple, "His Grace is a horologist of some renown who is working on a very important project with a fast-approaching deadline. But he also has three young wards who I gather are quite 'spirited.' The poor mites are orphans, so I suspect they need a good deal of nurturing as well as managing. But don't let *any* of that put you off. I know you will be brilliant and simply perfect for this position."

"I certainly hope so," said Emmeline. At least she had some idea of what she'd be dealing with. A bright nine-year-old with a penchant for frogs, and two exuberant boys, didn't sound like too much of a challenge to her. While Emmeline had told a little white lie about how she'd come by the lost toy soldier that belonged to Gareth—she'd simply found it inside her magical nanny's pocket; it hadn't been on the roof as she'd claimed—she was relieved the duke had believed her explanation and seemed to have formed a favorable opinion of her.

Mrs. Temple stood and rounded the desk, her pearl-gray silk skirts swaying in time with her light footsteps. She took both of Emmeline's gloved hands in hers and looked her up and down. "I can see you're perfectly attired in your Parasol Academy uniform today. Which is wonderful, because the duke would like to interview you this afternoon at three o'clock sharp. Because he's a horologist, I suspect he values punctuality above all else."

Three o'clock? Emmeline's gaze shot to the Boulle clock on Mrs. Temple's mantelpiece. It was already a quarter to three.

"Don't look so alarmed," said Mrs. Temple. "If you teleport, you'll get there in plenty of time. Which I'd strongly advise, considering it's still raining. London is a veritable quagmire at the moment."

"I'll fetch my cloak and umbrella and I'll be on my way," said Emmeline. "Fingers crossed *this* job works out."

Mrs. Temple smiled. "I have everything crossed for you, Mrs. Chase. Now go and work your magic on the duke."

Within five minutes, Emmeline was in Belgrave Square again. At least she *hoped* she was. As the bright whirling leylight dissipated and her equilibrium returned, she discerned that she was in a dark, cramped space—a stone police box. Through an iron grille in the door and a veil of scudding rain beyond, she could make out the pale pink blossoms of cherry trees and the facades of elegant, whitewashed terrace houses. Yes, this was definitely Belgravia; the residences didn't need a good scrub with carbolic soap like they did in other parts of London.

The door to the police box was locked, but it was but the work of a moment for Emmeline to use her leyport key to let herself out. As she stepped into the square, she opened her Parasol Academy umbrella . . . and then bumped straight into a uniformed bobby.

Oh, blast! There'd been no sign of *any* policemen yesterday.

The mustachioed constable, who couldn't have been more than one-and-twenty if he was a day, gaped at Emmeline in open-mouthed astonishment. "Miss, what on earth are you doin' in my box? You can't be loiterin' about in there! It's against the law!"

"I . . . er . . . I apologize if I startled you," replied Emmeline. She quickly pocketed her dismay and adopted a polite but distinctly professional demeanor. "I'm a Parasol Academy nanny. On official nanny business. So it's quite all right."

The young man's brows arrowed into a deep frown. "Parasol Academy nanny? I 'ave no idea wha' you're talkin' about, miss." All of a sudden, the bobby's gloved hand shot out from the folds of his black greatcoat and he gripped Emmeline's arm. "'Ere, you better come wif me back to the Yard then."

Emmeline gave an inward groan. It wasn't three o'clock quite yet, but the longer she stood out here in the rain, the worse for wear she would look when she knocked on the door of St Lawrence House. She did *not* have time for this.

Not only that, but Parasol nannies and governesses were *not* to draw undue public attention to themselves. Nor were they to bring the Academy's excellent reputation into disrepute. Unless, as per the *Parasol Academy Handbook*, Chapter 1, Section 7, Paragraph 20, there were exceptional circumstances that justified such an eventuality. She could *not* afford to make a scene.

"I take it you're new to the job, Constable?" said Emmeline with a perfectly pleasant smile, trying to keep her tone neutral rather than snippy. "Because if you are, you might be unaware that your superiors at Scotland Yard have given Parasol Academy nannies and governesses permission to use police boxes in the course of carrying out their official duties. So in actual fact, I haven't broken any laws at all."

The bobby's cheeks turned an indignant shade of red. "Now see 'ere, miss. I know what's wha' and what's not. An' I'm sure you're tryin' to sell me a great porky pie. I've never 'eard of the Parasol Academy."

"I assure you, I am *not* lying, Constable." Emmeline emitted a small sigh of frustration. Her skirts and boots were getting wetter by the minute and her patience was wearing thinner than one of her lawn shifts. "Now, if you'd be so kind as to let me go, I'll be on my way and no harm done."

But the bobby did not let go of Emmeline's arm. In fact, he began to tug her toward the end of Belgrave Square, away from St Lawrence House.

It just wouldn't do. Emmeline hadn't been able to talk herself out of the situation, so as a last resort, she was going to have to use her Academy-issued umbrella on the man.

"I'm sorry about this, Constable." Emmeline lowered her umbrella and gave the young man a quick nudge in the vicinity of his ribs with the silver tip—or, as it was called in the *Parasol Academy Handbook*, the Point-of-Confusion. At the same time she prodded the constable, she also muttered, "*Perplexio*," beneath her breath.

The effect of Emmeline's umbrella poke combined with the confusion incantation was immediate. All at once, the bobby stopped trying to frog-march her across the square. He came to a grinding halt and he released her arm. "I'm sorry, miss." He wiped a hand down his rain-damp face, then frowned at Emmeline from beneath the brim of his dripping helmet. "I seem to have . . ." He shook his head, his expression slightly dazed. "I can't quite recall . . ." He then squinted at Emmeline. "Do I know you?"

Emmeline smiled at him. "No, I don't believe so. I was asking you for directions to St Lawrence House. I have an appointment there shortly."

"Ah, the duke's residence." The constable pointed to the opposite corner of the square. "It's right over there, miss. You can't miss it."

"Thank you, Constable." Emmeline canted her head. "I bid you good day. I shall be sure to tell the duke how helpful you've been."

The bobby bowed. "Thank you, miss. Thurstwhistle's the name. Now you'd best get out of this rain so you don't catch cold. I bid you a good day too."

Emmeline didn't waste any more time. The constable's confusion would clear quickly if it hadn't already. He'd be all right. She hurried across the square and within a minute was standing outside the glossy black front door of St Lawrence House. To think that only yesterday, she'd been standing right here with a soot-smudged face, impulsively handing the duke a Parasol Academy business card.

And he asked for me. Me! Mrs. Emmeline Chase of Cheapside.

But remember, you're also a Parasol nanny.

Drawing a deep breath to quell a flurry of nerves and excitement, Emmeline grasped the door's smart brass knocker with her gloved hand and rapped three times. She'd taken a chance and perhaps now, with a little bit of luck, her path in life was about to change.

Chapter 4

In Which Knees Turn to Blancmange; And Then a Dialogue About Black Coffee, Rare Timepieces, Chronometers, and Other Matters of Great Import Ensues...

The front door of St Lawrence House swung open to reveal a smartly dressed, poker-faced gentleman with iron-gray hair and fiercely bristling muttonchops. "Yes?" he asked coldly.

The man's tone—Emmeline assumed he was the duke's butler—was so funereal and forbidding, a shiver slid down her spine. But she would not be deterred. She lifted her chin. "My name is Mrs. Emmeline Chase, and your master, the duke, has summoned me here for an interview," she said. "For the vacant nanny's position. I'm from the Parasol Academy."

The man's imperious gaze slid over her. "Weren't you here yesterday? I heard you'd somehow managed to get stuck on the roof like some common sneak thief."

Emmeline arched a brow. *Good grief.* Would she never get through the front door? "Yes, I *was* here," she said. "But as I mentioned, I have an appointment. His Grace is expecting me at three o'clock, and I'm sure you don't want to keep your master waiting. I've heard punctuality is important to the duke."

The butler looked down his long nose at her, but nevertheless, he opened the door wider to admit her. "Quite."

"Thank you," she said as she handed her wet umbrella to a liveried footman. "Mister..."

"Woodley," said the servant. "I am His Grace's butler." As soon as Emmeline had divested herself of her cloak, bonnet, and gloves, he added curtly, "Follow me." His long strides carried him across the black and white checkerboard marble floor, then up the grand sweeping staircase so swiftly that Emmeline had a hard time keeping up.

Upon reaching a shadow-filled, hushed hallway on the second floor, the supercilious Woodley bade Emmeline sit upon a chair beside a set of double oak doors. As she complied, the butler knocked, and then he disappeared into the room beyond when there was a murmured summons.

It was the duke. Emmeline immediately recognized the hot-chocolate richness of that lovely baritone. There was undeniable power and authority and musical beauty in that resonating voice. Not only the deep, meltingly warm timbre. There was also a certain exquisiteness in the perfectly refined vowels and the precisely clipped consonants and the undulating cadence. And all the man had said was, "Come in." She was certain if the duke began to recite Pythagoras's theorem or Newton's laws of motion, she'd be utterly enthralled.

Emmeline unnecessarily straightened the folds of her navy wool skirts and then stared at the rain drumming against a nearby window. Her heart was beating a fast tattoo as well.

She *must* compose herself. She didn't think she'd ever been quite so nervous in her entire life and she couldn't account for it. Nerves and an inconvenient physical attraction were her enemies right now. During her interview, she needed to be as cool and calm and collected as a frozen cucumber in midwinter. Above all, she needed to come across as professional. She *must* get this job.

Mrs. Chase, thank God you're here, came a cultured, avian voice, and a moment later, Horatio Ravenscar Esquire fluttered into the hall. He perched on the back of a neighboring chair and studied her with an obsidian eye.

Oh, responded Emmeline, blinking in surprise. *Why?*

The raven tilted his head. *After you left yesterday, all hell broke loose. While my master was out procuring an aquarium for Archimedes, Miss Harriet decided to conduct a trebuchet experiment.*

Emmeline's eyebrows shot up. *A trebuchet experiment?*

Horatio bobbed up and down and made a clicking sound in his throat that reminded Emmeline of a short chuckle. *Yes. Apparently Miss Harriet wanted to "test the effect of different counterweights on linear velocity." She selected the nursery for the field of testing, and flour "bombs" were the projectile of choice. One of Nanny Snodgrass's linen caps was purloined for the trebuchet's sling. And Nanny Snodgrass was the principal target.*

Emmeline winced. *Oh dear. I'm almost afraid to ask what happened.*

Horatio emitted another laugh. This time it was a full-throated chortle that sounded quite human. *Oh dear, all right. Even though nothing was damaged, everything and everyone in the nursery was coated in flour including Nanny Snodgrass. It looked like a snowstorm had whirled through the room.* The raven ruffled his glossy plumage. *While I rather enjoyed looking like a ghostly raven at first, I'm still trying to get the flour out of my feathers.*

I take it Nanny Snodgrass quit then? remarked Emmeline.

Horatio spread his wings and gave them a decided flap. *Actually no. When my master returned with the aquarium and found out that Nanny Snodgrass had threatened to use a birch switch to discipline his wards, he sacked her on the spot.*

Emmeline's mouth dropped open. *How shocking and awful that she would threaten to do such a draconian thing. I know*

His Grace's wards were misbehaving, but that is not the way to go about dealing with such a situation.

The raven puffed out his chest. *I know, Mrs. Chase. I know.* The bird suddenly cocked his head to one side. *I believe my master is ready to receive you. Good luck!*

A moment later, the butler reappeared. He saw Emmeline into the room—a study by the looks of it—and then the door shut behind her with a soft snick.

She was alone with the Duke of St Lawrence, and all at once, she felt discombobulated all over again. Like she'd just teleported into the room and everything was not quite right.

Today, the duke seemed all sorts of stiff and starchy, perhaps even disdainful. He stood ramrod straight in front of an enormous oak desk, his hands buried in the pockets of his perfectly tailored black frock coat, while upon his face, he wore an expression of chill remoteness while he looked everywhere *but* at her.

He hadn't been quite like this yesterday, had he?

Emmeline cleared her throat. "Good afternoon, Your Grace," she offered as brightly as she could, despite the fact she suddenly felt self-conscious beyond measure. Her confidence was further eroded when the duke's attention stayed fixed on a far corner of the room, as though she were a source of displeasure, or worse, someone not worthy of regard.

Emmeline wasn't sure if she felt insulted or disappointed. The man had summoned her here for an interview. She'd arrived on time. Her attire was spick-and-span, her hair under control.

Had he changed his mind? Had he already found someone else in the time between his meeting with Mrs. Temple and now?

Why on earth was he being so damned rude?

Emmeline's palms grew damp and she licked her dry lips. She knew the duke's wards were a handful, but she wondered if the man himself might be difficult to manage too. He was, in a word, mercurial.

Perhaps her initial, favorable impression of the Duke of St Lawrence had been completely wrong. Perhaps he *was* just like any other member of his elevated class—thoroughly snobbish and stuffier than the stuffed armchairs gracing his hearthrug. Then again, she was so horribly nervous, she might be misreading the duke and overthinking every little thing he said and did.

Scraping together the remnants of her rapidly disintegrating dignity, Emmeline drew a bracing breath in preparation to speak, but then the duke's piercing gaze swung to her. And that's when she realized that *she* was behaving like a total peagoose; she hadn't yet curtsied.

This man was a duke. A suitable display of obeisance was required.

Unlike yesterday, she had no excuse not to do so.

Even though her knees were quivering like a blancmange, Emmeline managed to execute a passable curtsy.

As for the duke, he at last inclined his head in acknowledgment and intoned a perfectly polite, "Good afternoon, Mrs. Chase. How do you do? Thank you for coming here at such short notice." Then his mouth quirked up at the corner in a hint of a smile. "I'm pleased to hear you arrived by the front door today."

"I . . . Yes I did, Your Grace. And you're very welcome. About me attending for an interview," replied Emmeline, relieved that there was still a sense of humor lurking beneath the duke's aloof exterior. "Mrs. Temple informed me that you visited the Parasol Academy and asked for me to apply. For the vacant nanny's position."

"Yes." The duke withdrew a gloved hand from his pocket and gestured toward the other side of the room where, to Emmeline's surprise, a sumptuous afternoon tea had been laid out on a low table by the fire. "Shall we, Mrs. Chase?" he asked. But then his brows descended into an uncertain frown. "Or should I call you Nanny Chase? What would you prefer?"

What would I prefer? Emmeline blinked. The duke actually did appear to be a trifle perplexed. Had she misjudged him? Was he, in fact, a little uncomfortable, perhaps even nervous? Was that the reason for his standoffish behavior?

Surely not.

She reexamined his expression, but she couldn't tell one way or the other. Nevertheless, she answered his question. "Mrs. Chase will do, Your Grace." She offered a small smile. "Nanny Chase if you offer me the position. I suppose it's up to you."

"Of course," he said.

Emmeline chose a velvet wingback chair, and the duke folded his long frame into the opposite seat. As he sat poker straight, one lean but muscular thigh draped over the other, Emmeline took a moment to study him a little more closely (surreptitiously of course) while she removed her kid gloves.

She supposed the precise cut of the duke's features only added to his general air of icy indifference. His cheeks, bracketed by neatly trimmed muttonchops, were so lean they were almost a little hollow. His thick, tousled locks tumbled across a high noble forehead toward heavy, black-winged brows and those remarkable arctic-blue eyes of his, framed by long sooty lashes (lashes Emmeline would practically kill for). There was not a trace of softness about his wide chiseled mouth, nor in the set of his rigid, sharply hewn jaw.

When the duke turned his head slightly, revealing his profile, Emmeline could see that the long line of his nose had an aquiline cast to it. Despite his off-putting manner, she *couldn't* deny that the duke was handsome. Although it would be far easier if she *could* ignore how attractive he was.

He was nothing at all like Jeremy, her late husband, who'd

been all devil-may-care smiles and charm personified. Emmeline almost snorted aloud. When they'd been courting anyway.

Besides, what did it matter whether the duke was her "cup of tea" in terms of looks and personality, or not? She wasn't looking for a husband. The Duke of St Lawrence could be as unpleasant as a spoonful of cod liver oil, or even a cup of hemlock, and she'd still take the job. *If* this interview went well...

Emmeline also noted that the duke hadn't removed his snug-fitting black kid gloves even though they *were* about to take tea. Which seemed rather odd. But everything about this particular encounter was peculiar, so Emmeline supposed she shouldn't be all that surprised. For instance, she didn't believe it was customary for a nobleman to share afternoon tea with a mere servant. Indeed, part of her was surprised that someone like the duke's housekeeper wasn't conducting her interview.

"Well then..." The duke's gaze dropped to the tea things on the table. Another frown. "I suppose we should get down to business. But would you like something to eat or drink first? Tea or coffee? Or a sandwich? The egg and cress ones are particularly good if you like that sort of thing. Or you might prefer a scone with strawberry jam and clotted cream. *Or* I could ring for something else. Lemonade or petit fours? Pastries?" The corner of his mouth twitched with the semblance of a wry smile. "It's probably a bit early in the day for a tipple of sherry or brandy."

Even though Emmeline wouldn't have minded something to eat—she'd missed lunch at the Academy—she didn't wish to prolong this already awkwarder-than-awkward interview. "I'm not one to tipple," she said. "With regard to the scones and sandwiches or anything else, no, thank you. But I wouldn't mind a cup of tea." *To moisten my dry throat and to give my stomach something to do other than churn.*

The duke tilted his head, and Emmeline took that as a sign that she was to play hostess like a well-bred society lady (which she was not) and pour. "Tea or coffee, Your Grace?"

"Coffee, thank you. I can't abide tea. Horrid stuff."

As Emmeline dispensed the beverage into a fine bone-china cup, the duke added, "I won't require milk or sugar. The coffee I enjoy is rather like me I suppose..." Another one of those twisted, almost wry smiles. "Broodingly dark, perhaps even inclining toward bitterness."

Although Emmeline was more than a little startled by the duke's frank admission, she managed to hand his coffee to him without rattling the cup in its saucer. *Dark and brooding and bitter?* At least he was aware of his own foibles...

"But don't let that put you off the position," the duke continued after he'd taken a sip of his drink. "Despite my numerous character flaws, which I will readily admit to, I believe I am a fair man."

Emmeline poured her own cup of tea and added extra milk and two sugar lumps. (Sugar could count as sustenance, couldn't it?)

Goodness. She hadn't expected any sort of forthright disclosures from a man like the duke. Although, it seemed the nobleman possessed a dry sense of humor which he wielded with great effectiveness now and again. And that wasn't a bad thing at all. In fact, the duke's self-deprecating openness had the effect of allaying Emmeline's own qualms. So much so, she looked at the duke over the rim of her cup and ventured, "While I appreciate your candor, Your Grace, I will confess that I'm beginning to have reservations nonetheless."

He cocked a brow in query. "You are?" His expression hovered somewhere between sardonic, incredulous, and grave, but Emmeline couldn't tell which emotion dominated. He was *very* hard to read.

"Yes." She took a sip from her cup then put it down. "I mean, how could I possibly work for someone who doesn't drink tea? I'm sure there are rules against it in the *Parasol Academy Handbook*."

Heavens, she shouldn't be saying things like this, but the duke was so stern and pompous this afternoon and some evil imp inside Emmeline wanted to needle him, just a little bit, just for fun. Just to see what he would do.

He stared at her for a long moment as if trying to work out if she *was* serious. But then his mouth twitched and something bright and burning flared in those pale frost-blue eyes. Humor or a spark of appreciation perhaps? "You're joking, of course," he asserted.

"Yes, I am." Emmeline suddenly decided she was enjoying herself. "My apologies if I've come across as too flippant. But sometimes certain things simply need to be said. Ground rules that should never be broken and boundaries that should never be crossed should be made clear from the outset."

"Another Parasol Academy tenet?"

Was that a note of amusement in the duke's voice? Emmeline hoped so. "Yes. But it also might be found under an alternative title: *The Principles of Sensible Living According to Mrs. Emmeline Chase.*"

"Well, your principles seem very sound to me," replied the duke with an approving nod. "And there's no need to apologize for injecting a bit of light teasing into the conversation. I'm inclined to be a little too . . ." His gaze darted away from her as he appeared to search for the right word. "Somber," he concluded.

He didn't mind Emmeline's teasing? Now *that* was a relief. There was hope she might secure this position after all. "Well, you did warn me about all the darkness and bitterness." She was unable to resist another tiny prod.

"I did." He lifted his coffee in a mock salute and took another sip. "To be perfectly frank, I think my wards could do with a little fun and flippancy in their lives. I do believe that some of the less desirable behaviors they've displayed of late are related to the fact their nannies to date have been rather too staid. And of course, I've not been overly 'present' either, what with my work and encroaching project deadline." He sighed. "All in all, they've not had an easy time of it."

Ah, at last they were down to business. Emmeline was on surer ground now. "Mrs. Temple mentioned they are orphans?" she prompted gently.

"Yes." The duke's frown returned. "It's all terribly tragic, I'm afraid. I've been told their parents died in a freak yachting accident in the English Channel. About a year ago. Their father—a distant cousin of mine whom I'd never met—fancied himself as a bit of a sailor. But a storm hit and"—the duke released a sad sigh—"it seems Mother Nature decided to take him down a fathom or two. The children went to live with an ancient maiden aunt for a while, but then she, too, passed away. Just last month in fact. So now they are with me."

Emmeline's heart clenched. "It's never easy losing a parent at any stage. But I think it's especially hard when children are so young. Your wards are lucky to have you."

The duke's brows lifted in surprise. "Why would you think that? You hardly know me, Mrs. Chase."

"While that's true, what I do know is that you went to see Mrs. Temple at the Parasol Academy. You obviously wish to hire a bespoke nanny who will provide exceptional care for your wards. Not every guardian—or parent—would do that. You clearly take your responsibility seriously and want only the best for these children."

The duke's gaze fell to his lap. With a gloved finger, he flicked a speck of nonexistent lint off his knee. "Indeed." There was a slight pause and then he added, "I take it that you are not daunted by the fact that my wards are rather . . . rumbustious? You saw that the oldest—Harriet—had upset Nanny Snodgrass with her pet frog yesterday."

Emmeline put down her tea. "Yes. I'm not one to listen to gossip, but I also heard about . . . the trebuchet incident a bit later on. And that Miss Harriet was the instigator of the so-called experiment."

The duke nodded as though he wasn't at all surprised that she knew. "Did your headmistress also tell you that before I employed Nanny Snodgrass, another nanny worked here? And that she only lasted a week?"

Emmeline shook her head. "No. She didn't mention that particular detail. May I ask why?"

"In the interest of being open and honest with you, the first nanny—a Miss Butterworth—resigned because Miss Harriet put a firecracker in the nursery stove. I'm pleased to say that no one was injured, but it was a serious incident."

Oh . . . Emmeline swallowed. "If I may venture an opinion, Your Grace, it sounds like Miss Harriet might be more than just a little bored. Perhaps she's also seeking your attention?"

"I agree," said the duke. "And while I have considered employing a governess for her, part of me thinks she very much needs someone who is both caring *and* capable of nurturing her interests. Someone with a keen intellect and a kind heart. I fear that I'm not particularly good with children, so wouldn't even know where to begin in that regard. As for seeking my attention . . ." His wide shoulders lifted and fell against the back of the wingback chair. "I'm afraid I have precious little of that to give to anyone at present."

Was that a note of regret threaded through the duke's voice?

Before Emmeline could ask if he was referring to the demands of his horological project, the duke asked her if she could replenish his coffee.

After she'd done so, he pinned his intense blue gaze on her and posed another question. "Mrs. Chase. How do you feel about corporal punishment for children?"

Even though Horatio had mentioned Nanny Snodgrass had been given her marching orders because she'd threatened to use a birch switch on the duke's wards, Emmeline almost dropped her brimming teacup. She eyed the duke, but as usual, his expression was largely indecipherable. "Of course, I'm vehemently opposed to it," she said firmly. This was definitely an *in for a penny, in for a pound* moment. "It's a barbaric practice that is proscribed by the Parasol Academy. If a nanny or governess used such punishment on their charges, it would be in clear violation of Rule 10 of Chapter 3 of the Academy's handbook. It would mean immediate revocation of a nanny's or governess's license to practice in the Parasol Academy's name."

The duke nodded his approval. "Just so. This handbook of yours sounds very comprehensive."

"It is," responded Emmeline proudly. "It covers all manner of things. From the best practices in caring for young children to modern pedagogy, curriculum considerations, and lesson planning for older charges. There are all sorts of regulations and safe practice recommendations around essential 'tools of the trade,' or our 'kit' too."

Emmeline was *not* going to mention leygrams and leyport keys, or that her uniform had magical pockets. And that her Academy-issued umbrella (and parasol, if the weather was fine) could be used to temporarily befuddle an assailant. Or that she could converse with certain animals, including the duke's very own pet raven. Doing so would contravene one of the Academy's main rules and break the oath a nanny or governess took when graduating: protect the Parasol Academy's secrets at all costs. The general public must *never* know that they practiced Fae magic in discharging their duties. Indeed, every graduate knew that Good Queen Maeve's Fae Charter might be repealed—and thus all their magical abilities would be removed—if that ever occurred.

Although Emmeline *could* mention that she always had a small, sheathed knife strapped to her ankle, inside her half boot... but perhaps not right now. "We take our duties as carers and educators *very* seriously," she added after a moment.

"Some might even say it's a calling. My dearly departed mother was once a Parasol Academy–trained nanny until she—" Oh no, Emmeline could *not* mention her father. "Until she resigned her commission, so to speak."

"It's in your blood," stated the duke.

"I suppose it is, in a way." Emmeline had never thought about it before, but there was some truth to it. "All Academy graduates are passionate about their roles and responsibilities. In fact, we are trained to guard our charges with our very lives if necessary. Parasol nannies and governesses receive extensive self-defense training. Anyone who attempts to harm those in our care had best be careful. *Very* careful."

Rather than looking entirely skeptical of her claim, the duke appeared thoughtful. "Your Mrs. Temple informed me that she protected the young Prince of Wales, Prince Alfred, and Princess Alice when Her Majesty was attacked last year."

"Yes. That's true."

The duke placed both feet on the floor and leaned forward, his forearms resting on his thighs, his gloved hands clasped. "I'm going to take you into my confidence, Mrs. Chase. I'm working on a grand and unique clock design for St Stephens Tower at the Palace of Westminster. There's a fierce contest going on between horologists to win the commission. And lately, I fear that a person or persons unknown have been attempting to sabotage the smooth running of my household. Things keep going wrong on a regular basis—events that have had nothing to do with trebuchet experiments or frogs. Unfortunately, domestic disasters seem to have become a regular occurrence at St Lawrence House and a generalized state of bedlam is more common than not. But it's not only that." The duke's expression grew troubled. "A few nights ago, when I was walking home from a Royal Horological Society meeting in Piccadilly, I had the distinct feeling that someone was following me."

"Oh, dick—I mean, good heavens," said Emmeline, alarm spiking through her. "Do you think it was a footpad?"

"I..." The duke's frown deepened. "I don't think so. Unfortunately, the night was terribly foggy and the fellow kept a discreet distance. At first. When he eventually drew close and my suspicions *were* aroused—he was practically on my heels at that point—I whirled around to confront him, but then he took off. So I only caught a fleeting glimpse of him. But I gained the impression that he was relatively well-dressed. He was cloaked and booted, and upon his head he wore a top hat."

"I'm glad you weren't robbed, or worse, physically assaulted," offered Emmeline, and the duke acknowledged her concern with a tilt of his head.

"I'll freely admit that the incident was both perplexing and to a degree, unsettling," he said. "Although, I always carry a cane with me when I'm out and about, so I'm easily able to defend myself." One of his shoulders hitched with a shrug. "At any rate, while I'm certain that no one would dare harm my wards, it's reassuring to know that the nanny who will be caring for them has extra skills up her sleeve."

"Should you employ me, Your Grace, I would do my best to protect your wards as though they were my own children." Emmeline meant every word that she said.

The duke nodded as though satisfied with her assertion, then straightened. "Of course, my suspicions that there's some insidious plot afoot to undermine me, or worse, do me some sort of mischief, might be completely unfounded. In any event, in order for me to complete my horological design and meet the deadline for submissions at the start of June, I need someone to entertain and educate these three rapscallions. Someone who *also* understands the importance of what I'm doing." The duke's direct gaze connected with Emmeline's. "Mrs. Temple mentioned that you once worked in an antique store that specialized in rare clocks and watches."

Emmeline swallowed. She would need to navigate this part of the interview carefully. She'd mention her father briefly, but then steer the topic in a slightly different direction if she could manage it. "Yes, my father once owned an antique clock store," she said. "But prior to that, he was a watchmaker by trade. So, I suppose my fascination with timepieces—especially those that are rare and old—is in my blood too. In fact, I attended a deceased estates auction at Pembridge's this morning where a late seventeenth-century Markwick pocket watch went for a song. I made a few bids, but an antique dealer by the name of Howell beat me to it."

The duke nodded, his expression solemn. "That's a pity. I collect pocket watches and I should like a Markwick for myself. *Howell*, you said?"

"Yes, his shop is in Chancery Lane, not far from the Inns of Court."

"Ah, I know it," said the duke. Then he cast her a half-quizzical, half-amused look from beneath his to-die-for lashes. It was *almost* a teasing look. "You make a habit of attending auctions, Mrs. Chase?"

"I . . . er . . ." *Blast and bother.* Emmeline hesitated, wondering how much information she should offer. She didn't want to appear secretive. But she also couldn't afford to say too much about her situation. Or rather, her father's. "It's a hobby of mine. I've always had a good eye for identifying valuable watches and clocks. If I can pick up a bargain here or there and then sell that item to another antique dealer for a little more . . ." She shrugged. "It's helped me to get by until I can secure a permanent position."

"Very clever," said the duke with an approving nod. Then he frowned. "Forgive me if I'm touching on a difficult subject, but Mrs. Temple led me to believe that you are a widow?"

Emmeline dropped her gaze and fiddled with the handle of her teacup. "Yes. My husband passed away almost three years ago. But now I'm *very* keen to secure work as a nanny. Or governess. I can certainly do both. The Academy prepares us for anything and everything."

The duke smiled. "It certainly sounds like it. Although, I *am* still bemused by the fact that you're trained in the art of self-defense. While you were quite nimble on your feet when I helped you down from my roof yesterday, you were less nimble when descending the attic ladder. And it takes more than a degree of agility to best an opponent in a fight."

Heat flooded Emmeline's cheeks as she recalled the moment she found herself on top of the duke, staring down into his shocked face. How her thighs had straddled his and how his hips had brushed—

Somehow, she wrested her thoughts away from the incendiary memory. To mask how flustered she was, she arched a brow in challenge. "You doubt my skill?"

"I . . ." The duke's gaze swept over her, assessing her appearance, and Emmeline's face grew even hotter. "A little," he said at last.

The wicked imp inside Emmeline that she could never quite keep in check made her say, "I'd be happy to offer you a complete demonstration to prove my assertions are true. That I would be able to fend off an intruder or an attacker—a kidnapper perhaps—and protect your wards."

The duke snorted. "You're claiming that you—a slip of a woman who can't be any taller than five foot four inches—could best me—a six-foot-two man—in a physical altercation?"

Emmeline raised her chin a notch. "I am, Your Grace." She nodded toward the fine Boulle clock on the marble mantelpiece. Then she frowned. She'd only been conversing with the duke a short while, yet the hands on the clock indicated it was almost half-past three. "Unless you don't have the time . . ."

The duke made a small scoffing sound in his throat. "I wouldn't refer to that clock. Most of the timepieces in my house seem to be running inaccurately at the moment. It's most frustrating, not knowing what the actual time is half the time."

Emmeline's heart pinched with sympathy. "I could well imagine. My Academy-issued pocket watch is as accurate as any chronometer, and it's always synchronized to Greenwich Mean Time."

The duke's gaze grew keen. "It is? I should add 'clock-setter' to your list of duties if I hire you, Mrs. Chase. But, I suppose if I *am* going to hire you, I should probably test your claim that you could defend my wards from the clutches of would-be kidnappers." The duke pushed to his feet, all six foot two inches of his intimidating-yet-glorious frame towering over Emmeline. He shrugged off his frock coat and draped it over the back of the wingchair.

"Very well, Mrs. Chase," he said with a sardonic cock of his brow. His gloved fingers beckoned her closer. "Do your best. Or worst. Whatever the case may be."

Chapter 5

In Which a Battalion of Hairpins and a Hem Cause Consternation; Cheapside Chivalry (or Lack Thereof) Is Discussed; The Tea Is Spilled... Again; The Duke Meets His Match; And an Explosion...

Xavier propped his gloved hands on his hips as he watched Mrs. Emmeline Chase rise to her feet then smooth her pinafore and skirts. A small smile played about her pretty pink mouth, and it took a herculean effort for him *not* to stare.

Which was not like him at all. The mere notion that his interest had been snagged by the nanny's physical appearance—a potential employee—was novel indeed. And also rather disquieting. Because he was *not* a lascivious sort of nobleman who ogled the servants. He certainly never dallied with them.

But just like yesterday, as soon as Mrs. Chase had entered his orbit, Xavier's whole world felt rather off-kilter. For one thing, he couldn't account for the fact that he was so transfixed by the young woman's glorious hair. Yesterday, at least a bonnet had covered most of her head. Today, she only wore some sort of flimsy lace and linen cap and her bright coppery locks had been pulled into a severe, matronly bun. No doubt a battalion of hairpins had been recruited to the cause.

During his entire conversation with Mrs. Chase—he should say interview, but it had felt rather more like a chat because he'd enjoyed the exchange thus far, immensely—he'd been forcing himself to look at her face, not her hair, lest he come across as peculiar.

Devil take him, even now as Mrs. Chase quite sensibly suggested that they move away from the afternoon tea things toward a less cluttered part of his study, Xavier's fingers twitched and flexed inside his silk-lined leather gloves with... with what?

Longing? Yearning? Desire?

The uncharacteristic impulse to throw off the nanny's silly cap—a pointless frippery that seemed as insubstantial as a spun-sugar cloud—and then pull out each and every one of those restraining hairpins so he could watch her burnished curls tumble down around her shoulders, persisted like an urgent itch he needed to scratch.

And he was about to get up close and personal with the beguiling nanny...

Get a grip, man. You're being goddamned ridiculous. As Xavier inwardly chastised himself, Mrs. Chase took up a position in the middle of the Turkish rug and rolled her shoulders as though she were loosening up her muscles before a bout of boxing or wrestling. She threaded her finely boned, elegant fingers together in front of her and cracked her knuckles.

It seemed she *was* entirely serious about demonstrating her self-defense skills.

Xavier frowned as he attempted to unravel the tangled skein of his emotions. He wasn't sure if he was impressed or amused or confounded. He certainly didn't feel as dark and bitter and brooding as he'd claimed to be a short time ago. Even though the afternoon was dismal and rainy, it felt as though Mrs. Emmeline Chase had brought a small measure of sunshine into St Lawrence House and had brightened Xavier's day.

Pleasantly baffled. That might be the right phrase, he decided as he loosened his starched cuffs and rolled up his sleeves in two precise folds. *Perhaps even a trifle mad. Because why on earth am I—*

"Your Grace," said Mrs. Chase, interrupting his convoluted musings. "I can see by your fearsome frown that you might be having second thoughts about this exercise. But I assure you, you won't hurt me."

"I..." Xavier met the nanny's blue-as-a-summer-sky gaze and saw no apprehension there. Only self-assurance and perhaps even a tiny spark of challenge. "Even though you've received self-defense instruction, it would be unchivalrous of me not to mention that like most gentlemen of my class, I've had years of training in boxing, fencing, and shooting. And I regularly engage in such activities to maintain my skills."

The nanny smiled and her gaze drifted to his chest and then to his linen-clad arms. Was she admiring his physique? Before Xavier could wrap his mind around such a strange thing, she said, "I can see that, Your Grace. And I'm not worried. Aside from receiving expert tuition at the Academy, I grew up in the vicinity of Cheapside. There are not many chivalrous gentlemen to be found in the streets around there. I can look after myself." Her pretty mouth curved into a smile. "But if it makes you feel any better, we can start with a simple, noncombative maneuver."

This lovely young woman used to live in Cheapside? The district wasn't far from Newgate Prison and Saffron Hill, one of the roughest, poorest areas of London. The insalubrious Fleet Ditch and its squalid slums weren't far away either.

It was becoming increasingly clear to Xavier that Mrs. Emmeline Chase was not easily daunted. He inclined his head. "Very well. I'm happy to follow your lead."

"Good." This time *she* beckoned him a bit closer. "I'll approach, but then at the last moment, I'm going to turn around and walk away from you. But I'd like you to grab my wrist to try and stop me. And I want your grip to be quite firm, like you mean business. Don't be all wishy-washy about it. I won't break."

"Wishy-washy?" Xavier couldn't suppress a smirk. "I've been called all sorts of epithets—both complimentary and unflattering—in my time, Mrs. Chase, but never that."

A bright red blush bloomed in Mrs. Chase's cheeks. "Oh, Your Grace. My apologies if I've offended you—"

He waved a dismissive hand. "No, of course you haven't. Here, don't *you* go all wishy-washy on me. I want to see the woman who used to stride down Cheapside and its environs, not the submissive servant. The nanny who takes on my wards—and my mercurial moods for that matter—will need a steely backbone."

Mrs. Chase nodded. "Understood. Let us proceed as I instructed." She took a few, quick steps closer to Xavier, then abruptly swung away from him. As she swiftly backtracked, Xavier caught her about the lower arm—tightly, but not *too* tight. He didn't want to hurt her or leave a mark. But no sooner had his gloved fingers wrapped around her woolen sleeve, she twisted her arm, gave a hard and precise yank, and then she was free and out of his reach. She'd deftly broken his hold at the weakest link—the point between his thumb and index finger. Even though it was a common maneuver, and he hadn't been particularly surprised, he was impressed by her speed and skill all the same.

Mrs. Chase grinned at him from the other side of the Turkish rug. "I know, I know. That wasn't anything particularly special. But I'm just warming you up."

"I don't doubt it," said Xavier. "Indeed, I'm keen to see what other tricks you might have up your sleeve."

"You should be more worried about what I've got concealed beneath my skirts," rejoined Mrs. Chase.

Before Xavier's mouth could even drop open, she'd flipped up the hem of her gown and the pristine white petticoats beneath to reveal one of her neat half boots in black kid leather,

her slender ankle encased in white hose, and the lacy edge of her drawers . . . the very things that had tormented him yesterday. But then he also noticed the pearl handle of a small, sheathed knife, held in place by a black ribbon garter.

"One must be prepared for anything, Your Grace," Mrs. Chase said matter-of-factly as she dropped her skirts back into place.

"Ahem . . . I . . ." Good God, the woman was going to put *him* to the blush. "Quite," he managed at last. "Just so."

He forced his gaze upward to meet Mrs. Chase's. "Are there any other hidden weapons I should know about on your person?" he asked, hoping the sudden rough edge to his voice wouldn't betray how rattled he was. "No pistols or swords or garottes or knuckle-dusters?"

Her blue eyes danced with mischief. "I have been known to deliver a tongue lashing on the odd occasion. But only when it's deserved."

Of course, Xavier's attention immediately fell to that pretty pink mouth again, and this time, he *could* feel heat flaring in his cheeks. Damn it. He didn't want to think about Mrs. Chase's tongue or her lusciously plump lips. Or her shapely ankles for that matter. How could he engage her services as a nanny if he kept having inappropriate thoughts about her?

"Now . . ." Mrs. Chase continued on as though nothing were amiss. As though she hadn't completely disarmed him already. "Let me demonstrate another evasive maneuver. I'll ask you to grab my arm in the same way . . . and then I'll restrain you."

"*Restrain* me?"

"I promise I won't hurt you," asserted Mrs. Chase.

No, she would simply floor him with those bright blue eyes and her words. And that hair. A coppery lock had managed to escape its pin prison and was caressing her ear.

Xavier swallowed and dragged his gaze back to her face. The nanny had spoken again, and he'd completely missed what she'd said. "I'm sorry. You'll need to repeat that."

She cast him an enigmatic smile. "I asked if you're ready, Your Grace."

He ran a hand through his hair then nodded . . . even though he wasn't sure at all. "Yes."

That smile again. It was maddening that Xavier couldn't interpret it. "Good. Remember to grab my arm as I turn away."

Like before, Mrs. Chase crossed the rug toward him, and as she drew close, some sort of strange electric frisson sparked down Xavier's spine. Curiosity? Anticipation?

Excitement?

He didn't have time to dwell on his feelings because Mrs. Chase was right in front of him . . . and then in the space of a heartbeat, she changed course. As she whirled away, he snagged her arm, halting her retreat.

Ha! He'd bested—

All at once, she turned back, her free hand clamped onto his wrist, and then she was somehow twisting his arm and shoulder up and around and applying pressure in such a precise and forceful way that he found himself losing his balance. In the blink of an eye, he was down on one knee, one hand on the floor, while his captured arm was immobilized and bent at an odd angle behind him. In fact, he could barely move, and if he did, it was *exceedingly* uncomfortable.

He was trussed like a Christmas goose and completely at Mrs. Chase's mercy.

Through the disheveled curtain of his hair, he glanced up at her. "Very clever," he said. "I did not see that coming."

She released him and as he straightened and pushed his hair out of his eyes, he suspected her smile was more than a little bit smug. He couldn't say that he blamed her.

"I'm convinced you can hold your own, Mrs. Chase," he began, but then she held up a hand.

"Not all attacks come from the front, Your Grace. Some are

stealthy and come from behind. To complete my demonstration, I'd like to show you how I'd manage in that sort of situation." She snared his gaze. "If you'll indulge me a little longer."

His masculine pride and his dignity had already been dented, so what more did he have to lose? And he couldn't deny that part of him was unabashedly intrigued by this woman and her seemingly endless arsenal of hidden talents. Perhaps the British Army or the Foreign Office should recruit Parasol Academy graduates into their service.

"Of course," he said. "What would you like me to do?"

She stepped close and turned so that her back was almost against his front. Indeed, she was so close, he caught the beguiling scent of her. A light floral fragrance (violets perhaps) and something else he suspected was simply "Mrs. Chase" drifted around him, and for one insane moment he struggled against the impulse to press his nose against the pale column of her elegant neck to inhale more of that sweet scent.

What the devil was wrong with him today?

Once again, he fought to pay attention to her directions.

"Now, Your Grace, I want you to slide your crooked arm about my neck, grip your own wrist with your other hand to make a noose, and then pull me backward like you mean to haul me off or even throttle me."

Xavier immediately stiffened. The mere idea of someone trying to do something so appalling to Mrs. Chase filled him with abhorrence and smoldering anger. Nevertheless, he complied and carefully slid his bent arm around her. He then clasped his own wrist in an uncompromising hold. At the same time, her hands rose and she gripped his bared wrists and forearms. Her touch seemed to tingle and burn the flesh beneath, but not in an unpleasant way. In fact, it was strangely exhilarating.

But perhaps that was simply because Xavier was not used to being so physically close to anyone. Especially a copper-tressed enchantress who smelled as sweet and delicate as a posy of violets, yet kept a knife strapped about her ankle and could bring a man to his knees.

She turned her head toward him and one of those damned silken locks almost brushed against his lips. "If this is to work, you'll need to grip me harder. Like you mean business, Your Grace."

"Very well." Xavier gritted his teeth and then tightened his hold, pulling her body flush against his. Thank God the nanny's skirts were voluminous, because if he had to maintain this position for too much longer, an untoward stirring in the vicinity of his trousers was bound to occur.

"Good," said Mrs. Chase, and before Xavier knew what she was about, she was bending her knees and tipping sideways, and he was following her down . . . right up until the moment she let go of his arms and grabbed him with surprising strength about the lower thighs. And then somehow he lost his footing, *again*, and found himself tumbling to the rug.

She tumbled with him, her body crashing into his, her skirts tangling with his legs as they rolled. The momentum of their collision carried them toward the sitting area . . . And then there was a clatter and a crash, and the next thing Xavier knew, he was flat on his back, covered in tea and coffee, and Mrs. Chase was straddling his hips.

Again. Like yesterday.

As Xavier stared up at the nanny, he realized he didn't care that vast patches of his linen shirt and silk vest were soaked through and uncomfortably plastered to his skin. Or that he might be lying on a mound of egg and cress sandwiches.

Rather, he became acutely aware that all the air had been sucked from his lungs.

But he wasn't winded. Mrs. Chase had somehow stolen his breath.

She was breathless too. She was leaning over him, her arms braced either side of his head. Her silly cap had fallen off and more of her curls, which had escaped the confines of her ruthlessly pinned bun, were practically tickling his cheeks. Beneath his gloved hands, which had somehow ended up about her waist, he could feel the quickened pace of her breathing as her rib cage expanded and contracted.

Her face was so close as it hovered above his, he could see her fine lashes were tipped with gold and that there were tiny flecks of gentian violet in the depths of her azure eyes. And that the scattering of freckles across her pert nose and flushed cheeks brought to mind cinnamon or nutmeg dusted across cream...

"I-I... I'm so, so sorry, Your Grace," Mrs. Chase stammered as she pushed herself up to a sitting position. She tucked her unruly hair behind her ears. "I assure you, it's not a habit of mine to sit upon—" She broke off and color suffused her cheeks. And then a frown knit her brow. "I hope I haven't hurt you."

"No. I'm perfectly fine." Well, that was a lie. Xavier's world had been turned upside down and inside out and he wasn't sure how long it would take him to recover his equilibrium.

But recover it he must. For the sake of his project and his wards. He could hardly employ Mrs. Chase if he were at sixes and sevens around her. He couldn't afford to be distracted when the deadline for his submission loomed.

Besides, it was the right thing to do. Maintaining his usual level of dispassionate, professional detachment when it came to interacting with his staff shouldn't be difficult. He simply needed to put some distance—especially physical distance—between himself and the nanny.

If he could do that, there was no doubt in Xavier's mind that she'd be perfect for the job.

To his relief, Mrs. Chase climbed off him, and then Xavier clambered to his feet.

"Oh dear. We've made quite a mess," murmured Mrs. Chase as she cast her dismayed gaze over the wreckage: the upended table, the scattered china, the squashed sandwiches and strewn scones, and of course the spilled tea and coffee that he was also wearing.

She retrieved her lacy cap and pinned it on her head while Xavier pulled out a kerchief from his trouser pocket and wiped his damp neck and torso. "How do you feel about birds?" he asked. "Specifically, ravens? Because I have one as a pet. He's named Horatio and he's rather..." He paused, searching for the right word. "Impudent. Large and loquacious would also be accurate descriptors. I wouldn't want him to put you off when you start."

Mrs. Chase's eyes widened. "Are you... are you actually offering me the job, Your Grace?" she whispered.

"Yes. I am. If you're willing to take it." Xavier studied her face, trying to gauge her reaction. He was suddenly and quite inexplicably as tense as a bowstring. If she said no...

The nanny bit her lip as though she were suppressing a smile. Or was she apprehensive? Xavier hated that he couldn't tell.

He was about to verbally nudge her for a reply when she said, "Well, to be perfectly honest, Your Grace, I'm not at all concerned that you have a large raven as a pet. In fact, I've already met him, and I think him a rather handsome and charming fellow. But I will admit that I'm a tad bothered to learn that you don't drink tea." She gave a small sigh, but there was an unmistakable gleam in her eye as she added, "But I suppose I can overlook that one small thing."

Relief welled inside Xavier's chest. "So, your answer is yes?" Even though he knew she'd been teasing him again, he needed to hear her say it.

Mrs. Chase clasped her hands beneath her chin and this time, she *did* smile. "Yes. It's an unequivocal yes. I will accept your offer."

Xavier nodded and his own mouth began to curl up at the

corners. "Excellent. I shall speak to Mrs. Temple about the contract—"

All of a sudden, the terrible sound of glass shattering penetrated the study and Xavier swore, quite loudly, before he could stop himself.

This nerve-jangling smash was immediately followed by a cacophony of other equally disconcerting, if not altogether disagreeable noises: a shrill female scream; a slamming door; the booming baritone of a man (possibly Woodley). And then there was the wince-inducing counterpoint to it all... the raucous squawking of Horatio. No doubt his redoubtable bird was in the midst of all the mayhem.

Xavier muttered another curse, this time beneath his breath. Dash it all. What the devil had happened now? What mischief had his three young wards got up to *this* time? Had they brought down the chandelier in the entry hall? Broken the stained-glass window above the landing on the main staircase? Smashed a pane of a glass-fronted bookcase in the library? Exploded another firecracker?

He caught Mrs. Chase's eye and noted her countenance had blanched. Damn it. He didn't want her to leave before she'd even begun.

"Your wards?" asked the nanny, sympathy in her gaze.

"I think so." Xavier started toward the door. "I can't hear Harry, Barry, or Gary howling or wailing, so I'll assume no one has been hurt. It sounds like the crash was close by."

CHAPTER 6

Concerning Ginger Beer, a Swarm of Gnats, Dust, and a Discussion About Puddles; And a Terrapin Finds a New Home . . .

Xavier strode out of his private study, following the sound of Horatio's squawks. Mrs. Chase followed close behind.

It didn't take long to find the locus of the disaster. It was in the nearby library. And the panes of one of the bookcase doors had indeed been broken.

As Xavier stood on the threshold, he took in the scene—or should he say the gigantic mess?—and its myriad details. Shards of glass—large and small—lay scattered about the Persian rug and some sort of pale foamy liquid was fizzing and bubbling and oozing out of the top of a dark brown bottle which sat in the middle of his desk. The foam also coated the front of the damaged bookcase and the tomes inside. It slid down the books' tooled leather spines and dripped from the shelves before pooling in a pale brown puddle on the floor below. This strange frothy liquid also trickled down the five faces that turned toward Xavier. A slightly sweet yet yeasty aroma—beer or ale, perhaps—permeated the air.

Harry threw Xavier a mulish look as she brushed a blob of froth from her nose (at least Xavier *thought* it was a mulish look; reading facial expressions with any degree of accuracy, especially in a fraught situation like this was *not* his forte), while Barry and Gary stared wide-eyed at Xavier from beneath the shelter of the mahogany desk. Woodley, wearing a thunderous scowl (now bald-faced anger was an emotion Xavier could reliably read), was mopping his forehead with a kerchief, while one of the younger housemaids, who was filling in as a nursemaid, gaped at Xavier in open-mouthed horror. And Horatio, upon seeing his master, ceased screeching and alighted on Xavier's shoulder.

"Batten down the hatches!" the raven cawed beside Xavier's ear. "Run! Hide! Duck! Take cover!" Then after the briefest of pauses, "Bottom's up!"

"Your Grace," began the butler at the same moment the maid, Fanny, exclaimed, "I'm so sorry, Your Grace, but Miss Harriet absconded from the nursery when I was darning a tear in one of Master Bartholomew's sleeves, and—"

"It seems she decided to explode a bottle of ginger beer," concluded Woodley with an arch of a grizzled brow. "It's like a volcano has erupted in here."

Harry shrugged and pushed her glasses up her nose. "It was only supposed to be a *little* explosion. More of a pop really. I wanted to see if I could make a ginger beer fountain. Something to entertain Bartholomew and Gareth, because they're bored witless and we haven't been to the park, or anywhere in fact, in ages. But I added too much bicarbonate of soda to the bottle, so after I replaced the cork, the pressure inside built up and—"

Xavier held up a hand. "Enough," he barked before closing his eyes and releasing a heavy sigh. He didn't like to raise his voice—and he most certainly didn't want to scare off Mrs. Chase—but when so many people talked to him at once, competing for his attention, a wave of irritation rose up inside him and a cloud of confusion invaded his mind. It was akin to being attacked by a swarm of gnats. It didn't help that he was already on edge because his usually pristine library had been turned into a complete and utter shambles.

He drew a deep, calming breath and recited pi to six decimal places in his head before he opened his eyes and spoke to his ward. "While I understand that you've been stuck inside St Lawrence House for far too long, Harry," he said, hoping he was using an appropriate degree of sternness, "I cannot dismiss the fact that you have ignored the rules I set out to keep you and your brothers safe. Did I not tell you yesterday that these scientific experiments of yours must cease? Can you not see that they are dangerous when you are a novice?" He gestured at the ruined bookcase and the mess in general. "Aside from destroying a perfectly good piece of furniture and its contents, you, or Barry or Gary"—for the life of him, Xavier could *never* remember the boys' actual names—"Fanny, or Woodley, or even Horatio might have been terribly injured. Judging by the amount of splintered glass lying about, I'm amazed you weren't torn to shreds." He plunged his brows into a deep frown to convey the depth of his displeasure and disappointment. "You do realize there must be consequences for your actions. Especially after yesterday when you catapulted flour all over the nursery."

Harry lifted her small, pointed chin and opened her mouth to respond, but Mrs. Chase stepped forward. "Forgive me for interrupting, but might I have a word with your ward, Your Grace?"

Xavier sighed. "Be my guest." He then turned to Woodley. "Might I suggest you speak with Mrs. Lambton about assembling a contingent of maids and footmen? It's going to take a considerable effort to clean *this* mess up."

Horatio, who was still perched on Xavier's shoulder crowed, "All hands on deck. All hands on deck."

The butler bowed. "I shall do so at once, Your Grace."

After Woodley quit the room, Xavier cast his gaze over the

ruined library once more. What on earth was he going to say to Harriet that hadn't already been said? He scrubbed a hand down his face as exasperation and a sense of hopelessness welled up inside him. He feared he was going to make a right royal hash of being a guardian.

But maybe, just maybe, Mrs. Chase might make things right.

He was certainly looking forward to finding out what sort of "magic" this Parasol nanny could wield.

She had the job! Emmeline could hardly believe it. Although, considering what had transpired in the library—and in the nursery yesterday—she would have her work cut out for her winning over "Harry, Barry, and Gary" and restoring some semblance of peace and order to St Lawrence House.

But then, if a Parasol nanny wasn't up to the task, then *no one* would be.

Emmeline caught the oldest ward's eye. "Miss Harriet, His Grace has asked me to be your new nanny."

The girl scowled at Emmeline. "You were the woman stuck on the roof. Bartholomew, Gareth, and I saw you. Why should I listen to someone who does equally silly and dangerous things?"

"Harriet," said the duke. His tone held an ominous note of warning. "You are already skating on thin ice. Where are your manners?"

Emmeline cast him a quick smile. "No, your ward makes a very good point, Your Grace." She turned back to the girl. "You're right. I shouldn't have been on the roof. It was a very dangerous and altogether foolish thing for me to do. And of course, you don't know me from a bar of soap, so you have every right to question my advice. But what I *do* know, is that His Grace is quite right. You cannot keep conducting these experiments. They are far too dangerous and destructive. How *would* you feel if Bartholomew or Gareth or Horatio or even

Archimedes got hurt? You cannot tell me that you wouldn't feel terrible."

The girl bit her lip. "I don't *want* anyone to get hurt. But being ignored"—she shot her guardian a resentful look—"and being locked up in a boring old nursery all the time with nothing to do also feels terrible."

"I agree. There's nothing worse." Emmeline pulled her silver watch from her pocket and passed it to the girl. "I tell you what, Miss Harriet, until I can think up some safer experiments to conduct, I have an idea for a horological study." She leaned closer to the girl and murmured, "Something that will help you get back into your Cousin Xavier's good books. It will be a way for you to make amends."

Harriet's eyes narrowed. "All right . . ."

"I shall tell you more about it shortly when I visit the nursery. But"—she exchanged a look with the duke before returning her attention to Harriet—"I think we need to get to the bottom of why His Grace's clocks are not running properly. My pocket watch keeps perfect time, so we are going to use that to help us set the correct time throughout St Lawrence House. Then we will monitor each timepiece accordingly. We'll need to keep records and make charts and schedules and all sorts of things to keep track of everything—some clocks need a wind every eight days, some clocks need a daily wind—so a notebook would be handy."

Harriet pushed her glasses up her nose. "I have one."

"Excellent. Will you look after my watch for me until I get to the nursery? I should stay here to help sort out things in the library. I won't be long, though."

Harriet nodded solemnly and pushed Emmeline's watch into a pocket of her ginger-beer-stained pinafore. "Very well, Nanny Chase. And I prefer Harry rather than Harriet."

Emmeline inclined her head. "I will see you soon, Harry."

After Harry collected Archimedes—the frog had been sheltering under the desk with Bartholomew and Gareth—the young maid, Fanny, ferried the children away. Horatio—after offering his silent congratulations to Emmeline—flew after them.

When Emmeline turned back to face the library, she found the duke was watching her. But his expression was inscrutable. "Harry likes you," he said simply. "She didn't poke her tongue out at you, or call you a wicked witch or something else equally insulting."

Emmeline arched a brow. "I should hope not. I might possess the ability to charm children, but I'm certainly not a witch. And I'm only a little bit wicked."

The duke blinked at her as though he couldn't quite make out if she were jesting or not. But then a deep rumbling laugh spilled from him. "My goodness, Mrs. Chase. You say the most peculiar things. But I think it's one of the qualities I like about you. And I think my wards will, too."

His shoulders then rose and fell with a weary sigh. "You don't have to do anything about this." He nodded at the library. "Woodley and the rest of the staff will take care of it. God knows, they've had a great deal of experience in dealing with enormous messes of late."

"It's quite all right, Your Grace," said Emmeline. "I want to make a difference in your life and that of your wards. Making things better is one of the main duties of a Parasol nanny." She offered him a tentative smile. "Besides, I wouldn't mind taking a peek at what books you have that might be of interest to children."

The duke's gaze wandered over the sticky shelves. "I'm guessing none at all. None that I can recall at any rate. And I grew up here." His eyes returned to Emmeline's face. "I'm happy to expend funds on books my wards might enjoy. I have an account at Hatchards."

Emmeline nodded her approval. "I shall let you know."

"Very well then, Mrs. Chase." The duke bowed stiffly. "No

doubt, I shall see you anon? I'm sure we'll need to speak about making arrangements to have your belongings moved to St Lawrence House." He frowned. "Of course, I've made the assumption that you wish to start here immediately. If that's not the case, I do apologize."

"There's no need for an apology. I do wish to start. Straightaway."

"Excellent. When you're ready, you shall find me in my study. Mrs. Lambton, my housekeeper, will help you with settling in. I'll also send a message to Mrs. Temple about your employment contract."

Emmeline bobbed a curtsy. She must remember her employer was a duke. "Thank you, Your Grace. You'll never know how grateful I am for this opportunity."

The ghost of a smile momentarily softened the duke's harsh features. "No, thank *you*, Mrs. Chase." And then the man turned on his heel and stalked stiffly away.

When the duke disappeared from view, Emmeline reached into her pocket. It wasn't a lie when she'd said one of her chief duties was to make things better. And considering the chaos in front of her—the smashed glass and ruined books and the sticky ginger beer foam coating everything—she would begin right now.

On rare occasions—in *exceptional* circumstances—the *Parasol Academy Handbook* permitted nannies and governesses to discreetly use "decalamitifying dust." It didn't always appear in one's pocket. One had to "ask" the Fae Realm for it. If and only if the incident was deemed a true calamity by the Fae—and one that should be rectified by such powerful magic—would the enchanted dust materialize.

Surely it couldn't hurt to call upon such a tool now. There *had* been an explosion of sorts.

While Emmeline could, in theory, employ the dust to put the whole room to rights—so it looked like nothing untoward had happened at all—it might invite *too* many inconvenient questions. It would be difficult to explain how one woman could clean up all the broken glass shards *and* repair the glass panes in the bookcases in next to no time. But she could at least remove the ginger beer residue and return the stained books to an unsullied state. If anyone *did* happen to ask her about the library's restoration, she'd claim that courtesy of her Parasol Academy training, she was a dab hand with a cleaning cloth.

More than anything, she wanted to impress the duke. She *did* want to make a difference in his life. And in the lives of his wards too.

Mind made up, Emmeline fisted her hand in her pocket, closed her eyes tightly, and with great reverence and sincerity, silently entreated the Fae to grant her the gift of the decalamitifying dust. And then her heart skipped as she felt a gentle tingling warmth in her fingertips which rapidly spread to her palm, making it buzz. *Yes.*

When Emmeline withdrew her fist, she *knew* that she held a small handful of magical silver powder. As she unfurled her fingers, the mound of dust sitting on her palm—no more than a spoonful—glittered and winked. Now she had been gifted it, she just had to deploy it with careful and clear intent. "*Decalamitify* ginger beer," she whispered, then gently blew.

The dust immediately dispersed, spreading outward and around the library in a great twinkling, starlike cloud. It engulfed the bookcases, the ceiling, the Persian rug. It blanketed the desk and the furniture and the mantelpiece. Everything was swallowed up in a sparkling haze. And then all at once, the cloud dissipated, revealing that the library was spotless. Well, free of ginger beer foam at any rate.

Emmeline gave an approving nod. What a pity she didn't think to use decalamitifying dust in the duke's study after they upset the afternoon tea table.

"You're not like the other nannies," came a small voice from behind Emmeline, and she almost jumped out of her skin.

Swinging around, she discovered that Bartholomew, the

middle child—no one had told her his age, but she suspected he was about six or seven—was standing in the hall.

Emmeline pressed a hand to her chest where her heart was pounding hard and fast. Oh, blast and drat and some other curse word she shouldn't even think of in the presence of a child. Had the boy seen her using the decalamitifying dust? Because that was a big no-no. A you-shall-be-expelled-from-the-Parasol-Academy-ranks-forevermore kind of offense.

She *really* should have shut the door.

Emmeline knelt down on the floor and looked into the young boy's eyes. "Hullo there, Master Bartholomew. What do you mean, I'm not like the other nannies?"

His small nose screwed up. "Well, for one thing, you're nice. And you smile a lot."

Maybe Bartholomew *hadn't* seen anything out of the ordinary. Emmeline breathed an internal sigh of relief. "Well, I should hope that I'm not like other nannies. That would be rather dull. To be like everyone else. And I believe that one should smile. And often."

"Cousin Xavier said you found Gareth's tin soldier," said the boy. "That it was on the roof and you put it in your pocket for safekeeping."

"I did," said Emmeline. It was only a small white lie.

Bartholomew's large brown eyes suddenly gleamed with a hopeful light. "Will you really take us to the park? In the rain?"

Emmeline smiled. "Of course. Who doesn't like jumping in puddles?"

Bartholomew nodded, then another look crossed his features. An expression that was bright-eyed eagerness tempered with hesitancy. "Is there something in your pocket for me, Nanny Chase?"

Oh my. What a sweet child. "I suppose that depends on what you need, Master Bartholomew."

The boy bit his lip. "I want Mama and Papa back," he said. "But I know you can't do that."

Emmeline's breath hitched and her heart suddenly felt like it was about to break in two. "No. I can't do that," she said gently. "I wish I could."

Bartholomew nodded. "I sometimes want a hug. Harry hugs me. But it's not quite the same."

"Well," said Emmeline, "if you ever need one of those, you can always ask me. I have an endless supply."

A small smile lifted the corners of the boy's mouth. "All right."

"Wait a minute. There *is* something in my pocket for you." Emmeline had the sudden urge to reach into the folds of her gown, and when she pulled out her hand, she was holding a small turtle with a lovely glossy shell. Sometimes Parasol Academy uniform pockets simply worked that way. They produced exactly what a child needed at the right moment.

Bartholomew's eyes immediately brightened. "It's a tortoise!" he cried. "I've always wanted one."

"I think it's actually a type of turtle. A terrapin." Emmeline lifted the creature to her ear. "He tells me his name is Aristotle and he would very much like to become friends with you and Archimedes. Oh . . ." She reached back into her pocket again and pulled out a glass jar. "I hope you're not squeamish, but I have some crickets here to feed both Archimedes and Aristotle. And when we go to the park tomorrow, I'm sure we'll find plenty of snails and worms for them too."

Bartholomew clapped his hands. "Hurrah!"

Emmeline passed Aristotle to the boy and then climbed to her feet. "Will you show me the way to the nursery from here?"

Bartholomew clasped her hand. "This way," he said, tugging her down the hall toward the stairs, and Emmeline smiled. She couldn't quite explain the unexpected glow suffusing her chest, but she suddenly felt like she'd found more than a mere "situation."

Of course, Emmeline sternly reminded herself as her young

charge led her past the door to the duke's study, *I mustn't let my guard down* too *much.*

She must always remember to keep her mind on the job. She mustn't let her thoughts stray to her enigmatic and far-too-attractive employer. She must quell the pitter-patter of her heart every time the Duke of St Lawrence walked into the room, or looked her way, or even uttered a word in that mesmerizing baritone of his.

Yes, she was a Parasol nanny first and foremost. She would be professional. She would carry out her duties in an exemplary fashion. Fraternizing with one's employer was forbidden by the Academy, and she could not afford to lose this job or her Parasol Academy licence for oh, so many reasons.

No matter what happened in the duke's chaotic household over the coming days, she would strictly adhere to one of the Academy's mottos. She would, "Keep calm and nanny on."

Chapter 7

Concerning the Hunt for an Egyptian Mummy and an Aztec Serpent in a Roman Gallery: An Unfortunate Fracas and a Volley of Impolite Epithets; The Rescue of a Priceless Black Beetle; And a Boiled Lobster Makes an Appearance...

"Should we go in search of the Aztec serpent? Upstairs in the Americas Room?" Emmeline asked Miss Harriet, who was fiercely studying the British Museum guide.

They were presently lingering in the museum's Roman Gallery in the shadow of a statue of the Townley Venus, working out their plan of attack for the remainder of their visit. But an hour remained before the Duke of St Lawrence returned with his carriage—Emmeline understood that he was at the Palace of Westminster attending to some sort of parliamentary or horological business—and there was so much they could see.

Of course, Emmeline was very much aware that while Harry was enamored with many of the exhibits, and would quite happily explore the museum all day, Bartholomew and Gareth would not. They'd only been here an hour and the boys were already growing restless. In fact, at any moment one or both of them might pay a visit to tantrum territory, or at the very least the state-of-stomping-feet or wobbling-lower-lip-land. All such destinations were to be avoided at all costs.

Harry, who'd been considering Emmeline's suggestion, frowned and pushed her glasses farther up her nose. "Hmmm.

No doubt Bartholomew and Gareth would like to see a serpent. They adore creepy-crawly, slithery things. I'd like to visit the Chantress of Amun's sarcophagus in the Mummy Room. It's upstairs too. I did enjoy the Egyptian Galleries—"

Harry got no further as a furious, high-pitched wail burst through the museum's hallowed and hitherto hushed halls. It ricocheted off marble busts and statues and the Roman Gallery's parquetry floor, and Emmeline's nanny instincts immediately kicked in.

Spinning around, her Parasol Academy uniform's skirts flaring wide, she quickly located the source of the commotion. So did all the other museum visitors milling about, but right at that moment, Emmeline didn't give a flying fig about them and their busybodying.

A handful of yards away, Gareth and Bartholomew had entered the field-of-fraternal-fisticuffs. Indeed, the boys were engaged in an all-out struggle that seemed to fall somewhere between an epic tug-of-war and a Greco-Roman wrestling bout. Whatever it was, it involved locked arms and white-knuckled fists and a lot of pushing and pulling and grunting. A flummoxed St Lawrence House footman—Bertie—who'd been tasked by Emmeline to watch over the young boys for a few minutes, waved his hands about while ineffectually muttering, "There, there. That's enough now, you two. There's no need to fight."

Oh, dickens on toast. After a fortnight of caring for the Duke of St Lawrence's high-spirited wards, Emmeline had quickly learned that there was nothing in the *Parasol Academy Handbook* that had adequately prepared her for the unvarnished reality: that her ingenuity would be constantly tested and her patience would become as frayed as a ball of yarn that had been attacked by kittens. It was a good thing that the children, like kittens, were really quite adorable.

As Emmeline hastened over to her enraged charges, the typical juvenile insults started to fly.

"Let go, you ninny-poop head! It's *my* beetle," cried Gareth, his chubby cheeks pink with indignation and exertion. His small fingers were wrapped about his brother's closed fists as he attempted to prize something—presumably the beetle in question—out of Bartholomew's grip.

"No, it's *my* beetle," bellowed Bartholomew, his brown eyes blazing. "It's for Aristotle. And it's nin-*com*-poop, you noddy numskull. Not ninny-poop."

Emmeline's lips twitched, but then she determinedly tamped down the urge to laugh at the boys' neologisms; it could not be denied that "ninny-poop" was a tad mirth-inducing. Instead, she summoned the required "very stern" frown as per the *Parasol Academy Handbook* guidelines.

Such a public display of rudeness and unruliness could not continue. Not only did it reflect negatively on Emmeline's skills as a much-vaunted Parasol nanny, but one or both of the boys might get hurt. Or the beetle for that matter. (*Good grief. Why fight over a beetle? And where on earth had they found one in the British Museum?*)

Emmeline lowered herself to her charges' level, kneeling upon the floor. "Now, now. Let's be considerate of each other and those around us," she said firmly but calmly as she attempted to catch each of the boys' gazes. "Petty squabbling does you no credit. And over a beetle of all things. I'm certain there are plenty in the gardens of St Lawrence House or Hyde Park. Besides, I'm sure neither of you wants to accidentally squash it, do you?"

Bartholomew at last wrested himself away from his younger brother's clutches. "It's not an *ordinary* beetle, Nanny Chase," he said, rolling his eyes. "It's a special black beetle. A *scab* beetle, and it's mine. I found it."

A scab beetle? *Oh no . . . Surely not . . .*

Emmeline swallowed as an awful thought struck her right between the eyes like a missile released from a slingshot. "Bartholomew," she said carefully in a low voice. "Where did you find it?"

He gestured with his chin. "Back there. In the room with all the stone tablets with the funny writing and the jars with the brains. And all the scab beetles."

"And the pinkses," added Gareth.

Pinkses? "You mean sphinxes?" asked Emmeline. "In the Egyptian Gallery?"

Both of the boys nodded. "Yes," said Bartholomew.

Emmeline drew a calming breath to subdue the tremor of apprehension in her belly. "Bartholomew, might I see this special beetle?"

The boy narrowed his eyes as he considered her request. "Very well." He uncurled his small fingers, and in the palm of his hand sat a priceless Egyptian artifact that had been carved from some sort of black stone. Feldspar or quartz perhaps.

Biting back a gasp of horror, Emmeline cleared her throat and murmured, "Boys, I'm afraid you cannot keep this beetle. It's a scarab and it's very old and very expensive and it belongs here. The museum guards would be very, very miffed if we tried to take it home. And His Grace would not allow it either."

Bartholomew's bottom lip protruded into a decided pout. "But there were lots of them on the shelf. And Aristotle likes beetles."

"Don't you think your terrapin would rather a real beetle?" asked Emmeline.

The boy shrugged. "I suppose."

"If you and Gareth would both like your very own scarabs, we can make some out of a special powder called plaster of Paris and water. And when they're hard like a rock, we can paint them whatever color you like." Emmeline donned an enthusiastic expression that would hopefully prove infectious. "You could even have a rainbow beetle."

"Really?" said Gareth, his face lighting up. "I want a rainbow beetle."

"I want a blue beetle," said Bartholomew.

"Wonderful." Emmeline held out her hand for the scarab, but as Bartholomew passed it to her, a booming bass tuba of a voice blasted through the air.

"'Allo, 'allo . . ." A heavy hand landed on Emmeline's shoulder. "Wot 'ave you got there, miss? Somefink tha' doesn't belong to you, I fink. You're nicked."

Oh, blooming bleeding blinking hell. Talk about leaping out of the frying pan and straight into a vat of boiling oil.

As Emmeline rose to her feet to face her accuser—a museum guard—she slid the scarab into her pocket. "I don't know what you mean, sir," she said in the smoothest, most I'm-not-at-all-guilty voice she could muster. She would protect her charges, and her reputation and that of the Parasol Academy—and of course, the Duke of St Lawrence's good name—using whatever means necessary.

She could *not* lose her job. She'd already paid off the turnkey at Newgate Prison after she'd received her first week's wages, and her father was as safe as he could be whilst in such a terrible place.

Aside from all that, she *was* good at nannying. And she liked working for the duke.

The museum guard, a solid middle-aged fellow with bushy side-whiskers and a mustache a bull walrus would be proud of, folded his bulky arms over his barrel chest. "Don't lie to me, miss, or fings will no' go well for you. I saw that scarab in your 'and, and one of 'em has been reported missin' from the Egyptian Gallery next door. Now"—he aimed an admonitory finger at her, almost poking her in the nose—"stop messin' me about and 'and it over, or I'll 'ave to lock you up in the guard's office while a bobby's summoned."

Well, *that* certainly wasn't going to happen. Not on Emmeline's watch.

Emmeline Chase, Parasol Academy nanny, needed to take charge. Raising her chin, she said to the glowering guard, "I assure you, sir, I do not have a scarab on my person." She held out both her white-gloved hands, palms facing upward. "See. Regardless of what you *thought* you saw, it seems you're quite mistaken."

The guard's eyes narrowed. "Well, you must've put it in one of your pockets or somefink." He thrust his chin belligerently. "Turn 'em out. Let's see wha' you've got stashed in those skirts o' yours."

Ugh. The guard was only doing his job, but right now, Emmeline wished she had her Academy umbrella at hand so she could give him a short sharp jab and momentarily confuse him. That would give her enough time to put the scarab back where it belonged. Unfortunately, and most inconveniently, her umbrella had been stowed in the museum's cloak room along with the children's gumboots and mackintoshes.

But all was not lost. Emmeline had one more trick up her sleeve that she could discreetly employ even in a crowded museum gallery.

She affected a resigned sigh. "Very well, sir," she said as she reached into her pocket. The cold, hard scarab sat at the bottom, but a small scent bottle had materialized above it. Curling her fingers about the cool glass, Emmeline withdrew her hand.

The scowling guard seized her wrist in an uncompromising grip and narrowed his suspicious gaze on the azure-blue bottle with its engraved silver lid. "'Ere, what's that? That's not a scarab."

Emmeline pressed the back of her other hand to her forehead à la swooning damsel. "I'm sorry, sir. It's a bottle of hartshorn. I'm suddenly feeling dizzy."

"Hartshorn?" repeated the guard, his brow concertina-ing in apparent confusion.

"Smelling salts or sal volatile," asserted Emmeline, uncapping the bottle with her thumb. "If you don't mind, I'd rather not fall into a dead faint and crack my head open like Humpty-Dumpty. That would be quite bothersome for everyone, don't you think?" She gave a little shudder for effect. "Just think of the mess."

The disgruntled guard gave a humph. "All right, then," he said, releasing his hold on her arm. "But no funny business."

"Hartshorn is perfectly harmless. See . . ." Emmeline waved the bottle—which really contained a potent "befuddling" perfume, *not* smelling salts—beneath the guard's nose. At the same time, she muttered beneath her breath the required Faerillion spell, "*Befuddlio.*"

The "befuddling" fumes—a faintly lavender-hued haze—wafted upward and the guard's gaze grew clouded and dreamy almost immediately. Then he shook his head and eyed Emmeline benignly. "Erm, can I 'elp you, miss?"

Emmeline donned her most charming smile as she pocketed the recapped bottle. "Why yes, good sir. If you could direct me to the Egyptian Gallery, I'd be most grateful. I'd like to show my young charges"—she beckoned Harry, Bartholomew, and Gareth closer—"the sphinxes. I've heard they are *not* to be missed."

"Of course." The guard gestured with his large thumb toward the far end of the Roman Gallery. "'Ead that way and then turn right into the Assyrian Transept. The Egyptian Galleries are dead ahead." He doffed his cap. "Good day, miss."

Breathing a huge sigh of relief, Emmeline grasped Bartholomew's and Gareth's hands, then caught Harry's eye. "Right, let's go, children. There's no time to delay."

And indeed, there wasn't. The befuddling perfume's effects would only last a few minutes at most. The pilfered scarab needed to be back where it belonged in case the museum guard recalled what had happened and gave chase.

Within a minute, the scarab was safely back on its shelf lined up with its five scarab chums (why such priceless ancient artifacts were not kept under lock and key, Emmeline would never know). Then their party of five—the three children, Bertie, and Emmeline—were scaling a set of stairs, heading for the Americas Room, on the hunt for Aztec serpents.

In an hour's time, when the Duke of St Lawrence returned to the museum to collect them, Emmeline could confidently declare that this excursion—the first she and the children had undertaken beyond a few trips to the park—had been a raging success. *Not* a complete disaster. (His Grace certainly didn't need to know it had been a *near* disaster.)

In fact, Emmeline was proud that for the past two weeks, she'd kept Harry actively engaged, and subsequently out of mischief, with their joint clock-monitoring project. Although, it was still unclear if anyone within the duke's household was deliberately tampering with his timepieces. While Harry used Emmeline's Academy pocket watch to diligently set the time on all the clocks throughout St Lawrence House to Greenwich Mean Time, they invariably still sped up or slowed down with alarming regularity. Even the eight-day clocks. It was most frustrating. *If* sabotage were involved, Emmeline would get to the bottom of it for the duke. She would not tolerate any underhanded goings-on within her employer's household.

Emmeline, with Harry's help, quickly located the two-headed Aztec serpent. Thankfully it was locked away in a glass display case, well out of reach of inquisitive fingers. As they all admired the intricately laid, tiny turquoise tiles that perfectly mimicked a snake's scales, the boys declared they wanted to make plaster of Paris serpents too.

"Of course you can," agreed Emmeline. She'd have to procure several shades of blue paint for the scarabs and the snake. Turquoise, cerulean, cobalt, arctic...

Blast and botheration. Why did her mind suddenly conjure up an image of ice-blue eyes fringed with thick black lashes?

And a rich, dark velvet voice that made her shiver in ways that had nothing to do with the cold London weather and everything to do with feverish middle-of-the-night fantasies. The sorts of dreams and yes, desires, that she hadn't experienced for a long, long time.

Emmeline determinedly pushed away her errant thoughts. As for the duke, he was not to blame for her inconvenient infatuation. He very much kept to himself, hiding away in his study, working on his grand clock design for Westminster Palace. On the handful of occasions when Emmeline *had* crossed paths with him in St Lawrence House, his manner had been scrupulously polite but distant. Nevertheless, she'd formed the impression that he wasn't *dis*pleased with the way she was executing her duties. At least thus far. If a nod paired with a brief enquiry such as, "Good day, all settled in then?" or, "I take it my wards are behaving themselves?" and on another occasion, "No explosions or other disasters of note, yet?" counted as approval.

The problem was, Emmeline couldn't tell. Indeed, in the carriage on the way to the British Museum, she'd begun to doubt the adequacy of her performance. The duke had been withdrawn, his expression stern as he'd stared out the rain-streaked window at the soggy London streets. Well, that was before he'd retreated behind the *Times* and Emmeline couldn't see much of his countenance at all apart from his slightly furrowed forehead and uncompromising black brows. In any event, Emmeline had started to fret that perhaps the duke *wasn't* impressed with the way she was managing his wards. Perhaps their youthful exuberance grated on his nerves. Gareth and Bartholomew, in particular, often had a difficult time sitting still and using "inside voices," and the closed space of the carriage only amplified their excitement.

However, Emmeline's concern was eventually allayed to a degree when she'd engaged the children in a game of I Spy to keep them entertained. While the duke kept his newspaper barricade in place, Emmeline was certain he'd paid attention to the proceedings and at various points, he even appeared amused. In fact, when Harry had declared that the person, place, or thing she'd chosen that began with the letter *A*—and *nobody* had been able to deduce after a solid ten minutes of guessing—was "antidisestablishmentarianism" (apparently it was a word on the front page of the *Times*), it was *that* particular remark that had provoked a smile from His Grace.

At least Emmeline *thought* he'd smiled. Surely the slight lift of his eyebrows, and the gleam in his eyes as they'd met hers over the top of his newspaper *were* indications of mirth.

As Emmeline studied the Aztec serpent's teeth—Bartholomew had asked her what they were made of—a foolish part of her wondered if she would ever again be the recipient of one of the duke's rare, dazzling smiles. Just like the one he'd given her during her interview when she'd amused him.

Ack. So much for her resolution *not* to think about the man in inappropriate ways.

She was about to ask Harry to check the precise location of the Mummy Room when someone called her name. And not just *anyone*. It was the Duke of St Lawrence, because Emmeline would recognize His Grace's baritone anywhere.

Despite her previous resolution to *not* behave like a silly adolescent girl, Emmeline's heart did an excited little jig, then a twirl as she turned to discover her employer, standing only a few feet away in the doorway of the Americas Room. His hands were firmly thrust into the pockets of his black frock coat while his pale blue eyes were trained directly on her in that far-too-direct, blush-inducing way of his. Indeed, she hadn't encountered such an intense look since her interview, and she was in no way prepared for it, so blush she did. From the tips of her neatly buttoned half boots to the roots of her red hair, she was suddenly engulfed in fiery self-conscious heat. She probably looked like a boiled lobster. *Ugh.*

As Emmeline dipped into a curtsy, she gave herself a stern mental poke and a pinch and a very cross frown. Not only was she a highly skilled nanny, but she was a *widow* for heaven's sake! She wasn't a swooning maiden. She'd been a married woman for two whole years and had been madly in love with Jeremy, her husband... until he proved unworthy of such finer feelings and that love had withered away.

But it had been such a long time since Emmeline had been held, let alone kissed. Yes, that was her problem. She wasn't made of stone like a sphinx or as dry as a desiccated mummy. She missed physical intimacy with a man, and the duke's looks were arresting. As long as she kept her indecorous yearnings in check, all would be well.

Oh, but now she was staring at the duke's beautiful mouth of all things, and he was speaking, and she'd been so caught up in her own ridiculous musings, she had no idea what the man had asked her.

"Y-Your Grace," she stammered. "My apologies, but I was woolgathering and missed what you said. I-I was not expecting to see you here and I..." She drew a breath to stop herself rambling. "Would you mind repeating your question?"

The duke canted his head in that poker-stiff, overly formal way of his. "No, I should apologize, Mrs. Chase. It seems my unexpected arrival has startled you. And I'm clearly intruding on your excursion."

"Oh no. Not at all," replied Emmeline. "Would you like to join us for the rest of our tour?"

"Oh, yes, do, Cousin Xavier," cried Bartholomew. "We've seen ever so many wonderful things."

"Yes, do," echoed Gareth, bouncing up and down on his toes. "Scabs and snakes and jars of brains and guts and gizzards and eyeballs."

"They're called canopic jars," corrected Harry. "And they were used for storing mummified remains of ancient Egyptians."

The duke's mouth quirked at one corner. "I cannot wait to hear more. But what say you, Harry? May I join your party?"

Harry considered her guardian over the top of her glasses. "As long as you don't mind dead people. We're seeing an actual mummy next."

The duke inclined his head. "I would very much like to see a mummy. After that, might I suggest that we visit the Horology Gallery? I've loaned the Museum a medieval astrolabe from my own private collection. I think you all might enjoy seeing that too."

Harry narrowed her eyes. "An astrolabe?"

"It's an ancient but quite sophisticated astronomical instrument that's essentially an inclinometer," explained the duke, "so it can be used to determine the azimuth of a celestial object..." His voice trailed away as he looked at Emmeline. "Perhaps you might be able to describe it in a more comprehensible way to my wards, Mrs. Chase?"

Emmeline smiled. "I would be happy to." She turned to Harry and her brothers. "An astrolabe measures the movement of the sun and the stars and the planets. Sailors once used astrolabes to help them navigate the seas on long journeys. Astrolabes can also measure time. I suppose it's a cross between a pocket watch and a compass."

The duke nodded his approval. "Just so, Mrs. Chase. You have a gift for explaining things to children."

Emmeline attempted to adopt a politely professional expression, even though she was preening a little underneath. "I should hope so, Your Grace. After all, I'm a Parasol nanny."

"I'm beginning to think a Parasol nanny is worth her weight in gold," returned the duke in a low voice. Then a small line appeared between his brows as he added, "I know I've been sequestered away in my study since you took up your post, but don't think I haven't noticed the wonders you've worked with my wards already. I haven't had such a productive fortnight in

Lord knows how long. At this rate, I'll easily meet the deadline for the clock design contest on the first of June."

Emmeline, her cheeks fairly blazing—she had not expected to receive so much praise all at once—cast the duke a grateful smile. "I'm pleased to hear you've found the peace and quiet you need to complete your work."

The duke's manner might be stiff, but his eyes held a subtle warmth as he said, "One must give credit where credit is due."

Relief suddenly whooshed through Emmeline, making her giddy. The duke *was* happy with her work performance thus far. Although, it wouldn't do to rest on her laurels.

If Emmeline were honest with herself, she *could* do more. For instance, she really should try to cultivate a closer bond between the children and their guardian. Today was a case in point.

While the duke's work was his main priority at present, she couldn't help but notice that he appeared to derive a modicum of pleasure when he *did* spend time with his wards, and vice versa. Indeed, he didn't seem in any hurry to end their museum excursion. She was certain he'd been amused by their earlier game of I Spy in the carriage.

When she had a quiet moment, she would put her professional thinking cap on and hopefully come up with a way to engineer further agreeable interactions. For one thing, both the duke and Harriet loved science, a mutual interest she could perhaps exploit. The boys, too, always lit up with smiles whenever the duke paid them any sort of attention.

Of course, Emmeline would readily acknowledge that she had a significant personal stake in ensuring everything continued to go well at St Lawrence House. It meant she would continue to receive the income she desperately needed to keep her father safe. She suddenly couldn't wait to visit her dear papa at Newgate Prison on her first full day off in a fortnight's time; so far, she'd only been able to share her good news via a letter.

As they all made their way to the Mummy Room, farther along the corridor, the duke pulled her from her ruminations when he remarked, "I'm intrigued, Mrs. Chase. How do you know so much about astrolabes?"

Caution held Emmeline's tongue for a moment before she responded. "Ah, a customer once brought one into the antique clock store where I used to work. For an appraisal and some repair work."

"The store your father used to own?" asked the duke, his tone mildly curious. "I wonder if it's a shop I've ever visited. What was it called again?"

Blast. Why did the duke have to remember *that* particular detail about her life? Emmeline didn't want to discuss the topic further in case she accidentally revealed too much about her father's current situation, so she said as nonchalantly as she could, "Oh, my father sold the business—it was in Cheapside—some time ago and he's retired now." It was only a *little* white lie. Evans and Sons had been liquidated by the bank and that was akin to being sold, wasn't it?

"Hmmm," said the duke, his expression thoughtful. "That's quite a shame. Like you, Mrs. Chase, browsing through antique clock stores is a hobby of mine too."

"Oh look, I can see the Chantress of Amun's sarcophagus," cried Harry, rushing toward the room ahead of them, her brothers in hot pursuit.

"Oh dear, duty calls, I'm afraid," said Emmeline. She cast the duke a quick apologetic smile (even though she wasn't sorry at all for the distraction) and hastened after her excited charges.

Heaven forgive her, never before had she been so grateful to visit someone who was deceased.

Chapter 8

Wherein There Is a Thoroughly Educative Discussion About Astrolabes, the Merits of Gumboots, and Umbrellas...

Gloved hands buried deeply in his pockets, Xavier followed his wards and Mrs. Chase into the British Museum's Mummy Room. Although, to his dismay, he only had eyes for the talented nanny.

Try as he might, he couldn't crush his altogether bothersome, highly inappropriate fascination with the woman.

His brain whirred with what it was that had him in such a thrall. Off the top of his head, there were a number of rather *obvious* things. She was bright, she was cheerful, she was engaging. She appeared to know exactly what his wards needed at the drop of a hat pin and could provide it—whether that be the answer to their myriad questions or the right words to quell an argument or to produce a misplaced toy or much desired item as if from nowhere. Or to be more precise, said item was usually pulled from the pocket of her Parasol Academy uniform at just the right moment, as if by magic.

It was like Mrs. Chase could see right into his wards' young minds and anticipate the very thing they wanted. He, on the other hand, had not a clue. Children were like a completely different species to him. Illogical and unpredictable and far too energetic, like a litter of mischievous puppies—endearing but still prone to creating unmitigated chaos.

From the very beginning, Xavier had struggled to make a connection with his wards. So had Nanny Butterworth and Nanny Snodgrass, for that matter. But Mrs. Chase had not only learned their names within the blink of an eye, but had miraculously tamed all three of them to the point they were docilely eating out of her palm!

Mrs. Chase's services were immeasurably invaluable to him, and he'd wanted the talented nanny to know that, hence his praise that she was worth her weight in gold. He hadn't missed her blush—the bright rush of pink into her freckled cheeks. But he was not certain what her flushed countenance had meant. Pleasure? Embarrassment? Awkwardness? A modicum of all three?

While Harry, Barry, and Gary seemed to belong to a different species, Emmeline Chase was like some otherworldly creature or being to Xavier. Unfathomable yet endlessly fascinating.

If truth be told, Xavier had been avoiding interactions with the young woman since she'd started working at St Lawrence House. Not because he didn't like her. Far from it. As he'd initially feared when he'd offered her the position, she might prove to be *too* damn distracting. And distractions—of any kind—were something he could ill afford.

He couldn't pinpoint exactly *why* this inconvenient obsession with Mrs. Chase had sprung to life. Only that it had, from the very moment he'd first laid eyes on her, sitting on his roof. (He still had no idea at all how she'd got there. It was yet another item to add to his steadily growing list of "Unsolvable Mysteries Related to Emmeline Chase.")

Xavier took up a position on the opposite side of the Mummy Room, leaning against the wall, watching Mrs. Chase as she asked Bertie to lift up young Gareth so he could better see the mummy in its sarcophagus. Noblemen were barely meant to even notice their staff, let alone cultivate any form of liking for them, Xavier reminded himself with a disconsolate sigh. Yet he'd engineered their shared carriage ride to be close to Mrs. Chase. To observe her rapport with his wards, he'd told himself. But that was the lie of the century.

Naturally, he'd tried very hard to pretend an indifference he didn't feel by looking out the carriage window or pretending to be riveted by his newspaper, when in actual fact, he'd been secretly entertained by his wards and Mrs. Chase's jolly games. And more than a little bit impressed by Harry's ability to both decipher and accurately pronounce "antidisestablishmentarianism."

If Xavier were *truly* honest with himself, he would acknowledge that he wanted to steal a little of Mrs. Chase's sunshine for himself. To hear her voice, her infectious laughter, glimpse the warmth in her summer-blue-sky eyes. To admire her coppery curls and the way they caught and changed color depending on the light. To catch a trace of her delicious violet scent.

And now, here he was, doing all those things as he lurked in the shadows of a British Museum display cabinet of ancient Egyptian relics, *gawking* like some covetous hobgoblin or a socially awkward schoolboy.

It was the sort of behavior that would have earned him a caning from the exacting tutor his father had once hired, Mr. Dickenson, to cure Xavier's "deficiencies of character."

You mustn't stare at others, Lord Westbrook. It isn't just rude, it's deviant conduct and not to be tolerated. Even after twenty years, Mr. Dickenson's caustic criticisms echoed through Xavier's mind. He could almost feel the sting of the cane on the palms of his hands and backs of his knees. Vividly recall the humiliation and impotent fury at his unjust treatment as it burned through his veins like acid.

Xavier's jaw clenched. Thank God the teasing his peers had

dished out at school hadn't lasted for too long. Even though he'd initially been dubbed "mad" and "weird," within a few months, it was also noted that the young Marquess of Westbrook was brilliant at mathematical equations. Once Xavier started to complete the work of his fellow classmates—in particular, the work of Marcus, Viscount Hartwell—the harassment stopped.

One thing Xavier knew to be true is that everything had its price. Anything could be bought, including a respite from torment. While Xavier despised his long-departed father and most of the "lessons" and "corrections" he'd been determined to impart through the odious Dickenson, this was one of the few messages that had truly stuck. That, along with always have a plan, and always be the smartest, most capable person in the room. And if you suspect you are not, hire someone who is.

When it boiled down to it, that was the real reason he'd employed Mrs. Chase. She was both smart and capable when it came to caring for children.

It wasn't because she was *pretty*.

Of course, it didn't hurt that she *was*.

Xavier focused on Mrs. Chase again (or Nanny Chase, as his wards loved to call her) as she patiently answered the children's myriad questions about the mummified Egyptian "chantress" lying peacefully in her coffin, presenting a benignly smiling painted face—her gilded mummy-mask—to the world.

Even as a grown man, Xavier had never been one to seek out company of the feminine kind. Like any male, he experienced base urges from time to time if he spotted a lovely face or neatly turned ankle or admirable cleavage. But he'd never acted on any of those urges. Not once in his thirty years had he done more than kiss a woman on a handful of occasions. Which utterly baffled his best friend, Marcus, who was the complete opposite in that regard. Marcus was an out-and-out rakehell, and no matter how many times Xavier had been dragged to one of his friend's "gentlemen's" clubs, or occasionally, an exclusive bawdy house, Xavier had steadfastly crushed any lustful stirrings, regarding them as ungentlemanly. Not only that, given his particular eccentricities with regard to touch, he'd always shied away from becoming physically intimate with a woman. Well, beyond a trifling kiss or two.

As a result, Xavier was confident that he wouldn't want to act on any untoward flickers of desire inadvertently sparked by Mrs. Chase. The problem was his and his alone to deal with. *His* burden to bear. Steering clear of the beguiling nanny had seemed like the best solution to his problem, although after a fortnight of doing so, it hadn't helped.

Xavier had quickly learned that completely avoiding Mrs. Chase was like trying to ignore an itchy spot that needed scratching. The more you disregarded it, the worse the impulse got.

So he'd told (lied to) himself that this short innocuous excursion would alleviate that persistent and annoying urge, so he could get on with his work without any distractions whatsoever. In fact, this whole endeavor had only made his "itch" worse.

Even now, he had to force himself to *not* stare at Mrs. Chase's face as he tried to read her expressions; as he devoured her every word, trying to interpret the nuances of what she'd said—whether she was serious or teasing.

She was presently explaining exactly what a mummy was to young Gary—*Gareth*, Xavier corrected himself—and the boy was scrunching up his nose.

"Ewww," he said. "You mean there are *real* bones under all those old bandages?"

"You didn't seem to mind the canopic jars," Harry remarked drily. "The bits and pieces in those were even more horrid."

"Perhaps it's time to move onto the Horology Room to see

the watches and clocks and the astrolabe," suggested Mrs. Chase brightly.

It was Bartholomew who wrinkled his nose this time. "Do we have to? I don't want to see a bunch of boring old clocks. There's lots of clocks at home. Can't we go to the park instead? You promised us a trip to the park, Nanny Chase."

"Yes. We want to play hopscotch and jump in puddles!" cried Gareth clapping his hands with boyish glee.

Xavier stepped forward. "I think your sister would like to see the astrolabe," he said, making sure he caught each of the boys' gazes in turn. "And it won't take long. *Then* we'll go to the park. Does that sound like an agreeable compromise for all parties?"

Bartholomew affected a heavy sigh. "All right, Cousin Xavier."

"All right," echoed Gareth, his small shoulders rising and falling in an equally dramatic sigh.

"I have no reason to object to that plan," added Harry. She squinted through her glasses at the museum map. "It looks like the Horology Room is on this floor and quite close. Only a few doors down, halfway along the next corridor."

"Excellent," said Xavier, inordinately pleased with himself for successfully fielding an argument. "It's all settled then."

"Thank you for stepping in, Your Grace," said Mrs. Chase as they all followed Harry, their apparent museum guide, out of the Mummy Room. "Although, you really don't need to come to the park with us. I'm sure you're very busy—"

"Not at all," he rejoined. "I could do with some fresh air."

"Well, if you're sure," she said. "We'd be delighted to have you accompany us."

The smile the nanny suddenly gifted Xavier loosened something inside his chest and some sort of unexpected emotion he couldn't have put a name to, even if he tried, tumbled through him. It was like Mrs. Chase had reached into him and found some tiny, loose piece of thread, and with an effortless tug, she'd begun to unravel his tight control.

The strange sensation was unsettling yet exhilarating at the same time. He cleared his throat. "I'm sure the delight will be mutual, Mrs. Chase," he said in a voice that was strangely graveled. "Perhaps some of your magic is starting to rub off on bitter old me."

The nanny didn't say anything as she kept pace with him, her hands clasped primly behind her back. If he were to hazard a guess, Xavier would say that her expression was pensive, perhaps even a trifle apprehensive, but dash it all, he couldn't be sure. He hoped he hadn't said or done anything to upset her. Or maybe it had been his gruff tone. Despite Mr. Dickenson's endless elocution lessons to eliminate the woodenness from his manner, all these years later, he still had an inordinate amount of difficulty judging whether the way he spoke was quite right for the occasion or not.

Bertie walked with Bartholomew and Gareth while Harry forged ahead. However, when they all reached the Horology Room, Mrs. Chase broke her silence. Turning to Xavier, she said quietly, "I know it's probably not my place to say anything, but I don't think you're as bitter and brooding and difficult as you believe yourself to be, Your Grace." Her eyes as they met his were strangely soft, like a misty summer's morn. "In fact, you remind me of warm hot chocolate."

Warm hot chocolate? Xavier's mouth fell open. Before he could formulate any sort of reply—which was hard to do when one was completely lost for words—she moved away, catching up to Harry, who'd already found the ornate brass astrolabe in its glass-fronted display cabinet.

Was *gobsmacked* a word? If it wasn't, it should've been, because that's exactly how Xavier felt right now. Literally smacked in the gob, not to mention flabbergasted and dumbfounded and astounded and confounded and whatever other words appeared in a thesaurus under the entry *stunned*.

When Xavier eventually joined his wards, Bertie, and Mrs. Chase by the astrolabe cabinet, the nanny also appeared to be a tad astounded, but for an entirely different reason. "Your astrolabe is beautiful, Your Grace," she said in a voice touched with awe. "I've never seen one quite so large or lovely. The detailed scrollwork is marvelous. And it's English, you say?"

"Yes," said Xavier proudly. He was on surer ground now, not stranded in the middle of *Where-the-deuced-hell-am-I-land*. "I believe it was constructed around 1300. If you look closely at this tympan or plate"—with a gloved finger he pointed out a particular spot on the face of the astrolabe—"you can see that *Lundoniarum*—Latin for London—is marked precisely at fifty-two degrees."

"I want to know how it works," said Harry.

"I have a smaller astrolabe, French in origin, back at St Lawrence House that I can show you some time," said Xavier to his ward.

Harry regarded Xavier over the tops of her spectacles. "I would very much like that," she replied in her usual solemn manner. Although, was that a spark of interest or excitement in her eyes? Xavier liked to think so, and he suddenly felt inordinately pleased.

Aloud he said, "Excellent. When there's a clear day or night—"

He got no further as a familiar, entirely too brash, and undeniably tiresome voice blared through the room like a foghorn.

"Well, well. If it isn't His Grace, the Duke of St Lawrence. Fancy meeting you in the Horology Room, old chap." This was followed by a nerve-grating guffaw; it was the kind of boisterous laugh that one might expect to hear in a tavern at the end of the night or emanating from a raucous crowd at a bare-knuckled boxing match.

It was *not* appropriate for a place like a museum. But then, the man who'd invaded the Horology Room, Sir Randolph Redvers, was hardly ever appropriate. At least in Xavier's opinion.

Xavier turned slowly, fists clenching at his sides. "Sir Randolph," he said, employing a curt tone. "I don't see why you should be so surprised to find me here, considering at least a third of the museum's watch and clock collection presently on show is mine."

Sir Randolph, a fellow horologist and rival contestant in the race to secure the winning design for the Westminster Palace clock, grinned widely at Xavier from the other side of the room. Xavier tried not to wince at the man's abominable sartorial choices. On this occasion, the bold-as-brass baronet was attired in a black frock coat paired with garish plaid trousers in shades of red, umber, and saffron. His dark auburn hair was slicked back with so much Macassar oil, Xavier thought the man's head rather resembled a horse-chestnut conker. (In fact, Xavier suspected the man had about as much sense as a conker.)

Hovering beside the baronet was the British Museum's curator, Mr. Brimble. A spare-framed man of middle age, Brimble was overshadowed by the grand proportions of the broad-shouldered, square-jawed, heavy-browed Sir Randolph.

"I'm so sorry to disturb you, Your Grace," said the curator as he wrung his bony hands. His bald pate and forehead, sheened with perspiration, shone in the glow of a nearby wall-mounted gaslight. "But Sir Randolph has recently become one of our patrons—and a most generous one at that. He's expressed a desire to view our horology collection with a view t-to rejuvenating it."

Xavier cocked an eyebrow. "I see."

"Yes." The baronet marched toward Xavier then took up a wide stance, as though he owned the room and everything in it. Rubbing his large hands together he declared, "I think it might be time for an overhaul of what's on display. It all seems a bit—" Pausing, his dark brown gaze drifted over the display cabinets before he added with a grimace, "Quite frankly, it's all looking a bit tired and stale and mundane. But no hard feelings, Your Grace?" He bared his teeth in another wide grin. "Out with the old and in with the new, as they say. You can't fight progress, hey what?"

Xavier narrowed his eyes. Good God, the man was nothing

but a pompous windbag who dispensed banalities as though they were pearls of wisdom. Sir Randolph had joined the Royal Horological Society but a year ago, and Xavier did not think much of the man. His bluff arrogance, his need to be the center of attention—to dominate and assert that he was better than everyone else—irritated Xavier no end.

"Change for change's sake is hardly what I'd call progress," Xavier said coldly. "I'm sure the museum only displays timepieces that have historical significance and demonstrate innovation in the field of horology. I'd wouldn't call anything here tired or stale or mundane."

Mr. Brimble offered Xavier a bow along with a small smile. "Thank you, Your Grace."

Sir Randolph snorted. "I think I will have to agree to disagree with you there, my friend. Although . . ." The odious man's gaze shifted and settled on Mrs. Chase, who'd been standing quietly with Harriet, Bartholomew, and Gareth the entire time. "It was remiss of me to say *everything* here is mundane." He gave the nanny a rakish wink.

To Xavier's surprise, Mrs. Chase didn't blush or drop her gaze in response to the baronet's blatantly flirtatious manner. No, she placed her hands protectively on young Gareth's shoulders and raised her chin as though in challenge. Her eyes glittered dangerously, like a lioness about to spring into action. If Xavier were a betting man, he'd wager there was an element of don't-even-think-about-coming-anywhere-near-me-or-my-charges in her eyes.

It was at that moment that Xavier knew he could count on this woman to protect anyone in her care. She was not easily intimidated and would be a force to be reckoned with. Of that he had no doubt.

For his part, Xavier was livid. How dare bloody Sir Randolph Redvers subject one of his female staff members to that sort of lascivious look and uninvited personal remark? Not just in front of her employer, but in front of children and the museum's curator.

The hide of the bastard!

Xavier's knuckles cracked as his fingers curled into even tighter fists. Right at this moment, he'd love to plant a facer right in the middle of the despicable baronet's nose. Or smack him fair in the gob to wipe the leering smile off his face. (Yet another reason why *gobsmack*—or any suitable morphological variation thereof—should be a word.) But physically assaulting another man, no matter how provoking he was, wasn't appropriate behavior either. Xavier would not create a scene in the middle of the day in the British Museum in front of his wards and his staff.

He was better than Sir Randolph Redvers. He wouldn't stoop so low.

Crushing down his ire, Xavier drew a calming breath, then addressed the baronet and the curator directly. "I think it would be best if any further discussion about the horology collection is adjourned until the next Museum board meeting later this month," he said in the sort of ominously cold, ducal tone that made most men quiver in their boots.

As he expected, Mr. Brimble turned as white as parchment paper while Sir Randolph merely raised an eyebrow and made a scoffing noise in his throat.

"If you insist," said the baronet, his eyes hard. "That won't stop me making my own assessment of what's on offer."

"So be it," replied Xavier. Softening his expression so it wouldn't be so forbidding, Xavier turned to Mrs. Chase, Bertie, and his wards. "Right, let's move on, shall we? The park awaits."

Mr. Brimble bowed stiffly. "Good day, Your Grace."

Sir Randolph donned his usual grin that smacked of false cheer. "Tally-ho then, Your Grace. I expect I shall see you anon."

More's the pity, thought Xavier. Although aloud he simply said, "Quite."

However, as he passed by Mr. Brimble he added in a low voice, "Whatever donation Sir Randolph is making to the museum, I'll double it," before continuing on his way. If Sir Randolph Redvers heard him, he didn't much care. Xavier would have the last say on the topic of the horology collection, of that he was certain.

Chapter 9

In Which There Is Discussion About a Particular Bottom; A Pilgrimage to a Park; Splishy-splashy Hopscotch; And a Disturbing Epiphany About Stone Age Men and a Non-Celestial Orbit...

Once they were well away from the Horology Room, Mrs. Chase remarked for Xavier's ears only, "I shouldn't say anything, but I cannot help it. What a horrid man Sir Randolph is, Your Grace." She gave a little shiver of apparent disgust.

Xavier cast her a sideways glance. "Oh no. You've got him all wrong, Mrs. Chase," he rejoined. "He's really not a bad sort of chap. As long as you disregard his arrogance, his bad manners, and his bullish ways in general."

She gave a short laugh. "Or his overly familiar manner. He reminds me of the sort of conceited clodpole who believes his attentions are desired by women." She shook her head and muttered as though to herself, "What an enormous ass."

"One could safely say Sir Randolph is a big-headed, braying blowhard who has more money than sense," said Xavier. "A veritable Bottom."

Mrs. Chase laughed again, her eyes dancing with merriment. "Sir Bottom seems very apt. One wonders if Shakespeare had someone like Sir Randolph in mind when he wrote the part for *A Midsummer Night's Dream.*"

"Perhaps," agreed Xavier, returning her smile. They'd reached the museum cloakroom and Mrs. Chase was suddenly caught up with helping the children don their wet-weather garb. The afternoon had grown dark and Xavier suspected the heavens would open up before too long.

Even though he'd pulled on his greatcoat, beneath his silk-lined clothes he shivered. He had his silver-topped cane with him, but he'd left his umbrella in the carriage. While he'd offered to accompany Mrs. Chase and his wards to the park, he dreaded the idea of getting soaked. But he also didn't want to miss the opportunity to converse more with the nanny.

Just to make absolutely sure she is *the right fit for my wards,* he told himself as they ventured outside into the museum's forecourt where a mizzling rain was falling. *It's my duty. I can grin and bear a little rain in aid of a good cause.*

"Where will we find your carriage, Your Grace?" asked Mrs. Chase, scanning Great Russell Street. She'd donned a heavy wool cloak of navy blue, and her fair countenance was shadowed by the brim of her bonnet and her wide umbrella. Harriet, Bartholomew, and Gareth stood beside her in their bright yellow mackintoshes, matching hats, and gumboots, like three little ducks all in a row.

Xavier turned up the collar of his greatcoat against a chill wind that was blowing a fine misty veil of rain across the puddle-strewn pavement. "It's a short walk away, down toward the corner of Montague Street. It's a shame we don't have a key into the private garden in Russell Square around the corner. I'm not sure if we'll make it to Hyde Park or the park in Belgrave Square before it rains cats and dogs."

Mrs. Chase cast him an enigmatic smile. "I say let's try our luck with accessing Russell Square, Your Grace. There might be another nanny out and about who'd be kind enough to admit us. And if it starts to pour, we can all beat a hasty retreat to your carriage."

Xavier agreed and they all trooped down the street in the direction of Russell Square. "Is there some sort of secret nanny club we mere mortals don't know about?" he asked as they paused to cross Montague Street. He could already see the Russell Square garden gates up ahead.

Mrs. Chase laughed. "Perhaps. I could certainly say that is the case for Parasol nannies and governesses. Our handbook clearly states that supporting one's fellow graduates is a core responsibility. We're rather like a military corps in some respects. Upon graduation we all swear oaths to not only protect the children in our care to the very best of our ability, but to always have each other's backs."

"I must say, you're very fond of this handbook of yours."

"As a Parasol graduate we are duty bound to follow its rules. Anyone who does not risks expulsion from the Academy. And that is something I would never do."

"I admire your commitment to the cause, Mrs. Chase," said Xavier. And he meant it.

As Mrs. Chase accompanied Harry across the road—Bertie escorted the boys—Xavier had the oddest urge to take one of the nanny's hands and tuck it into the crook of his elbow like any gentleman would when escorting a young woman anywhere. But he didn't. Mrs. Chase was an employee. He was a duke. And never the twain shall meet.

Instead, he gripped his cane in one hand and thrust his other hand into his pocket.

It didn't take long to reach Russell Square, and by the time they did, the light shower had stopped, a fact Xavier was rather glad about. As luck would also have it, there was another Parasol nanny who was leaving the private park with her young charges who, upon seeing Mrs. Chase, was happy to admit them all.

Once Bartholomew, Gareth, and Harry were busy playing a spirited, very splishy-splashy game of hopscotch—Mrs. Chase had produced a piece of chalk from her pocket, which Bertie used to draw the hopscotch squares on a damp section of flagged paving—Xavier racked his brains, trying to think of a way to draw the nanny into conversation again. Should he find out more about her background? Her family? Chat about her father's antique clock store? Some of the auctions she'd been to? More about her own childhood? Any other interests she might have beyond timepieces? Or perhaps he should confine the conversation to his wards.

He was not one to take part in any sort of social chitchat, even at the best of times. Especially with a member of the opposite sex, let alone a staff member.

He barely conversed with his valet, Babcock, or his butler. Aside from his friend Lord Hartwell, Horatio, his raven, was probably the individual he spoke to the most.

Xavier grimaced. *Good Lord.* He was fortunate that no one had yet dubbed him *Mason the Misanthrope.*

He glanced at Mrs. Chase as she diplomatically settled a dispute between Harry and Bartholomew; apparently Bartholomew was sure that Harry had hopped out of bounds, whereas Harry was adamant she hadn't because the chalk hadn't smudged.

Egad, how he admired Mrs. Chase's talent for reading people and situations and knowing exactly what to do and say. Whereas he was often lost for words.

Perhaps he should discuss the matter that was uppermost in his mind. But in doing so, he might unsettle the nanny. Although he had broached this particular subject at her interview, and he already knew Mrs. Chase wasn't easily daunted. In fact, she might even offer to help. She could easily knock a man off his feet. Not only that, but she kept a sheathed, pearl-handled knife strapped to her ankle . . .

Agitated by his uncertainty—and a far too enticing vision of a black ribbon garter surrounding a slender lower leg encased in white hose—Xavier tapped the toes of his boots with his cane... until his circuitous, uneasy thoughts were interrupted by the nanny herself.

"I have a confession, Your Grace. It's-It's rather unfortunate. And more than a little embarrassing to be making such an admission so early in the piece. Although, you may have noticed the issue already...."

Xavier looked up to find Mrs. Chase regarding him with her large blue eyes. He tried to read whether her words matched her expression, but he failed. She could be worried, but she might also be teasing him. "I'm not sure what you mean," he said.

She drew a breath. "Despite our best efforts—both mine and Miss Harriet's—the clocks at St Lawrence House keep slowing down and speeding up. And I ..." She released a small sigh, and a fine line appeared between her brows. "I am utterly perplexed. There's no rhyme or reason to it. Not that I can fathom."

"Yes, I've noticed," replied Xavier. "But rest assured, I do not blame you, Mrs. Chase. It is a mystery that seems quite unsolvable."

The nanny nodded. "Yes, I've taken to calling it the 'Great Clock Mystery' in my own mind. Miss Harriet and I will continue to set all the clocks to Greenwich Mean Time with my Parasol Academy pocket watch each week, but I suspect I shall have to find another project to occupy her. Something a little more challenging or scientific. Perhaps both." She cast him a look from beneath her gold-tipped lashes that was a confusing combination of artful and coy—at least to Xavier. "I do think Harry might be genuinely interested in learning about your French astrolabe, Your Grace. Her eyes fairly lit up when you mentioned the possibility."

"And my offer was genuine," returned Xavier as an unexpected feeling—an agreeable but odd sensation akin to warmth—spread through his chest. The idea that his eldest ward might be interested in the intricate workings of an astrolabe was... pleasing? Was that the right word? Indeed, he was beginning to see glimpses of himself in Harry, and he suspected Mrs. Chase had seen that too. The nanny's ability to read him—to see past his dispassionate exterior and ofttimes awkward manner—was an altogether novel experience.

It was also slightly unsettling.

Xavier cleared his throat, suddenly feeling unusually self-conscious. "I'm afraid we *will* have to wait for clearer skies though," he added, avoiding the nanny's far-too-perceptive gaze, squinting at the heavy clouds above them instead. "In the meantime, perhaps that visit to Hatchards you mentioned is in order. Remember I have an account there and you can purchase whatever books you need."

Mrs. Chase inclined her head. "I shall plan a trip for tomorrow. If you can spare a carriage, of course."

"Of course," said Xavier, acknowledging her reply with his own head tilt.

They lapsed into silence again as they watched the children play, and Xavier wondered if his tone had been too gruff. Or his lack of eye contact had offended the nanny. But after a few minutes, Mrs. Chase ventured, "I take it there have been no other untoward happenings at St Lawrence House over the past two weeks, Your Grace? I haven't heard anything. But then, I don't know the other servants all that well yet. Naturally it takes time to build up the sort of rapport that invites confidences." She bit her lip and dipped her head so her bonnet shielded her face. "Oh dear. It sounds like I'm the sort of servant who indulges in idle gossip. I'm really not. But if I do hear anything useful..."

"I understand. I know what you mean," said Xavier. "And I especially appreciate that you are so willing to help me get to the bottom of whatever is going on in my house." His attention flitted away and settled on the bronze statue of the Duke of Bedford at the far end of the square's garden.

Out of the corner of his eye, he registered that the nanny nodded. "My duty, first and foremost, is to you and your wards. So if I do hear or see anything suspicious—such as anyone tampering with the clocks, or anything else at all that doesn't seem quite right—I shall let you know straightaway."

"Thank you. Actually"—Xavier made himself catch the nanny's gaze—"there is something I need to tell you." He drew a steadying breath, not because he was worried about what he was about to disclose. No, he had to steel himself to not get distracted while he maintained eye contact with the young woman. "Early this morning, I was informed by Mrs. Lambton that St Lawrence House may have been broken into."

"Oh my God! I mean *goodness*," breathed Mrs. Chase, her face paling. Then she frowned. "But you said, *may* have. There's doubt?"

"Yes, there is. Apparently the cook, Mrs. Punchbowl, noticed that the door into the kitchen was unlocked and slightly ajar when she commenced her usual duties—she lights the stove in preparation for the day at six o'clock sharp. Woodley swears that the entire house was secure last night before he retired at eleven p.m. And the night footman claimed the kitchen door was locked when he did a round of the house three hours later at two a.m. So some time in the next four hours, someone unlocked and opened the door. However, it appears that nothing has been stolen or tampered with or broken in the house."

"I take it that includes the lock on the kitchen door? It wasn't broken?"

"No, it's fine," said Xavier. "A key is needed to both unlock and relock the door."

"Who in your household has a key for the kitchen door?"

"Aside from me, Mrs. Lambton, Mrs. Punchbowl, Woodley, and whoever is rostered on as the night footman until three a.m. When he's done his final round, the set of keys is left in the cloak room adjacent to the entry hall."

"Hmmm, so really anyone at all *in* the house could have accessed that set between three and six a.m.?"

"Yes, you're right. For what reason, I have no idea."

Mrs. Chase tapped a gloved finger against her chin. "Could it have been one of the servants stealing outside and returning in the early hours before dawn—like a maid or footman—sneaking off for a tryst?"

Dragging his gaze away from the nanny's mouth (*I. Must. Not. Stare.*) Xavier said, "I have no idea." Which was true. "It's never happened before though. Which doesn't mean one of the servants hasn't recently found a sweetheart."

"Hmmm. The only other explanation I can think of is that an outsider—a would-be thief or saboteur—picked the lock to the kitchen door. Which is entirely possible."

"Can you pick locks, Mrs. Chase?" Xavier wouldn't have been surprised at all if the woman could.

"Oh no. Parasol nannies and governesses have many talents, but lock picking isn't one of them." Mrs. Chase's expression grew serious. "But why would anyone break in and not take anything? Unless . . ." Her brows dipped into a deeper frown.

"Unless it was another instance of someone trying to unsettle me in a new way?"

She gave a nod. "A rival horologist perhaps? Someone like Sir Randolph?"

Xavier shrugged. "I have no way to tell. I don't know much of anything at all. I feel like I'm stumbling around in the dark, tripping over things that have been deliberately placed in my way to unnerve me. And I can't find a dashed candle or lamp that will shed light on the situation." Then he sighed. "I haven't involved the local constabulary because there would be nothing much to report. My cook discovering an open door is hardly a crime. All the other doors and windows throughout the house were secure, too."

Mrs. Chase's expression changed. Xavier thought it might

be her "pensive" look. "At my interview, Your Grace, you mentioned someone followed you home after a Royal Horological Society meeting not that long ago. Have there been any other incidents of that nature since then?"

"No..." Although, Xavier couldn't shake the odd feeling that maybe they were being observed right at this moment. The hairs stood up on the back of his neck as though a chill wind had blown past, and again, his gaze drifted around the enclosed park of Russell Square. As far as he could see, they were ostensibly alone in the gardens, but beyond the black wrought-iron fence surrounding the square, there was an endless parade of passersby and trundling carriages and carts and hansom cabs. Even the occasional omnibus rumbled past. No particular individual stood out. No one appeared to be watching him or his wards or Mrs. Chase or Bertie. It was clear his imagination was playing tricks on him.

But still... Xavier's grip tightened on his cane. Inside was a sheathed rapier. With one click of a button on the silver handle, he could release the weapon. And he was an excellent swordsman, if he did say so himself.

Mrs. Chase broke into his thoughts. "Perhaps you should have hired me to be your bodyguard or private investigator, Your Grace."

She was joking of course. Xavier could definitely see the sparkle in her eyes. "I'm starting to think I should have," he replied with a wry smile.

It was Mrs. Chase who looked away this time. At that moment, there was a cry.

Young Gareth had tripped and fallen. He was sitting in a puddle, clutching his leg and wailing.

"Nanny Chase, Gareth needs a plaster," called Harry as the young woman rushed over to her injured charge.

"I have one here," said Mrs. Chase calmly. Heedless of the wet, muddy ground, she dropped low and began to tend to

Gareth's skinned knee. Once the plaster was applied, she gave the boy's head a pat. "It looks like you get a piggyback ride back to the carriage, my brave young man. If Bertie will oblige."

She looked up at the footman and he grinned down at her. "I will, Nanny Chase," he said. And then he winked.

Was Bertie flirting with the nanny? Was there something in the air today that was making men wink at Mrs. Chase? Something catching, like a cold?

Of course not, you dunderhead. Mrs. Chase is an attractive widow with a bright friendly manner. It's inevitable that men will notice her. You've noticed her.

Deep down, Xavier knew that *he* was being an ass.

However, recognizing that he was an ass while experiencing some hitherto unknown emotion—something sharp and hot and dangerous—did not make it any easier for him to crush his primitive Stone Age instincts to dust. Not when they were stomping around inside him like a troglodyte, giving him the insane urge to unsheathe his rapier and skewer the strapping young footman—or at the very least, whack him on the arse with his cane—for daring to flirt with Mrs. Chase while on the job. Right under the nose of his employer! The cheek of the man.

And then Xavier was struck by an even more insane thought.

He was *jealous* of the footman. Since when had Xavier Mason, the Duke of St Lawrence, turned into the sort of man who was afflicted by jealousy? And over such a trifling incident?

Of all the things that had happened today, perhaps that was the most sobering, astonishing event of all. Along with the fact that no matter how hard he tried, Xavier could not stop wanting to be in the orbit of Mrs. Chase.

By the time they got back to his carriage, Xavier had identified what his problem was and he told himself so. *Mrs. Emmeline Chase, once noticed, cannot be unnoticed. Of course, you engineered this whole outing, hoping her allure would dissipate. Hoping her magnetic pull would dwindle the more accustomed you became to her presence.*

Except his plan hadn't worked at all. Ignoring Mrs. Chase—waiting for her shine to fade so she became ordinary or unremarkable or mundane enough to blend into the background—was like trying to ignore the sun or the stars or the moon in the heavens.

Mrs. Chase was the opposite of ordinary. She was endlessly fascinating.

Oh, it was then that Xavier knew he was in deep, deep trouble.

It would be a miracle if he'd be able to concentrate on his work now.

CHAPTER 10

Concerning Alchemy, Puff Balloons (Not Loonies), Dodecahedrons, Bird's for Baking, and Cockeyed Paintings...

"Today's topic of study is... the alchemy of baking," announced Emmeline to her three expectant charges, all suitably attired in serviceable cotton pinafores to protect their clothes.

They were presently gathered in St Lawrence House's kitchen along with Fanny, the maid who'd become an "under" nurserymaid of sorts, and Mrs. Punchbowl, the duke's cook.

"What are we making?" asked Harry, her eyes alight with interest. But then her bottom lip dipped into a moue of displeasure. "I hope it's something we *can* actually eat. Scientific experiments are all well and good, but it would be nice to produce something that's edible."

"Oh, it's definitely edible," confirmed Emmeline. "But there is also science involved."

It had been almost two weeks since their excursion to the British Museum, and Emmeline had done her very best to keep the children entertained and out of mischief. They'd all paid a visit to Hatchards and purchased armfuls of books and charged them all to the duke's account. They'd made plaster of Paris snakes and beetles and snails, much to Gareth's and Bartholomew's delight.

While the astrolabe demonstration had not yet eventuated due to the constant inclement weather—overcast skies, foggy nights, and rain made it impossible to view the heavens—the duke had kindly loaned Harry a microscope to keep her active mind engaged, and she loved it.

Emmeline had also endeavored to take the children to the park every single day—the boys especially needed outdoor time to release their boundless energy—but not today. It was teeming buckets, blowing a gale, and altogether freezing cold and miserable. Emmeline had thus decided a cozy kitchen adventure was in order.

"We're actually making something that's dear to my own heart." Emmeline caught each of the children's gazes. "A treat my own dear mama made for me when I was young, and it was cold and dark and raining just like today. Drumroll . . ." With a pair of wooden spoons, she tapped out a rapid tattoo on the polished oak counter like a regimental drummer. "We're making puff balloons!"

"Puff balloons!" exclaimed Mrs. Punchbowl, her brown-as-currant eyes narrowing. "Never 'eard of 'em."

"They're essentially a fried scone," explained Emmeline. "To serve them, you *must* drizzle them with lashings of golden syrup. There's only one way."

"Yummy scrummy!" cried Gareth. "Puff balloonies in my tummy!"

"Puff bal-*loons*, not loonies," corrected Harry. To Emmeline she said, "They do sound positively scrumptious. Do they explode if you blow them up enough? Like a balloon?"

Mrs. Punchbowl scowled and placed her fisted, flour-dusted hands on her ample hips. " 'Ere, I'll 'ave no explosions in *my* kitchen, Nanny Chase. I remember wha' 'appened in the library and the nursery afore you started 'ere."

Emmeline raised her hands in a calming gesture. "Now, now. There'll be no explosions of any kind whatsoever. The scones do puff up a little—that's because of the addition of the baking powder—but they don't blow up. However, one must exercise great care during the cooking process because they're fried in very hot lard. I shall enlist the help of Mrs. Punchbowl when it comes to that part. We shall make the dough, and once the puff balloons have cooled—we don't want any burned tongues—we shall eat them for afternoon tea."

"Hooray!" shouted the boys, and Harry grinned.

The making of the puff balloon batter commenced. Flour was sieved into a large bowl with a little salt and Bird's Baking Powder—Bartholomew had to be reassured that the white chalky substance in the baking powder tin was *not* made of crushed bird bones but bicarbonate of soda and cream of tartar. Then everything was mixed together with enough milk to form a lumpy, very tacky dough.

"Oooh, it *is* sticky," declared Gareth as he helped shape the messy mixture into a rough rectangle on the floured kitchen table.

"It's tastes awful," said Bartholomew, wrinkling his nose in disgust after he'd licked a dough-coated finger. "Like glue."

"Ah, but it hasn't been fried or drizzled with syrup yet," Emmeline reminded him. "Now"—she picked up a bread-and-butter knife—"what shape do we want our puff balloons to be. Circles or squares?"

"Squares," said Gareth.

"Round like balloons," said Bartholomew.

"Dodecahedrons," said Harry. But there was a mischievous twinkle in her eyes.

"You'll get more scones out of the dough if Nanny Chase cuts squares," added Mrs. Punchbowl.

"Squares!" chorused all three children.

Emmeline laughed. "Very well."

Within the space of fifteen minutes, Mrs. Punchbowl had fried all the scones until they were puffed and golden and light as air. After hands were washed and the kitchen had been restored to its usual state of spick-and-span, the children sat down to a feast of golden-syrup-drenched puff balloons.

"These are wicked good," said Bartholomew around a mouthful of sticky scone.

"Best thing ever," agreed Gareth, licking his fingers.

"Do you think Cousin Xavier would like a puff balloon or two?" asked Harry.

Mrs. Punchbowl shook her head. "I'm afraid 'is Grace doesn't like sweet food, poppet. Plain, 'olesome food is more 'is cup o' tea. Speaking o' which"—she glanced at the kitchen clock—"'is Grace is due for 'is afternoon pot o' coffee and serve o' shortbread."

"Shortbread? I thought you said His Grace didn't like sweet things," said Emmeline. During her interview, there had certainly been an array of all sorts of treats laid out, but looking back, Emmeline couldn't recall the duke having anything other than his strong black coffee.

"Oh, the shortbread isn't for the duke," said Mrs. Punchbowl. "It's for 'Oratio. That raven." She laughed, her cheeks growing as rosy as apples. "'E'll eat almost anyfink."

Emmeline couldn't help but laugh too. Over the last few weeks, she'd been making a concerted effort to get to know the other staff members at St Lawrence House. Fanny was sweet and Mrs. Punchbowl was jovial. Bertie always had a ready smile and a wink for her.

Woodley was his usual po-faced self. Horatio fluttered in and out of rooms and chatted to Emmeline now and then. As for the raven's enigmatic master...

The duke, still very much engrossed in his work, kept to himself all day, every day, until later in the evening after the children retired for the night at eight o'clock. Then he would summon Emmeline to his study, and he would ask her about how his wards were getting on, before checking if she'd noticed anything untoward or unusual, particularly about the behavior of the other staff.

In quiet moments, Emmeline would readily admit to herself that it was the favorite part of her day, chatting with the duke. Even though it shouldn't be—he was her *employer*.

But he was witty and self-effacing and charming in a subtle way. He even seemed to relish hearing all about his wards—what they'd been learning about, their latest antics—and she hadn't expected that.

She felt listened to and seen, like the duke valued her observations and opinions. She felt like she *mattered*.

It had never been like that with Jeremy. Once he'd wooed her and wed her, his interest had begun to wane almost immediately. A thespian and aspiring playwright, he'd spent far too many hours either idling away in their Cheapside lodgings, "working" on his plays, or rehearsing and performing at Freddy's music hall.

Except, "writing, rehearsing, and performing" also meant drinking far too much and having affairs with other women while Emmeline worked long hours at her father's store.

Needless to say, it was a time Emmeline would rather forget. While she'd grieved for Jeremy and what they'd once shared, she couldn't say she wasn't still bitter and angry about his betrayal of their wedding vows and of the precarious financial position he'd left her in. But if he *hadn't* drunk too much and accidentally fallen through one of the stage trapdoors to his untimely demise at the age of six-and-twenty, she wouldn't have embarked on the course she was on now. Life had certainly taken her on a strange journey.

Training at the Parasol Academy, and now working for the mercurial Duke of St Lawrence, certainly kept Emmeline busy enough that she didn't dwell on all the old awfulness of the past. Although, she couldn't help but feel a *tad* guilty about "spying" on the St Lawrence House staff and then talking about them all behind their backs with the duke. On the other hand, she genuinely wished to get to know some of the other servants. Perhaps even make a friend or two because she would admit to feeling a trifle lonely whenever she had a spare moment to herself. She missed her dear friend Mina Davenport. She even missed the hustle and bustle of student life at the Academy. So it wasn't simply an intelligence-gathering exercise to discover who was responsible for the odd goings-on in the house. Emmeline truly wished to form new connections.

Once the children had had their fill of puff balloons—the last one had made it onto the duke's afternoon tea tray, even though His Grace wasn't likely to eat it (and Horatio might)—Emmeline asked Fanny to escort the children back to the nursery. Emmeline needed to clean her uniform. After making puff balloons, she'd managed to get flour and sticky syrup on her sleeves and pinafore, and it wouldn't do.

As per the *Parasol Academy Handbook* guidelines, a nanny must be "neat as a pin at all times." A besmirched uniform was highly frowned upon and must be "unsmirched" discreetly and as soon as possible. To save time, Emmeline would employ the *Unsmirchify* incantation in the privacy of her room rather than changing into a completely new pinafore and gown (which would take far too long considering she had to grapple with twenty fiddly jet buttons down the back and several sets of tight laces).

Less than ten minutes later, her appearance restored to the required standard, Emmeline was about to return to the nursery when she heard a decidedly feminine screech emanating from that direction.

Alarm prickled along Emmeline's spine. Was that Fanny or one of the other housemaids? Thinking that perhaps Archimedes the frog or Aristotle the terrapin had escaped from their aquarium—or at the very least, a mouse or rat had sneaked into the house—Emmeline hurtled pell-mell out of her room and found Fanny outside the nursery gawking at an empty hallway.

"What's wrong? What's happened? Are the children all right?"

Emmeline demanded in a great rush... and then the hair at her nape stood up when she noticed that every single one of the paintings lining the walls had been tipped to a forty-five-degree angle.

It was decidedly odd and unsettling, and there didn't seem to be any rhyme or reason to it.

Emmeline's gaze darted to the nursery door. Three small faces poked out.

"What happened to all the pictures?" asked Bartholomew, his brown eyes wide.

"They weren't like that when we came upstairs five minutes ago," remarked Harry with a frown.

Somehow Emmeline managed to sort through her own scrambled thoughts to come up with an explanation that seemed logical and wouldn't distress the children. "Oh, I expect Horatio has been flying about the house, stirring things up for fun. It would be easy enough for him to upset a painting."

"Naughty Horatio," said Gareth, his young voice brimming with disapproval.

"Indeed," said Emmeline. She glanced at Fanny, who was whey-faced and seemed struck dumb, at least momentarily. "Children"—she pulled out a small bundle of sticks from her pocket and passed them to Harry—"why don't you play spillikins with these for a few minutes while Miss Fanny and I put these pictures to rights?"

"All right..." Harry looked a little skeptical. "Maybe Miss Fanny needs a cup of tea."

"Yes, I expect she might," agreed Emmeline. "Could you ring for one, Harry?"

As soon as the nursery door shut, she grasped the maid's arm. "Tell me why you're so shaken, Fanny. Do you know who did this?" She gestured at the paintings.

"It's the *ghost*," the maid whispered fearfully.

"What ghost?" asked Emmeline. She couldn't disguise the doubtful note in her voice.

Fanny at last met Emmeline's gaze. Her frown was a mere hair's breadth from annoyed. "*You* know. The ghost that tampers with all the clocks and opens locked doors in the middle of the night. And makes the pipes leak and puts rats in the walls... *That* ghost."

"Oh," said Emmeline. "Surely not. I'm certain there must be a logical explanation for all these peculiar occurrences. It could very well have been Horatio this time." Of course, Emmeline didn't believe the duke's raven was responsible at all, but she had to at least attempt to nip these unhelpful rumors in the bud. "With all this terrible rain, he has been cooped up inside for quite a while."

Fanny shook her head. "I don't think so. You haven't been here long enough to witness everything, Nanny Chase. It *has* to be the ghost of St Lawrence House. Most of the maids think it's the ghost of the old duke—His Grace's father—who roams the halls, especially at night, upsetting things. Apparently he was a right grumpy old sod. Whereas some of the footmen think—" The nurserymaid bit her lip. "I shouldn't say anything."

"What do they think, Fanny?" Emmeline prompted gently.

The maid dropped her voice to a whisper again. "They think it might be His Grace who's doing these odd things. Did you know that in the past he was called Mad Mason and Lord Weirdbrook? Before he inherited the dukedom."

What? "That's awful," said Emmeline, her heart cramping even as indignation spiked. "And not true."

Fanny pouted. "He *does* have some peculiar mannerisms. And habits. The way he's so obsessed with clocks and watches... According to Babcock, his valet, the duke refuses to wear anything but silk-lined clothes. And the way he either looks you right in the eye or barely regards you at all... I mean, *I* can see why some people might think he's a bit touched in the head."

Anger bristled inside Emmeline, but she strove to keep a neutral expression as she said, "Fanny, I hope that you won't spread that sort of horrid gossip about the place. I especially won't have that kind of talk in my domain, the nursery. Or anywhere near the duke's wards, for that matter." She softened her tone as she added, "I know I've only been here a short time, but His Grace has been nothing but kindness personified. Aside from that, don't you think many of us have our own little eccentricities? Mr. Woodley is a case in point. Does he ever wear any other facial expression other than 'undertaker'?"

Fanny laughed at that. "Yes, Nanny Chase. I promise I won't spread malicious talk. I happen to like His Grace, too, despite his quirks. He wouldn't do this." She gestured at the paintings. "He prefers everything to be ordered, not messy. I still think it might be a ghost." She gave a little shiver as she murmured more to herself than to Emmeline, "Nothing else makes sense."

"If it's a ghost, I'd prefer that he or she were more useful and helped out by picking up the children's toys in the nursery from time to time. Or even helping the housemaids dust," said Emmeline.

Fanny readily agreed. The maid returned to the nursery to supervise the spillikins game while Emmeline sought out the duke. She wanted to report on the latest strange occurrence sooner rather than later. On her way downstairs to the second floor, it was evident that several other paintings—stern portraits of the duke's ancestors no doubt—had also been tilted on an angle. *Curious and curiouser,* thought Emmeline as she paused to examine a pewter-haired gentleman with a hawkish nose, forbidding scowl, and a high-point collar so stiff and sharp looking it could have easily poked out an eye if one got too close.

Emmeline reached the second floor. It had to be one of the servants who'd tampered with the paintings in the hall rather than an intruder. There was always a footman stationed at the front door, and the kitchen door that served as a staff entrance was always locked. (Well, except for the night it had been mysteriously *un*locked.)

But who would do this and why? Was it to disturb the duke's peace of mind so he couldn't get his work done? Was someone trying to portray him in a bad light? And to what end? Could it be that the duke was right? That someone like Sir Randolph Redvers was paying off one of the staff members to create disturbances in St Lawrence House?

Emmeline had no idea. But what was happening wasn't right. Her charges might be in danger if the saboteur went too far. It was her duty to protect the Duke of St Lawrence's wards, no matter what.

An unscheduled visit to her employer was in order. There was no time to delay.

Chapter 11

Involving Sticky Badgers and Sticky Beaks; Bird-wittedness and Brazen Moves; Champagne, Meringues, Cream, and a Far Too Tempting Invitation...

As Emmeline suspected, His Grace was in his study. Bertie, who was on "guard duty" in the hall, gave her a wide smile before he knocked on the door and announced her arrival.

As soon as Emmeline entered the room, Horatio, who was on his perch behind the duke's desk, bobbed up and down and cawed a soft greeting. *Nanny Chase*, he remarked in her head. *So lovely to see you. I enjoyed the puff balloon pudding you made immensely. Although I am now stickier than a badger who's plundered a beehive...* For effect, the raven wiped his glossy black beak on his polished mahogany perch then ruffled his feathers.

Yes, it's an inevitable hazard I'm afraid, returned Emmeline. *But I'm very pleased to hear you enjoyed it, Horatio.* Concerned that *she* might appear to be bird-witted if she regarded the duke's raven for too long, Emmeline transferred her attention to her employer and dipped into a curtsy.

As for His Grace, he'd already placed his silver fountain pen in its stand, pushed aside his work, and had risen to his feet as though Emmeline were a fine lady who'd come to visit. It seemed to be a habit of his—treating her as though she were someone from his exalted class—and she was always surprised (and secretly more than a little flattered) by his gentlemanly manners.

It made Emmeline feel special, and the warm flutters she felt in her belly whenever he behaved in such a way had everything to do with the fact he was kind. (And nothing at all to do with the fact he was austerely handsome and respectful. Or the delicious richness of his voice which always turned her insides to a mushy puddle.)

"Thank you for seeing me, Your Grace," she began at the exact same moment he said, "To what do I owe this unexpected pleasure, Mrs. Chase?"

Emmeline laughed, then her face grew hot when the duke held her gaze in that very direct way of his. Like he was interested in her and couldn't stop studying her expression. Or he was trying very hard to discern her thoughts.

Hoping the duke wouldn't notice the telltale color in her cheeks—Emmeline had honestly never blushed so much in her entire life—she reminded herself why she'd come. "I know we usually talk in the evenings, but something unexpected has occurred," she said. "Another difficult-to-explain household disturbance. It's nothing disastrous, and your wards are perfectly fine, but I thought you should hear about it right away."

"I see," said the duke, his brows descending into a deep frown. He gestured to the wing chairs in front of the fire. "Shall we be seated for this discussion?"

Emmeline agreed and once they were settled, she proceeded to describe the "upset paintings incident." She also gave an abbreviated account of Fanny's disclosure about the ghost of St Lawrence House. "Fanny also told me that some of the staff think—" Emmeline paused and bit her lip. She would need to choose her next words carefully. The last thing she wanted to do was upset the duke by being tactless.

"Yes," prompted the duke. "Go on, Mrs. Chase." His mouth tipped into a wry smile. "Although I suspect I know exactly what you are about to say. Is it something to do with my mental fitness? Or lack thereof? That various staff members often whisper that I might be as mad as a hatter?"

Emmeline grimaced. "I'm afraid so, Your Grace."

"And what do you think about that idea?" he asked, watching her carefully.

"I think it's utter nonsense," returned Emmeline firmly. "Not to mention terribly rude. And I told Fanny so. I also advised her not to repeat that sort of gossip."

The duke inclined his head. "Thank you for nobly defending me. Although, rumors of that nature have been circulating about society for quite some time, so I'm not surprised nor offended. My singular tastes and undeniable obsession with horology have marked me as . . . different. Even amongst my peers."

"You're not a usual sort of duke," said Emmeline with a smile meant to convey her understanding.

"Exactly," said His Grace, the faintest trace of an answering smile playing about his wide chiseled mouth. "I suppose the most noteworthy thing about this particular 'painting' incident is that the perpetrator has decided to wreak mischief in the middle of the day rather than in the middle of the night. Which is a particularly brazen move, I must say."

"It *must* be someone on your staff," asserted Emmeline. "Nothing else makes sense."

The duke steepled his gloved fingers beneath his chin. "Yes . . . Of course, I'll question Woodley and the footmen stationed at the front door. And Mrs. Punchbowl, who's always in the kitchen. There are daily deliveries—food, newspapers, coal, and mail—so any number of strangers visit the house. But given everything else that's occurred over the last few months, it stands to reason that the mischief-maker is someone who not only works but resides here."

"I'm reasonably certain it isn't Fanny," said Emmeline. "She did seem genuinely shaken when I found her in the hall outside the nursery. It was her shriek that alerted me to the fact that something was wrong in the first place. Unless she ducked out of the nursery and tampered with the pictures when I was repairing my appearance upstairs."

"It does seem unlikely," agreed the duke. Then his gaze combed over Emmeline, slow and assessing. "Along with the need for you to repair your appearance. You always look immaculate, Mrs. Chase."

"Not after making puff balloons, I'm afraid," said Emmeline with a sigh. "I was rather floury and syrupy."

"Ah, the puff balloons." The duke smiled. "Horatio did enjoy the one that was sent up. I was almost tempted to try it after I'd heard you'd made it. But alas, I do not enjoy sweet fare."

"That's quite all right," said Emmeline. "Your wards enjoyed cooking them at any rate."

"I'm sure they did." There was a slight pause in which the duke regarded Emmeline, his expression deeply thoughtful. "I told a lie before, Mrs. Chase. Your appearance is always immaculate . . . except for one thing." His attention settled on the top of her head.

Emmeline self-consciously touched her utilitarian coiffure. Was her coiled bun coming undone? Had some of her curls escaped? Her untamable locks were the bane of her existence. "My apologies if my hair is not quite right," she began, but the duke held up a hand.

"It's not your gorg—It's not your hair that's the problem," he said. "It's that godawful nanny's cap that the Parasol Academy makes you wear. If I had my way, I'd burn the ridiculous thing. It's as pointless as a broken compass. Why anyone thought that something that resembles an exploded meringue would make a good hat, I'll never know."

Emmeline couldn't contain her laughter. It fountained out of her like a frothy spill of champagne from an uncorked bottle. "Oh, Your Grace, I do happen to agree with you. But as per the *Parasol Academy Handbook*—"

"You have to wear it," finished the duke with a sigh. "Tell me, Mrs. Chase"—his blue eyes, now glowing rather than ice-cool, bored into hers—"do you *always* follow the Academy's rules?"

"I do," Emmeline declared with a decided nod. (A little white lie.) "I must." (Not a lie.)

"Ah, but you are in my house now, Mrs. Chase." The duke's voice grew deeper. His blue gaze more intense. "Shouldn't you follow *my* rules?"

Emmeline's pulse accelerated like a runaway train, clickety-clacking so loudly, she wondered that the duke didn't hear it. "I-I will always try to, Your Grace," she stammered. "As long as your rules are not in direct opposition to the Academy's." Although, deep down, Emmeline feared that her commitment to certain parts of the Academy's prescriptive handbook—such as its strict uniform policy—could very easily falter. In fact, right at this moment, her resolve was wavering like a candle flame guttering in a draft.

She sat up straighter as though the mere act of improving her posture would somehow reinforce her willpower. Yes, her determination was like steel, and not at all weak like a soggy biscuit that had been dunked in a cup of tea one too many times.

"Hmmm." That small, disgruntled rumble implied the duke was not particularly pleased with Emmeline's response. His gloved fingertips drummed on the arm of his leather chair. "What if I proscribe the wearing of that abomination you call a nanny's cap while inside the walls of St Lawrence House?" he continued. He cocked a brow as though presenting her with a challenge. "I won't tell the Academy if you don't. No one will know. Why don't you take it off right now . . . ?"

Scorching heat flooded Emmeline's face. She felt as though

the duke had asked her to strip naked, not just take off her cap. But perhaps such indecorous thoughts had invaded her mind because the man himself was currently dishabille—coatless and necktie-less with a loosened collar and rolled-up shirtsleeves. Indeed, the entire time she'd been in the duke's study, Emmeline had been secretly wondering how the duke would look, sans clothes. Oh, she was a naughty, wicked nanny. A frustrated widow who hadn't had any sort of fulfilling "relations" for far too long. Thank heavens her employer couldn't read her direct thoughts.

"I-I suppose I could dispense with my cap," murmured Emmeline, raising her hands to the top of her head. "I wouldn't want to displease you, Your Grace."

As she began to carefully remove the half-dozen hairpins that kept the confection of linen and lace in place, heat flared in the duke's eyes. Was it a spark of triumph? Desire?

Surely not. Emmeline's imagination was simply running wild down all sorts of libidinous paths that in the end would only trip her up. She was far too fanciful, and her inappropriate thoughts were bound to get her into trouble if she didn't rein them in. And quickly.

One should *not* lust after one's employer. Like and respect and admire, yes.

Desire, no.

No, no, no, with an enormous dollop of never, ever, ever on top.

She couldn't risk her position here. She needed the money. Her father needed the money. She must be ruthless. Mercenary. She must not put a foot wrong. Not when there was so much at stake.

The duke smiled like the cat who'd lapped up an entire bowl of cream when Emmeline was capless. She didn't think she'd ever seen him smile in that way before. Like a rake. Like a man who'd gotten his way and was pleased beyond measure.

She tucked her cap and hairpins into her pocket then said in a voice that was far too breathless, "Well, I hope my appearance now meets with your approval, Your Grace."

"It does." His voice, low and soft and intimate, stroked over her, making her shiver. "Very much."

Oh, my days. Emmeline didn't know where to look or what to say. In the ensuing silence, the only things that could be heard were the ticking of the mantel clock and the crackle of the fire. And perhaps the wild thud of her heart against her ribs.

Emmeline smoothed her damp palms down her skirts as she tried to school her thoughts into some semblance of order. To not think about the duke in ways that she shouldn't. She most certainly *wouldn't* look at the duke's thighs and the way the fabric pulled tight over the hard muscles. Or the fact that his rolled-up cambric sleeves revealed his lean, corded forearms with their fine dusting of hair.

To think those lean strong arms had been wrapped around her at her interview . . .

It was a memory she'd been steadfastly trying to avoid, but when she was alone at night, it would slip into her mind, taunting her, teasing her until she took matters into her own hands to relieve her pent-up, physical tension. She wasn't an innocent young virgin. She was a widow and she had needs, damn it! And the duke was a very attractive, intriguing, powerful man . . .

Emmeline had the sudden, completely mad urge to want to see the duke's bare hands. He always wore fine black leather gloves that seemed molded to his flesh. If she peeled off those gloves, what would she find? He had long, almost elegant fingers and she imagined his nails were well-kept. Would there be a fine sprinkling of hair on the backs of his hands too?

Oh God, now she was wondering what he could *do* with those hands. How it would feel if he inched up her wool skirts and pristine white petticoats and rested his large palm against her drawer-clad thigh. Skated his fingertips up higher, higher, until he found her—

No. What happened to no, no, no, with an enormous dollop of never, ever, ever on top, Emmeline Chase? Remember Chapter Five, Paragraph 3.2, Part a) of the Parasol Academy Handbook? *The bit about fraternizing with one's employer. That it's entirely and utterly <u>forbidden</u>!? (Yes, it was even underlined in the handbook.)*

Emmeline swallowed. Closed her eyes and drew a deep breath. *Think about something irksome. Something horrid and annoying. Like burnt toast and rotten potatoes for tea. Like enormous spiders and dog-eared pages or impossibly knotted bootlaces. Or anything written by Charles Dickens.*

Once she was feeling less discomposed (that is, her lust was locked away securely behind a bolted door) Emmeline faced the duke. "Well, I shall continue to keep an eye out for the St Lawrence House saboteur," she said. "It's such a shame that I didn't catch whoever it is in the act earlier on. Although, if the saboteur is getting bolder, perhaps he or she will reveal their hand before too long."

The duke released a sigh. "We can but hope."

"Right... If there's nothing else..." Emmeline moved to the edge of her seat.

The duke took her cue and rose as she did. But instead of dismissing her, he said, "Ah, but there is something else, Mrs. Chase." He held out a gloved hand like he was inviting her to dance. "Come. I have something I want to show you."

Chapter 12

In Which Drawers Catch on Fire; Jib Doors and Jabs and Jibes Are Featured Along with Cursory Curtsies, Codfish, and Grenades...

Emmeline's breath hitched as she stared at the duke. Did he really want her to place her hand in his?

He must. When she looked into the duke's ice-blue eyes, there was an unmistakable spark of challenge there again. And she couldn't very well refuse her employer. Could she?

Despite her earlier resolution *not* to be affected by the duke, Emmeline's heart began to pound. She reached out and as soon as the duke's leather-clad fingers engulfed hers in a warm grip, a ripple of unwanted yearning slid over her skin, raising gooseflesh beneath her clothes. Making the tips of her breasts harden and push in the most unseemly manner against her linen chemise and corset. Clearly, the errant lust she'd locked away not five minutes ago had not been subdued at all. It had opened one eye and was stirring restlessly, muttering curses at her while rattling the door handle, trying to escape.

Blast and bother! This was so very dangerous. Even though she'd sternly reminded herself that she shouldn't "fraternize" with the duke, it seemed that when push came to shove, she was prepared to capitulate and dive right in.

But maybe she was being fanciful and reading things into the situation that simply weren't there. *Taking the duke's hand means nothing at all. It's no different to any man offering you his arm. It's what gentlemen do all the time,* she told herself. But then another voice whispered, *Liar, liar, drawers on fire. Dukes don't usually offer nannies their arms, do they, Emmeline Chase?*

"Where are we going?" she managed as the duke tucked her hand into the crook of his elbow as though he were about to escort her into a ballroom or into dinner. "I might need to get back to the nursery . . ."

"You'll see," said the duke matter-of-factly. As though what they were doing was completely de rigueur. "Besides, I'm sure Fanny can cope on her own for fifteen minutes."

Any additional protest or excuse that Emmeline could think to mount quickly dissipated as the duke led her across the plush Turkish rug to a towering pair of mahogany bookcases on the other side of the room. The dust-free shelves contained row after row of leather-bound volumes, their spines all perfectly aligned. Emmeline didn't have much of an opportunity to peruse the titles as the duke reached into one of the shelves with his free hand and slid out one of the books. All at once, the bookcase closest to the desk began to move.

It was a secret door. A jib door!

Emmeline gasped as the whole bookcase swung silently inward on well-oiled hinges, revealing another room beyond—an enormous chamber not unlike a museum gallery. The next thing that struck Emmeline was the ticking. The very air thrummed with the soft rhythmic sound of countless timepieces, diligently marking the passing of endless seconds and minutes and hours.

"I thought you might like to see my personal horology collection," said the duke as he ushered Emmeline into the room. After relinquishing her hand, he added in a manner that seemed to be both diffident and proud, "I also wanted to show you the electromechanical clock prototype I've been working on for the upcoming exhibition at the Crystal Palace next month."

Personal horology collection? Now that was an understatement if Emmeline had ever heard one. This hidden room was like a horological treasure trove. Unlike a pirate's den though, this chamber was ordered and neat and stunningly beautiful. It was filled with tiered gilt and glass display cases that were teeming with watches. The burnished oak-paneled walls were lined with every kind of clock imaginable. There was a row of impressive longcase clocks standing to attention along one side of the gallery. Another shelf-lined wall showcased innumerable carriage and ormolu mantel clocks. Sundials, chronometers, and a magnificent brass sextant upon an ornate stand dominated one corner. There was even a German cuckoo clock.

Wherever one's eye fell, there was the glow of brass and gilt and polished wood, and the sparkle of crystal and glass, and enamel, and jewels. This homage to horology was nothing short of breathtaking.

Emmeline's mouth must have been hanging open in wonder because she had to close it in order to speak. "Your Grace," she murmured, her voice laced with awe. "I had no idea this room was here. I feel like I've been transported to a magical domain. And yes, I'd love to see your electromechanical clock. I'd consider it an honor."

She spun around slowly, trying to take in every single detail of the magnificence surrounding her. The floor was white marble veined with fine lines of green and gray. The soaring vaulted ceiling, which was supported by four fluted marble columns, was a tribute to the night sky. It was painted a deep velvety blue, providing the perfect backdrop for depictions of the sun and the moon and various constellations, all exquisitely rendered in gold and silver. A gilt banner above the jib door proclaimed *Tempus Rerum Imperator*: *Time, the Ruler of All Things*.

In front of a row of tall casement windows stood a long oak desk-cum-workbench that ran along the entire length of the room. As Emmeline drew closer, she could see that its surface was covered with a variety of metallic tools of all shapes and sizes, tools that she immediately recognized as paraphernalia associated with watch- and clock-making; the sorts of tools her father had used in his own Cheapside workshop.

A pewter-handled magnifying glass and a jeweler's eye loupe lay at the very end of the bench beside a gilt pocket watch; it lay open, its delicate insides exposed.

"I like to tinker," explained the duke as Emmeline, still openly gawping, wandered the length of the workbench. "While I love collecting rare timepieces, bringing my own designs to life is even more fulfilling."

As Emmeline touched a fingertip to a razor-sharp steel wheel—the cutting disc—of a topping machine, she laughed. "Oh, I don't know," she said. "This seems to be a bit more than tinkering to me. This looks like a serious occupation. I'm wildly curious though, Your Grace. You're a nobleman. A duke, no less. How did someone like you learn so much about the art of watch- and clock-making?"

The duke pushed his hands into his trouser pockets and shrugged. "I hired a master affiliated with the Worshipful Company of Clockmakers guild to train me. Privately of course. For several years, I was very much the apprentice. But now I like to think I know enough to create my own timepieces that are both sophisticated and unique. And beautiful."

This last word was uttered as he looked directly at Emmeline.

Oh. My. Goodness. Trapped in the duke's piercing blue gaze, Emmeline's toes curled in her boots. Her face was as blazing hot as a furnace. He couldn't mean that *she* was beautiful. Because she wasn't. Oh, she knew she was attractive-*ish*. She had a pleasing enough figure (at least Jeremy had told her so before he'd grown bored with her and moved on to other women) and regular features. She had all her teeth and they were relatively straight. But she also had an unfashionably freckled countenance (that no amount of lemon juice would repair) and garish copper-red hair. She was not a conventional "beauty" by any means.

And then, of course, she was a nanny, not an accomplished, gently bred, aristocratic (virginal) young lady, the sort of woman a duke would pay court to. Unless the duke wanted to pursue her for *other* reasons... which hardly seemed likely. His Grace didn't seem like a rakish, lecherous sort of man—the type of odious employer who waylaid maids in stairwells and pressured them for favors. Someone like Sir Randolph Redvers for instance. Now, if a man like the baronet ever propositioned Emmeline, she would not hesitate to jab him sharply in the nether regions before she told him to roughly self-insert his nannying post where the sun doesn't shine.

But Emmeline firmly believed that the Duke of St Lawrence wasn't like that. Moreover, his praise and interest were not unwelcome. Even though Emmeline didn't understand why the duke wanted to spend so much time with her—she'd be a fool to deny that he didn't—*she* was the one in danger of developing a ludicrous infatuation with the man.

She certainly wouldn't do the unthinkable and fall in love.

Now *that* would be a disaster of epic proportions.

To break the wire-taut silence that followed the duke's pronouncement, to encourage the duke to shift his unnerving focus onto something else, Emmeline gestured helplessly at a nearby display—a magnificent carriage-style clock—sitting atop a marble pedestal that was at least three feet tall. The clock itself appeared to be about the same height. "Did you make this clock by any chance? It is exquisite."

"Ah," said the duke, drawing closer. His gaze moved to the clock. "I did. And it's actually my electromechanical prototype. It's a smaller version of what I have in mind for the Westminster Palace clock."

"Oh..." Emmeline circled it, admiring the mother-of-pearl face and elegant hour hands inlaid with turquoise enamel. The lustrous gilt case and its swinging brass pendulum. Even its regular tick sounded refined; its cadence was as measured as the Queen's. "You must have spent hours and hours working on it. I don't know a lot about electromechanical clocks though. They are not all that common." Then she laughed. "I've always imagined that to work, they have lightning rods attached."

The duke released a huff of laughter too. "Not quite. My clock is powered by a Faraday-type of electromagnet. When the pendulum slows—every thirty swings or so—it comes into contact with the magnet, which then gives it a little push." The duke rocked back on his heels. "I won't bore you with the details, but I'm rather proud of it if I do say so myself. It's the one clock in this entire house that is incredibly accurate. Go on." He gestured at the clock with his chin. "Compare the time on your Parasol Academy pocket watch to the time on this specimen. I'd wager my clock is marking Greenwich Mean Time just as perfectly."

Emmeline pulled out her own watch from her gown's pocket. "You're right," she said after a moment. "Your clock is keeping excellent time."

"Ultimately, I envisage connecting a number of clocks via a wiring system to this wonderfully accurate electromagnetic clock—the 'queen' clock. So the other 'courtier' clocks would do the monarch's bidding." The duke grinned. "Or if it were a nanny clock, she would make sure her junior clocks are on time."

Emmeline returned his smile as she slipped her watch back into her pocket. "I like the sound of that. I gather you'll patent your clever design, Your Grace?"

The duke placed a hand on the side of his prototype and

gave it a pat. "That is the plan. It would mean that all the clocks in an entire household or place of work—whether it's a factory or bank or college or any other type of business—would be perfectly synchronized. I imagine it's a system that would be quite useful. I can't be the only person in Christendom who desires such accuracy."

"That would be marvelous," said Emmeline. "The Westminster clock, it needs to be incredibly accurate, too, does it not? To win the commission?"

"It does," said the duke. "Although, rather than powering it by an electromagnet, I've another idea involving telegraph wires."

"Telegraph wires?"

"Yes, I've been toying with the idea of connecting the Westminster clock directly to the chronometers at the Royal Observatory at Greenwich. A signal could be sent—an electrical pulse—along already existing telegraph wires to the Palace of Westminster to make sure the clock doesn't lose time. I've yet to consult George Airy, the Astronomer Royal, but I believe it could be done."

"How ingenious," declared Emmeline. "It sounds very much like using ley—" She broke off, horrified that she'd almost disclosed one of the Parasol Academy's greatest secrets—that the Fae's leyline magic could be harnessed for sending te-ley-grams and teleporting. Drawing a breath, she tried again. "Isn't it the case that *telegraph* wires transmit electric signals over lines or wires to send telegrams? It sounds like that would work remarkably well."

"It should. In theory," said the duke. Then his brow furrowed with concern. "I hope I'm not boring you to death, Mrs. Chase."

"Oh no. Of course not. Bore away, Your Grace. I mean, I'm not bored at all. I'm fascinated. Truly. And I'm delighted that you've shared so much of your work with me. I promise I won't tell a soul about any of your brilliant plans."

The duke inclined his head. "It's been my pleasure, Mrs. Chase.

And I know you'll be discreet. Perhaps it's because of your Parasol Academy training, I believe that I can trust you. And because you understand my passion for horology, I feel as though I've known you for a lot longer than a handful of weeks." Then to Emmeline's surprise, the duke's cheeks grew bright with color. "My apologies. I sometimes say things that I shouldn't. I hope I haven't made you feel uncomfortable in any way."

"No, not at all. I like—" Emmeline bit her lip. She'd been about to say that she liked the duke, but then *she* would be guilty of saying something she shouldn't. "I enjoy working for you, Your Grace, and your wards are delightful. Which reminds me. I probably should return to the nursery." She hesitated, her feet seemingly glued to the marble floor. She didn't want to leave, but she knew she should, for so many reasons.

Her gaze drifted wistfully over the duke's worktable and his fascinating collection of watches and clocks. Harry would love it here, examining all the timepieces, learning about them all. This room was undoubtedly a sanctuary for the duke, but he'd invited her, Emmeline, to see it. Would he share it with his clever young ward?

There was only one way to find out. And she wouldn't be doing her job properly if she *didn't* make the suggestion.

Buoyed by her conviction to further nurture the bond between the duke and Miss Harriet, she said, "I know you are terribly busy, Your Grace, but do you . . . do you think you might have time in your schedule to show this room to Harry? I'm certain she would love to watch you as you create or repair a timepiece. To learn how watches and clocks work. Or you could simply show her the astrolabe, even if you cannot demonstrate its use until the weather is fairer."

In the silence that ensued, the duke studied her face. Emmeline had no idea what he was thinking until he said, "I don't see why not. In fact, I think I might like that too."

Emmeline's heart leapt. "Really?"

The duke smiled. "Yes, really."

"Wonderful. Well"—Emmeline shifted her gaze to the jib door—"I'll be going then."

The duke sighed heavily. "Yes, I suppose you should. Lord knows, I've kept you long enough. But I do want to thank you for letting me know about the saboteur's latest escapade. If Woodley hasn't already asked the staff to put the paintings to rights, perhaps you could ask—"

At that moment, the jib door moved a fraction and Woodley's voice filtered through the small gap. "Your Grace. My apologies for interrupting. But you have a visitor waiting outside your study."

The duke frowned. "Visitor? I'm not expecting anyone. And why in Jove's name have you let them in?"

"It's your uncle, Your Grace," said Woodley. "Lord Peregrine."

The duke strode toward the door and swung it wider, revealing the grim-faced butler. "Yes. I know my uncle's name," he said, his voice bristling with annoyance. "What does he want?"

"To speak with you, Your Grace. He says it's an urgent matter. And he doesn't wish to spend too long here as his son has another pending appointment. Mr. Mason is currently waiting downstairs in the entry hall."

"That suits me," muttered the duke. Glancing back at Emmeline he said, "Mrs. Chase. I don't want you to feel awkward so—"

"Xavier? Are you in there? It's your uncle." Lord Peregrine Mason possessed a voice as deep as a well, and his consonants were so sharply enunciated, they could have sliced flesh to the bone. "I don't wish to waste my time, idling out here in your blasted corridor. And Algernon needs to be elsewhere—"

"Lord Nevergrin. Never-never-never-grin," squawked Horatio from the study.

Nevergrin? Emmeline had to bite the inside of her cheek to stop herself laughing at the raven's jibe. The duke's uncle must be quite horrid to have earned such a nickname.

Although, the duke wasn't grinning. In fact, his scowl was so fierce it looked as though he was about to encounter someone exceedingly unpleasant. Turning back to Emmeline, he said in a low voice meant only for her, "It's probably best if you stay here while I deal with my uncle. He's a patronizing prig at the best of times."

"Of course, Your Grace," replied Emmeline in an equally soft voice. "Perhaps I could set some of your clocks to the correct time while I wait?"

The duke inclined his head. "Thank you. That would be appreciated. The winding keys and cranks are with each device."

As he stepped into the study, calling for his uncle to enter, Horatio fluttered over his master's head into the Horology Room. He settled on top of the duke's electromechanical clock prototype and cocked his head, his dark beady gaze connecting with Emmeline's. *Thought I'd keep you company while we wait for the insufferable Lord Nevergrin to leave,* he said. Then he ruffled his glossy black feathers. *It's either that or I'll be tempted to drop something rather nasty on the man's shoulder. Now don't look at me like that, Nanny Chase. The pompous pillock deserves it. If you eavesdr—Pardon me. If you* accidentally *hear the conversation taking place in His Grace's study, you'll see that I'm not wrong.*

Is Lord Peregrine really that bad? asked Emmeline. While she knew that she shouldn't listen at keyholes—or jib doors—the duke hadn't fully closed the bookcase, so there was a small gap allowing the conversation currently taking place in the study to drift through into the Horology Room.

Nevergrin is the absolute worst, asserted Horatio. *He's essentially a bully. The equivalent of a morose thundercloud. Or an upset belly. He does nothing but produce a lot of loud, use-*

less, and unpleasant grumbling. Which is very much like the old duke, his late brother.

How dreadful! The duke's own father had been a bully? Emmeline's heart swelled with sympathy for her employer. His childhood must have been terribly unhappy if that were the case.

To distract herself from imagining the duke as a sad and lonely and distressed little boy—the sort of child she'd been trained to both nurture and protect—Emmeline took out her pocket watch. She should get on with setting the duke's clocks. But her vision had blurred, and she couldn't make out the position of her watch's hands.

All of a sudden, Lord Peregrine's booming baritone invaded the room. "What do you mean you don't have them here, boy?"

Boy?! Emmeline stiffened with anger. The Duke of St Lawrence was *not* a child. *How dare—*

The duke's voice cut through her thoughts. "I might be your nephew, but you will treat me with respect in my own home, sir. Otherwise, I shall have you thrown out into the street along with my cousin."

There was a snort. "You wouldn't dare."

"Oh, believe me, I would dare, *Uncle*. And I don't care who sees. Now"—the duke paused as though he was drawing a calming breath—"if you hadn't so rudely interrupted me, I would have been able to inform you that the St Lawrence sapphire and diamond parure that you wish to borrow for your wife is in a locked safe at my bank, Coutts and Co. I can send a message to the bank manager, asking him to release it into your care for the period it is required."

"Humph..." The duke's uncle was silent for a moment. Then he said, "Your Grace, wouldn't it be simpler if you handed all the St Lawrence jewels over to me for safekeeping? Then my lady-wife can wear them whenever she pleases. And I won't have to come begging."

"I'm not as curmudgeonly as Ebenezer Scrooge, Uncle Peregrine, if that's what you're implying."

Lord Peregrine emitted a low grumble. "That's not what I'm implying at all. The point is, you're not the marrying kind. You've told me that yourself often enough. And even if you were, you'd have a hard time convincing any woman of sound mind to accept your suit given your . . . reputation."

"Well, thank you very much, Uncle." Bitterness laced the duke's voice.

"You cannot say it isn't true. You know as well as I that if you don't wed and produce an heir, the dukedom will eventually pass to *my* son."

"No doubt you and Cousin Algernon would both like that."

"It has nothing to do with *liking* it," returned Lord Peregrine hotly. "It's the way it is. You should hear the rumors flying about the clubs."

This time the duke snorted. "Let me guess. Everyone is whispering about Mad Mason again? Or have they come up with some new insult now that I'm the duke? Insane St Lawrence perhaps? Or St Lawrence the Lunatic?"

"You have no idea how embarrassing it all is," returned Lord Peregrine, his tone scathing. "The pitying looks I receive whenever your name comes up in conversation. And your aunt and cousin too when they're out and about. You're the albatross of the family, Xavier. Your father, God rest his soul, should have had you committed to an asylum for your own good years ago. And I told him so, on more than one occasion I might add. Your obsession with horology is more than unhealthy, it's bizarre. Not only that, but your plan to design the Westminster Palace tower clock is utterly nonsensical. As if someone like you—a man who's clearly crackbrained—could ever come up with—"

Emmeline had had enough. Without thinking, she pushed

through the gap in the jib door and marched into the study. "Oh, pardon me, Your Grace," she said, glancing between the duke and his vile visitor. "I had no idea that I was interrupting you and your . . ."

Tilting her head and narrowing her eyes, she directed her attention to the duke's uncle—a tall gray-haired man with a high forehead and a long beak of a nose—then waited for an introduction that she was in no way entitled to. Oh, she was being so very insubordinate, and breaking every single etiquette rule in the book (and not just the *Parasol Academy Handbook*), but she didn't care. Her employer—a good man with a brilliant mind—was being grossly insulted, and she would defend him, come what may.

"This is Lord Peregrine," supplied the duke, his expression inscrutable. "My uncle."

"Nevergrin Nevergrin," chanted Horatio as he fluttered back into the study and landed on his perch. His black eyes gleamed with wicked glee as he regarded his master's uncle.

Ignoring the raven's shameless but amusing taunts as best she could, Emmeline murmured, "My lord," and bobbed the most cursory of curtsies to Lord Peregrine. As she boldly met the man's gaze, she could see that he was bristling with irritation.

And then it struck her. This was the monocled, hawk-nosed gentleman whose portrait had been knocked askew on the stairs. She had a mind to keep knocking that painting sideways when no one was looking, simply to spite the horrid aristocrat.

As though he'd discerned her less-than-agreeable thoughts, Lord Peregrine made a scoffing sound in his throat before returning his attention back to his nephew. "For God's sake, don't bother with an introduction, Xavier. I have better things to do than to meet the hired help."

"Yes, thoroughly insulting one's relatives is such a worthwhile endeavor," returned Emmeline. "And far be it from me, the hired help, to deny you the opportunity to continue to do so, Lord Peregrine. I'm sure His Grace appreciates your unvarnished candor and unstinting concern for his well-being. Because we all know how salubrious a prolonged asylum stay would be."

"Well, I never," exclaimed the ignoble nobleman. Outrage transformed his features; his countenance turned an alarming shade of puce while his mouth snapped open and shut like a landed codfish gasping for air.

Giving Lord Peregrine her back—Emmeline didn't give a jot that she'd upset the man—she curtsied to the duke. "Your Grace. I shall return to your charges."

And then she quit the room before her simmering anger made her do something else reckless like upending the duke's coffeepot over Lord Nevergrin's head.

Bertie, still stationed at the door along with Woodley, called a faint farewell, but Emmeline didn't stop. She merely gave a brief wave as she hastened down the hall.

Brava, Nanny Chase. Brava! Horatio had followed her. When Emmeline reached the main staircase, the raven landed on a newel post and she halted.

She drew a calming breath. *I hope I haven't lost my job.* Regret and worry had started to seep in, dampening her fiery indignation.

Oh no. You won't have, replied the raven, his cultured voice reassuring. *There's no love lost between His Grace and Lord Nevergrin. My master does not like him. Not one little bit.*

Emmeline clasped her hands together. Unease continued to gnaw away at the pit of her stomach. *All the same, I wonder if I've made myself an enemy. In hindsight I feel it was unwise of me to cross His Grace's uncle.*

Horatio fanned out his tail feathers. *Pfft, I wouldn't worry. Lord Nevergrin is full of bluff and bluster and not much else. His Grace is your employer. His opinion is the only one that matters.*

Emmeline knew Horatio spoke sense. Loyalty to her employer had sparked her outrage and surely the duke would see that. She was fretting unnecessarily.

Probably.

At least, she hoped so.

This wasn't the first time that her unruly tongue had gotten her into trouble.

Her gaze wandered along the stairwell. Lord Peregrine's painting was still askew. Even though it was petty of her to think so, she'd like to leave it that way.

Emmeline tapped her chin as she studied the peer's sneering portrait. Evidently, the duke had two potential enemies with motive and considerable means. His uncle, Lord Peregrine, and Sir Randolph Redvers. Of course, there might be any number of rival horologists aside from Sir Randolph who might want to discredit the duke in order to win the Westminster Palace clock contest. Algernon Mason, Lord Peregrine's son, would eventually inherit a dukedom if his cousin Xavier, who had neither wife nor heir, was declared non compos mentis and committed to an asylum.

She sneaked down the stairs to the first-floor landing to catch a glimpse of Lord Peregrine's son. He was sitting rigidly on an overstuffed wingchair in a nook in the entry hall. Even a screen of cascading fronds from a pedestal-mounted palm couldn't hide the tight look of impatience on the hawk-nosed gentleman's face, or the fact he was tapping his polished leather toe on the tiles.

Well, whoever it was that bore the duke ill will must have deep enough pockets to be paying one of the St Lawrence House staff members to do their dirty work. Emmeline didn't *think* Fanny was involved in the most recent incident of sabotage, even though she had been in the hallway outside the nursery. The maid's distress had seemed genuine. But for the right price, another staff member might very well be creating mayhem. He or she might also be spreading rumors about a ghost being responsible for the mysterious goings-on. It was a clever ploy that would divert suspicion away from the real culprit. If the staff were frightened of the idea of a malevolent phantasm roaming the halls, they'd be less likely to investigate anything that went bump in the night, or any time at all for that matter.

Emmeline regarded the duke's raven again. *Horatio, you fly about various parts of the house throughout the day. Have you ever noticed anyone on staff behaving oddly or doing something they shouldn't?*

The raven cocked his head to one side as though giving due consideration to the question. *No, I haven't seen anything, I'm afraid.*

Hmmm. Emmeline ventured another question, one she probably should have asked weeks ago. *Have you ever observed anyone tampering with His Grace's clocks?*

Again no, replied the raven. *Woodley and the head footman usually set the clocks about the house. Unless you and Miss Harriet have done so instead. Various housemaids polish and dust them. But I cannot tell the time so I wouldn't know if anyone was setting the correct time or changing it to an incorrect one.*

Emmeline sighed. *Well, if you do notice anything strange occurring—anything at all—you'll be sure to tell me, won't you?*

Horatio bobbed up and down. *I certainly will, Nanny Chase.*

Emmeline thanked the raven, then she started to climb the stairs, heading back to the nursery. She would ask the duke later on this evening about who could access his hidden Horology Room and if those clocks had been losing or gaining time.

As long as Horatio was correct and the duke *wasn't* upset with her for overstepping . . .

What if the duke *didn't* summon her for their usual evening consultation?

Oh, hell's bells. Emmeline knew she'd be useless—a tangled bundle of frayed nerves—for the rest of the afternoon and evening, fretting about whether or not she'd be dismissed. She wouldn't be able to do her job properly. She wouldn't be able to give her charges the care and attention they deserved.

She stopped, then spun around on the landing, reversing course. Then stopped again and put a hand to her forehead.

Double hell's bells. She was whirling about so much, she was getting dizzy.

The only way to find out what the duke was thinking was to go right back to his study. She *must* not lose her job. Why, tomorrow was her first day off and she was so looking forward to visiting her father and sharing all her good news with him in person.

She must apologize to the duke for eavesdropping and for her boldness. At once.

Although it would probably be best to wait until Lord Nevergrin left.

Horatio, she called.

The raven, who was still perched upon the newel post below, stopped preening his feathers and looked up, his expression inquiring. *Yes, Nanny Chase?*

I have a favor to ask.

With a few flaps of his enormous wings, Horatio soared up to the next floor, then landed on the railing close to where Emmeline waited. His dark eyes glinted as he strutted toward her. *Do you want me to spoil Lord Nevergrin's clothing with a well-aimed guano grenade after all? I'd be more than happy to do it.*

Despite her concern about being sacked, Emmeline couldn't stifle a laugh. *No, but when the man leaves, perhaps you could fly up to the nursery to let me know. I need to speak with your master again and I'd rather do so when the coast is clear.*

The raven's reply, a short croak, could have passed for a snort. *Spoilsport. But very well. I'll do it. As long as you share some of Archimedes's and Aristotle's crickets with me. A bird cannot live on shortbread and puff balloons alone.*

Done, returned Emmeline. *There might even be a few worms and snails thrown into the mix too.*

You certainly know the way to a raven's heart, Nanny Chase. Before long, I have no doubt you'll have found your way into His Grace's as well.

Even though Emmeline felt a blush rising, she quipped, *Does your master like worms and crickets and snails too then?*

No, but he does seem to have developed a penchant for feisty freckled redheads. Don't pretend you haven't noticed the way His Grace looks at you.

And with that, the raven took off, heading in the direction of the duke's study, leaving a flabbergasted nanny in his wake.

Chapter 13

In Which There Is a Discussion About Awkward Insertions, the Principles of Sensible Living, Breaking Rules, Umbrella Thwacks, and Hidey-Holes...

"Your Grace?"

For the second time this afternoon, Xavier looked up to find Mrs. Chase in his study.

He frowned as confusion and concern warred with a bright burst of pleasure at seeing her again so unexpectedly. She'd quit the room not fifteen minutes ago in a flurry of righteous indignation and navy-blue skirts, and he had no idea what had brought her to his door this time. Glancing at her face, he couldn't read her mood. Apprehensive, perhaps?

Then he admonished himself for staring like a dolt. Pushing to his feet, he beckoned her farther into the room. "Mrs. Chase. What is it? Has something else happened? I haven't heard any screams or explosions."

"No. I..." Her voice trailed away before she rallied and met his eyes. "I came to see you because I..." She swallowed and lifted her chin, her manner determined. As though she were about to face a judge or a general. "Even though you and Lord Peregrine are not on the best of terms, that is no excuse for what transpired in this room before. I did not acquit myself as a Parasol Academy graduate should have. I inserted myself in a conversation that I had no business being in. I was rude to your uncle. I've disgraced my name, broken the Parasol Academy's rules and put the Academy's esteemed reputation at risk. And no doubt, I've angered you. Therefore, I've come to offer my unequivocal apol—"

"Stop right there, Mrs. Chase." Xavier held up a hand. "While you might have breached your Academy's rules, do you recall the conversation we had during your interview in this very room almost a month ago? Do you remember what you said about your own principles?"

"I . . ." The nanny frowned and clasped her hands at her waist. "Yes. I think I do."

"I recall that discussion. In detail. In fact, you said, 'sometimes certain things simply need to be said,' did you not? You even called your personal creed *The Principles of Sensible Living According to Mrs. Emmeline Chase*. And *I* happen to like it. I think your way of looking at the world is very sound."

The nanny blushed. "I also said that there are some ground rules that should never be broken and boundaries that should never be crossed. And I did both of those things."

Xavier crossed his arms over his chest. "Are you seriously arguing with me, Mrs. Chase?"

"No. I . . ." She gave a short laugh. "To be perfectly honest, I don't know what I'm doing or what's gotten into me today."

"Well, I do," said Xavier. "You were defending me. You stood up for me. And I was nothing but impressed."

"Oh . . ." Mrs. Chase's gaze dropped to the floor before she looked up through her lashes at him. "So you honestly don't mind that I listened in on your private conversation and then insulted your uncle?"

"It's not behavior I would ordinarily condone. But I understand why you did it. Lord knows, my uncle deserves it. As I said, he's a patronizing prig."

The nanny pressed her lips together as though she was attempting to suppress a smile. "I also wanted to say that I'm so sorry you had such a difficult childhood. That your upbringing wasn't easy."

Xavier looked away this time. "No. It wasn't."

He probably should dismiss Mrs. Chase. Send her back to the nursery. He recognized that he'd already been too familiar with her this afternoon. Asking her to remove her nanny's cap so he could better see her beautiful coppery hair had been one thing. But then offering her his hand and then escorting her into his Horology Room—because how could she refuse when he was her employer?—was a step too far. Men in his position shouldn't behave that way. He still couldn't work out why he'd crossed his own line and stepped out of bounds.

But . . . though he might be grossly inexperienced when it came to interacting with the opposite sex, he'd noticed certain things about Mrs. Chase and the way she'd responded to his requests and his nearness. His touch. She hadn't shied away. She hadn't told him off—and he knew she was more than capable of speaking her mind if she felt strongly about something.

Yes, he'd noted the delicate flush in her cheeks when he'd wrapped his gloved fingers around hers. The increased pace of her breathing. He was as certain as he could be that she hadn't been put off by his nearness.

She'd definitely been awestruck when she'd explored his Horology Room and studied his electromechanical clock.

That clock was one of the things Xavier was most proud of. Unlike his past or the fact that almost everyone thought he was "crackbrained." Yet Mrs. Chase didn't seem to think he was mad. He was nothing but grateful that she genuinely wasn't discomfited by his eccentricities and ofttimes off-putting manner.

Before Xavier could stop himself he said, "Just before you arrived, Mrs. Punchbowl sent up a fresh pot of coffee from the kitchen. Would-would you like to stay for a short while and have a cup? I feel as if . . ." How should he put this? He made himself look Mrs. Chase in the eye. "I don't know why. I can't explain it, but I have this need to talk to you—confide in you— about my family. About why I am the way that I am. At least to some extent. Perhaps it might even help us to work out the identity of my invisible enemy. If you know more about me and my history."

When Mrs. Chase didn't say anything, he rushed on. "Of course, you don't have to. You shouldn't feel obliged to listen just because I'm your employer. But I would appreciate your thoughts."

The nanny hesitated, worrying at her lower lip with her teeth, but only for a moment. "I would love to stay, Your Grace," she said softly. "Not because I feel it is my duty, but because I want to." Lifting her chin, she added in a firmer tone, "Whatever affects you also affects your wards. I *want* to help in any way that I can."

"Very well. Shall we be seated?" Xavier brought the coffee tray over to the fireside, and once they were both settled in chairs and armed with brimming coffee cups, he fell to contemplating how to begin.

Apart from his best friend, Marcus, Lord Hartwell, no one knew what he'd been through. His childhood was a quagmire of painful memories and without a doubt there were details he didn't wish to burden Mrs. Chase with. He didn't want her pity. But, inexplicably, he did want her to understand him. He wanted to be vulnerable in a way he never had before.

He sipped his coffee, the brew as bitter and dark as his recollections about his youth, then he put the cup aside. Steepling his fingers beneath his chin he said, "I'm not the most eloquent of men, Mrs. Chase. So I hope you'll bear with me while I find the words I need. It's not easy revisiting times one would rather forget. That being said, I feel it is important that you know certain things. It's not a secret that many think I'm mad."

"I know you're not. I've never thought that and the more time I spend with you the more I find that I'm . . ." She trailed off, her cheeks pinkening as she bit her lip as though she were about to say something she shouldn't. "We all have our idiosyncrasies. I don't see anyone accusing Sir Randolph of being eccentric or mad because he's a horologist. It isn't fair that society, and even your own family, think that there's something wrong with you."

"We both know life is rarely fair though." He sighed heavily. "Though, I do worry that at some point, all these aspersions about my soundness of mine may result in Harry, Bartholomew, and Gareth being removed from my care. And I would hate for that to happen."

"Oh, surely not," said Mrs. Chase. "I, for one, would defend you, most fiercely."

"Thank you," said Xavier with a solemn smile. The nanny's support—her faith in him as a parent finding his way—was deeply appreciated.

He was about to tell her so when Mrs. Chase's eyes lifted to his. "I hope you'll forgive me for bringing up a difficult subject, Your Grace, but Lord Peregrine mentioned that he thought your father should have sent you to an asylum. But he didn't."

Xavier couldn't contain a short huff of laughter. "Only because my father didn't want the family name to be damaged beyond repair. No, my father was an autocratic, distant sort of man who always strove to keep up appearances, no matter what. He didn't want to confirm what the rest of society whispered about—that his only son was at best peculiar and eccentric, and at worst, insane. No, his way of dealing with his problematic son was to ignore the rumors, preferring to sneer at them rather than give them any credence. Especially after I'd graduated from Oxford and was seen about town on a more regular basis. The gossipmongers began to have a field day."

He shrugged a shoulder and brushed a piece of lint off his

trouser leg. "As an adult, the talk, all the cruel whispers, have never particularly bothered me either. Until now... Now that there seems to be a plot afoot to actively undermine me and to tear whatever remains of my reputation to shreds. The opinions of those that matter—men like the Astronomer Royal and Charles Barry, the architect of the new Palace of Westminster, and even Her Majesty—could very well affect whether I'm awarded the St Stephen's clock commission or not. Who would trust the plans of a madman?" He looked at Mrs. Chase. "I want this commission so very badly. Not for the fame but for the deep satisfaction it would bring me. To see *my* clock at the top of that huge tower beside the Thames, proclaiming the precise time for all of London to hear, for years and years, now that would be marvelous. The dream of a lifetime made real."

"It undoubtedly would," said Mrs. Chase softly. "The talk about you being mad might stop too."

"It might." Xavier cast the nanny a cynical smile. "One would hope so, but alas, I don't think it will. Not after all this time. And I'm very much set in my ways." Xavier sipped his lukewarm coffee then released a sigh. "My father tried very hard to change me though. When I was nine, a few years before I was packed off to Eton, he hired an exacting tutor. A man by the name of Dickenson who was tasked with employing 'any means necessary' to make me behave like a 'normal' boy. One who looked at others the right way and spoke the right way—with inflection and not in the manner of an automaton. Who engaged in the right sorts of activities and didn't obsessively study clocks and pull pocket watches apart to see what made them tick."

Mrs. Chase's expression was grave. Xavier sensed that compassion and sadness weighted her words as she said, "That all sounds so horrible, Your Grace. I'm so sorry."

He shrugged. "It was a long time ago. The odious Mr. Dickenson and my even more odious father are both gone now."

"And your mother? You haven't mentioned her," said Mrs. Chase gently. "Of course, you don't have to. My own dear mother passed away unexpectedly when I was sixteen—a virulent influenza claimed her—and even after all this time, I still find it difficult to talk about her."

"No, it's all right," said Xavier. "My mother..." He straightened a seam on the back of his glove while he waited for a peculiar tightness at the back of his throat to ease. Then he began again. "My memories of her are hazy at best," he said, "but by all accounts she found my father to be an altogether unpleasant man too. She left him—absconded to the Continent with her lover in fact—when I was seven years old. My father, who was supremely annoyed with her rather than heartbroken—I gather it was a marriage of convenience and neither of them loved the other—eventually initiated divorce proceedings, but then I was told she died six years later. My father sent a letter during my first year at Eton to inform me of the fact."

"Oh, Your Grace... She left you behind and you never saw her again?" Mrs. Chase bit her bottom lip, which had begun to wobble ominously. And good God, was there the shimmer of tears in her eyes? Xavier hadn't meant to make her cry.

"You mustn't feel sorry for me," he said a little too gruffly. "All of these youthful trials and tribulations are over and having never experienced affection, let alone love, I hardly missed it. And it wasn't as though my mother could take me with her. I was the heir to a dukedom and my father would have hounded her until he had me back."

"I know." The nanny drew a shaky breath. "But the thought of a child—of *you*—feeling so alone, with no one on your side, no one who truly cared..." The light in her eyes grew fierce. "If your father were still here, I'd give him a piece of my mind. I'd even consider giving him a thwack on his behind with my umbrella. Of course I wouldn't really," she hastened to add. "But I'd be vividly imagining it."

Xavier's mouth twitched as he pictured the nanny wielding

her umbrella like a weapon. "He deserved a good thwack or two at the very least. Believe me, my thoughts have been far less charitable."

For the longest time, Xavier had avoided thoughts about his parents. He'd never really thought of them in terms of being a "family." One that was supportive and caring at any rate. Looking now at Mrs. Chase, seeing her with his wards, he'd begun to catch glimpses of what a family *could* be. How uplifting it could be to spend time with others who accepted you for who you were and made you smile. When you didn't have to hide your true self and pretend to be something or someone you weren't. Perhaps not all families were the same.

Xavier released a sigh and shifted in his seat. Mrs. Chase was effortlessly weaving her delightful joie de vivre through the life of his wards, and in turn, his too. But at the end of the day, she was still his wards' nanny. *Best not to think of her in an overly familiar way*, he reminded himself sternly as he took a sip of his drink. That path was undoubtedly fraught with danger, for both of them.

When he looked up, Mrs. Chase was smiling at him. "May I ask . . . is there a reason why horology has always fascinated you?"

Xavier hesitated. He rubbed his gloved forefinger and thumb together as he worked out what he wanted to say. He didn't want to burden Mrs. Chase with too much awfulness—he'd probably disclosed too much already—so he simply said, "There was, many years ago, a towering walnut longcase clock in St Lawrence House's library. It's broken now and stored in the attic, but when I was very young—I was quite small for my age—I liked to use the storage cupboard at its base as a hidey-hole. I loved the sound of the chimes. The way they echoed through the case and made the very wood vibrate."

He didn't add that he'd used the space to avoid his father when he was in one of his raging, thunderous moods and his parents were arguing, because that sounded far too sad.

"We didn't always stay here in London though. The family's

ducal seat in Kent, Kingscliff Castle, features a magnificent central clock tower. And that tower was a place I retreated to... when things were difficult. I used to watch the enormous clock's cogs and wheels for hours and hours. I can't explain it, but I found the activity thoroughly absorbing." He gave a wry smile. "I still do."

"Kingscliff Castle and its clock sound beautiful," said Mrs. Chase. Her blue eyes were soft and warm and luminous. "It's by the sea, isn't it? At Kingsgate?"

"Yes... How did you know?" asked Xavier, his curiosity sparking. "Have you been there?"

"When I was a child, our family—my mother, father, and brother—used to holiday at the seaside. Usually at Margate or Ramsgate. But sometimes we would venture farther south to Kingsgate." Mrs. Chase smiled. "Just think, I might have been playing on the shore while you were watching from your tower, Your Grace."

Xavier made himself smile back. "Perhaps." Again, he'd omitted part of the narrative. That his flint-hearted father had banished him to the clock tower on numerous occasions as a cruel and unusual punishment for any sort of "misdemeanor." For complaining that his clothes were uncomfortable—that the fabric was scratchy, or his stockings were knobbly or that his shoes pinched. Or for not eating particular foods at mealtimes because they didn't taste or feel right and made him gag. Or if he became upset when his clothes got wet or dirty. Young Lord Westbrook was deemed fussy and ungrateful and stubborn. At other times he was labeled irrational and infuriatingly difficult.

An impossible child. An incumbrance.

Xavier clenched his fist upon the arm of the chair as resentment and sadness rolled through him. That clock tower had been cold and lonely and a terrifying place to imprison a far too sensitive seven-year-old boy. Not only was it high above the ground, but there were no creature comforts—only a hard stone floor to sit upon. Xavier's only companions had been the gulls and the sea wind that blew straight off the English Channel. In wintertime, that merciless wind wailed through the battlements, its icy teeth tearing at him until his own teeth chattered.

Little did his father know that in the end, the clock—its rhythmic ticking, its sonorous chimes, its synchronous movements—had become a source of comfort for Xavier. A refuge from turmoil. The clock was predictable in a way his father and the world around him had never been.

It was Mrs. Chase who broke the silence and drew Xavier away from his tumultuous musings. "I've been thinking, Your Grace. Does the St Lawrence House saboteur ever tamper with your electromechanical clock or any other timepieces in your Horology Room?"

"No..." Xavier frowned. "I've never really thought about it before, but you raise a very good point. Aside from me, only a very small handful of staff are permitted entry into the room, namely Woodley and, twice a week, Mrs. Lambton, who oversees the maids who clean in there." He nodded toward the jib door. "Nothing has ever gone missing. The watches and expensive watch parts are all under lock and key. Woodley usually sets the clocks while I'm in the room, and many of the watches are dormant."

"I see." The nanny gave him a quizzical look. "But you opened the jib door using a secret latch. So feasibly anyone who knows about that latch could open the door at any time."

"Not quite," said Xavier. "The jib door must be unlocked with a key for the mechanism to work. I'd unlocked it earlier this morning."

"So only you, Woodley, and your housekeeper have a key?"

"No. Just me and Woodley. If I'm not here, he lets Mrs. Lambton and the maids in."

Mrs. Chase nodded, seemingly satisfied. "So the saboteur is only meddling with the clocks in the main part of the house."

"It would seem so," agreed Xavier. "I employ a staff of thirty. Twenty-two reside in the house. It's horrible to think that someone I trust wishes me ill."

"Yes." Mrs. Chase moved to the edge of her seat. "I will let you know if I observe anything else unusual or untoward. I've been getting to know some of the maids and Mrs. Punchbowl and Mrs. Lambton. Bertie, your footman, too. I keep hoping that someone will have a slip of the tongue, or I might catch them in the act of doing something they shouldn't."

She'd been talking with Bertie? Xavier frowned. He shouldn't mind. He had no business feeling chagrined. But he was. Jealousy pricked at him like a thistle.

"I'm glad that you have settled in here so well," he said after a moment. "And I probably don't say it enough, but you're doing a marvelous job with my wards."

"Thank you. Your faith in me means a lot considering how I behaved earlier." Mrs. Chase stood and Xavier rose too. "I *really* should be getting back to the nursery."

"Yes. I suppose so." He didn't want the nanny to go but he couldn't think of a reason to make her stay.

"Well, thank you again for everything." The nanny took a step toward him. "It goes without saying that I think you're a marvelous employer."

All of a sudden, she reached out and touched Xavier's bare forearm, and before he could stop himself, he flinched and hissed as though he'd been burned. And perhaps he had been. Although not in the way Mrs. Chase probably supposed.

"Oh. Oh, I'm sorry, Your Grace." She snatched her hand away and clutched it to her breast. "I shouldn't have done that. And to think that I came here to apologize for acting inappro—"

"No. No, it's not that." Xavier drew a steadying breath as bone-deep want clashed with his ingrained aversion to any sort of unexpected physical contact. "You simply took me by surprise. I'm not used to others touching me. If I initiate the interaction, or if I know it's coming, I'm quite all right." He threw her a smile. "If you recall, I didn't mind our sparring session when you demonstrated your self-defense skills."

She winced. "I also accidentally fell on you the first time we met. You couldn't have expected that. It's a miracle you offered me an interview at all."

Xavier caught her gaze in his. "Mrs. Chase, you are perfect for this post in every way."

You're perfect for me . . .

Where the devil had that thought come from? Xavier swallowed and tugged at his waistcoat. Dropped his attention to the floor as a bittersweet ache stirred in his chest and heated his blood. If he took a step closer to Mrs. Chase, pushed his legs against her stiff skirts, wound one of her coppery curls around his gloved finger, how would she react? Would she draw closer? Tilt her face up toward his? Would her eyes become heavy-lidded and her gaze unfocused and dreamy as her attention drifted to his mouth?

But then what, Xavier? Then what? You're a virgin, for God's sake, and she's a widow who'd undoubtedly have expectations that you might not be able to meet. Aside from all that, she works for you. As a nanny. Pursuing a physically intimate relationship with Emmeline Chase—asking her to become your mistress—would be demeaning and she deserves so much more than that. No matter how much you yearn for her, it is not *an option.*

The sound of the door softly snicking closed told Xavier that he was alone again with his prized watches and clocks.

Strange how for once that didn't seem enough.

Chapter 14

In Which There Are Two Pleasant Excursions, One Involving a Sword Fight and the Other a Bout of Fisticuffs; And Ice Is Required to Put Out a Smoldering Fire . . .

When Emmeline awoke the next morning—her first day off since she'd started working for the Duke of St Lawrence—she spied an envelope sitting upon the rug beside the door. But it wasn't any old envelope. It was a leygram, and Emmeline knew exactly who it was from even before she slipped from beneath the bedcovers and all but hurtled across the room. Mina Davenport must have responded to the leygram Emmeline had sent last night.

Her breath quickening, Emmeline retrieved her blue, leylensed quizzing glass from her reticule, then tore open the missive.

My dearest Emmeline,
I would love to see you today! I've been dying to hear how you've been getting on at St Lawrence House. I even have some very good news of my own to share. (Now I know you'll come.)
See you around noon at the Academy!
Your friend always,
M.

Emmeline smiled as she hugged the softly humming leygram to her chest. Even though the morning was dull and gray and it was sure to rain, she wouldn't let the dismal weather dampen her spirits. After she spent an hour or two with Mina, she'd pay a visit to Newgate to see her poor darling father. Mrs. Lambton had paid her wages yesterday, so now that Emmeline had a purse full of coins, she would also be able to give the turnkey his next installment of protection money.

All in all, it was going to be a wonderful kind of day.

Once she was dressed in her own attire—her least worn widow's weeds and matching black poke bonnet—Emmeline collected her reticule, gloves, and Parasol Academy umbrella (strictly speaking, she wasn't supposed to use it if she were "out-of-uniform," but she hadn't another umbrella and she didn't want to get wet if it rained), then headed for the door.

Although she *could* have teleported to the Parasol Academy, she decided it would be best if she went on foot. It was but a twenty-minute walk and she wouldn't need to worry if her kid half boots and black wool hem ended up getting wet or muddy. She also needed to consider the to-do she might cause if she simply disappeared from the environs of St Lawrence House without anyone seeing her leave. There didn't need to be any more mysterious goings-on causing consternation and upset.

After she'd farewelled Fanny, who was taking charge in the nursery, and then Bertie, who was on duty at the front door, Emmeline crossed Belgrave Square, waving to young Constable Thurstwhistle in his police box before she rounded the corner onto Upper Belgrave Street.

As she walked, she tried not to think at all about the duke and everything that had transpired yesterday in his study. In particular, that moment when he'd murmured in his deep, all-too-delicious voice, "Mrs. Chase, you are perfect for this post in every way." And in the seconds immediately afterward when his gaze had briefly touched her mouth before falling away to the floor.

She could have sworn he'd been thinking about kissing her. She'd felt the thrill of it shivering through her, making her breath catch and her lips tingle and the most secret parts of her body softly pulse. For one mad moment—the tiny space between one wild heartbeat and the next—she'd contemplated throwing her arms about the duke's neck and pressing her mouth to his. But then sanity prevailed, and she'd beat a hasty retreat, rushing back to her room, where she'd splashed cold water onto her burning cheeks in a frantic effort to compose herself before she returned to the nursery.

The duke hadn't summoned her to his study again later that night and she'd been half disappointed and half relieved.

No, it's all for the best that you keep your distance from the Duke of St Lawrence, she firmly reminded herself as she strode across Eaton Square. *You've been spending far too much time with the man. Learning far too many intimate details about him. You need to stomp out this inappropriate infatuation. You are* prim. *You are* proper. *You are* an exceptional nanny.

Yes, she just needed to remind herself what was most important. What was at stake. She needed to be the best, most *professional* Parasol Academy nanny she could be so she could help her father. Because she could not achieve the latter unless she embraced the former. And if that meant keeping her distance from her employer—both physically and emotionally—she would. She must.

Resolve restored to corset-steel hardness, Emmeline continued on her way, not even pausing to converse with a friendly group of chattering pigeons clustered at the southern end of Eaton Square Garden, or a fine black carriage horse who threw her an amiable snort and mental "hullo." By the time she reached the Parasol Academy, she was quite out of breath (and not to mention a tad embarrassed about it). As per the *Parasol Academy Handbook*, Chapter 9, Paragraph 2, Section 1b), she must be as fit as a fiddle in order to effectively discharge her duties as a bodyguard should the need ever arise. While chasing children about required a good degree of physical stamina, Emmeline conceded that she might need to schedule time for a brisk, early morning walk each day. And perhaps the occasional physical training session at the Academy. Sword-fighting, boxing, wrestling, along with accurate shooting and knife-throwing, were skills she must maintain. She could do with a brushup on her rope-climbing and knot-tying skills too.

Emmeline found Mina in their old dormitory room. As soon as she crossed the threshold, her friend rushed over to envelop Emmeline in an enormous hug.

"My darling friend, I've missed you so much," Mina cried.

Emmeline released a small laugh even though guilt pinched. Mina Davenport was usually calm and composed and not a demonstrative sort of person at all. She *must* have missed Emmeline. Quite a lot. "I'm only a short walk away," she said. "Not the other side of the English Channel or at the North Pole."

"That may well be the case," said Mina, "but don't tell me you haven't been horrendously busy from the crack of dawn until late at night with nary a moment to spare."

Emmeline couldn't lie. "Looking after three precocious children does have its challenges. I'm lucky my employer is very understanding."

Mina's hazel eyes gleamed with speculation. "The very eligible and mysterious Duke of St Lawrence, no less. Everyone at the Academy has been talking about him since you left to take up your post."

"Oh yes," said Emmeline, wondering what "everyone" *had* actually been saying about the duke. No doubt there'd been all sorts of unkind whispers about him, but Mina was far too tactful to elaborate. "I don't see him all that often," she added, even though that was an out-and-out lie. "He very much keeps to himself, working on his horology projects."

Mina suggested that they both take seats by the window. "Is it true that he intends to enter a design into the Westminster clock tower contest?" she asked as she smoothed her perfectly pressed skirts into exact pleats.

"It is." Emmeline eyed her friend. "There certainly *has* been a lot of talk about the duke, by the sounds of it."

Mina's cheeks grew rosier than a spring rose garden. "Well, not every graduate is employed by someone in such an elevated position. He's practically royalty."

"I suppose he is," agreed Emmeline. She'd never really thought of the duke that way before. She barely remembered to curtsy most days. "But he's also..."

She was about to say *kind and thoughtful and clever*, but then she realized she'd have to explain how she knew so much about a man who she claimed she barely saw at all. "While he's a very singular sort of gentleman, he's also very reasonable. And while his wards do keep me on my toes, they are also a delight. But enough about me. In your leygram, you mentioned that *you* had some news."

"I do." The gold flecks in Mina's eyes glowed as she said, "Mrs. Temple has secured a position for me. In Hertfordshire, so not so very far away. I start in a week's time."

"Oh, that's wonderful. Congratulations!" declared Emmeline, claiming her friend's hands and giving them a squeeze. "Tell me everything right now before I expire on the spot from an overdose of curiosity."

"I'm to be the governess for an only child—a boy, aged seven, who's also a viscount," said Mina. "His godmother—Lady Grenfell, a dowager countess—wishes him to start formal lessons, but she feels he's not the sort of child who would respond well to a male tutor. The boy—I *should* say Lord Fitzwilliam—lost his parents a year ago and Lady Grenfell feels he needs a teacher who will be sensitive and nurturing."

"You will be absolutely perfect," said Emmeline, smiling at

her friend. "And no doubt your mother and sister will be pleased for you too."

While Mina's family wasn't in the same dire financial straits as Emmeline's, most would consider them "genteelly impoverished." Mina's late father, a vicar and the younger son of a baronet, had passed away, leaving Mina's mother with a meager inheritance, which included a small cottage in the Cotswolds and not much else. Even though Mina and her younger sister, Dorothea, had elevated fraternal grandparents, they were essentially dowry-less. So when Mina had been bequeathed a Parasol Academy scholarship by an ancient maiden aunt, she'd jumped at the opportunity to study at the much-esteemed college. It meant Mina would be able to help support her mother and Dorothea.

Emmeline and Mina chatted for a while about books they'd like to read and plays they'd both like to see (even if they couldn't afford to purchase any new novels or tickets for a London theater performance), and then they eventually decided to repair to the Academy's fencing saloon for a bout or two with foils.

As they quit the change rooms—there was always an ample supply of suitable fencing attire for graduates to use so one didn't have to risk ruining one's clothes (rips and tears were inevitable)—Mrs. Temple appeared in the hall.

"Mrs. Chase, how lovely to see you," declared the headmistress with a warm smile as she tripped toward them, her pearl-gray skirts softly whispering about her ankles. "How have you been getting on with the Duke of St Lawrence and his wards?"

Emmeline smiled. No doubt Mrs. Temple already knew how she'd "been getting on"—the canny headmistress would have been in contact with the duke to make certain that Emmeline's performance was at the very least, satisfactory, if not exemplary.

"Everything is going splendidly," replied Emmeline. "I'm enjoying the work immensely."

"Excellent," said the headmistress with a decided nod. Then she glanced at her silver watch, which was always pinned to her bodice. "I would stay to chat longer, but alas, I have to attend a board meeting at our brand-new St Giles orphanage."

While only the well-to-do could afford a Parasol nanny or governess, the Academy had long been involved in many philanthropic endeavors. Since its inception, it had established orphanages, a foundling hospital, and a home for unwedded mothers in London. Mrs. Temple had also recently opened a number of charity schools in London's poorer areas.

All Academy graduates learned that these benevolent institutions were created because of a specific clause within the Academy's secret Fae Charter: The Parasol Academy must protect and nurture as many children as possible, no matter their circumstances. Emmeline wholeheartedly supported such good deeds. Perhaps she could mention the Academy's philanthropy to the Duke of St Lawrence. His wards were orphans so he *might* consider making a donation.

Mrs. Temple continued on her way, and then Emmeline looked at her own watch. She needed to get going too.

On the doorstep of the Academy, Mina hugged Emmeline goodbye. "I promise that I'll send you a long leygram as soon as I've settled into my new position at Highwood Hall in Hertfordshire."

"I'll hold you to that," replied Emmeline with mock sternness, "otherwise I'll be teleporting into your new wardrobe in the middle of the night."

"Goodness, we can't have that. Knowing you, you'd end up in the Hall's goldfish pond or stranded in a tree or the coal cellar."

Emmeline laughed. "You will never let me forget about that time I ended up in the Thames, will you?" Thank goodness Mina didn't know about her most recent teleportation mishap.

"Well, you can't be fabulous at simply everything," said Mina. "Otherwise, what hope do the rest of us mere mortals have? I'm still smarting after that royal trouncing you gave me in the fencing saloon. And you said you were out of practice. What rot."

"My reflexes might be sharp, but I assure you, my physical stamina is waning. The only reason I'm hailing a hansom cab rather than walking is that I need to get to—"

Dickens on toast. Emmeline pressed her lips together. She couldn't believe that she'd nearly let slip that she needed to get to Newgate Prison before visiting hours ended. Walking the three-and-a-half miles into the City of London would take far too long. "I'm eager to purchase a few odds and ends at Covent Garden and I'd like to get there before it rains," she amended, nodding at the sullen gray clouds above them to make her point.

What she'd said wasn't a complete lie either. She did intend to visit the market first to pick up some provisions for her father.

"Well, enjoy, my dear friend. I'd offer to come with you, but I promised another student that I would help her master some of her incantations." Mina lowered her voice. "She can't quite manage the *Unsmirchify* spell. Instead of cleaning up spills and messes, the whole spoiled item of clothing disappears into thin air. Which is *very* awkward. A nanny or governess should not be parading around in her drawers and corset."

"Oh dear. How mortifying that would be," said Emmeline.

"And *so* not manners," agreed Mina. "From day one of our training, we swear to adhere to the Parasol Academy's motto, 'We're prim, proper, and prepared for anything.'"

"Very true." Emmeline gave a decided nod. Next time she had improper thoughts about the duke, she would repeat the Academy's mantra to herself. It would be the equivalent of a mental pinch. Hopefully, if she said it enough times, it would sink in.

* * *

"Good God, Xavier, what's gotten into you today?" demanded Marcus Cavendish, Viscount Hartwell, rubbing his abused jaw. "That facer of yours nearly knocked my back teeth out."

Xavier grimaced. Although a purple bruise was already blooming beneath his friend's light stubble, he knew that Marcus probably wouldn't mind *that* much. No matter Lord Hartwell's state of dishevelment, or the degree of scandal attached to his name, he always seemed to be popular about town. After all, the fellow was a rakehell and had a wicked reputation to uphold. If he were bruised, even bloodied or slightly broken, there'd still be women lined up offering to kiss him better.

"My sincerest apologies," said Xavier, tugging off his boxing glove and flexing his throbbing fingers. "I think I nearly broke my knuckles too." He wiped his glove-free hand over his perspiration-beaded brow then plucked his damp silk shirt away from his chest. For the last hour, he'd been sparring with his best friend at the exclusive Belgravia Boxing Saloon for Gentlemen, and now that they'd paused their friendly bout, he was dying to strip off his sweat-drenched clothes and take a bath. While he positively loathed the sensation of damp clothing against his skin, bathing did not bother him at all.

In fact, indulging in a long hot bath might give him the opportunity to relieve some pent-up physical tension in another way. Because boxing with Marcus clearly hadn't worked. His overzealous punch was an indicator that his simmering sexual frustration was about to boil over. It appeared that was the drawback of being a thirty-year-old male virgin with a beguiling nanny in his employ.

Egad, he'd turned into a randy March hare with energy to burn and no satisfactory way to expend it. Would that he was the sort of man who could accompany Marcus to a high-class bawdy house. Or a society ball to find an obliging widow who didn't give a fig about the unflattering rumors that dogged him.

He could also simply get drunk. But alas, he wasn't the sort of man who overindulged in alcohol either. No, immersing himself in the world of horology and exercising hard were about the only ways he could quell the fire in his veins. (And occasionally finding relief by his own hand.) Except, none of these methods were working. At all.

He was a horse about to bolt. A storm about to break. A pistol about to explode.

For the first time in his life, Xavier decided that being a virgin was the absolute worst. And he didn't know what to do about it. He certainly wasn't going to slake his misbegotten lust by attempting to seduce his wards' nanny. It wasn't her problem to fix.

It was his issue entirely. Still, being saddled with his virginity had been his cross to bear for a long, long time. Xavier supposed that if he did "his duty" and wed, his irksome and rather inconvenient "problem" would be solved. But he had decided years ago—even before he'd inherited the dukedom, in fact—that he'd rather poke a cravat pin in his eye than hunt for a suitable wife for the sole purpose of fathering the requisite heir and spare. Indeed, he was certain that finding a dodo bird on the isle of Mauritius would be a far easier feat than hunting for a bride in London's ballrooms. Given the rumors surrounding his rightness of mind, no doubt it would be a torturous, demoralizing process, and all things considered, one he'd rather avoid. Besides, his life was so bloody complicated right now, he simply didn't have the time, let alone the inclination to get married.

He certainly didn't want to secure the services of a mistress. The idea of paying a woman to be intimate with him—of reducing such an encounter to an impersonal transaction—didn't sit well with him at all. He wanted his first time to be—

Gah! Dash it all to hell! He didn't know what he wanted.

Xavier yanked off his other boxing glove and began unwinding the silk binding from his abused knuckles. He wished he could think of a way to alleviate his "problem" without betraying his principles. He wanted Mrs. Chase with an acuteness that was almost unbearable, yet he didn't want to want her. He enjoyed her company, admired and respected her, but this bone-deep yearning to have her in a physical sense was not respectful at all.

He supposed it had always been the case, right from the very start. Like a bright shooting star falling from the zenith, she'd landed on his roof and, rightly or wrongly, he'd burned to know her in every sense of the word.

Oh, he was in a bad, bad way.

Marcus tossed him a towel. "Shall we call it a day, my friend?"

Too discomposed to manage a coherent verbal response, Xavier grunted his assent then blotted his face. Devil take him. He was grunting now?

He really was devolving into a troglodyte.

Marcus threw himself down onto a nearby wooden bench and his bare shoulders rose and fell on a huge sigh. "I suppose I should be grateful that I'm not sparring with the new Marquess of Kinsale." He gestured with his chin toward the towering bruiser of a man on the other side of the room who was proceeding to pound a punching bag into next week. Although, considering the power of the chap's mighty blows, maybe it was into oblivion.

Xavier cocked an eyebrow. "Kinsale, you say? He hails from Ireland then?"

"He does," said Marcus. "Phineas O'Connell is his name and he's originally from Dublin. I met him recently at an out-of-town boxing match in Surrey about a fortnight ago. It seems he inherited the marquessate quite unexpectedly and he doesn't wear the title comfortably." He winced slightly. "The chap also has a marked stammer. I don't give a jot, but I do wonder if that's part of the reason he's not keen on meeting other 'toffs,' so to speak."

Xavier nodded. "I could understand why an Irishman with a stammer might be reluctant to enter society."

"Indeed." Marcus's eyes were soft with understanding. At least Xavier interpreted his friend's expression as sympathetic. "Like you, Lord Kinsale is quite the loner. I imagine he feels like the proverbial fish out of water at society events. Even so, I've been meaning to invite him to White's and show him around town. Make a few introductions." He caught Xavier's eye. "You and I both know what it's like when one is new and doesn't quite fit in."

Marcus was alluding to their early days at Eton. It was a time Xavier would never forget. He cast another glance at the marquess. "He looks like he could hold his own though. He certainly knows how to throw a punch."

"Rumor also has it that Lord Kinsale used to be a prize-fighter. Speaking of rumors"—Marcus rose and threw a towel about his shoulders—"I should let you know that that bastard Sir Randolph Redvers has been spouting all kinds of lies about you and your mental fitness. Again. Those who know you well realize it's nothing but horse bollocks."

Xavier gave a small snort of laughter. "So that means you and you alone. To be perfectly honest, I'm not surprised that Sir Randolph is behind this current rumor campaign. My uncle paid me a visit yesterday and mentioned the gossip going around the clubs."

"Peregrine? That bitter old bellend?" Marcus flicked his towel against his thigh. "His son Algernon is a complete tosser too."

"I won't disagree with you," said Xavier. "About the only thing I can do to counteract the rumors is to rise above it and do well, despite all the slings and arrows hurled my way."

They watched Lord Kinsale pummeling the punching bag for another minute, then Marcus said, "How *is* your Westminster clock design coming along? And your electromechanical clock prototype?"

"I'm making steady progress with both," said Xavier. "Actually, I have a new nanny who's effectively managing my wards, so that's helped immensely. Although there are still odd household occurrences from time to time that disturb my concentration." He related the latest events to his friend.

Marcus frowned. "Hmm. I don't like the sound of that break-in. And someone followed you home not that long ago if I recall. You need to take extra care, my friend."

"Believe me. I am," replied Xavier. "I keep hoping that there *isn't* a sinister plan afoot to discredit me. That it's all in my head. But as time goes on, I know something is wrong. I can feel it."

"You should always trust your gut. Have you considered hiring a private detective?"

"Yes, but I have nothing specific to share that would be helpful." Mrs. Chase was already taking on an undercover role within St Lawrence House. Xavier supposed he could have someone look into Sir Randolph's activities, to see if he had recently paid anyone to follow him about or break in to St Lawrence House. But he also didn't see much point in hiring an investigator to watch the baronet at all hours of the day and night when there were barely any breadcrumbs to follow. He needed something concrete to go on. "I'm rather hoping the problem will resolve itself in time," he added. "Once I submit my clock design—if my suspicions are correct—then all this domestic mayhem and skullduggery will end. That's what I keep telling myself anyway."

Marcus eyed him gravely. "I hope so. And it goes without saying that I'll help in whatever way I can. You only need to ask."

"Thank you. Your support means a lot. It always has."

The viscount ran a hand through his tousled light brown hair. "I know you'll be keen to head home, but let me introduce you to Lord Kinsale first."

The marquess's training session appeared to have ended, as he was presently unwrapping his bandaged knuckles.

"Kinsale," called Marcus as they approached the dark-haired mountain of a man. "How goes it?"

The marquess turned and his emerald-green eyes darted to Xavier before settling on Marcus. "W-Well enough," he said. The soft Irish lilt in his voice was more evident when he added, "How-How-How are you?"

"Good. Good..." Marcus's smile widened as he affected Xavier's introduction. "Lord Kinsale, this is the friend I was telling you about. Xavier Mason, the Duke of St Lawrence."

The Irish peer tilted his head by way of a bow. "Your Grace," he said. "P-P-Pleased to m-m-m-meet you."

Xavier would have extended his hand to shake the marquess's, but he wasn't wearing any gloves. So he simply inclined his head as well. "It's good to meet you too. Though I wouldn't bother addressing me so formally. Xavier will do." While it was customary for noblemen to be referred to by their titles, even when conversing with close acquaintants, Xavier had always disliked the practice, given his titles and his surname had always been distorted into vile nicknames.

The Irishman arched a black brow. "Xavier it is. I prefer to go by me Christian n-name too. Phineas. But most of me acquaintances call me Ph-Ph-Ph—" He broke off and drew a deep breath. "Phinn."

"Phinn," repeated Xavier. "You were certainly giving that punching bag a sound thrashing. Marcus was just telling me that you were a prizefighter."

Phinn's mouth quirked with a sardonic half smile. "Aye, I was, Your Gra—I mean, Xavier. For f-four years."

Studying the Irishman's face, Xavier could see that his nose was slightly crooked, as though it had been broken. There was also a scar bisecting his left eyebrow. Xavier idly wondered if Mrs. Chase would think the man ruggedly handsome. Was that the right way to describe the Irish peer? Xavier would readily own that he couldn't tell whether other men were physically attractive or not. He also had no idea if women considered *him* to be attractive. Or more to the point, if Mrs. Chase did.

Of course, it shouldn't matter what the nanny thought of his looks. Although, she often blushed around him... The problem was, Xavier was never sure why. Perhaps she did so because he had a habit of regarding her too closely and for too long. Then again, her apparent discomfiture might be caused by something else entirely. Some reason he couldn't fathom because he was an inexperienced, largely clueless male. To Xavier, Mrs. Chase was as mysterious and unfamiliar as the universe, yet equally as beautiful and thoroughly absorbing.

Bloody hell. He was thinking about the woman again. He'd become quite obsessed with her.

Marcus and Phinn had begun to make plans to visit White's and Boodle's later that evening. When asked if he would like to join them, Xavier hesitated. He should, but he also had a lot on his mind. And Marcus would no doubt want to introduce Lord Kinsale to some of London's less genteel gentlemen's "clubs."

Xavier certainly wasn't in the mood for drinking or gambling or consorting with high-class courtesans. But then, he supposed he never was. He'd rather go hunting for rare pocket watches at auctions and antique jewelry stores.

A watch-hunting expedition would also be a good distraction. Perhaps then he'd stop fantasizing about making love to a flame-haired nanny with sky-blue eyes and a smile that could light up the darkest day.

Given the smoldering fire in his veins, an ice-cold bath rather than a piping hot one wouldn't go astray either.

Chapter 15

In Which Paths, Umbrellas, and Swords Cross; And Chivalrous Knights (or Perhaps an Avenging Angel) Make an Appearance...

Emmeline shivered as she followed a sour-faced prison guard through the fetid, ice-cold corridors of Newgate Prison. In one hand she carried a wicker basket of provisions that she'd purchased at Covent Garden. In her other hand, she held a posy of dried lavender, which she pressed to her nose. Wedged tightly beneath one arm was her trusty Parasol Academy umbrella.

Carrying her umbrella always gave her an added sense of security whenever male prisoners hurled insults or horrid propositions her way. While they were safely behind iron bars, it didn't make them any less intimidating. And one never knew what sort of prison guard one would encounter. If they got a bit handsy, she could easily give them a poke with the Point-of-Confusion. Or at the very least, a well-aimed smack on the knuckles. (Both were far safer options than pulling out her sheathed ankle knife. Getting arrested for threatening a prison guard would be too inconvenient for words.)

Emmeline was certainly grateful that her father—perhaps because of his age and the nonviolent nature of his crime—had been incarcerated in a solitary cell. If he'd been locked up in one of the enormous group cells, he would not have fared well. As it was, every time she saw him, he was more gray-faced and weaker than the last occasion.

But he won't be here for much longer, she reminded herself. Newgate must be the earthly equivalent of Hades. Emmeline was surprised that there wasn't a sign declaring, "Abandon all hope, ye who enter here," above the prison's front entrance.

Obviously, there were any number of ways that Emmeline could break her father out of Newgate. If she had no qualms about breaking a multitude of Parasol Academy rules, she could simply wear her uniform and then use her leyport key to teleport her father to someplace far away.

But then he'd have to live in hiding for the rest of his days, and with all the publicity generated by the suspicious disappearance of a prisoner, the Academy would undoubtedly find out and she'd be expelled. Her name would be mud. She'd never practice as an Academy nanny again. She might even be arrested for effecting the escape of a prisoner.

She simply couldn't do it.

The guard stopped outside one of the studded iron doors and grunted as he inserted the key into the lock. "There you go, miss." He held out his hand and Emmeline dropped the required "contribution" of a few shillings into his palm. "I'll be back in 'alf an hour."

The door swung open, its hinges grating and the bottom edge scraping over the uneven stone floor, and then Emmeline was pushing into the dim and dank interior. As the cell door slammed shut behind her with a resounding metallic thud, Emmeline's gaze lit on her father.

He was sitting on the edge of his narrow pallet bed, blinking as though he'd just woken up. His graying hair and clothes were disheveled and the lines bracketing his mouth and creases around his eyes were deeply etched. "Emmeline . . . is that you?" he asked in a voice as raspy as the prison door hinges.

"It is, Papa." Emmeline deposited her things on a narrow stone bench built into the wall, the only other piece of "furniture" in the cramped chamber. As always, she would try to be cheerful, even though her heart was breaking.

As Edward Evans rose on unsteady legs, Emmeline took a few steps across the filthy floor and embraced him. "It feels like forever since I last saw you," he said thickly.

"I know. And I'm sorry it's been so long." Emmeline couldn't hide the catch in her voice when she noticed how bony and frail her father's frame felt beneath her gloved hands. Heavens above, even his breathing had a weak, rattling quality. It hadn't been like that the last time she'd visited. "But I'm here now," she said, drawing back. "It's my day off."

"Yes. You must have greased the palm of the turnkey well enough because I got your letter. Working as a nanny for the Duke of St Lawrence, eh? I'm so happy for you, my girl. Your mother would have been so proud." Her father suddenly lapsed into a coughing fit. "Sorry," he said on a gasp, his eyes watering. "I can't shake this awful cold."

"Don't be sorry," said Emmeline, guilt slicing into her heart. She should have come sooner. She should have asked the duke if she could have a half day off every fortnight rather than a full day once a month.

She returned to the wicker basket, removed the folded blanket that covered it, then pulled out the medicinal tonic she'd purchased from an apothecary. "Here, try some of this, Papa. It should help ease your cough," she said as she handed him a dark brown bottle. "And then you can have some of the bread and cheese and gammon I brought. Apples too."

Edward Evans moved closer to the only source of light in the cell—a narrow window set high in the stone wall—and squinted at the label. "Wortley's Chest Tonic," he read, then emitted a short wheezy laugh. "Am I supposed to drink it or rub it on my chest?"

Emmeline gave his shoulder a light playful slap. "Drink it, of course. The apothecary informed me that it contains a bit of laudanum. At the very least, it should help you sleep better at night. I bought a blanket as well. And some socks and a scarf. They're all wool. A little coarse, but hopefully they'll keep you warm." She placed everything on the end of her father's bed then returned to the basket. "And last of all, I have a book for you. Sir Walter Scott's *Ivanhoe*. It's secondhand but all the pages seem to be there."

Her father took the novel and pressed it to his chest. "I shall enjoy every word, my dearest daughter. The days are long and dreary, and it will provide me with some much-needed entertainment."

"Oh, Papa." Tears welled in Emmeline's eyes, blurring her vision. "I promise you that I will get you out of here. The Duke of St Lawrence pays me well to look after his wards. As soon as I have sufficient funds—hopefully within a month—I'll arrange for you to be transferred to the debtors' prison, Giltspur Street Compter. I've heard it's much nicer there."

"Don't cry, my Em," said her father, his own eyes suspiciously wet. "I know that I'm thinner, and I can't shake this cough, but there's life in these middle-aged bones yet. And you have no idea how grateful I am for all that you're doing. You're a good girl. Always have been. Unlike . . ."

Unlike Freddy, her brother. "Has Freddy visited you lately, Papa?" asked Emmeline gently. She knew he'd done so shortly after their father had been incarcerated. He'd promised to revive his music hall, the Oberon, and had surmised it wouldn't be too long before patrons began pouring in again to see all sorts of plays and melodramas and musical acts. But that had been months ago. Emmeline had seen neither hide nor hair of Freddy since Christmastide.

Her father released a wheezy huff of laughter. "No. I imagine he's too riddled with guilt. One would hope he's making a go of the Oberon, considering all of the money I threw at it."

Emmeline sighed. "I should try to see him. While I'm worried about him, I'm also angry about what happened. How it's *your* business that failed. It isn't fair."

"It was my decision to take out that second mortgage. To invest in his dream," said Edward. "I chose to risk my store. Obviously, in hindsight, it was foolish of me to do so. But I did have hopes Freddy could turn things around. You never know, he still might."

"Perhaps." Emmeline wasn't convinced. Her brother wasn't a bad man. But he was undoubtedly flawed. He could be thoughtless and indolent, and Emmeline believed he was far too laissez-faire when it came to managing the Oberon. He was far too chummy with the music hall's staff, and Emmeline wondered if some of the Oberon's takings had been pilfered. It was clear that Freddy's propensity for too much "wine, women, and song" and not enough "nose to the grindstone" had led them to this pass.

Emmeline perched on the stone bench and her father sat on his bed. She regaled him with stories about the duke's delightful wards and roguish raven, and before she knew it, her half hour visit was over and the prison guard was at the door. Emmeline hugged her father goodbye. "Promise me you'll use that tonic and wrap up warmly. And don't let any of the food I bought you go to waste. Oh, and I want to hear about your favorite part of *Ivanhoe* when I next visit."

Her father's eyes twinkled with amusement. "Yes, Nanny Chase. I promise I will."

Emmeline smiled. "Good." It hurt her heart to leave, but at least her father appeared to be in much better spirits. "I'm going to ask the duke if I might have two half days off per month rather than one whole day. Then I can visit you fortnightly."

"I would love that, Emmeline." Her father's expression was a mixture of hopeful and grave. "But only if it won't inconvenience the duke. Don't put your position in jeopardy. I'm not worth—"

"'Ere, I 'aven't got all bleedin' day, you lot," grumbled the guard from the doorway. "It's time to go."

Ignoring the guard, Emmeline said, "Of course you're worth it, Papa. I'll send word as soon as I know when I can see you again." She gave her father one last quick hug, collected her umbrella and reticule, and then the guard was unceremoniously ushering her through the prison to the main entrance.

Once Emmeline was out on the street again, she turned her face to the lowering sky and inhaled a deep lungful of fresh air. Well, relatively fresh compared to the awful miasma lingering inside Newgate's thick stone walls. The clouds above might be as dark and swollen as bruises, but she felt considerably less disheartened than before. There was hope on the horizon. Her father *would* be all right.

She began walking toward St Paul's Cathedral. The bells were ringing and she was drawn by the bright melodious peals. It reminded her of the bells of St Mary-le-Bow's near her old family home in Cheapside. Of halcyon days when her mother and father were both happy and well, and her brother, whilst full of mischief, was caring. When she and Freddy had shared puff balloons by the fire and had laughed and squealed as they'd tried to wipe their syrupy sticky fingers on each other.

Emmeline's eyes grew misty as the bittersweet memories flooded her mind. *At least you have happy childhood memories,* she reminded herself. *Unlike the poor Duke of St Lawrence. Or the numerous children who don't have parents or even a home to speak of.*

She made another resolution to speak to the duke about donating to some of the Parasol Academy's causes.

Emmeline was just giving her dried lavender posy and a handful of pennies to a young match girl by the stairs of St Paul's when a large shadow loomed over her, claiming her attention.

"Emmeline?"

Freddy! Emmeline swung around and discovered her brother standing right beside her. While surprise jolted through her like an electrical charge, her heart twisted painfully as her gaze traveled over him.

Her brother was looking very much worse for wear compared to the last time she'd seen him. His cheeks were hollow and there were shadows beneath his gray eyes. His ginger hair, crammed beneath a battered tweed cap, was far too long, his clothes were rumpled, and his boots were scuffed and muddy. One of the buttons on his sack coat was hanging by a mere thread.

"I thought it was you." Freddy looked her up and down, his eyes hard and assessing. Different. "Still wearing your widow's weeds, I see. I didn't think you were that devoted to Jeremy."

"It was quite the opposite actually. He wasn't that devoted to *me*," returned Emmeline, unable to hide the bitterness in her voice. "The only reason I'm still wearing widow's weeds is because I can't afford new gowns. Not when I've been paying for father's upkeep in prison."

"And where have you been getting the money for that, pray tell?" demanded Freddy. "What have you been up to?"

"Well, if you'd seen me or Papa recently, you'd have learned that I graduated from the Parasol Academy not so long ago. I'm now working as a nanny." Emmeline wouldn't say *who* she worked for. She'd protect her employer's name at all costs. "What are you doing here anyway? Have you finally decided to visit poor Father?"

Freddy gave a disgruntled huff as he kicked at the lowest step of the cathedral that towered behind them. "I've been thinking about it. Look, it's not been easy for me, Em. I'm trying my bloody hardest to get the Oberon back on its feet. You might have paid *me* a visit every now and again to see if you could do anything to help."

"I think our family has done enough," returned Emmeline

angrily. "Or have you forgotten about Papa's sacrifice already?"

At last Freddy's expression turned remorseful. "Of course I haven't. I just..." His voice trailed away and so did his gaze. His attention shifted to the bustling road, then to the entrance of St Paul's. "Every night I lie awake, hoping to God that Father is all right. But there are several creditors snapping at my heels. The mortgage payment on the premises is overdue, and I'm late paying some of the cast. In fact, the lead actress in my current pantomime, *Puss in Boots*, has walked out." His expression grew pleading. "I'm getting desperate, Em. You could always sing and dance a bit. You're attractive enough. Do you think that in the evenings you could nip away and—"

Emmeline had to close her mouth (which had dropped wide-open) before she could reply. "Freddy, you *cannot* be serious. Of course I can't just 'nip away'"—she made a sweeping motion with her umbrella to emphasize her point—"to appear in one of your shows. My employer pays me well to do what I do. I will *not* jeopardize my position. I've worked too hard and Papa's counting on me. Not only that, but I *love* my work."

Freddy suddenly grabbed her arm. His gray eyes were as hard as steel as he said tightly, "Be that as it may, you're going to have to come with me. If I can't put on a show, then the Oberon *will* close its doors. And I can't afford that. I won't go to prison. I *need* your help."

Emmeline could easily twist away from her brother's grasp, but she wanted to make a few things very clear before she did so. "The only one I have allegiance to right now is our father," she said heatedly as she poked Freddy in the chest with the handle of her umbrella. "I've promised him that as soon as I have enough money, I will get him out of Newgate and into a dedicated debtors' jail. Something that isn't quite so like hell on earth. So you'll forgive me if that's what I'm focusing on right now. Not digging you, a grown man, out of a hole of your own making."

A muscle worked in Freddy's jaw and something like fear flickered in his eyes. Or perhaps it was anger, because his fingers dug harder into Emmeline's arm. "I'll drag you all the way back to Shoreditch if I have—"

All at once there was the unmistakable rasp of a metallic blade being unsheathed and the wickedly sharp point of a sword appeared beneath Freddy's chin.

"Unhand Mrs. Chase this instant, before I remove your appendage with this," growled a deep voice. A *familiar* voice that resonated with the power of crashing waves or rolling thunder.

"Your Grace," gasped Emmeline. Her heart stuttered, not knowing whether to slow down or speed up, because sure enough, the Duke of St Lawrence had somehow materialized on the steps of St Paul's Cathedral. For all the world he looked like some avenging angel about to smite down her brother. From beneath the shadow cast by the brim of his top hat, his glacial blue eyes burned with an almost otherworldly ferocity that stole Emmeline's breath clean away.

Freddy must have known the duke meant business because he immediately let go of Emmeline's arm and raised both hands, palms forward in a placatory gesture. "No harm done," he said to the duke before his attention darted to Emmeline. "I take it you know this man, Em?"

Emmeline swallowed. "I do." She turned to the duke. "Your-Your Grace. This is my brother, Frederick Evans. I'm perfectly fine. You don't need to run him through. You can put your sword away."

The duke hadn't taken his eyes off her brother the entire time Emmeline had been speaking. Even though his sword was still aimed at Freddy's chin, he lowered the tip a fraction. "He might be your brother, Mrs. Chase, but he has the uncivilized manners of a lout." To Freddy he said, "Apologize to your sister at once, Mr. Evans. And mean it."

Freddy swallowed, his Adam's apple bobbing nervously. "I'm sorry, Emmeline. I shouldn't have grabbed you like that.

It was unforgivable. I'll–I'll work something out to keep the Oberon afloat."

At that, the duke resheathed his rapier inside his silver-topped cane.

"I accept your apology," murmured Emmeline. "And I'm certain you will. You're clever enough."

Her brother's mouth tipped into a broken half smile. "I hope you're right, Em," he said gravely. He tilted his head in the duke's direction and doffed his cap. "Your Grace? I wish I could say it's been a pleasure . . ." And then Freddy turned on his heel and marched away, disappearing down a dark, narrow laneway that ran toward the back of the prison.

"Mrs. Chase. Are you all right?" The Duke of St Lawrence's entire demeanor had changed. His eyes were no longer filled with cold blue fire but shadowed with concern. His voice was low and imbued with a velveteen softness that bordered on intimate.

Emmeline swallowed, her throat suddenly tight. Her breath seemed to have snagged somewhere in her lungs. Snatching a quick breath, she managed, "I'm a little rattled but unharmed." In truth, she was a tangled mess of emotions. She was upset about her brother and the dire financial straits he was still in. Anxious that her father was unwell and all alone in the dark, gray-stoned hell looming behind her. But the burning question in her mind was: How much had the duke heard of her exchange with Freddy? His voice and gaze were gentle, so maybe he *hadn't* heard much. Nothing that might result in her being dismissed, at any rate.

She was also undeniably unsettled because the duke was standing so very close. So close, she could detect his expensive woodsy cologne and the fresh scent of his starched collar. He smelled so wonderful, she wanted to press her nose into his neck and inhale deeply. Feel the solid warmth of his chest beneath her palm . . .

She resolutely crushed the errant impulse like a bug beneath her bootheel and instead, pressed a hand to her throat where her pulse was fluttering wildly like a trapped butterfly. "To be perfectly honest, Your Grace, I could do with a nip of sherry. It's been a trying afternoon."

The duke nodded. "Come then," he said, offering his arm. "I know just the public house we can go to."

Chapter 16

Concerning a Rather Telling Encounter at a Chophouse; Followed by a Disconcerting Dash with a Damsel-not-in-Distress...

Ye Olde Fleet Ale and Chophouse was located halfway down a poky side alley off bustling Fleet Street. It was not the sort of place Xavier usually frequented, but it wasn't far from some of the antique clock and jewelry stores that he liked to explore in and around nearby Temple Bar, Chancery Lane, and Ludgate Hill. Like today. The added bonus of the chophouse—aside from the fact it served an excellent steak and kidney pie—was that it was but a short walk from St Paul's Cathedral.

Xavier didn't think Mrs. Chase was about to swoon or faint—she didn't seem the type—but she'd requested a fortifying nip of sherry, so she'd undoubtedly prefer to have it sooner rather than later.

He found a table for them by the fire in the chophouse's main taproom, and once they had their drinks—Xavier had ordered brandy for himself—he settled onto the ladderback chair beside his far-too-pale nanny.

He watched Mrs. Chase take a sip of her sherry—an excellent amontillado—and she exhaled on a soft sigh. When a flush of pink suffused her lightly freckled cheeks, the tension in Xavier's own body began to abate.

"Thank you, Your Grace," she said, catching his gaze. "I'm not sure what you saw or heard outside St Paul's . . ." She bit her lip as she toyed with her glass. "My brother is going through a difficult time at present. He's not himself."

"And no doubt you are having a testing time too, Mrs. Chase," said Xavier gently, "considering your father is in prison. I can't even imagine the terrible stress you've been under."

"You heard that?" she whispered, her expression stricken. At least Xavier thought that might be the correct word to describe her reaction. Her countenance was horribly pale again and her eyes had widened. Her fingers had tightened about her glass too. "I . . ." She trailed off, her gaze dropping to the tabletop. "I'm sure you have questions. Lots of them." Then she hoisted up her chin and met his eyes again. "I've kept a rather large, rather awful secret from you, Your Grace. And the Parasol Academy. And for that I'm truly sorry. But I want you to know that my father's situation has not compromised my ability to competently discharge my nannying duties in *any* way."

"Many individuals who are incarcerated in a debtors' prison rarely end up there because they are bad people, Mrs. Chase. Ill fortune can strike anyone at any time."

Mrs. Chase gave a small huff. "In this case, my father's ill fortune has a lot to do with my brother's poor decision-making." And then she disclosed that her brother owned a struggling music hall in Shoreditch—the Oberon—and that even though their father had sacrificed his own business to bail out her brother, there were still creditors dogging the young man. Her gaze was suspiciously misty as she said, "I don't know what will become of Freddy. I don't want him to go to jail too. I-I can't support both of them. Not on my wage, as generous as it is." Then she pulled out a dainty lawn kerchief from her pocket and dabbed at her eyes. "My apologies for turning into a watering pot, Your Grace. I'm not one to burst into tears."

"Mrs. Chase," said Xavier, imbuing his voice with as much compassion as he could muster. "I want you to know right now that your position is not in danger. You are a good person with a noble and kind heart, and since I employed you, my life and the lives of Harriet, Bartholomew, and Gareth have been so much calmer and brighter. You're like a burst of sunshine breaking through the clouds. I'd rather cut off my own arm than lose you."

"Oh," murmured the nanny. "Thank you. No one's ever said anything quite so . . . so heartfelt and lovely to me before. Or quite so dramatic." Her lips quivered with mirth. "Though I'd settle for you losing a little finger or toe. I'm not sure I'm worth a whole arm."

Xavier laughed. "Yes, I really didn't think that declaration through, did I?"

"Nevertheless, I know what you meant. The sentiment behind it. I'm grateful for your understanding." Mrs. Chase's lower lip trembled again but not with amusement. To Xavier's dismay, her eyes brimmed with tears. One drop slid down her cheek, and he had the sudden, uncharacteristic urge to reach out and brush it away with his gloved thumb.

He curled his hands into fists on the slightly sticky tabletop to keep from doing so. "You're very welcome," he said gruffly. He wished he could take all of Mrs. Chase's worries away. Seeing her in tears made his chest ache in the most peculiar way.

He had no idea what that meant.

Of course you do, you dolt. It means you're beginning to care for the woman. The stiff and starchy and unfeeling Duke of St Lawrence does *have a heart after all. And desire. Bucketloads of desire, considering what you thought about while taking a bath this afternoon. And what you did while thinking it.*

Bloody hell. That could only mean . . .

Xavier picked up his brandy and knocked it back in two swift mouthfuls. As the fiery liquor burned its way down his throat, he pushed away any and all thoughts of what the logical, analytical part of his brain had been about to tell him. If he didn't say it, even in his own head — then it wasn't true.

Dukes did not feel affection—of any kind—let alone desire for their nannies. Or love. He almost snorted. As if he, the cold and bitter Duke of St Lawrence, knew what love looked like. He was certain he wouldn't recognize love even if it marched up and planted a punch right between his eyes.

Yes, the very notion of him being in love with a woman, now that *was* mad. And he wasn't mad, or insane, or a lunatic.

Xavier Mason was rational and remote. Cool, calm, and collected like an iceberg floating in a frozen arctic sea. As impervious to emotion and illogical urges as a carved marble statue or even an abandoned tin soldier. He'd been weak this afternoon and had given in to his carnal cravings. But that was then, and this was now.

He was in control, not falling head-over-heels for Emmeline Chase.

His equilibrium restored and firmly in place, Xavier glanced at his pocket watch. It was getting late and night would be falling soon. The chophouse was already filling up with workers who'd finished for the day and were seeking a drink and a bite of dinner.

Sliding his watch back into the pocket of his frock coat, he said, "Shall we head back to Belgrave Square? But then I'm assuming that's what you want to do. Technically, it is still your day off."

Mrs. Chase smiled. "It is, but I'm a trifle tired. I wouldn't mind going ho—I mean, back to St Lawrence House. I take it your carriage is nearby?"

"Alas, no," said Xavier as he escorted the nanny outside. He didn't take her arm this time, simply walked alongside her with his cane firmly in one hand while he buried his other hand in his coat pocket. "I wasn't sure where I would end up or how long I would be, so I caught a hansom cab. I can hail a cab now if you'd rather not walk too far."

Mrs. Chase turned her face to the darkening sky. "The rain is still holding off. I wouldn't mind walking for a while." She cast him a smile. "A Parasol nanny needs to make sure she's fighting fit."

They continued down Fleet Street in companionable silence for a few more minutes before the nanny ventured, "It's probably none of my business, Your Grace, but you didn't mention why you were in the vicinity of St Paul's Cathedral and Newgate Prison this afternoon."

"No. I didn't," said Xavier. "But I'm happy to share why." He explained that he'd also taken the afternoon off from any sort of work and had been indulging his passion for watch-hunting. "I visited Pembridge's on Ludgate Hill, but alas, there wasn't another Markwick pocket watch or anything as unique or valuable up for auction."

"That's a shame," said Mrs. Chase. "Did you come across anything else that caught your eye?"

Apart from you? The words were on the tip of Xavier's tongue but he pressed his lips together so they wouldn't spill out.

Devil take him. It didn't matter how many times he gave himself a stern talking-to, or outright denied his fascination for the nanny, his obsession persisted like a fever in his blood that he couldn't shake. Aloud he said, "Not really. But I enjoyed the excursion all the same."

"I'm glad," she said. A few minutes later, Xavier was surprised when she drew exceedingly close to him. He was even more astonished when she threaded her arm through his and tugged him down. "Your Grace, I hope you'll forgive me for taking liberties," she murmured close to his ear, "but I believe we're being followed."

"Are you sure?" returned Xavier. Even so, his body tensed and his grip tightened on his cane.

"As sure as I can be." The nanny's voice was quiet but edged with determination as she continued. "There are two of them. One is broad-shouldered and burly. The other is leaner and shorter but no less menacing. I noticed them watching us in the chophouse and they've been keeping pace with us. They might be common cutpurses, but then again, maybe not. They definitely have an air of 'up to no good' about them."

Xavier resisted the strong urge to look over his shoulder. Cold anger began to brew in his blood, even as thunder rumbled in the distance. It wouldn't be long before it rained. "There's only one way to be certain," he said. "Up ahead, there's a small lane—Middle Temple Lane—off to the left that leads down to the Temple Church and the Inns of Court."

"I know it," said Mrs. Chase.

"We'll duck down there and see if they follow us. Are you all right with that?" Xavier studied the nanny's face in the growing gloom, but he couldn't detect any fear in her expression. "Feel free to say no. It could be dangerous if they mean either, or both of us, harm. I can simply hail a hansom cab."

"No. This is important." Mrs. Chase's voice was firm. "I feel certain these men are shadowing you. If we can confront them and extract information from them, you might find out who's behind this sustained campaign to intimidate and discredit you, once and for all. Besides"—her mouth lifted in a faint smile—"I can hold my own in a fight if it comes down to that."

"I don't doubt it," said Xavier. Which was true, but the gentleman in him was loath to put this young woman in danger, no matter how fearless she might be or how proficient she was in the art of self-defense. He prayed these men *weren't* hired thugs and there wouldn't be a physical altercation.

Perhaps they were both simply starting at shadows.

Except they weren't. As soon as Xavier and Mrs. Chase entered the narrow lane, Xavier could hear heavy footsteps behind them. The round, domed building of the Temple Church was up ahead on their left. Perhaps they could duck inside and catch a glimpse of the men without confronting—

At that moment the heavens opened up and it began to pour.

Heavy, ice-cold raindrops pummeled them, and Xavier gritted his teeth. He would soon be soaked to the skin and he didn't have time to be distracted by his strong dislike of damp fabric clinging to his body.

Then all of a sudden, Mrs. Chase opened her umbrella. Huddling closer to him, she thrust the canopy over both their heads. "I have an idea," she murmured, her deliciously warm breath fanning over his cheek. "Do you trust me, Your Grace?"

"Implicitly," he returned without hesitation.

The lane they were following was coming to an end up ahead. It diverged—one path veered to the left, leading one around the outside of the church. The other branched to the right, tracing a path between tightly packed barristers' chambers. From previous excursions, Xavier knew it ended in a closed courtyard.

"Turn right," urged Emmeline, increasing their pace. No sooner had they dashed around the corner, she was pushing him beneath a stone archway into a narrow recess—a tight alleyway—between two buildings. It was such a small, cramped space, Mrs. Chase was crushed hard up against Xavier's chest. It was a wonder the umbrella fit.

A frisson of panic shot through Xavier. They were effectively squashed. Trapped. Sitting ducks with no room to move or fight back. Beneath the tattoo of the hammering rain, he could hear the resounding wet slap of approaching footsteps on the pavement. Men running. Drawing ever closer. "What are you do—" he began.

"Shhh." Emmeline pressed a gloved finger to Xavier's lips. Then she whispered the strangest word he'd ever heard. "*Cloakify.*"

Cloakify? Xavier didn't have time to think on it further as an enormous peal of thunder boomed and reverberated down the lane. A strange haze—a soft purple-hued mist—seemed to envelop them and meld with the shadows. Was it a trick of the light? Something to do with the tempest breaking over London? The electricity in the air?

Surely it hadn't anything to do with the peculiar word he'd thought Mrs. Chase had uttered.

Glancing out from beneath the brim of Mrs. Chase's umbrella, Xavier spied one of their pursuers, silhouetted in the entrance to the alleyway where they hid.

Damn.

Holding his breath, all senses on high alert, Xavier pressed the catch on the top of his cane. He wouldn't hesitate to draw his rapier—or use it—if he had to. But to his astonishment, the man—the thug—didn't seem to be able to see him or the nanny.

How could that be? Perhaps the shadows, the mist, and the deep gloom of the alcove were enough to completely hide them.

Lightning flashed, briefly illuminating the stranger. The heavily built brute was scowling, peering into the gloom as rain sluiced down his face. A prominent scar carved a path across one cheek, right down to the corner of his mouth. "Where did they go?" he called over his shoulder, back toward the church.

The second man appeared beside his partner. "Bleedin' 'ell," he grumbled. He was wearing the simple garb of a workman. A cap and ill-fitting sack coat, loose trousers and heavy boots. "We can't 'ave lost 'em."

The first man removed his beaver hat and combed a hand through his close-cropped hair. "Looks like we 'ave." He glanced back toward the Temple Church, then to his left where the closed courtyard lay.

"Do you fink they've taken shelter in one of these legal toffs' rooms? Or the church?"

"Maybe. But we're not supposed to be creatin' a fuss that will get noticed." Thunder growled again as the scarred stranger jammed his hat back on his head. "Righto. Not much point in searchin' for Lunatic St Lawrence now. We're sure to 'ave put the wind up 'im at least. The guv'nor oughta be 'appy about that if nuffink else. There's no sense stayin' out 'ere when it's rainin' like the end of the world is nigh."

The thugs disappeared from view and Xavier released a relieved sigh. *Thank God.* And thank heavens for Emmeline's quick thinking, pulling them into a darkly shadowed recess and using her umbrella to hide them.

"Who do you think the 'guv'nor' is?" murmured Mrs. Chase, claiming his attention again. She was still pushed up against him, his legs crushing her skirts. The soft mounds of her breasts were pressing into his chest.

Xavier swallowed. Hard. How the hell was he supposed to think, let alone speak in this situation? "I'm not sure," he managed roughly. "It could be Sir Randolph. Maybe my uncle or cousin. Or someone else entirely."

"I'm sorry that oaf called you such an awful name."

Xavier shrugged a shoulder, the fabric of his frock coat scraping on the bricks at his back. "It's nothing I haven't heard before."

One of Mrs. Chase's hands, the one not holding the umbrella, was lying against the front of his coat. Right where his heart thudded wildly against his rib cage. "That doesn't make it all right, Your Grace," she said softly.

"No. It doesn't." He drew a breath, intending to suggest they leave. But he found himself frozen to the spot. Reluctant to move.

Transfixed by whatever magical spell the nanny was effortlessly weaving beneath her umbrella.

The sheeting rain was still pouring down all around them. Thunder grumbled and lightning flickered but Xavier barely noticed. Even though there was scarcely any light in the alley where they sheltered, he could just make out the pale oval of Mrs. Chase's face, framed by her coppery curls and the brim of her black bonnet. The soft gleam of her large eyes.

His gaze dipped lower. The gentle curve of her lush mouth . . .

His banked desire stirred. His blood, already afire from the chase and the act of steeling himself for a fight, seared through his veins, awakening the peculiar ache—stark yearning—in his chest again.

He licked his lips. "Mrs. Chase," he whispered huskily. He *shouldn't* kiss her. He shouldn't be taking advantage of this woman—any woman—in this situation.

But this was Emmeline Chase. The delicious figment of his dreams. The calm center of his spiraling universe.

"Emmeline..." His whisper was edged with a need so sharp, she must hear it.

"You want me," she murmured.

Was it his imagination, or did she tilt her face up toward his? Was she really inviting him to—

There was a shift in the air. A crackle of electricity. A quickening of breath—both his and Mrs. Chase's—and the sharpening of all Xavier's senses. Everything around them suddenly seemed to be limned in a silvery-lavender light.

"Do you want to kiss me, Your Grace?" Mrs. Chase's fingers curled into his lapel. The tip of her pretty pink tongue swept over the plush pillow of her bottom lip, leaving behind a soft sheen of moisture. Her delicate feminine scent—violets and perhaps vanilla and something that was essentially Emmeline—floated around him, teasing him.

Dear God. Xavier couldn't resist such a sweet temptation. He'd been trying so hard for so long to *not* give in to his desire. Telling himself all sorts of lies and inconvenient truths, like she was an employee, and he was a nobleman with a duty of care. But in this particular moment when his pulse was careening out of control and Mrs. Chase was all but offering her mouth to him, his resolve was dissolving faster than a sugar lump in a cup of coffee.

He raised a hand—sweet Lord, he was so nervous, he was trembling—and dared to cup Mrs. Chase's cheek. To cradle the gentle curve in his gloved palm. To brush a raindrop off her satin-smooth skin with the pad of his thumb. "I know that I shouldn't, but yes, I do want to kiss you," he all but groaned. "Most desperately. Most ardently."

Her breath drifted over his mouth, warm and humid in the frosty air as she reached up and slid her hand behind his neck. Her fingers threaded through his hair. "Then what are you waiting for?"

That was a very good question, and damned if Xavier could mount a single objection that actually mattered.

Bending his head, he brushed his lips over Mrs. Chase's in an experimental glide. A tentative exploration. It had been forever since he'd kissed a woman, and he prayed that he still possessed a modicum of finesse. She'd been married. She would know everything there was to know about the art of kissing.

Even so, despite his lack of recent practice, he would try to make this good.

No, better than good.

He wanted to sweep Emmeline Chase up and away, carry her heavenward to the stars.

Mrs. Chase's—no, *Emmeline's* lips—were as smooth and slippery as the finest silk, and as Xavier deepened the pressure of his mouth on hers, she yielded. Parted her lips and released a soft breathy moan. And Xavier felt like he'd been set alight.

Fire raced through him like molten quicksilver, straight to his loins. Sparks flared behind his closed eyes. He dropped his cane.

One of his hands grazed a path along Emmeline's slender shoulder and he hauled her closer. At the same time, Emmeline tugged him down, and the press and slide of her mouth grew harder, her movements urgent, as though she wanted more from him.

She wanted him to taste her. He could sense it.

Gathering his courage, Xavier gently pushed his tongue between her lips, delving into the warm, slick recess. Explored her with languid strokes. And when she caressed him back, her sinuous tongue boldly curling around his, he groaned in appreciation.

She tasted like heaven and honey and the sherry she'd been drinking. He'd always believed that he didn't like sweet things. But he hadn't tasted Emmeline Chase.

Xavier suddenly wanted to press his lips against her neck. Slide open the buttons of her gown and trace the soft freckled flesh above the neckline of her chemise, the hollow above her collarbone . . . and lower . . . His fingers flexed against the side of her breast, and she arched into him like a cat, wanting more.

God help him, he wanted more too.

When they at last drew apart, both of them were breathless. Indeed, Xavier's head was spinning like he was intoxicated while other parts of him were throbbing. He was both satisfied and unsatisfied. Caught between what he longed to do with this remarkable woman, and what was the *right* thing to do. How could something that felt so natural and wonderful be so wrong in all other respects?

But wrong it was. He was a duke. She was a nanny. He'd taken advantage of her when she'd been in a vulnerable situation. Even though she'd invited him to kiss her, in his mind, it still felt like he'd pressed her for an illicit favor, and in the heat of the moment when her guard was down she'd consented.

As guilt rushed in, extinguishing any lingering embers of pleasure inside Xavier, one thing was clear. This couldn't go any further. This could never happen again.

"Mrs. Chase . . . I'm sorry. I shouldn't have—"

The nanny shook her head. "Don't apologize. We were both . . . not ourselves. I'm to blame for what we did as well. We'd been in danger and-and we were both simply overwhelmed by relief. It was a natural reaction. A completely expected response considering the extraordinarily tense situation we were both thrust into." She drew a breath and held his gaze. "That being said, perhaps . . . perhaps it would be best if we both tried to forget what happened. Lock it away in our minds in a compartment labeled 'this never occurred.' If the Parasol Academy hears about this. Any of this . . ." She shivered. "I could lose my license to practice. I can't afford for that to happen."

Ah, so she regretted what they'd done too. And for good reason.

Xavier nodded. "I understand. And your secret—all your secrets—are safe with me. Duke's honor." He placed a hand on his chest, in the spot where Mrs. Chase's had been right before they'd kissed. "We shall never speak of this again."

He couldn't promise that he wouldn't *think* about it though.

"Thank you, Your Grace." Nodding toward the laneway, she added, "It's stopped raining. Shall we return to St Lawrence House?"

Xavier retrieved his cane. "I think that would be most sensible."

Once they were safely installed inside a hansom cab and on their way back to Belgravia, the nanny ventured, "Your Grace, I'm afraid that I have another small favor to ask."

Xavier immediately pulled his attention away from the window. He'd been focusing on the snarls of traffic and the passersby on the Strand, rather than fixating on the only woman he really wanted to look at. "Anything," he said.

Mrs. Chase was sitting opposite him and the light from a passing gas lamp flickered across her face. Her manner seemed apprehensive as she said, "Instead of taking one day off per month, might I . . . might I have two half days? So that I can visit my father once a fortnight. He's not been well of late, and I'm worried about him. If it's all right with you. I wouldn't want to put you or your wards out."

"No, that's perfectly fine," said Xavier. "I'm sorry your father is ill."

"It's only a cough," she said. "You know, the cells are cold and damp and . . ." She shrugged. "He has a tonic and a new blanket. He'll be all right." She appeared to rally and summoned a smile. "Thank you again, Your Grace. Many employers wouldn't be so considerate."

"Family is important," said Xavier gravely. Since his wards had come into his life—since Mrs. Chase had entered his life—he was beginning to understand that much at least, even if a finer emotion like love remained a mystery to him. "We must look after those we care about. Indeed, I can see how much you care about your father, and that is to be commended. Not only that, but worrying about his well-being is bound to have an effect on you too. I don't like the idea of you being so troubled all the time."

A small line appeared between Mrs. Chase's brows. "At the chophouse, I assured you that my performance had not and *would* not be affected by my family's ongoing trials and tribulations."

"I know that, and I believe you. It's just that seeing you hurt—" *Hurts me.* Xavier broke off before he uttered those two very small but telling words. "You work very hard. And I'm sure Fanny will manage without you two afternoons per month," he concluded.

Xavier had told himself over and over again that he would *not* acknowledge any softer emotions when it came to Mrs. Chase. He'd continually reassured himself that he knew nothing of love. The giving or receiving of it. So his heart *couldn't* be in danger if it was an organ that was essentially broken. Frozen and hard and unfeeling.

It seemed that maybe he'd been wrong.

At least he'd stopped himself from saying anything too mawkish. No doubt Mrs. Chase would start to believe that he *was* actually mad.

Turning his gaze back to the window, Xavier tried very hard to resurrect his aloof and difficult, tending-toward-bitter side.

He set his jaw and focused on the passing streetscape and how poorly sprung the hansom cab was. How lumpy the worn leather seat felt and how irritating it was to be looking through a grimy windowpane. How his damp trouser legs clung uncomfortably to his shins and calves and that inside his wet leather shoes, his toes were half-frozen. How he hated wet shoes.

With all his might, he attempted to concentrate on everything *but* the fearless and passionate young woman sitting across from him. Or the fact he could still feel the exact place where she'd rested her hand upon his chest. How the flesh beneath his silk-lined cambric shirt seemed to glow with a subtle warmth. As though her sunshine was melting away the ice encasing his heart and breathing life into his bones.

Somehow that simple touch had marked him, and Xavier knew that he would never be the same again.

Chapter 17

Wherein Night's Plutonian Shore, Antidisestablishmentarianism, Calculus, Bottom-bums, Prickles and Tingles Are Briefly Featured; Followed by Heartfelt Hugs (But an Absence of Blubbing) and a Strong Desire for Defascination...

"'Quoth the Raven "Nevermore,"'" said Miss Harriet to Horatio. "Now you say it, please."

The raven was sitting upon one of the window ledges in the nursery, his head cocked to one side as he studied the duke's ward. "Nevermore, nevermore," he croaked, bouncing up and down. "Night's Plutonian shore, Lenore. Nevermore!"

Harry groaned and dropped her forehead onto the book in front of her. "Grrr. I suspect Horatio is being uncooperative on purpose, Nanny Chase," she said when she raised her head. "We both know he can say much harder things than the lines I'm trying to teach him."

"Antidisestablishmentarianism nevermore!" cried Horatio before he fixed a wickedly gleaming eye on Emmeline. "Nevermore, nevermore!"

Emmeline laughed at the bird's verbal antics. Harry had been trying to teach the raven certain lines from Edgar Allan Poe's famous poem "The Raven" for the last half hour. But the cheeky bird was steadfastly refusing to cooperate. "Perhaps he needs a little more of an incentive," she said, putting aside the mathematical equations she'd been marking: Harriet had completed a series of calculus problems; Bartholomew was in the process of mastering basic addition; and Gareth had been matching geometric shapes. "You could perhaps feed him a beetle or two. There are still a few left in the bottom of Archimedes and Aristotle's aquarium."

Archimedes, who was sitting on the desk beside Harry, croaked as if in protest.

That would be a good start, replied Horatio as he looked directly at Emmeline.

"I think you should teach him more words like ninny-poop," said Gareth with a giggle.

"Ninny-poop nevermore," taunted Horatio. "Bottom-bum, bumpety-bump."

Both Bartholomew and Gareth immediately began skipping around the nursery, clapping wooden blocks together and chanting, "Bottom-bum, bumpety-bump. Bumpety-bump."

"Nevermore!" chorused Horatio.

Emmeline rolled her eyes at the raven. *Now look what you've done, Mr. Ravenscar.*

Oooh, Mister *Ravenscar, is it?* The raven fluttered over to the aquarium. *You know what will make me stop?* He sauntered around the glass tank, tail feathers wagging, then tapped on the side with his beak. *Rat-a-tat-tat.* Aristotle immediately retracted his head, legs, and tail into his shell.

I don't know if I should reward such willfully mischievous behavior, admonished Emmeline. Rising from her seat, she addressed the still-chanting boys and their sister. "I think we should put on our coats and hats and go outside into the garden. It's a lovely afternoon."

"Aww, can't we go to the park?" asked Bartholomew.

"Perhaps tomorrow," replied Emmeline. In truth, she was a trifle reluctant to venture outside with the children at present. Last time they had—the day before last they'd visited the private park in the middle of Belgrave Square—Emmeline had felt as though they were being watched. Her skin had prickled with uncomfortable awareness, and she would be silly not to pay attention to that feeling. Even the *Parasol Academy Handbook* stated that one shouldn't ignore any preternatural sensations of apprehension such as prickles and tingles and raised hair on one's nape or shivers down one's spine. At one point, she'd even thought she'd glimpsed her brother, Freddy, through the trees, just beyond the wrought-iron fence that enclosed the park. But then she'd convinced herself that her mind was playing tricks on her. Because surely Freddy would've said hullo. They'd had words, but he was still her brother.

Seeing three sad faces, Emmeline added, "After a good run around, we could make a picnic of our afternoon tea. And as for Horatio"—she sent the raven a mock glare—"he can find his own beetles along with his manners."

Spoilsport, returned the raven. But he didn't look or sound the least bit repentant.

Outdoor clothes donned, Emmeline escorted the children downstairs. After a quick visit to the kitchen to have a word with Mrs. Punchbowl, they continued on to the sizable walled garden at the back of St Lawrence House. It was Fanny's afternoon off, so it was just the children and Emmeline. Oh, and Horatio of course.

As for his enigmatic owner... Emmeline's gaze strayed to the duke's study on the second floor. According to Bertie, His Grace had quit St Lawrence House at an early hour to attend to "some important business matters," so that explained why she hadn't seen him today. Since their intimate encounter—their *kiss*—five days ago, she'd barely crossed paths with the duke at all.

Which was all for the best. Emmeline had meant every word when she'd suggested that they should both forget what had happened beneath her umbrella. Although, doing so was easier said than done.

When she *did* happen to see the duke—usually when she was in the company of the children—she donned a politely professional mask, when really, deep down, she was a confusing mixture of sharp yearning and even sharper schoolmarmish admonishment.

Though, putting aside all contrary feelings, Emmeline *was* pleased that the duke had taken a few of her recent suggestions on board and had begun to make a little time in his busy schedule for his wards. In the last few days, Harry had visited his hidden Horology Room, and due to the finer weather, the promised astrolabe demonstration had eventuated. The girl had been fairly bouncing with excitement when she'd reported to Emmeline that she was going to help Cousin Xavier repair a pocket watch.

The duke had also taken the children to the garden the day before, to discuss the construction of a special pond for Aristotle and Archimedes. It had been Bartholomew's idea that the frog and terrapin might like a holiday outside during the warmer months, and their guardian had readily agreed to the proposal. It was heartening to witness a closer bond developing between the duke and his wards even if she, Emmeline, had to do the opposite and keep herself at a respectable distance. Her duty, first and foremost, was to her charges after all.

When the children commenced an exuberant game of tag, Emmeline settled on a stone bench by a rose arbor. Ordinarily she would have joined in the game, but today she was feeling rather listless and despondent. For no particular reason she could fathom.

Little liar, she thought. Like a disgruntled child denied their after-dinner pudding, she was out of sorts because *she* hadn't been spending any private time with the duke like she used to. She hadn't been summoned to His Grace's study in the evenings, but then she'd nothing of note—no odd domestic incidents—to report. Everything had been calm. Nothing had gone awry. Well, aside from all the clocks not being able to keep time. That was still an ongoing issue.

The biggest lie she kept telling herself was that the kiss she'd shared with the duke had meant nothing. It had been *everything*. It had been the sweetest yet most passionate kiss she'd ever experienced in her life. Even now, she could still feel the warmth of the duke's lips, the soft but sure caresses of his velvet tongue. The delicious groan he'd made when she'd dared to taste him back. The hard heat of his body crushed against hers.

Perhaps the most intimate detail, the part she treasured the most, was the fact the duke had whispered her first name, his tongue and lips curling around each sound, making it his own.

She sighed and idly plucked a pink rosebud from a nearby bush and brushed it against her cheek. The worst part was, *she* was the one who'd encouraged the duke to kiss her. It had been beyond foolish to do so. What he must think of her, practically throwing herself at him like that.

She'd also broken several Academy rules all at once.

Number one: She'd deployed the *Cloakify* spell in the presence of the duke.

Number two: She *hadn't* cast the spell in order to protect her charges.

Number three: With malice aforethought, she'd taken advantage of the fact that she and the duke had been invisible beneath her umbrella, and because no one could see them, that had emboldened her to act on her wanton impulses.

Oh, she was a bad, bad nanny. The antithesis of prim and proper.

She *had* been prepared for anything though, and she'd successfully hidden both herself and the duke beneath her umbrella to keep them from harm. The thugs that had pursued them had declared that they'd only intended to put the "wind up" the duke for their "guv'nor," but what did that really mean? If they'd cornered her and the duke, would they have attempted a physical attack? The duke was armed with a rapier, and she'd been armed with her trusty umbrella, her fists, and her wits.

Emmeline liked to think that she and the duke would have emerged relatively unscathed from a confrontation with those men. But one never knew.

Despite the warmth of the sunny spring afternoon, an icy tremor slid down Emmeline's spine and she wrapped her arms about herself. If anything had happened to the Duke of St Lawrence... If he'd been hurt. Or worse...

Emmeline's heart contracted painfully. She couldn't bear to think about such an eventuality. And *that* was another warning sign. Another alarm bell ding-a-ling-a-linging in her mind, telling her that she was beginning to care for the man in a way that she absolutely couldn't afford to.

She didn't know what to do. A sensible woman might ask for a transfer to remove herself from the situation. But she couldn't abandon her charges, not when they seemed so settled and happy.

Focus on doing your duty. Follow the Parasol Academy Handbook's *guidelines to the letter. Nurture and protect the duke's wards. The duke is a charismatic and handsome distraction. Nothing more.*

It was a pity there wasn't a chapter in the *Parasol Academy Handbook* dealing with ways to control or even quell one's unseemly emotions. It was all well and good for Chapter Five, Paragraph 3.2, Part a) to proscribe fraternizing with one's employer, but not particularly helpful when one was hurtling pell-mell into disaster.

Now, a spell that one could cast on oneself—a *Defascinating* (that sounded quite painful) or *Unsmittening* incantation—would be incredibly useful. The *opposite* of a love spell.

Love? Emmeline's breath caught as horror and dismay blasted through her. Her fingers crushed the rosebud. *Was* she falling in love? Being "in lust" with the duke was one thing, even cultivating a tiny tendre for him was natural, but to be *in* love?

No. *Emphatically and unequivocally no.*

Never-in-a-million-years, no-no-nopity-no.

Just no.

All of a sudden, Gareth came running over. His hat had fallen off and his cheeks were flushed pink with exertion. "Nanny Chase, Nanny Chase! Can you play hide-and-seek with us now?"

Emmeline pushed to her feet. Her knees were unsteady, but her voice mercifully wasn't as she said, "I would love to. Who's going to count—"

"Nanny Chase?"

Emmeline's attention swung to the terrace. The French doors were open and standing on the threshold was the housekeeper. "Yes, Mrs. Lambton?" she called.

The housekeeper crossed the flagstones and descended the stone stairs. "His Grace has requested your presence in the drawing room," she said as she drew close. "I will watch his wards while you are away."

"Oh. Very well. Is everything all right?" As far as Emmeline knew, the drawing room was rarely used. Since she'd started working at St Lawrence House, she'd only set foot in it to check on the clocks. To be invited there by the duke was exceedingly unusual.

"I believe so," replied Mrs. Lambton.

Gareth pouted and curled his small fingers around Emmeline's. "You'll come back, won't you, Nanny Chase?"

Emmeline gently ruffled the child's already tousled hair. "Of course I will. As soon as I can." She caught Mrs. Lambton's eye. "I've already had a word with Mrs. Punchbowl. Afternoon tea should be appearing shortly." She smiled at Bartholomew and Harry who'd wandered over. "I believe there's apple teacake and egg-and-cress sandwiches on the menu."

"Hurrah," cried Bartholomew.

That sounds far more palatable than beetles, remarked Horatio from his perch in a nearby beech tree. *As much as I'd like to have a stickybeak in the drawing room, I think I'll stay here with the children, Nanny Chase.*

Emmeline inclined her head in the raven's direction. *Very well. But don't have too much cake. You know it will give you a stomachache.*

Horatio released a string of deep-throated caws that sounded very much like a chuckle. *Yes, dearest Mama*, he said. *Now run along. You don't want to keep the master waiting.*

By the time Emmeline arrived outside the closed drawing room door, her pulse was racing, and she was more than a trifle breathless. Not from hurrying (she'd recently introduced a two-mile early morning walk schedule to her daily routine) but from nerves.

Bertie was standing to attention outside the shiny oak-paneled doors along with another young footman named Ollie.

Bertie gave her a wink. "I hear His Grace wants to see you, Nanny Chase."

"Yes," replied Emmeline, summoning a smile. "Do you know why? Was he in a good mood?"

Ollie gave a small snort. "When is he ever?" he muttered. "All I ever get is icy stares and frosty orders."

Emmeline frowned. "His Grace isn't like that, Ollie. You should show your employer more respect. It's . . . it's just his way."

"Looks like someone is sweet on His Grace," teased Ollie. "Poor Bertie, it seems you'll have to start making calf's eyes at someone else on staff. Just don't let Woodley or Mrs. Lambton catch you."

"Shut up, Ollie," grumbled Bertie. A red flush crept up his

neck and he tugged at his high collar. "I hope all goes well in there, Nanny Chase. His Grace has someone else with him, by the way. I didn't catch his name."

Oh? Before Emmeline could think to ask anything else, Bertie and Ollie were opening the double doors to admit her to the drawing room beyond.

It was a spacious room that was elegantly furnished; everywhere the eye settled there was polished wood and touches of gleaming gilt and plush fabrics in hues of soft cream and muted green. But Emmeline paid little attention to these details.

No, all her attention was claimed by the duke and the pale, gray-haired gentleman beside him.

"Papa!" Emmeline cried, her heart leaping with joy. And then she was rushing across the room to hug him, gathering him close and squeezing tight. "Is it really you? Are-Are you really free?" Her throat was so clogged with emotion, she almost couldn't get the words out.

"My sweet Em," her father murmured in an equally choked voice as he hugged her back. "Who'd have thought it, eh?" Coughing a little, he released her, then cast the duke a watery smile. "And it's all thanks to your employer. It's clear the Duke of St Lawrence is a fine gentleman with a kind heart."

Emmeline bit her lip to stop it wobbling. She *would* not blub. Blubbing was not allowed. She was certain that was written somewhere in the *Parasol Academy Handbook*. (Besides, she looked horrid with red eyes and a drippy nose. She was very much a messy crier not a pretty, dainty crier.)

"He is. He does," she eventually managed, after the impulse to dissolve into tears had abated. Then she risked a glance at the duke.

He was by the fireplace, his stance as rigid as one of the fire irons, his hands behind his back. And he was looking at her with a curious expression: His gaze was soft but his mouth was set in an uncompromising straight line.

Was he struggling to fight back tears too?

Surely not.

"Thank you, Your Grace," said Emmeline. Her voice quivered only a tiny bit. "I don't know how you managed to make this happen, but I am nothing but grateful. Eternally grateful in fact."

The duke inclined his head, his expression grave. "Think nothing of it," he said gruffly. "I would have arranged for your father's release sooner but there were a few things that required sorting out first. The wheel of justice turns slowly."

A few things that required sorting out...

Emmeline suddenly felt like she'd been struck by a thunderbolt. "But—Don't tell me, Your Grace, did you cover my father's debt so that he might be released?"

The duke hesitated as though taking a moment to choose his next words. "It doesn't matter—"

"You did!" cried Emmeline and she clapped her hands to her cheeks. "Oh heavens. It must have cost you an absolute fortune. You didn't have to—"

"No, you certainly didn't have to," added her father. "But I'm thankful that you did."

Emmeline drew a shaky breath. Of all the things to happen of late, she hadn't expected this. While she was relieved, she was also shaken to her core. The duke's generosity was... It was too much. "It goes without saying that we will pay you back, Your Grace."

"Yes, that goes without saying," repeated her father.

The duke shook his head. "That won't be necessary."

"But—" began Emmeline but the duke cut her off.

"No buts, Mrs. Chase. Arguing with me will get you nowhere." The duke turned to look at her father. "If it makes you feel any better, when you *are* feeling up to it, Mr. Evans, I shall employ you as my personal horology assistant. The Great Exhibition is only a fortnight away and I'd appreciate your help with the setting up of one of my clocks in the Crystal Palace—it's a new electromechanical design. How does that sound?"

Her father beamed. "I would be delighted."

"Excellent." The duke's mouth turned up in a rare wide smile. "Then it's all decided."

"Evidently," said Emmeline. But she was smiling too.

How could she not? She didn't think she'd stop smiling for the rest of the year.

Chapter 18

Comprising a Brief Description of a Room with a View and a Horny Toad; Followed by a Short Account of How to Manage a Particular Domestic Disaster; And Concluding with a Disconcerting Discussion About Nightcaps and Gloves...

No truer words were ever spoken than *home is where the heart is.*

Indeed, St Lawrence House suddenly felt exactly like that to Emmeline—a true home in every sense—now that her father was safe and sound. The rest of the duke's staff appeared to readily accept Edward Evans into their fold, and Woodley, without even raising an eyebrow, allocated him a cozy bedroom of his own not far from the butler's pantry on the ground floor. It had its own little fireplace with a comfy armchair on the hearthrug, and the single bed had a wonderfully soft mattress. The kitchen was nearby, so delicious cooking smells floated in, and there was a casement window with a view of the back walled garden. With the window open, bees could be heard droning lazily in the lavender and borage hedge.

Her father declared he couldn't have been happier and more content.

Emmeline, while overjoyed at the sudden reversal in her father's fortunes, was torn. The duke had not intended that she or her father would feel indebted to him, but she couldn't help it if she did. Just a little.

Actually, a lot.

As she took dinner with her father and the rest of the duke's servants around the vast oak table in the kitchen—Fanny had returned and had kindly offered to supervise teatime in the nursery while she was away—Emmeline supposed that she would eventually become accustomed to the idea that she didn't owe the duke anything. That he'd taken it upon himself to free her father out of the goodness of his heart and had no other agenda. She would also endeavor to be as professional as she could be. Which meant, she must not entertain any more improper thoughts, daydreams, or fantasies about her employer. She most certainly wouldn't revisit their kiss in the rain.

This time, she really, truly, cross-her-heart-and-hope-to-die meant it.

After her father was all settled in his room for the night (he was quite content to read *Ivanhoe*), and the children had gone to bed, Emmeline retired to her own bedchamber.

She donned her plain white flannel nightgown (Parasol Academy issue, of course), then unpinned her hair before wrangling it into a plait. When she was a newly wedded bride, Jeremy had always liked her to wear her hair out when she came to bed. She supposed she should have known he was being unfaithful when he started not to care how she dressed her hair at night.

Revisiting his betrayal always used to bring tears to Emmeline's eyes and a fresh ache in her chest. She'd even believed at one point that she wasn't enough for a man. That she was somehow lacking. But after her Parasol Academy training, she knew this to be a falsehood. She was a strong, intelligent, hardworking, good-hearted woman who hadn't wed a charming prince but a right royal horny toad who was so weak-willed, he hadn't been able to keep his trousers buttoned.

She deserved better than the likes of Jeremy Chase. Not that she was looking to ever get married again. She had a career now and that was all she needed to make her feel fulfilled.

Odd to think that her employer, a duke, seemed to respect and care for her well-being more than her husband ever had.

With a sigh, Emmeline slid between the chill sheets of her single bed. Even though it was April, it was still cool in the evenings. She was regretting the fact that she hadn't thought to prepare a warming pan of hot coals like she had for her father. The night air seemed to exacerbate his cough, but he'd taken his tonic and when she'd bid him goodnight, he was rugged up in bed before a toasty fire. Emmeline trusted that in time, his chest would clear altogether.

Emmeline put aside her copy of the *Parasol Academy Handbook* (she'd been rereading the chapter on maintaining professionalism) and tucked her quizzing glass into its case (the special blue lens was needed to read the contents of the handbook, otherwise the text looked like nonsense). Then she snuffed out her bedside candle and snuggled down beneath the bedcovers. Thoughts of what she'd do with the duke's wards tomorrow filled her head as she watched her own fire dying down in the grate. If the weather held fair, perhaps they could make a trip to London Zoo. In the morning, she'd check with the duke if he could spare a carriage. It was too late now.

Besides, during dinner, the duke's valet, Babcock, had reported that His Grace had gone out for the evening—to attend a Royal Horological Society meeting and thence to a late dinner with a good friend, Viscount Hartwell, at one of their clubs. He wasn't expected back before midnight.

Blast. Emmeline sat up in bed. In all the excitement that had accompanied her father's arrival, she'd completely forgotten about checking on the clocks about the house; it was clock-winding day for all the larger timepieces which were on an eight-day schedule. Of course, Woodley might have taken on the task already. But she was the one who possessed the most accurate pocket watch.

Sliding from her bed, Emmeline relit her candle, then flipped open her watch. It was half past eleven. It shouldn't take her too long to check on all the longcase clocks and mantel clocks in the main rooms. Even if she made sure the vestibule longcase clock and the clocks in the duke's study were all on time, that would be a start. It was the least she could do, given everything the duke had done for her father.

Emmeline pulled on her Parasol Academy navy-blue dressing gown (complete with a magical pocket—one's charges might need help during the night) and cinched it firmly about her waist. Then she donned her Academy-issued muslin and blond lace nightcap to add an air of "matronly" respectability to her appearance. Aside from the night footman, most of the staff would be abed. But still, it was always best to be appropriately attired, no matter the occasion.

It's a pity that the Parasol Academy Handbook *doesn't contain an incantation for setting clocks and watches to Greenwich Mean Time*, thought Emmeline grumpily. *Now* that *would be exceedingly helpful.* She eyed the hefty tome accusingly as she thrust her feet into her slippers. To her astonishment, the handbook's blue leather cover shimmered, like a scattering of stardust had drifted over it.

It was almost as though the handbook was beckoning to her.

Curious, Emmeline got out her quizzing glass then flipped open the handbook. And then she gasped. The book had opened onto a page that contained an entry entitled: *Timepiece Incantation to Reset Persistently and Irritatingly Irregular Clocks and Watches (to Ensure the Smooth and Efficient Running of the Household).*

What. On. Earth?

She must be dreaming. No, a firm pinch applied to the underside of her wrist confirmed she was wide-awake.

Emmeline knew this book inside out and back to front. Every word, every line was as familiar to her as the back of her own hand. She had never, ever seen this spell before. She flipped back and then forward a few pages. Yes, this was the chapter covering incantations and this was the subsection related to *Managing Domestic Disasters of All Kinds.*

Excitement bubbling in her veins, Emmeline bit her lip as she contemplated the possibilities. What harm could it do to try out this spell? It wasn't as though she'd be traveling through time, or moving it backwards or forwards, or changing the very fabric of existence itself. She was simply setting clocks and watches "to ensure the smooth and efficient running of the household." Apparently, one only had to perform the spell once, and the "ensorcelled" timepieces would remain synchronized to Greenwich Mean Time unless someone physically reset them.

Emmeline took a minute to commit the method and Faerillion incantation to memory, and then, pocket watch in hand and magical words all but dancing and fizzing on the tip of her tongue, she quit her bedroom. According to the handbook, she could only reset the clocks within a single room, not every clock in the house all at the same time. To that end, she'd start in the duke's study.

Emmeline took the servants' stairs to the second floor. Upon entering the study, she found that it was deserted—as she had expected. Horatio usually spent the night on a perch in the duke's suite, and if the duke had returned to St Lawrence House early, no doubt he'd retired for the night too.

Apart from a soft golden puddle surrounding a gas lamp on the duke's desk, the only other sources of light came from the glowing coals in the hearth, a pair of gaslight wall sconces, and a stray moonbeam that had managed to slip through a gap in the claret-red velvet curtains at the casement window. But Emmeline didn't mind. Performing magic in discreet corners and in the shadows was the Academy's preferred mode of practice anyway.

She took up a position in the very center of the room. According to her pocket watch, the duke's mantel clock was running five minutes late while the longcase clock in the corner was two-and-a-half minutes fast. It just wouldn't do.

Holding her watch by its silver chain, Emmeline extended her arm and began to gently swing the timepiece back and forth, back and forth like a pendulum. When it began to spin in tiny circles on its own, she crossed her fingers for luck (this was an untried spell after all), drew a fortifying breath and then murmured the magical words, "*Setify Greenwich Time.*"

Almost immediately, a silvery-blue sphere of light enveloped the watch. It grew and spread rapidly until the entire room was filled with an ethereal iridescent glow. Emmeline felt like she was bathing in shimmering moonlight. And then almost as quickly, the light faded. When Emmeline compared the time on her pocket watch to the time showing on the mantel clock and the longcase clock, all three timepieces were perfectly synchronized.

"Well, that worked rather well, if I do say so myself," she murmured proudly. It was like her pocket watch had become the "queen" clock and the other clocks were "courtier" clocks. While the duke's electromechanical clock prototype in the adjacent Horology Room was a remarkable feat of ingenuity, she rather thought the Parasol Academy's spell was wonderfully effective too.

It was definitely time to move on and sort out the other household clocks. It also occurred to Emmeline that if any of the clocks in the house *did* lose or gain time from now on, it would confirm that a household member *was* behind the tampering, that it wasn't a mechanical fault of the clocks themselves.

She was just quitting the room when she heard a snick and a soft whoosh behind her. There was the rustle of fabric, and the study grew slightly brighter.

"Mrs. Chase?"

Spinning around, her pulse quickening, Emmeline discovered the Duke of St Lawrence standing by the open jib door that led into his Horology Room.

"Y-Your Grace," she stammered breathlessly as she bobbed a curtsy. "I-I had no idea that you were in here. Or at home for that matter. I didn't mean to intrude. I-I popped by t-to reset the clocks. So they wouldn't bother you by chiming or bonging at different times. I know how that annoys you so."

Oh dear. She was babbling but she couldn't seem to stop herself. "I-I suppose I should get on with resetting the others." She took a step toward the door.

"No, don't worry about them," said the duke. He was coatless and his necktie and collar were loose. In one hand he held a cut-crystal tumbler of an amber-hued liquid. Brandy perhaps. "It's too late for that. The rest can wait until tomorrow."

"If you're sure . . ." Reaching behind her, Emmeline felt for the door handle. She was in her nightclothes. She should go. "I shall bid you goodnight then, Your Grace."

But the duke didn't seem ready for her to leave. He gestured toward the fire with a gloved hand. "Why don't you stay? Sit with me awhile. It feels like ages since we last spoke." He paused and then his eyes narrowed. He ran his assessing gaze over her from the top of her cap-clad head to the tips of her blue velvet slippers. "I'm sorry. I can see you're dishabille. If you'd rather not, I would understand."

Heat flared in Emmeline's cheeks. "I . . ." All sorts of reasons *not* to stay formed in Sensible-Emmeline's head. But Not-So-Sensible-Bold-As-You-Please Emmeline discarded them and said instead, "I would like that, Your Grace. As long as I might have a sherry."

Emmeline held her breath. *Did I really have the effrontery to say that? I really did. Oh no, I really—*

The duke's eyes gleamed with an emotion Emmeline couldn't quite place. "Certainly, Mrs. Chase," he said. "As long as you take off that godawful cap."

Emmeline touched the lace edge framing her face. "I think it looks quite fetching." A lie of course, but she was already in danger of falling under the duke's spell and her nightcap made her feel like she was playing the part of the prim-and-proper-all-kinds-of-respectable nanny, even though she feared that deep down, her far more wanton-and-wicked self was preening and flouncing, waiting in the wings for her chance to sneak on stage. "It helps keep my hair in place," she added for good measure.

"It makes you look like one of my old maiden aunts," grumbled the duke. "Great-Aunt Agatha, to be precise. There's a portrait of her on the first-floor landing, not far from my Uncle Nevergrin's."

Emmeline crossed her arms and adopted a stern-nanny frown. "I'm sure you didn't employ me because of my looks, Your Grace."

The duke gave a snort of laughter. "Very well. You have me there. Take a seat, Mrs. Chase, and I will try to put up with the visual abomination of yet another cap that should be consigned to the fire."

Emmeline selected her usual wingchair (oh dear, she did indeed have a usual chair) and the duke returned with her sherry. Before he claimed his own seat, he threw a few logs on the grate and very soon there were bright flames and sparks leaping up the chimney.

"So tell me how your father is settling in," the duke said in a conversational tone as he sat across from her. "And I'd like to hear how my wards are doing." Leaning back in his chair, nursing his brandy glass in his gloved hands, he propped his feet on a footstool and fixed his gaze on Emmeline.

Emmeline set aside her untouched sherry and proceeded to do as the duke had requested. She gave an account of how contented her father was and relayed his wards' academic progress as well as a few amusing anecdotes about the latest harmless nursery shenanigans. The duke gave her permission to take a carriage to the zoo on the morrow and then they lapsed into silence. Emmeline would have liked to have said it was companionable silence, but there was a strange vibration in the air. A crackling energy.

Perhaps a few remnants of the time spell lingered. It couldn't be anything else . . .

The duke tossed back his brandy and sighed. "I'm afraid I'm in one of my bitter-as-black-coffee moods tonight."

"I'm sorry to hear that," said Emmeline. "Babcock mentioned you were attending a Royal Horological Society meeting?"

"Yes, I went." The duke smiled tightly. "Sir Randolph was there being his usual asinine self. George Airy, the Astronomer Royal, attended too. He sounds very interested in my electromechanical clock prototype. He's keen to see how it all works at the Great Exhibition."

"That sounds promising," said Emmeline. "Did something else untoward happen? Did someone follow you again when you left?"

"No. Nothing like that. That's not the reason for my somber mood." The duke paused. "After the meeting, I went to another club with a friend. I should have known better. Gentlemen's clubs are not my cup of tea. Not my cup of anything really. You walk in the door, thinking that you're going to be served a fine brandy"—he lifted his glass and examined the glowing amber liquid within—"but then you discover it's absinthe. A tentative sip promises pleasure but all you're left with is a bitter taste in your mouth and a gnawing, hollow feeling in your gut."

Emmeline frowned. Was the duke a little in his cups? Given Jeremy's propensity for drink, she knew the signs well. She studied the duke's face. He was certainly brooding and melancholy, but his words weren't slurred. His eyes were clear, not glassy. His movements weren't lacking in coordination, or very slow and deliberate, as though he were concentrating on not being clumsy. "I'm sorry," she said.

He arched a brow in query. "For what?"

"I don't like seeing you so out of sorts. I was . . . sympathizing."

His mouth twitched. "Well, seeing you in that cap isn't helping my mood. I wish you'd relent and take it off."

Emmeline straightened in her seat. "It's regulation," she said firmly, even though her wicked self was practically lifting her skirts and flashing her ankles offstage.

The duke snorted. "Rules again. Rules have their place of course. God knows, I have enough of my own." He took a sip of his brandy then set it aside. "Rules, structure, schedules, strict habits, I thrive on them. They are essential for my peace of mind. Take these gloves for instance." He held up a hand and examined the fine black leather that practically resembled a second skin. "Touching anything, unless it's as smooth as satin or a polished surface, feels excruciatingly uncomfortable to me. Rough textures in particular set me on edge, making me grit my teeth. It's almost as though I'm listening to fingernails constantly scraping down a chalkboard. I can't suppress the sensation. My silk-lined gloves make my days . . . bearable."

"How dreadful." Emmeline's heart ached with sympathy. "I can't even imagine what that would feel like. And obviously, I *have* wondered why you wear gloves all the time. Thank you for the explanation."

The duke caught her gaze. Held it. "I've seen you watching my hands. You're probably curious about whether I ever take my gloves off."

Emmeline retrieved her sherry and took a hasty sip. "I . . . I might be . . ."

"I do. Sometimes," he said, his deep voice a dark velvet stroke reaching toward her, coaxing her closer. "Especially if there's something feather-soft and silky that I long to touch." He extended his index finger and traced a seam on the arm of his leather wingchair. "I'll make a deal with you, Mrs. Chase. I'll remove my gloves right now if you remove your cap..."

Oh, if she acquiesced, Emmeline was sure to feel like she was making a bargain with the devil himself. But it seemed she could not resist temptation, even though there were a thousand sensible reasons—most of them delineated quite clearly in the *Parasol Academy Handbook*—not to give in. "Yes," she murmured before she could stop herself. Offstage Emmeline began to sashay about, hips swaying. "I agree."

The duke's chiseled mouth curved into a wicked smile. "Excellent. We have a deal."

Chapter 19

*In Which a Deal Is Adhered to; A Confidence Is Shared;
And the Duke Receives a Much-Desired Lesson...*

Oh goodness, what had she agreed to?

Her breath catching, Emmeline watched as the duke held up his right hand and deftly tugged on the glove's fingertips, loosening the snug fit of the leather before he pulled it off altogether. He tossed the glove onto the table beside his discarded brandy, then proceeded to remove the other one with equal efficiency. "There you are, Mrs. Chase," he said, amusement brimming in his voice as he held up his bare hands, turning them this way, then that. "Aren't you in awe?"

Emmeline swallowed. "They are very handsome," she murmured huskily. It wasn't a lie. Just as she'd imagined, the duke's hands were strong yet elegant looking. His fingers were long, and his nails were neatly trimmed into precise crescents. Fine black hairs dusted the backs. She could even see the outline of a vein or two. She bit her lip as images of what he could do with those hands—those fingers—tumbled through her mind. Her face grew hotter than the dancing fire before them.

He chuckled, the sound rich and delicious. "Handsome hands. I'll accept the compliment, Mrs. Chase." Then his gaze grew darker. Hotter. "Now your turn. Off with your cap."

"Very well..." Emmeline tugged at the ribbon beneath her chin then pulled off the matronly head covering and tossed it beside the duke's gloves. "There. Will that do?"

The duke's gaze wandered over her, tracing the line of her plait, which hung over one shoulder. He didn't answer her question. Instead he murmured, "I had no idea your hair was so long. It really is wondrous to behold."

Emmeline had the sudden urge to unbind it and let it tumble loose about her shoulders, but she didn't. The slippery slope she was on was getting slipperier by the second. (So were particular parts of her person, which was clearly a warning sign that Offstage Emmeline might put in an appearance at any moment. And who knew what *she* would do?)

"Thank you, Your Grace," she managed. Then the mantel clock and longcase clock both heralded the hour in perfect unison. It was midnight. "I suppose I should be going to bed. Or I'll be sure to turn into a pumpkin."

"Well, we wouldn't want that." Ever the gentleman, the duke rose to his feet as she did. "I wish you sweet dreams."

Emmeline knew her dreams would be anything *but* sweet. They'd be hot and delicious and would heavily feature the duke's bare hands doing all sorts of wonderfully wicked things to her body. She reached for her discarded cap on the table beside the duke's gloves, just as the duke did too. Their fingers brushed, and a sizzling heat rushed up Emmeline's arm, engulfing her entirely.

Both of them sucked in startled breaths. Their gazes collided.

"Emmeline," the duke whispered huskily. His warm fingers curled around hers, tugging her closer. "Sweet Emmeline."

In the next moment, Emmeline was in the duke's arms, kissing him hungrily. She gripped the duke's wide shoulders while he clasped her face. One of his hands slid to the back of her head, his fingers spearing into her hair, wreaking ruin on her loose braid.

Oh, dear Lord. If the study were burning, Emmeline wouldn't have cared. Neither did she care that anything within her resembling prudent thought or prim behavior had gone up in flames. All that mattered was this dizzying kiss and the glorious feeling of being wanted by this man.

Of having her desires satisfied. Wanton Emmeline was practically performing backflips and cartwheels and somersaults across the stage.

They broke apart. "We shouldn't," she whispered, want thrumming fiercely though her veins, gathering low in her belly and making her nipples peak and ache. It took everything within her *not* to throw off her dressing gown and undo the buttons of her nightgown, baring her breasts to the duke's gaze. To his touch. His kisses . . .

"Yes. You're right. We said we wouldn't kiss again after the first time. That we'd forget all about it . . ." The duke was rubbing the curling ends of her plait between his fingertips. He swallowed. "We shouldn't."

His burning blue eyes lifted to hers. "But I can't help it. I want you so very much. It's like I've taken a tiny sip of something utterly divine, and now I want the whole damn bottle."

A heartbeat later, they were kissing once more, tongues tangling, hot ragged breaths melding. Emmeline's heartbeat pounded in her ears, and lust throbbed between her thighs. She pressed herself against the duke's long, lean, hard body like a wild creature in heat. Her fingers tugged clumsily at his shirt, pulling it free from his trousers. And when her palm found his taut abdomen, a deep groan rumbled in his throat.

Through the velvet of her robe and fabric of her nightgown, she could feel the duke's great need for her. There was no doubt in her mind that he wanted her as much as she wanted him.

But, but . . . Something sharp and thorny and thistlelike—a bothersome burr of a thought—pricked at the back of her mind. She needed to make something clear.

"Your Grace—"

"Xavier," he all but growled. "When we're being intimate like this, you must call me Xavier."

He dragged his lips across her jawline. Nipped at her earlobe then soothed the spot with his tongue. Oh, she couldn't think when he did that. "Xavier," she murmured. "I . . . I want to go further than kisses. I want more than a little taste. And I know you do too. But I need . . ." She inhaled a shaky breath and caught his heavy-lidded gaze. "Before we do anything else, I need you to know that this isn't me offering myself to you as a form . . . as a form of payment . . . for what you did for my father today. I'm not like that. I don't want you to think badly of me."

"What?" The duke—Xavier—drew back. His black brows had slanted into a frown. "Of course I don't think that. I would *never* expect that from you or any woman. You don't owe me anything, Emmeline. I'm *not* the sort of nobleman who demands sexual favors. I certainly don't want you to be with me out of gratitude, or worse, because you feel obliged to." He stroked her cheek with the back of his fingers. "And I would never, ever think ill of you. I have nothing but the highest regard and admiration for you."

Emmeline nodded. "I believe you," she murmured.

"Good," said Xavier in that irresistible, dark-melted-chocolate voice of his. "Just be with me. Just this once. That's all I ask. Let me kiss you, touch you." He dragged his hot mouth across her cheek, nuzzled her ear, making her shiver. "We're here because we both want to be," he murmured thickly. "Because we both need to ease this distracting, interminable ache that exists inside both of us." Drawing back, he tipped her chin up with the crook of his finger. "Agreed?"

Helplessly ensnared in his smoldering gaze, Emmeline nodded. "Yes," she whispered. The duke knew exactly how she felt because he felt it too. If she didn't do something to appease the unspent desire sparking inside her, she might very well expire.

Just this once.

Once will be enough. Surely. And what harm could it do?

No one else will know. Just the duke and I.

Emmeline curled her fingers around Xavier's side, tracing the smooth curve of his lean ribs. When he flinched a little, she frowned and withdrew her hand. "Do my caresses bother you? You told me once that you didn't like unexpected touching."

"No." He smiled down at her. "Not at all. I'm simply not used to having someone else touch me *there*. And I've just discovered I'm ticklish in that area."

Emmeline laughed softly. "The great Duke of St Lawrence is ticklish? Good heavens." She wound her hands about his neck. "And how does it feel to touch me? Without your gloves on?"

Xavier bent his head and rested his forehead against hers. "Amazing. Glorious," he murmured. His bare hand rested against her neck, his thumb stroking her nape. "Your skin is as soft and smooth as cream. Your lips feel like satin. Your tongue is like velvet and your hair reminds me of the finest silk. I want to sift it through my fingers. Bury my face in it. Watch the strands change color in the firelight."

Oh my . . . "I'm beyond flattered," Emmeline whispered. Jeremy had never said such beautiful things to her. And he was a playwright. A man who was supposed to be adept with words.

"It's true," said Xavier. And then he was kissing her again and Emmeline was spinning, spinning, spinning away into the stars. At some point, Xavier pulled her down with him onto his wingchair so Emmeline was sitting across his lap. When eventually they drew apart, both of them panting, Emmeline was smiling but Xavier wasn't.

"What's wrong?" she murmured, cupping his jaw. His night

beard abraded her fingertips. "Are you having second thoughts about . . . about us being together like this?"

Xavier caught her hand and kissed her palm. "No, it's not that. I need to tell you something. Something that you should know about me."

"Well, I know you don't have a secret wife hidden in the attic," she said. "I've been up there."

Xavier laughed too. "No, nothing as dramatic as all that. It's a little embarrassing though." Then he inhaled a deep breath as though he were about to hurl himself over a cliff into a freezing cold ocean. "I've . . . I've never been with a woman before."

Oh . . . Emmeline touched his lean cheek where a muscle had begun to tick. "Are you telling me that you're a virgin?"

Xavier grimaced. "I'm afraid so. If you don't want to go any further after all, because I lack experience, I would understand. I am but a novice when it comes to lovemaking. You're a widow and in your eyes, I might be woefully inadequate."

Emmeline cradled his face between her hands. "First of all, the way you kiss—by the book—I would never have known. And secondly"—she leaned forward and brushed her lips over his. "I don't mind at all. In fact, I'm honored that you've entrusted me with your secret."

His mouth hitched in a smile. "I've studied of course. Read books, as you mentioned, detailing methods. Techniques. I've pored over salacious etchings. I've also kissed several women."

Emmeline raised an eyebrow. "At these gentlemen's clubs?"

"Yes. And on the rare occasion I've attended a ball, I've kissed an obliging widow or two. But nothing more than that."

"Well, *this* particular widow is very obliging," said Emmeline softly. "You're a clever man, and I also suspect a very fast learner. Given your attention to detail, I'm absolutely certain you'll be a wonderful lover."

"I can but try. I'm not even certain that I want to lose my virginity tonight. I don't want to put you in a position where you'll have to worry about . . ." He swallowed. "I don't want to ruin you by getting you with child."

"I never fell pregnant when I was married," said Emmeline. The words didn't sting as much as they used to. While she adored children, and had always hoped she'd be a mother herself one day, she'd come to accept that for her, it simply wasn't to be. She might be a nanny first and foremost, and must appear to be chaste, but she was also human. And oh, it had been such a long time since she'd been with a man. But it was more than that: She so wanted to find pleasure with *this* man.

She looked up through her eyelashes at Xavier. "Naturally, one doesn't have to play at couch-quail to be satisfied."

The duke gave a soft laugh. "Play at couch-quail. I like that. And I'm aware there are many ways to share physical pleasure." Xavier's expression changed. His gaze grew heavy. Hotter. *Intentional.* "May I?" He raised a hand, his palm hovering over the swell of one of her breasts. "May I touch you here?"

Moved by the fact that this man, a *duke*, would ask her permission, Emmeline nodded. "I would love it if you did," she whispered.

And then she closed her eyes as Xavier's hand closed over her. Gently kneading, testing the feel of her through the fabric of her nightclothes. Running his thumb over the taut, straining peak beneath. Rubbing and teasing and pinching and *ooooh* . . .

It wasn't enough. Her body demanded more.

Her fingers trembling, Emmeline clumsily pulled open her robe and slid the mother-of-pearl buttons of her nightgown's bodice undone. Guided Xavier's hand inside so his warm bare flesh was touching her bare flesh. Desire rose in a great wave and Emmeline whimpered.

"Let me see you." Xavier groaned, and when she obliged, parting the fabric so her breasts were exposed, he groaned again. "You're beautiful," he whispered raggedly, his gaze drinking her in, savoring her nakedness like she was a veritable feast, and he was a starving man. "I'm in awe."

He feathered a caress over her collarbones and then his long fingers stroked and delicately plucked at her nipple. Circled her sensitive flesh, raising goose bumps and provoking delicious shivers. All the while he nuzzled and nibbled at her neck, and it wasn't long before Emmeline was shifting restlessly in his lap.

"Kiss me here," she all but pleaded, touching where his wicked fingers played.

The duke's growled reply came almost immediately. "With relish..."

If Xavier hadn't told Emmeline that he was a novice, she would never have known. His greedy lips, his sinuous tongue were hot and eager, and it wasn't long before Emmeline was moaning in utter abandonment, arching her back, clutching at his head, flagrantly pressing herself into his mouth.

The soft core of her was now throbbing and needy and she slid up the hem of her nightgown in blatant invitation. "You can touch me here too," she whispered. "If you want to..."

Xavier lifted his head. "Oh, believe me," he rasped. "I want to. But I don't want to fumble about, guessing what you like. You must teach me. I want to learn what pleases you."

Emmeline's cheeks grew hot and so did the slick juncture between her thighs. "Very well," she whispered. She couldn't refuse this man when there was such raw, naked need in his eyes. Such earnest longing.

Covering the duke's hand with her own once more, she showed him how to stroke her. How to tease and torment and relentlessly nudge her toward the edge of bliss. His gliding, circling fingers grew more confident, more knowing, and as pleasure built, Emmeline let him take control. Holding on to his strong wrist, she shamelessly undulated against his hand until pleasure welled and rushed through her in a hot pulsing surge.

And then Xavier was kissing her, absorbing her soft shuddering gasp of release, as he wrapped her up in his arms.

When the ripples of bliss at last began to ebb and her faculties returned, Emmeline straightened a little and murmured, "You are quite the student, Your Grace. But I don't think the lesson has quite ended."

The duke frowned down at her. "What do you mean? I thought you... Did you not achieve satisfaction? The way you gasped and then went boneless in my arms—"

"Shhhh." Emmeline pressed a finger to his lips. "I did, and it was magnificent. What I mean to say is, it's my turn to demonstrate how a woman can please you." She cast him a coquettish smile as she wiggled her derriere a little. "You certainly feel up to it."

"You certainly feel up to it..."

God's blood. Xavier clenched his jaw as a hot pulse of lust bolted through him. Never in his life had he felt so aroused or so alive.

So *wanted.*

"Well, I've never had a half-naked woman in my lap before," he said in a voice that was none too steady. "Come to think of it, I've never even had a fully clothed woman *in* my lap until tonight."

A light peal of laughter fell from Mrs. Chase's—no, *Emmeline's*—kiss-swollen lips. "That's not quite true," she said, her bright blue eyes dancing. "The first two times we met, I ended up straddling you. Surely that counts."

Xavier tucked a loosened lock of her silky hair behind her shell-like ear. He didn't think he'd ever grow tired of touching her hair. "How could I forget?" he murmured.

She adjusted her position slightly and he couldn't contain a hiss.

"Oh, I'm sorry," she murmured. "Did I hurt you?"

He laughed. "No, but I *am* in agony. I'm sure you can tell I'm about to burst."

She smiled a siren's smile and one of her hands crept between their bodies. Her fingertips slid beneath his shirt and pressed against the waistband of his trousers. "I can fix that."

Xavier frowned. "Only if you truly want to. I would never presume..."

"Oh, I want to," replied Emmeline, her lovely voice husky with desire. "I want to very much."

Slowly, teasingly, she unfastened the fall of his trousers and without hesitation, clasped his hot, heavy, throbbing length. On a half-anguished, half-relieved groan, Xavier's head fell back into the corner of the wingchair. Closing his eyes, he gave himself over to Emmeline's wicked ministrations. Her fingers were deft and sure as she worked him into a frenzied lather, his raging lust gathering force with each stroke and squeeze and...

Oh God, he was undone.

Gripping the arms of the chair, Xavier quaked and groaned as he lost complete control. Exquisite pleasure broke over him, crashed through him like a massive cataclysmic wave, stealing his breath and obliterating every single thought except one...

Emmeline. My sweet Emmeline...

Gathering her close, he pressed a kiss to her temple. "My valet is going to kill me," he murmured huskily into her vanilla-and-violet–scented hair.

Emmeline's shoulders shook with laughter. "Quite possibly." She pressed a kiss to his throat and his jaw then sat up. "Perhaps we should have thought ahead and made use of a handkerchief."

"I have one in my pocket if you need one."

"So do I," said Emmeline. "But I have a better idea."

Xavier cocked a brow. "Really?"

Emmeline smiled mysteriously. "Yes, really. But you must

shut your eyes and promise not to peek. No matter what happens." She poked his chest. "On pain of death."

Both bemused and intrigued, Xavier chuckled. "By Jove. Whatever you're going to do sounds like serious business indeed." Nevertheless, he complied with Emmeline's request.

No sooner had his eyelids fallen closed, he felt Emmeline shift slightly and whisper something completely nonsensical. "*Unsmirchify.*"

Almost immediately there was a soft humming sound. A faint tingling warmth passed over his skin and the very air around him seem to be illuminated for a brief second.

What the deuce?

"You can open your eyes now, Xavier."

Xavier did and then sucked in a startled breath. The aftermath of his release had completely disappeared. His entire person was spotless. And so was the nanny's. Her nightgown was done up and not a hair was out of place.

"How? Wh-What?" he stammered. "What on earth do they teach you at the Parasol Academy?"

"All Parasol nannies and governesses are trained in advanced cleaning techniques," she said, climbing off his lap.

"Advanced cleaning techniques?" Xavier stood too. Even his trousers were done up and his shirt tucked in. "Is that a euphemism for witchcraft?"

She laughed. "Surely you're not suggesting that I'm a witch, Your Grace? We both know that witches aren't real. Just like ghosts and trolls and mermaids don't exist."

She was right, of course. And suddenly the scientist in him didn't much care that he didn't have a logical explanation for what had happened. The universe itself contained countless untold mysteries after all.

Emmeline Chase had magic in her voice and her fingers, her eyes and her smile. Who was he to question that?

He pulled her into his arms. "Well, you've done a good job

of bewitching me tonight, Mrs. Chase," he said softly. "I don't know what you did or how you did it, but I'm grateful that I won't need to face the wrath of my valet."

She fiddled with the points of his collar. "I had a wonderful time too," she said almost shyly. Or was there regret in her tone? She wouldn't meet his eyes.

He stroked a finger down her nose. "I know this must be a once-only occasion. You have a reputation you wish to maintain and I . . ." He caught her chin gently and tilted up her face so she couldn't escape his gaze. "While I loved what we did—and I'm touched beyond measure that you were so very patient with me, showing me things that I'd never experienced before—I cannot offer you more than this. I'm very much a confirmed bachelor. And as for anything else—"

"There's no need to explain, Your Grace." Mrs. Chase's mouth lifted into a wry sort of smile. "I understand, more than you know. You're a duke. A blue blood. I'm a nanny from Cheapside. While I've broken far too many Parasol Academy rules tonight, I want to assure you that I will continue to do my very best when caring for your wards. My duty to them will not be neglected."

"I know it won't," said Xavier. "You are nothing but conscientious."

All of a sudden, the lights in the gaslit wall sconces began to flicker.

Xavier narrowed his eyes. *How odd . . .*

The next moment, the gaslights went out completely.

Mrs. Chase was frowning too. "I wonder if only the lighting in here has been affected, or if the gaslights have stopped working throughout the house."

"There's only one way to find out."

Xavier exited his study, the nanny following close behind. The wall sconces in the hall had all gone out too. Everything was bathed in deep shadow.

"I'll have the issue thoroughly investigated tomorrow," said Xavier. His gut tightened. Had the saboteur struck again? "I'll also accompany the night footman on a round to check everything is secure."

"Are you worried something untoward is happening? Another break-in attempt perhaps?" Emmeline sounded concerned but not alarmed.

Xavier rubbed a hand down his face. "I hope not. The problem is, I don't know."

"I'll check on your wards on my way back to my room," said Emmeline.

"Would you like a candle?" asked Xavier.

But the nanny shook her head. "There's enough moonlight to light my way," she said. She reached out as though she were about to touch his arm, but then her hand fell away. "Take care, Your Grace," she said softly.

"You too, Mrs. Chase. Goodnight."

As Xavier watched the nanny retreat down the darkened hallway, heading for the servants' stairs, he clenched his ungloved hands. Regret and melancholy swirled in his belly and rose up to tighten his chest. Constrict his throat.

Damn it.

If things were different . . . if he were just Mr. Xavier Mason and not the Duke of St Lawrence, then he wouldn't have to set aside the woman who made him feel like the king of men. Who made him feel seen and valued and not like a carnival spectacle to be whispered about and laughed at. To be shunned by many despite the fact he was a "blue blood."

But *if only*s were useless, he reminded himself sternly as he headed downstairs to seek out the night footman. Best to draw a line under this night, firmly shut the door on it, and focus on his other passion, horology. Clocks and watches and the science behind them—his plans to make a name for himself as a first-rate horologist, to be the best in his field and the brilliant designer of the "King of Clocks" at Westminster Palace—would be more than enough, even if those dreams would never keep him warm at night or offer him blissful violet-scented oblivion.

Would that he could extinguish his dreams featuring Mrs. Chase.

After tonight, Xavier was certain that they would stay with him until the end of his days.

Chapter 20

Concerning a Great Exhibition, a Hot-Air Balloon (not Puff Balloon), Plaid-Clad Cocks, Pink Fountains, Lemonade, and Leeches...

"Unfortunately, another maid has left in the night without a word, Your Grace," announced Woodley in doleful tones.

Xavier scowled at his own reflection in the full-length bedchamber mirror. That would make the third in two weeks. *Damn it.*

Xavier's valet, Babcock, made a tsking sound. "Flighty things," he said, adjusting Xavier's necktie. "A few flickering lights and they flee like startled rabbits. It's quite ridiculous if you ask me."

"Mrs. Lambton suspects at least half the female staff members think it's the St Lawrence House Ghost who's responsible," said Woodley. "So yes, it's quite ridiculous if not outright irrational behavior. There's no accounting for the foolishness of females."

"I think that's a gross exaggeration and oversimplification," said Xavier gruffly. "Take Mrs. Chase and Mrs. Lambton for instance. They are far from foolish or irrational."

"My apologies, Your Grace," said Woodley. "You are quite right. There are exceptions to every rule."

Xavier gave an internal eyeroll. He knew from experience

that changing the butler's mind about women was as futile as trying to plug a whale-sized hole in a tugboat. It was time to steer the conversation back on course. Considering Xavier had been avoiding Mrs. Chase lately—keeping her at arm's length seemed the sensible thing to do since their late-night tryst a fortnight ago—he'd been garnering his intelligence about any odd goings-on within the walls of St Lawrence House in other ways. "Is there any news on what's wrong with the gas lighting?"

Woodley sighed heavily. "I'm afraid not, Your Grace. The man from the gasworks company reported that there's nothing wrong with the lines inside or outside the house. It's all a bit of a mystery."

"It's a dashed nuisance, that's what it is," grumbled Xavier.

He picked up his cold cup of morning coffee from the dressing table, then set it aside with a grimace. At this rate, there'd be no servants left at St Lawrence House by Christmas. Not only that, but it looked like he'd be working by candlelight to get the Westminster clock design completed in time for the first of June deadline. He really couldn't afford to waste precious time worrying about yet another raft of domestic disasters. Especially not today.

It was the first of May, and at long last, the Great Exhibition at Hyde Park was opening to great fanfare. Xavier's superbly accurate electromechanical clock was installed in the Crystal Palace—in fact his "Queen of Clocks" had pride of place at the entrance of the enormous glass pavilion—and he was filled with both pride and nervous anticipation. If Her Majesty and Prince Albert marveled at his latest invention, then the Astronomer Royal would have to take note. Xavier might even be in the running to win a Council Medal for innovation or one of the many Prize Medals for craftsmanship.

That sort of recognition certainly couldn't hurt when Xavier's unique design for the Westminster clock was considered.

That was the plan at any rate. And then perhaps Sir Randolph Redvers wouldn't be strutting about the next Royal Horological Society meeting like a plaid-clad cock o' the walk.

When Babcock stopped fussing over Xavier's attire, a Savile Row black suit paired with a silver-gray silk waistcoat and a black silk topper—the valet had insisted the Duke of St Lawrence must look his best for such a grand occasion—Xavier descended to the entry hall below. As per his request, he found Mrs. Chase waiting with his wards. Fanny the under-nurserymaid, and the two footmen, Bertie and Ollie, were also in attendance. Even Horatio was present. The only one absent was Mrs. Chase's father, Edward; Woodley had informed Xavier that the man was poorly this morning. Xavier would send for his own personal physician if the man's condition didn't improve soon.

Xavier glanced at the nanny. She looked a little wan, too, come to think of it. Perhaps she was worried about her father. He would ask her how she was feeling in a quiet moment.

Turning to his wards, he greeted Harry, Bartholomew, and Gareth in turn. "Are we all excited about attending the Great Exhibition?" he asked. "I can see you're all in your very best attire."

"We are beyond excited, Cousin Xavier," declared Harry. Behind her glasses, her brown eyes were alight with unfettered enthusiasm. "I cannot wait to see all the latest scientific inventions and the Crystal Palace itself. The *Times* mentioned that it's three times longer than St Paul's Cathedral, ten stories high, and there's a fountain made of four tons of pink glass!" She lifted up a Great Exhibition guidebook and pencil. "I'm going to make notes about everything. I also have a list of things I most want to see."

"I want to see the dinosaurs," said Bartholomew, bouncing on his toes. "And the Queen."

"Nanny Chase says there'll be a puff balloon," said Gareth. "Can I go flying in it?"

"Up, up, and away," crowed Horatio from the gas chandelier above their heads.

Mrs. Chase laughed. "While I believe there *will* be a hot-air balloon at the Exhibition's opening—at least according to the newspapers—I'm not sure if His Grace knows the answer to your question about riding in it, Gareth," she said. "But I'm certain there will be plenty of other things to marvel at. Scientific inventions, dinosaurs, and the Queen at the very least. And of course, His Grace's magnificent Queen of Clocks."

Xavier's cheeks grew unaccountably hot at receiving the young woman's praise. To cover his discomfiture, he checked his pocket watch—it was a quarter to ten—and suggested that they all get going to make sure they arrived in time. While Hyde Park wasn't that far away, Xavier had heard that a crowd of over twenty-five thousand was expected.

Once they'd trooped outside to where a matching pair of ducal town coaches awaited, Xavier approached Mrs. Chase. "I'd like you and the children to travel with me," he said. "I know I shouldn't worry so much, but in light of recent events, I'd feel better if you all stayed close." It wasn't a complete fib. Then again, if he were honest with himself, he would acknowledge his eyes were yearning to surreptitiously feast upon the woman.

The nanny dipped into a curtsy. "Of course, Your Grace."

Even though Mrs. Chase's cheeks were paler than usual, Xavier thought she looked particularly fetching today. She was attired in her regulation Parasol Academy uniform of a navy-blue wool gown, but instead of wearing a snow-white cotton pinafore, she was sporting a navy shoulder cape trimmed with black, military-style frogging and a matching bonnet tied with black silk ribbons beneath her pert chin. Rather than her umbrella, she carried a dark-blue parasol trimmed with frothy white lace.

As far as he could tell, she wasn't wearing one of her hideous caps. Although if there was one hidden beneath her bonnet, he supposed she had to wear it because she was out in public, representing the Academy.

Once they were all installed in one of the town coaches—along with Horatio, who'd decided to perch on Xavier's shoulder—Xavier regaled his wards with a brief summary of the morning's proceedings and what they could expect to see.

"As Nanny Chase mentioned, there will be a hot-air balloon launch at eleven o'clock sharp. And then the Queen and Prince Albert will be arriving at noon. I hear there will be a cannon salute and a choir, and once all the official business is over, you'll be able to explore all the exhibits. I believe there's over one hundred thousand items on display," said Xavier.

"One hundred thousand," breathed Bartholomew. "Gosh, I can't even count to a hundred yet."

Young Gareth screwed his nose up. "I can only count to ten," he said, then proceeded to demonstrate his skill by counting his small fingers.

"I want to visit the machinery room most of all," said Harry. "I'd especially like to see Dr. Merryweather's tempest prognosticator, which uses leeches to forecast the weather, and the velocipede—it has wheels and pedals and you can ride on it. Oh, and there are daguerreotypes of the actual moon!" She held up her notebook. "See. They are all on my list."

Xavier laughed. "I don't think we'll have time to see *everything* that's on display in one day, but Nanny Chase and I will endeavor to show you as much as we can."

"We will indeed," agreed the nanny. "As long as all three of you promise to be on your best behavior while the official proceedings take place. I don't want to witness any unruly shenanigans, especially when Her Majesty arrives."

"We promise. We promise," all three children chorused in unison.

"That goes for you too, Horatio," said Mrs. Chase sternly as she pointed at the raven. "And you are not to go anywhere near Dr. Merryweather's leeches. I saw that gleam in your eyes when Harry mentioned them."

To Xavier's surprise, his raven tilted his head as though in acquiescence. "Yes, Nanny Chase," he cawed. "Whatever you say, Nanny Chase."

"Good," said Mrs. Chase with a firm nod. She sat back in her seat and sat primly with her parasol across her lap.

No doubt she had to be on her best behavior too. It was Xavier's understanding that Queen Victoria had once employed Mrs. Felicity Temple, the headmistress of the Parasol Academy, and that's why the college had been awarded a Royal Charter. It would reflect badly on the Parasol Academy if one of their nannies couldn't effectively manage the behavior of her charges.

Xavier, for one, had no doubt at all that Mrs. Chase would do a stellar job today. Harry, Bartholomew, and Gareth had already come a long way. In a handful of weeks, they'd gone from rumbustious ruffians to well-behaved and delightfully engaged children.

Better yet, they were happy, and seeing them all so content gave him great satisfaction. No, it was more than that. He enjoyed spending time in their company too.

With respect to his wards, employing Emmeline Chase had been the best decision Xavier had ever made.

Although, when it came to his own peace of mind, Xavier was starting to feel like he was as tormented as an opium-eater. Right in front of him, sedately dressed in navy-blue wool, her lightly freckled face surrounded by a bright nimbus of copper hair, was the one thing he wanted, but for so many sound, logical reasons, couldn't have.

Xavier turned his gaze away to stare disconsolately out the window. The day was fine, but he suddenly felt as though a somber cloud had passed over the sun and blotted out all the light. If he weren't careful, before too long he'd likely resemble the fabled ghost that roamed the halls of St Lawrence House. The problem was, besides throwing himself headlong into his work, he had no idea what else to do in order to assuage his obsession with Mrs. Chase.

His plan, so far, to conquer his incessant yearning for her company, was failing on a scale as spectacular as Napoleon's fall at Waterloo.

"Nanny Chase, is that *really* Queen Victoria?" asked Bartholomew in a loud whisper. His nose wrinkled as though he was far from impressed. "If it is, she's rather short. But she has kind eyes."

Emmeline, the children, the duke, and the rest of his small retinue of servants were all gathered near the Duke of St Lawrence's "Queen of Clocks" as the royal party admired it. (Upon their arrival, Horatio had flown off to cavort about Hyde Park.)

The duke's clock stood in the central gallery midway between the western entrance of the Crystal Palace and the magnificent pink glass fountain, and it seemed to be attracting a lot of attention judging by the oohs and aahs. (In Emmeline's mind, oohing and aahing could only be a good thing.)

Emmeline bent low and whispered back to Bartholomew, "Yes, that is the Queen. And her height doesn't matter. I have no doubt she is very wise and fair-minded. Those are the qualities that are most important when you are a ruling monarch."

"I reckon Harry could be Queen. Or even you, Nanny Chase," said Gareth, looking up at her. "You're smart. And prettier."

Emmeline was about to say that one's attractiveness shouldn't be a prerequisite for anything much at all, when the Duke of St Lawrence leaned close to her ear and murmured, "Of course, you *are* right. But then so is Gareth."

Blushing, Emmeline turned to look at the duke, but he was moving away to speak with a smartly dressed, middle-aged gentleman with graying hair, muttonchops, and a pair of silver-framed spectacles perched on his nose. The Astronomer Royal. The duke had pointed him out earlier during the official opening ceremony.

Emmeline thought he looked suitably impressed with the duke's clock. If anyone deserved accolades for his ingenuity, it was the Duke of St Lawrence. In Emmeline's mind, he also deserved accolades for being wise, fair-minded, *and* attractive in a disconcerting, steal-your-breath sort of way. *Not* being infatuated with the duke was still proving to be an impossible feat, especially after their passionate study tryst.

However, now was *not* the time to be dwelling on the unattainable and all the if-onlys and what-might-have-beens. Emmeline needed to stay focused on looking after Harry, Bartholomew, and Gareth. There were thousands of people congregating inside the massive Crystal Palace, and it would be quite easy for the children to get lost.

Despite the crowds, Emmeline had spotted several other Parasol Academy nannies and governesses—their uniforms made them hard to miss. There was even a Parasol nanny discreetly minding two of the Royal children who'd accompanied the Queen and Prince Albert to the Exhibition's opening.

Her fellow Parasol graduates had all smiled and tilted their heads at Emmeline before returning their attentions to their own charges. In a way, it was reassuring to know that if anything untoward should happen today—if God forbid Harry, Bartholomew, or Gareth *did* wander off—she might have other well-trained Parasol Academy sisters to call upon for help.

Emmeline also had her Academy-issued parasol at hand; like her umbrella, it had a very useful Point-of-Confusion at the tip. Hopefully she wouldn't have to use it or her sheathed ankle-knife. Or any other items related to the physical protection of her charges. The duke was a wealthy man, with a target on his back already. She couldn't afford to let her guard down, even for a split second.

Who knew what devious types might be skulking about in the crowd?

At that moment one of London's premier skulkers—Sir Randolph "Bottom" Redvers—skulked into view. Although considering the odious man's abrasive guffaw preceded his actual appearance—combined with the fact he was wearing another garish plaid suit in shades of purple, green, and egg-yolk yellow (the baronet's tailor really needed his eyes checked)—she would have to concede that he wasn't *skulking* per se. Especially since he was also surrounded by several toadying gentlemen who were equally as loud in both demeanor and attire.

Emmeline didn't recognize any of his acquaintances. Not that she was expecting to see the two thugs who'd chased after her and His Grace almost three weeks ago. But it never hurt to keep one's eyes peeled for danger. Just as it didn't hurt to trust one's gut or one's hackles if they began to prickle. Prickling hackles most of all, as per the *Parasol Academy Handbook*, Chapter 1, Section 8, Paragraph 12.

As soon as the royal party moved away—Emmeline did wonder if Sir Randolph's sartorial choices had precipitated the retreat more than his overbearing manner; the Queen was known to be fond of tartan, but surely not *that* sort of eye-wateringly offensive pattern—the baronet approached the Duke of St Lawrence's clock. He cocked his head to one side and his narrowed eyes ran over it from top to bottom as though he were a sergeant major examining his troops.

"So I hear this is the Queen of Clocks," Sir Randolph announced in trumpeting tones to no one in particular. "It's pretty enough. If you like that sort of fussy design." He made a show of peering at the plaque beneath the clock that described its unique features. "And it's electromechanical you say, Your

Grace?" he threw over his shoulder at the duke. "And incredibly accurate?" The baronet pulled a gilt pocket watch from his purple silk waistcoat, flipped it open, then smirked. "*Almost* on time. A valiant effort, St Lawrence. Who knows, with any luck, your clock might even be in the running to win a Prize Medal. Which would be a feat in and of itself given your reputation."

"My reputation as a horologist speaks for itself," replied the duke frostily. "And my clock keeps perfect time."

"Well, I for one, am *most* impressed," said the Astronomer Royal to the duke. "Indeed, I suspect your design is innovative enough to be considered for a Council Medal." He tilted into a bow. "I look forward to seeing your final design for the Westminster clock when submitted, Your Grace." And then he moved off into the crowd, wandering after the Queen and her retinue. Thank goodness Sir Randolph did too.

Gareth tugged at Emmeline's sleeve. "Nanny Chase, I would like some lemonade, please."

"And I would like to see the dinosaurs," added Bartholomew. "Then the cat circus."

"The performing cats and the dinosaur exhibit are outside, according to the Exhibition guide," said Harry, her nose in the booklet. "But if we go through that door"—she pointed over her shoulder—"we'll be in the machinery room. We could go there first."

Bartholomew pouted. "That's not fair. And machines are boring."

"I'm really, really thirsty," complained Gareth.

Oh dear. Sensing a three-pronged mutiny on the horizon, Emmeline drew a deep breath. "Why don't we all have lemonade first? There's a refreshment court close by, behind the exotic plant conservatory over there. Then we can work out our plan of attack for the rest of the day. Rest assured, everyone will get to see what they want."

Harry gave a dramatic sigh. "Very well, Nanny Chase."

"I suppose so," conceded Bartholomew.

"Hurrah! Lemonade!" cried Gareth, clapping his hands.

"Well done, Mrs. Chase," said the duke as they made their way toward their destination in the exhibition hall's north transept. The boys walked ahead with Bertie and Ollie while Harry, her nose still in the Exhibition guidebook, strolled beside Fanny. "Are you sure you didn't study diplomacy at the Parasol Academy?"

"Actually, there is a chapter on fielding arguments and fair negotiation strategies," Emmeline replied, her eyes on her charges.

"If it will make your life any easier," he said, "I could take Miss Harriet along with Fanny to see the machinery while you take the boys outside to see the cat show and dinosaurs."

Emmeline glanced at the duke as they wandered past a grove of elm trees. "If you're sure, Your Grace. If you have other noblemen and dignitaries you wish to meet with, I'm sure I can manage. Especially since I also have Bertie and Ollie to help with the boys."

The duke's mouth slanted into a lopsided smile. "Oh, so is this your subtle way of telling me you don't need me, Mrs. Chase? I know when I'm not wanted."

"I . . . That's not . . . I apologize if—" Emmeline broke off as she realized the duke was laughing at her. "You're lucky I don't give you a spank with my parasol, Your Grace," she said with a quelling look.

The duke cocked a brow. "I thought you didn't believe in corporal punishment?"

"For children. Impertinent dukes however . . ." Emmeline playfully wagged a finger.

"And what about impertinent nannies?" teased the duke, his eyes dancing with mischief. "What should be done with them?" He spun his cane, then tossed it from one gloved hand to the other.

"I shall not rise to your bait, Your Grace," said Emmeline primly. "I will *not* comment on how you might use your cane on my person. Nor your sheathed sword." Ooh, but she was stepping well outside the dictates of decorum now. It was a good thing the duke's wards were ahead and out of immediate earshot, but she couldn't seem to keep her undisciplined tongue in check.

"What about my *un*sheathed sword?" returned the duke in a low voice.

Did His Grace really just say that? Emmeline blushed and laughed at the same time. To steer the conversation in a different, more sedate direction she ventured, "Now if you're challenging me to a bout of fencing, I'm game for that, Your Grace."

"You fence?"

"Yes indeed. I could do with some regular practice. Although I prefer the foil, I could make do with a rapier at a pinch."

"Gadzooks, is there anything you cannot do?"

She threw the duke an arch smile. "I cannot fly. But I think you already knew that."

"Honestly, Mrs. Chase, I'm not even convinced of that anymore," said the duke. "I still don't know how you came to be on my roof. Or how you managed to clean—" Color crept along the crests of his high cheekbones. "My apologies. We agreed that we would not speak of that evening. I cannot forget it though. No matter how hard I try."

"I know," said Emmeline softly. "I'm much the same."

The duke sighed. "And of course, I shouldn't be talking to you about it now. Or openly flirting with you in public. It's just that you seemed a bit out of sorts earlier on, and I wanted to see you smile. When you do, it makes me feel . . ." His words trailed away, then he stopped walking. Turned to face her. "Forgive me."

Emmeline stopped too. They'd reached the tropical "conservatory" and the shadow of an enormous palm frond cast the duke's austere features half in light, half in shadow. "There's nothing to forgive, Your Grace. I—"

Emmeline halted, her breath catching. In the crowd, a few yards away, she spied a ginger-haired man with a tweed cap pulled low on his brow. Their eyes met fleetingly, then he was gone again, swallowed up by the milling throng.

Freddy?

"What is it?" The duke reached out to clasp her arm. "Is something wrong?"

"Oh, it's-it's nothing. I simply saw a man with red hair, and for a moment I thought he was my brother. I-I could have been mistaken. He's gone now."

The duke looked around. "Are you sure it's *not* him?"

"I doubt that Freddy could afford a ticket to the Great Exhibition," said Emmeline. "And even if he managed to secure one, I suppose it's by-the-by. I feel like half of London is here." She glanced toward a clearing up ahead—the refreshment court. "I see that Bertie and Ollie have secured a table for our party. Time for lemonade, Your Grace?"

"This conversation isn't over, Emmeline," said the duke in a low voice. His hand lingered on her arm. "You and I, we have unfinished business."

Beneath her uniform, Emmeline's flesh tingled and a frisson of heat washed through her from head to toe. She had no idea in what direction the duke meant to steer any future discussions—they both knew that nothing could come of their brief erotic encounter, no matter how incendiary their attraction, or genuine their fond regard for each other.

But for now, she'd have to set her feelings aside and focus on taking care of the duke's wards. Not all the ways she could break more rules with the duke.

Today of all days, Emmeline felt all the way to her bones that she must be prepared for anything.

Chapter 21

Wherein There Is a Visit to a Dinosaur Court, Nanny Chase Gives Chase, Followed by a Discussion About Hoydens, Hellions, and Worm's Meat...

After much negotiation—during which several glasses of fizzy lemonade and sticky iced finger buns were consumed—it was decided that the children's first stop would be Dr. Merryweather's tempest prognosticator. Lured by the prospect of seeing weather-predicting leeches—as well as a garment fashioned from poodle fur, a "talking" electric telegraph, and a taxidermy display featuring animals engaged in everyday domestic scenes such as frogs shaving and kittens sipping tea and playing the pianoforte—both Bartholomew and Gareth agreed the dinosaurs and cat circus could wait until they'd explored inside for a while.

At least that was the plan. Emmeline had her fingers crossed that the duke's wards would remain agreeable for a few hours. It *was* an exciting day out, after all.

By the time they emerged outside and began to make their way toward the "Dinosaur Court" on the banks of the Serpentine, the boys were fairly bouncing like a pair of jack-in-the-boxes. "Can we climb on the dinosaurs?" asked Gareth. A small crowd was already amassed around the exhibit. A good number of children were swarming over the huge concrete sculptures—sitting on their backs and their heads, even swinging from their necks. "Or are the dinosaurs too sore? I don't see any bandages though."

"They're not *real*, silly," said Bartholomew. "So they can't be sore. They're *statues* of dinosaurs. And there are no more dinosaurs left on earth anyway. They're all dead. Like dragons."

"There's a *Megalosaurus*, a *Hylaeosaurus* and two *Iguanodons*," read Harry from her guidebook as they waited on the edge of Rotten Row for a dignitary's carriage to pass.

"An Igoo-nana?" repeated Gareth. "Did they eat bananas?"

"I don't know," said Emmeline. "Perhaps it's something we can research when we return to St Lawrence House."

The duke grimaced. "I'm not sure if I have any paleontology texts."

They crossed the road and hovered on the edge of the small throng, waiting for an opportunity to move closer. After a few minutes, Bartholomew began to transfer his weight from one foot to the other. "Oh no. I think I drank too much lemonade," he complained.

"There are retiring rooms over that way," said Harry helpfully. She pointed to a low building by a grove of trees not far from the Crystal Palace. "The guidebook says it only costs a penny to use them. They are divided into male and female sections."

"I shall take you," said the duke. "Bertie will accompany us if that is all right with you, Mrs. Chase. You'll still have Ollie and Fanny."

"That's perfectly fine, Your Grace," said Emmeline. "We'll be here, communing with the dinosaurs."

Not long after the duke, Bartholomew, and Bertie had moved off, a loud squawk heralded the return of Horatio. He landed on the branch of a nearby beech tree. *Hullo! Did you miss me?*

Of course I did, replied Emmeline. *I consider you one of my very best friends.*

By Jupiter, if I could blush, I would, returned the raven. He puffed out his glossy black chest. *Because we're friends, I thought I should let you know that Lord Nevergrin, his snooty-nosed wife, and their ne'er-do-well son Algernon are here today. I watched them arrive a short time ago. They were heading for the Crystal Palace.*

Emmeline glanced toward the children, Ollie, and Fanny. Harry was reading her guidebook while Gareth held Fanny's hand. Ollie was scratching the back of his neck and staring off into the distance toward the retiring rooms. The footman was a strapping young chap like Bertie, and Emmeline supposed he could see over the heads of the strolling crowd. *Thank you for the warning*, she said to Horatio. *Hopefully the duke won't cross paths with his uncle, aunt, or cousin.*

Horatio ruffled his feathers. *I'd be happy to drop a guano grenade or two on any one of the blighters. Or swoop down and knock off their hats. Lady Peregrine's is particularly atrocious. That would quickly send them home.*

Emmeline had to cover her mouth with a gloved hand to stifle a laugh. *I'll keep it in mind.*

She turned her gaze back to the children. And then she frowned in confusion. Not *children*. One child. Just Harry.

Cursing herself for being distracted by her conversation with Horatio, she picked up her skirts and hastened across the clipped lawn toward Fanny and Ollie. "Where's Gareth?"

Fanny turned this way and that. "He was here a moment ago, Nanny Chase. I swear."

"You were holding his hand," Emmeline said. "Did you not notice when he let go? Which direction he went?"

The young woman shook her head. "No. I-I don't know. He can't have gone far."

Harry, who'd tucked her guidebook away in a pocket, was

biting her bottom lip. "I'm worried," she said. "It's not like Gareth to go off on his own. Gareth!" she called. "Gareth!"

Ollie started forward, moving toward the dinosaur exhibit. "Maybe he's hiding behind the dinosaurs. I'll look."

Horatio fluttered onto a lower branch of the beech tree. *Never fear, Nanny Chase, I'll look about the Park. I have a bird's-eye view.*

Thank you, my fine feathered friend.

Emmeline rushed around the edges of the crowd, calling Gareth's name, looking for his light brown hair and blue coat.

She would not panic. She would not panic. He *must* be nearby.

Even so, her heart was pounding and her mouth was as dry as cold ashes. One thing that had been drummed into Parasol Academy students from day one was that you must *always* be on alert. Always be on your guard, especially in public places.

She'd become complacent and had relied on Fanny too much.

But self-recrimination could wait until later. Finding Gareth was her priority.

"Mrs. Chase?" The duke caught her arm and Emmeline almost stumbled against him. His black brows had arrowed into a ferocious frown. "Is something amiss?"

Her heart in her mouth, Emmeline stated the dreaded truth. "Gareth has wandered off, Your Grace."

The duke swore beneath his breath. "How long has he been missing?" he demanded, his grip tightening.

Tamping down a surge of rising fear—she was trained for this, she was prepared for any eventuality—she filled the duke in on what had happened.

"Do you think he wandered over to the Serpentine?" he asked, his fiercely concerned gaze scanning the crowd and the surrounding parkland. The lake's still, mirrorlike surface glinted in the sunlight.

Oh God! If he'd slipped in... "I have no idea," Emmeline replied, unable to disguise the tremble in her voice. "Horatio—" She broke off. *Curses.* She couldn't mention Horatio was flying about looking from above. "I'm sorry. I'm rambling. We need to mount a proper search. Every second counts."

Bartholomew had begun to cry, and Harry was as pale as a ghost. Emmeline's heart contracted painfully. She wanted to comfort them, but the best thing—the *only* thing to do was find Gareth. And as quickly as possible.

Ollie reappeared, red-faced and panting. "He's not on or around the dinosaur statues."

"Damn it," muttered the duke. He caught Emmeline's eye. "Right. Here's what we'll do. Fanny can stay here with the children while—"

A loud screech from above drew their attention heavenward.

Horatio!

I've spotted Gareth, Nanny Chase, called the raven. *A few hundred yards off. He's with a brute of a man in a tweed coat and brown beaver hat, heading toward the Albert Gate. Or possibly Hyde Park Corner. I'll swoop the kidnapping bastard and peck his misbegotten eyes out. This way!*

Not if I get to him first, thought Emmeline, her blood boiling.

Horatio shot off and Emmeline picked up her skirts and bolted after the raven. Fueled by fury and righteous indignation, her feet took flight. "Gareth's been taken," she called over her shoulder, back at the duke. "By a man. Follow me!"

Not caring if the duke kept up with her or not, Emmeline sprinted across the grass, ducking and weaving through knots of Exhibition-goers as she went. Her Academy parasol was tucked beneath her arm and she would take immense delight in poking Gareth's kidnapper to kingdom come. If she could manage it, she'd get a few well-placed whacks in too for good measure. On his backside and between his legs. About the ears too. How dare he take Gareth!

How dare he!

There. Up ahead. A brown beaver hat and tweed coat. Wide shoulders that looked vaguely familiar... Could it be the scarred brute who'd chased her and the duke down Temple Close?

The hat went flying as Horatio swooped down like an avenging avian god from on high. The man tried to beat him off with a flailing arm, but the raven was too nimble. The bird launched a second attack and a woman screamed and a man shouted.

"Gareth," cried Emmeline, ignoring the burning in her pumping legs and her lungs. "I'm coming!"

She was so close now, she could see the little boy. Even though Horatio had attacked the kidnapper, he still held on tightly to Gareth's hand.

"Not for long you won't, you swine," muttered Emmeline to herself, skidding to a halt behind them.

With all her might, she prodded the man's back with the end of her parasol as she muttered, "*Perplexio*, you bastard."

But then the brute swung around to face her. Rage contorted his features. Blood trickled from a raven-inflicted scrape above one eyebrow. "Ow! That hurt, you bloody bitch," he cried.

Damn, the Point-of-Confusion had not worked! The scar-faced stranger was not pleasantly perplexed at all. He looked like an incensed bull about to gore her.

But he'd let go of Gareth at least. "Run," she urged the boy as she and the fuming henchman faced each other like combatants in a wrestling ring, sizing each other up.

Then the man swore and paled. Took a step backward, away from her. Glancing over her shoulder, Emmeline caught a glimpse of the duke, running full tilt their way.

Curses. The kidnapper was going to scarper.

Not on her watch. He had questions to answer. Not only that, but he needed to be locked up.

"Go to Cousin Xavier," Emmeline called to Gareth as she launched herself at the kidnapper's legs, knocking him to the ground in a rugby tackle. They grappled briefly and then rolled over—once, twice, three times—ending up in the dust of Rotten Row, Emmeline landing on top. Her skirts were tangled in the kidnapper's legs and he was gripping her shoulders with bruising force. And then all at once the thug landed a glancing blow on her jaw. Her head was instantly abuzz, her vision blurry.

Bleeding bastard! She balled her hand into a fist and punched him back, her fist connecting with his nose. Or maybe it was his eye. Before she could get another blow in, the brute twisted his body, throwing her off, and then he was scrambling to his feet and hurtling away, heading for the Albert Gate and the busy street beyond.

Damn and blast and bloody quadruple bleeding hell! Frustration surged through Emmeline as she clambered to her feet. She wanted to give chase, but her head still spun with dizziness and she feared she wasn't up to it. She bent over, her hands on her knees, shoulders heaving. She was not going to pass out or throw up. She must not.

"Emmeline..."

The duke. Emmeline forced herself upright and pushed a lock of tangled hair out of her eyes. Somewhere along the way she'd lost her bonnet, and the right side of her face was throbbing and stinging like it had been attacked by a swarm of angry bees. But none of that compared to the fury and frustration swirling in her belly. And a good dose of guilt and humiliation because she'd failed in her duty. "Your Grace," she managed between snatched breaths. "How... How is Gareth? Where is he?"

"He's confused and shaken but otherwise all right," said the duke. "He's with Bertie and Horatio, just over there." He pointed toward an ancient oak and sure enough, Gareth was there, safe and sound. "I believe Ollie and Fanny are still waiting with Harry and Bartholomew at the Dinosaur Court."

The duke then reached into the pocket of his frock coat and withdrew a handkerchief. "Here, Mrs. Chase," he said gently, his eyes filled with concern. "You might need this for your lip."

Emmeline took the fine piece of white linen and dabbed gingerly at her mouth. *Oh, dickens on toast.* Her bottom lip was split and bleeding. No wonder it was stinging. "I'm sorry," she said and then blinked rapidly as her vision grew blurry. Behind the duke she could see that a group of nosy parkers had gathered. She mustn't make a bigger scene than she already had by bursting into tears.

"What do you have to be sorry for?" asked the duke. "You are not to blame for the actions of a thug hired to intimidate me and those I care about. The man who lured Gareth away, I saw it was the same dog who chased us down Middle Temple Lane. All this occurred because of me. Not you."

"I was distracted," admitted Emmeline as a tear dripped onto her cheek. Annoyed with herself, she hastily dashed it away. "I should have had my eyes on Gareth the whole time. I was careless and that is unforgivable."

"It makes you human. And thanks to your Parasol Academy training, you also saved my ward," said the duke softly. "I've never seen someone run so swiftly or tackle a brute twice their size so fearlessly. You are a force to be reckoned with, Mrs. Chase. Now"—he reached out and gently touched her shoulder—"let's gather everyone together and return to St Lawrence House."

"Are you sure? I don't want to ruin the rest of everyone's day—"

"Mrs. Chase," said the duke, his voice imbued with warning. "You're hurt. There will be no arguments. Besides, I need to talk with the Metropolitan Police about the incident. The kidnapper and whoever was behind this attack need to be brought to justice." He glanced about. "Actually, I'm surprised there aren't more bobbies around—"

"Nevergrin! Nevergrin!" Horatio squawked from the oak tree. "Nevermore!"

Oh no. Emmeline did *not* want to have an encounter with the duke's uncle right now. Nor the man's wife or son. She was sure the duke didn't either, judging by the sudden ferocious cast of his features.

Turning, Emmeline faced a sneering Lord Peregrine at the front of the small crowd of onlookers. On his arm was a middle-aged woman wearing an enormous hat that resembled a strutting peacock, considering the number of azure and turquoise feathers cascading from its crown. On her other side was a younger, narrow-framed gentleman, Algernon Mason, whose expression was not dissimilar to his father's. But then, Emmeline knew she must look a fright given the fact her hair was tumbling down, her face was battered, and her uniform was covered in dust and grass stains.

It was the woman—Lady Peregrine no doubt—who spoke first. "Is this the rude creature you spoke about, Peregrine? She's a *nanny*, you say?" She made a tsking sound. "What a disgrace. She looks like the worst kind of hoyden." Fixing her gaze on the duke, she added, "I really don't know what you were thinking to employ her, Your Grace."

Hoyden? Emmeline bit her tongue as a wave of impotent fury and mortification rolled over her. While part of her wanted to defend herself, she knew that if she lashed out, she'd only make things worse.

Algernon Mason sniggered. "Lud, hoyden is far too polite an expression if you ask me. What the deuce has she been doing? Brawling in public?"

Lord Peregrine raised his monocle and raked Emmeline from head to toe with a scathing look. "I believe she's a graduate from the Parasol Academy for Exceptional Nannies and Governesses." Then he snorted. "Exceptional? I'd say she's the opposite."

A muscle flickered in the duke's cheek as he glared coldly at his relatives. "Are you quite finished with your unjust character assassination? This nanny just saved my ward from the clutches of a kidnapper. She deserves a medal, and a commendation from Queen Victoria, not ridicule."

Huzzah! Bravo! cheered Horatio from the sidelines. *About time His Grace defended you, Nanny Chase.*

Lady Peregrine sniffed. "If you say so, Your Grace."

"I do. And it's my opinion that matters, not anyone else's. Especially not yours, dearest Aunt, Uncle, Cousin," returned the duke, his contempt for them clear. Indeed, Emmeline was certain that the definition of the word "disdainful" in the *Imperial Dictionary* contained a reference to the Duke of St Lawrence in that moment.

As if from nowhere, Sir Randolph materialized at the front of the crowd. "Oh, I don't know. Hoydens have their place," he said with a chuckle, winking at Emmeline. "And hell-raising hellions. In fact, I quite like the idea of a feisty redhead who's not afraid to get down and dirty—"

Faster than a striking bird of prey, the duke shot forward and gripped the baronet by the throat. His eyes were hard and burning, his words as sharp as glacial ice as he ground out, "Say one more word about her and I'll knock the living daylights out of you, you pathetic piece of worm's meat." Then he thrust Sir Randolph away with such force, the man ended up on his backside on the grass.

Ignoring the shocked gasps around them, the duke tugged his coat cuffs back into place then returned to Emmeline. "Come, Mrs. Chase," he said, placing a hand at the small of her back. "Let's go home. I'd say we've both had enough of this rabble."

"I won't disagree," she murmured as they turned away from the gawking, gossiping crowds. Returning to St Lawrence House would also give her time to regroup before she was called to account before the headmistress of the Parasol Academy.

This hitherto-fine-now-rapidly-turning-into-a-horrid-mud-puddle day wasn't over *quite* yet. Such a pity she couldn't cast an *Unsmirchify* spell to clean up the whole terrible mess.

Although, not *all* messes were terrible, she decided when Horatio flew past and called out to her, *Don't worry, Nanny Chase. The Nevergrins are about to experience my wrath.*

Then a few seconds later, *Guano grenades away!*

As enraged male shouts and a woman's screech filled the air, Emmeline tried very hard not to smile . . . at least for a full half second.

Well, Lady Nevergrin *had* called her a hoyden.

Chapter 22

In Which Brandy Is Sipped, Tea Is Not Taken, and a Delicate Matter Is Broached...

Upon returning to St Lawrence House, Xavier sent for his own physician, Dr. Fotheringham, to examine Mrs. Chase's injuries, and then to assess the health of her father. According to Woodley, Edward Evans was still coughing, short of breath, and weak, despite resting in his room for the best part of the day.

While the doctor was busy with his patients, Xavier went to his study and helped himself to a fortifying glass of brandy. It wasn't even three in the afternoon, but he needed something to quell the roiling fury in his veins.

There was no doubt in Xavier's mind that the kidnapping attempt had been orchestrated for the sole purpose of throwing his life into turmoil so he wouldn't be able to finish his Westminster Palace clock design. Because who would be able to concentrate on anything at all after something so terrible had happened? The scarred brute who'd taken Gareth needed to be apprehended and prosecuted. But whoever was behind this wicked, insidious plot to disrupt his life and threaten, or even harm, those he cared about needed to pay too.

It might be his uncle, but in his gut, he was certain Sir Randolph Redvers was the "guv'nor" the thugs who'd chased him and Emmeline had been talking about. But he had not a jot of proof.

He sloshed more brandy into his glass, downed it in two gulps, then wiped the back of his gloved hand over his mouth.

Most of all, he wanted to throttle Sir Randolph for so vilely insulting Mrs. Chase. And he would love nothing more than to tear apart the kidnapper for physically hurting her. He knew she would be all right, but to see her disheveled and bruised and bleeding had made his heart ache and his blood boil.

This time, Xavier's enemy had gone too far. Sitting on his hands now would be unconscionable. To that end, when he'd arrived home, he'd sent word to Scotland Yard that he wished to report an attempted kidnapping of a child. Mrs. Chase had informed him that the Parasol Academy headmistress might very well turn up on the doorstep to speak with him about the "incident" in Hyde Park as well.

Even though he was not looking forward to that particular conversation, Xavier, of course, would do nothing but sing Mrs. Chase's praises. He thanked God she'd been able to rescue Gareth. There was no doubt in his mind that the only reason she'd been able to was because of her expert training.

On the way home in the town coach, Gareth had told Xavier and Mrs. Chase that the man with the scar had coaxed him away by offering to take him on a balloon ride. Or "puff-balloon" ride as Gareth had put it. "He was a bit scary looking, but I really, really wanted to go," the boy had explained. "He said that you were already there in the puff-balloon basket, Cousin Xavier. And Bartholomew. I didn't want to miss out."

Xavier wondered how the kidnapper had known that that would be the perfect lure for the young boy. He cast his mind back over the events of the day; there'd been talk of hot-air balloon rides before they'd set out for Hyde Park—while they'd all been assembled in the vestibule if his memory served him correctly. Aside from Bertie, Ollie, Fanny, and Woodley, there'd been any number of servants—both maids and footmen—bustling about in the background. Though Fanny had been the one who'd let go of Gareth's hand while they'd been waiting for a turn to see the dinosaurs.

Xavier huffed out a sigh and stared unseeingly out the window. It seemed unlikely that the young nurserymaid would be responsible for such a heinous betrayal—to be in league with a brutish scar-faced thug who was at the beck and call of the mysterious "guv'nor." Nonetheless, as soon as Mrs. Chase was free—Dr. Fotheringham was currently examining her injuries—he would seek her opinion.

While he didn't want to jump to any erroneous conclusions about Fanny, it would be wise to proceed with caution. For his own peace of mind, he'd asked Mrs. Lambton to watch over the children in the nursery while Mrs. Chase was otherwise occupied.

If anything had happened to Gareth, or any of his wards...

Or to Emmeline Chase...

Xavier gripped the window ledge so tightly, his knuckles cracked. Then it hit him. After what had happened in Hyde Park today, he would have to do something he didn't want to, at all. Even though it was logical and practical and best for everyone.

He must send his wards and Mrs. Chase away.

The idea hurt so much, it was akin to being punched in the gut. The pain of it practically winded Xavier. For a moment he considered pouring another brandy, but he needed a clear head for what had to happen next.

Coffee, as dark as his mood right now, would have to do.

Emmeline sat in the small window seat of her bedchamber and studied the square below. The duke's physician, Dr. Fotheringham, had come and gone, and she couldn't deny she was feeling a bit sad and sorry for herself.

And worried. Any moment now, a leygram might turn up in

her room, requesting her presence at the Parasol Academy to account for what had happened this afternoon. Or Mrs. Temple might suddenly arrive at St Lawrence House. The headmistress would undoubtedly want to speak with the duke too. Scandalous news traveled faster than any other sort of news, and what could be more scandalous than a story about a Parasol Academy nanny grappling with a man in the middle of Hyde Park on the opening day of the Great Exhibition? An event not only attended by Queen Victoria, Prince Albert, and the who's who of British society, but dignitaries and industry leaders from around the world.

Emmeline could almost see the newspaper headlines now:

Parasol Academy Nanny Creates Chaos at the Crystal Palace!

Or worse...

Brawling Parasol Academy Nanny Makes a Great Exhibition of Herself in Hyde Park!

An icy tendril of apprehension crept down Emmeline's spine. Because she'd failed to keep a proper watch over sweet Gareth today, if Mrs. Temple and the Academy Board decided that her actions had brought the Academy's name into disrepute, the repercussions could be catastrophic.

In fact, she could very well lose her license to practice as a Parasol nanny. She could also lose her job altogether if the duke began to have second thoughts about her conduct today.

To be parted from the duke...

To never see his wards again...

To be a desperate and practically destitute widow once more...

Emmeline brushed a tear away from her cheek.

It was an eventuality she couldn't bear to contemplate. Especially given the ill health of her father.

Emmeline was terribly anxious about him. Dr. Fotheringham, who'd paid a visit to her father before he'd examined her

(Emmeline had insisted, despite the duke's decree) had reported that "Mr. Evans has developed a serious ague of the lungs." The physician had prescribed a new tonic to ease his cough, an abundance of rest, and if at all possible, a sojourn in the country or at the seaside to escape the unhealthy miasmas of London.

Thanks to the duke, the first two recommendations were definitely doable. The third would be almost impossible. She couldn't afford to send her father away. She couldn't employ anyone to care for him. She certainly wouldn't ask the duke for more help. He'd done enough for her and her father already.

Focus on one thing at a time, Emmeline. Falling into despair and panic will not *help you at this point. You need a clear head.*

She sighed heavily, then winced. Her face really did hurt like the devil. While she'd changed into a clean uniform and pinafore and redressed her hair (with her proscribed lacy nanny's cap in place in case Mrs. Temple arrived), there was no way to disguise her swollen, cut lip or the purple bruises blooming on the right side of her jaw and cheek. She was lucky she hadn't lost a tooth or that her jawbone hadn't been dislocated or broken. That hired thug certainly packed a punch.

Other parts of Emmeline hurt too. She had scraped knees and bruised ribs. Her thigh muscles were stiff and sore from running so hard. Even though she'd been wearing gloves, they'd only been fashioned from cotton and the knuckles of her right hand were abraded and bruised. She'd even broken five fingernails. *Five!*

A vengeful part of Emmeline hoped that the punch she'd landed on the kidnapper had at least given him a black eye.

But she'd do it all again in a heartbeat. She'd do *anything* to protect the children in her care. Slay dragons, even fight evil Queen Mab herself if she ever dared set foot in the nursery. Yet, it was Emmeline's fault that Gareth had been taken.

That's what hurt the most of all.

A familiar tingling sensation that Emmeline always associated with the Fae's leyline magic rushed over her and she watched the mat before her door expectantly, her heart tripping over itself with trepidation. Sure enough, a leygram materialized, the parchment envelope glowing with a faint silvery-blue mist for a few seconds before dissipating.

Drawing a deep breath, Emmeline pulled her quizzing glass from her uniform's pocket then crossed the room to pick up the missive. It wasn't a surprise that it was from Mrs. Temple, indicating she would arrive at St Lawrence House in the next few minutes. In fact, because she was on official business, she was teleporting into the Metropolitan Police box in Belgrave Square. She'd speak with the Duke of St Lawrence first, then Emmeline would be called.

A few minutes later, Emmeline caught sight of a petite woman marching with sure steps across the square far below. She couldn't see the pedestrian's face—it was hidden by a pearl-gray parasol trimmed with lace—but Emmeline knew it was Mrs. Felicity Temple.

Glancing at her pocket watch, Emmeline saw that it was precisely three o'clock.

Who'd have thought that such a pleasant-sounding, innocuous hour—the time when one took afternoon tea or naps—could very well be the hour of her professional doom.

When the summons came twenty minutes later—one of the housemaids knocked on her door to relay the message—Emmeline descended to the drawing room with heavy footsteps and an even heavier heart.

She would tell the truth. She wouldn't paint herself in a better light or sugarcoat her actions. The *Parasol Academy Handbook* hadn't prepared her for a situation like this, but attempting to minimize her own failure would not help.

Upon entering the drawing room, Emmeline found Mrs. Temple sitting alone by a large bay window with a tea tray set out before her.

The headmistress immediately put down her cup and rushed over to greet Emmeline. She gathered up Emmeline's hands and gave them a light squeeze. "Oh, Mrs. Chase. Just look at you." Her concerned gaze traveled over Emmeline's face. "The duke said you'd been hurt, and he wasn't exaggerating. Are you sure you're up to speaking with me?"

Emmeline breathed a small internal sigh of relief. Mrs. Temple didn't *seem* displeased with her. Not yet at any rate. "Yes, I am, ma'am," she said. "I think it's best for everyone if we talk sooner rather than later."

"Very well, if you're sure." The headmistress gestured toward the pair of shepherdess chairs by the window. "Come and sit and we can go over what happened in Hyde Park. I'm afraid it's Parasol Academy protocol when a major incident involving one of our nannies or governesses occurs. Especially when one of her charges has been endangered and the event is very much in the public eye."

"Yes. I understand," replied Emmeline as she took a seat. Mrs. Temple offered to pour her a cup of tea, but she politely declined, claiming her lip was too sore. In truth, her stomach was churning far too much. While Emmeline was reassured that she wasn't in any immediate danger of being hauled over the coals for misconduct, until she knew for certain her job and license were safe, her nerves would be all ajangle.

"Now," said Mrs. Chase, "the Duke of St Lawrence and I have had a good talk and we both want to reassure you that you are in no way to blame for what happened today. The attempted kidnapping of little Gareth Mason was *not* your fault."

"What the duke doesn't know is that I was speaking with his raven, Horatio Ravenscar Esquire, when Gareth was taken," said Emmeline dolefully. "I wasn't watching his ward closely enough. I'd entrusted his care to the nurserymaid-in-training."

"Who let go of his hand and didn't watch where he went or who he spoke to." The headmistress's expression was grave but kind. "Mrs. Chase, you are being too hard on yourself. How long did you converse with Horatio? Whom I have just met, by the way, and what a charming fellow he is."

Emmeline thought back. "I'd say a minute. At the most. But a minute is all it takes sometimes."

Mrs. Temple shook her head. "We cannot have our eyes glued to each and every child twenty-four hours a day, for every single second. I understand one of the duke's footmen was in attendance too."

"Yes, but—"

"No buts. Your continued self-flagellation will not help protect the duke's wards. What you must do is provide a thorough account to the Metropolitan Police when they arrive. In fact, the duke has requested that Scotland Yard detectives investigate the matter. He believes young Gareth's attempted kidnapping may be linked to a domestic sabotage plot."

"I believe he's correct," said Emmeline. And then she gave (a slightly edited) account of everything strange and sinister that had occurred since she'd taken up her post. (The *only* incident she was particularly vague about was the time she and the duke had been pursued by the guv'nor's two hired henchmen. Mrs. Temple didn't need to know that she'd cast the *Cloakify* spell, then kissed the duke in the rain. It would not be wise at all to divulge she'd broken yet two more Parasol Academy rules, thus risking the immediate cancellation of her nannying license.)

Mrs. Temple nodded and *hmm*-ed throughout Emmeline's narrative and at the end, she said, "Yes, that aligns perfectly with everything the duke told me. It is of great concern to me, and His Grace, that there's been an escalation in the types of attacks occurring. An attempted abduction is terrible indeed. Thanks to your brave actions and quick thinking, you rescued young Gareth."

"Horatio helped." Emmeline explained how the raven had scouted for Gareth in the crowd in Hyde Park and that's how she'd been able to locate the boy so quickly.

"And it's most admirable that you've cultivated such a wonderful relationship with the duke's pet. Which is another reason why I don't think it was a terrible thing that you were chatting to the raven today."

Emmeline winced. "The publicity surrounding this is going to be awful, isn't it? And what will Queen Victoria think, considering she issued the Academy a Royal Charter?"

"Oh, Her Majesty thinks you are marvelous, Mrs. Chase. A credit to the Parasol Academy. I've already spoken with her and there's nothing at all to worry about on that score. As for publicity—I will be providing an official statement to the newspapers. Any headlines and articles that appear in the coming days will portray both you and the Academy in a positive light. If they do not, I'm certain Her Majesty will have something to say about it."

"Oh goodness." Emmeline at last let out a shaky but relieved sigh. She could hardly believe it. Everything was going to be all right—

"However," said Mrs. Temple, "there is another matter—something of quite a delicate nature—that I need to broach with you."

"I see," said Emmeline carefully, even though she didn't. "It sounds . . . serious."

Mrs. Temple's clear silver gaze met hers. "One of the other Parasol nannies who was present in Hyde Park today, she did notice something a little odd and felt duty-bound to report it. It's nothing *you* did, Mrs. Chase, but it was noted that the duke placed his hand on your back in a most familiar way as he escorted you from the Park."

Oh . . . Emmeline couldn't stop the telling flare of heat that crept up her neck into her cheeks. "I-I don't recall that His Grace did that. I *was* rather shaken after my impromptu wrestling match with my charge's kidnapper."

"I'm sure you were in a bit of pain too," said Mrs. Temple, her voice soft with sympathy. But then her expression firmed. "While the duke was no doubt concerned for your well-being, this nanny *also* said that he became quite incensed when a gentleman in the crowd verbally insulted you and made vulgar insinuations about your virtue. In fact, the duke gripped him about the neck then threw him to the ground."

"Yes. That did happen," said Emmeline. "It was Sir Randolph Redvers, a rival horologist who was rude to me. The duke suspects that the baronet might be behind this sabotage plot. I suppose it's only natural that he'd had enough of the man who could have orchestrated the kidnapping of his ward. I don't think there's anything more to it than that." (Oh dear. Another lie. Was there a special Fae hell for fibbers?)

"I see," said Mrs. Temple. She picked up her cup of tea, took a quick sip, then put it down again with a precise click. "In light of the duke's actions, and the fact it is clearly not safe for his wards to stay in London at present, I suggested to His Grace that he might consider sending you and the children away for a while. And he agrees."

"He does?" murmured Emmeline faintly as astonishment momentarily stole her breath. Then she cleared the throb of emotion suddenly clogging her throat and said as firmly as she could, "Of course." Because what else could she say? It wasn't as though she hadn't been contemplating *worse* outcomes a short time ago. She hadn't lost her license or her job altogether. She should be relieved, not trying to stem the prick of tears.

"I know you will understand it's for the best." The headmistress's expression grew kind. "You are an attractive, vivacious young widow, Mrs. Chase. It's understandable that the duke might become enamored of you. There's a reason the Parasol Academy has a strict, no fraternization policy. We don't want anyone's judgment to be compromised, and romantic entanglements tend to do that."

"That's not . . . I don't think . . ." Emmeline pressed her lips together then winced because of the resultant sting. "I'm sure the duke doesn't harbor any sort of tendre for me."

Oh, that was the biggest, fattest lie she'd ever told. She was definitely bound for Fae Fibber Hell.

And then a voice at the back of her mind whispered, *The duke is going to send you away. So perhaps he* doesn't *feel anything for you. Maybe you've been misreading the whole situation.*

And then she told herself to stop being such a selfish, self-pitying ninny-poop. This wasn't about her. This was about the children and what *they* needed. Her feelings, or the duke's for that matter, did not signify.

Mrs. Temple cast her another sympathetic look. "That might be true, but I rather think some time away is all for the best. No doubt His Grace will have more to say to you about where he would like his wards, and you, to reside."

Emmeline clasped her fingers together in her lap and her abraded, swollen knuckles protested. "Yes. I'm sure he will," she said far too brightly, ignoring the pain in her hand and in her heart.

Nothing to see here. Nothing's amiss. I'm really not about to burst into tears.

"Which is why I will leave you now." Mrs. Temple rose to her feet and Emmeline did too. "You did well today, Mrs. Chase," she said with a kind smile. "I trust you will continue to shine as one of our best and brightest Parasol nannies." Reaching out, she touched Emmeline's arm. "I shall see myself out."

As the door closed behind the headmistress, Emmeline sank onto her chair again.

She didn't feel shiny at all. She felt as glum and miserable as a raincloud on a midwinter's day.

A tear escaped and this time, she didn't wipe it off her cheek. Even when it touched her split lip and made it sting.

The duke was going to send her away, and she didn't think she could bear it.

Because she loved him.

Chapter 23

Descriptive of a Very Significant Encounter and a Goodbye; Perhaps...

Xavier stood before the closed drawing room door, his forehead resting on the polished wood panels.

He should go inside. He needed to speak with Mrs. Chase. But he didn't want to.

Not because he didn't desire her company. He did, he always did. But because what he had to say to her were words he did not wish to utter. But he must. For the sake of Harriet, Bartholomew, and Gareth, he must.

He had an obligation. A duty of care. His wards deserved the very best life could offer, and he wanted to keep them safe.

He wanted to keep Mrs. Chase safe too.

That was the thought that gave him the push to do what he needed to do even though his heart was already hurting like hell. Like the devil himself was skewering him through the chest with a burning-hot poker. And the pain was only going to get worse.

Reaching out a gloved hand, Xavier opened the door.

Mrs. Chase was sitting by one of the large bay windows at one end of the room, looking out onto Belgrave Square. And

God damn it, she was wearing that vile lacy cap again. Probably because she'd been interviewed by the headmistress of the Parasol Academy and needed to comply with their strict uniform policy.

She must have been lost in thought because she hadn't heard him enter. He cleared his throat. "Mrs. Chase."

Her attention immediately focused on him. And oh God, her large blue eyes already contained shadows. It seemed Mrs. Chase was the only person he was able to reliably read.

He approached her and she stood and curtsied. Yes, he'd been correct. She was apprehensive, perhaps even melancholy. Mrs. Temple must have already said something to her about her need to leave London. He wasn't sure if that was going to make this conversation any harder, or easier.

There was only one way to find out.

"Mrs. Chase," he repeated at the same time she "Your Graced" him. A smile quivered at the corner of her poor abused mouth.

If he could take her pain away, if he could make everything better, he would. Which was why he had to put his own needs aside and say, "I want you to take my wards to Kingscliff Castle in Kent. You'll all be far safer there, away from all this"—he waved a hand—"this chaos revolving around me. I don't want anything to happen to Harry, Bartholomew, or Gareth. Or to you. Especially after today."

She nodded. "I understand. Mrs. Temple already broached the subject with me. The last thing you need is to be distracted by concerns about the children's safety. It's just that . . ."

"Yes?" Xavier took a step closer.

The nanny's gaze dropped to his necktie, which suddenly felt far too tight. "I shouldn't even be saying this, but it will be hard to go," she murmured.

Was that a catch in her voice?

Xavier swallowed to loosen the constriction in his own throat. "It won't be forever. Just until I've submitted my plans to the Astronomer Royal at the start of next month."

"That's assuming Sir Randolph is behind this terrible campaign to hurt you," she said. "If it's Lord Peregrine, these attacks might continue for some time."

"That's true." Now that Xavier had cooled down, he couldn't fault Mrs. Chase's logic. He reflected on the events of the day.

What if his uncle *was* the mastermind behind this insidious plot to paint him as mentally incompetent? What lengths would he go to in order to gather additional "evidence" in order to instigate a lunacy investigation trial?

His uncle had been present in Hyde Park when Gareth had been kidnapped. He'd also witnessed Xavier's subsequent attack on Sir Randolph. He might very well challenge the Duke of St Lawrence's sanity on the basis of those two incidents alone. Not only could he accuse Xavier of not being able to take care of a child properly, but that he'd lost control and had physically attacked a "gentleman" in front of a crowd of people in broad daylight.

It was all rubbish of course, but facts could certainly be twisted to suit agendas.

Xavier sighed heavily. There were so many uncertainties and no clear answers.

"Whether it was Sir Randolph or my uncle, or another unknown party altogether who orchestrated Gareth's kidnapping today, it's still impossible to say," he said. "But I'm hopeful that Scotland Yard will turn up something useful. In the meantime"—Xavier made himself smile—"you could view your time away as a summer holiday by the seaside. Like the ones you used to take with your family. In light of Dr. Fotheringham's advice—he spoke with me a short time ago—it appears your father would benefit from convalescing in more salubrious climes. The fresh sea air will do him a world of good."

It sounded like he was trying to convince himself more than Mrs. Chase that this was a good idea. Although he'd told her that this time apart would only be for a month, somehow it felt like more than that. Something more significant.

It felt like he was ending something that had scarcely even begun.

Xavier's head began to buzz uncomfortably with all the things that had been left unsaid because she was a nanny and he was a duke.

He suspected that Mrs. Chase knew that too.

His suspicions were confirmed a moment later when she ventured, "Yes. You're right of course, Your Grace. But I can't help feeling that this is more than a temporary goodbye."

She met his gaze again, her expression stoic yet impossibly sad. "Mrs. Temple reminded me that fraternization between employers and employees is forbidden. I think she suspects there might be something going on between us, an inappropriate attraction, and for so many reasons, we both know that we can never have anything more. Sending me away is sensible. It will give both of us the opportunity to . . . to put some distance between us. So we have the time and space to return to our own respective corners of the chessboard, so to speak."

Xavier's gaze lingered on Mrs. Chase's face, taking note of her features, the set of her mouth, the shadows in her eyes. *We both know that we can never have anything more . . .*

He'd never been quite sure how Emmeline Chase felt about him beyond a degree of fondness and a strong physical attraction, but that one simple word "more" indicated that she might have developed deeper feelings for him.

That she'd started to fall in love with him.

His heart wanted to soar, yet it was plummeting down, down, down to the depths of despair.

"Emmeline," he said, "a few weeks ago, I told you that I have the highest regard and admiration for you. And of course, my desire for you has been abundantly evident. But, I'm afraid all that was a lie. I . . . What I feel is *more* than that too."

"Oh . . ." Hope or joy—some bright spark—flared, then just as quickly faded in Mrs. Chase's lovely blue eyes. "I did wonder if you might care for me, even just a little," she said softly, almost timidly. "Although, judging by your expression, I suspect there might be another 'but' or 'however' coming."

Xavier tried to smile but it was a challenge to make his mouth work the way he wanted it to. "You are correct," he said gently. "I *do* feel something for you—an emotion that transcends mere lust and regard and a budding affection. *But*, I honestly don't know if I can call it love. And that's what you deserve, Emmeline. A strong and abiding love from a good man whose heart is alive and beating and sure. I'm not certain that I can give you what you need."

Even though Emmeline was frowning, she reached out and touched his arm. "You are a good man. You are a much better man than the one I married."

Xavier shook his head. "I'm sorry, but how can you know that's truly the case? *I* don't even know that. I've always been a man of science and logic, and when I try to analyze my own emotions and actions and responses, I simply cannot. My hesitancy, my reluctance to put a name to what I feel about you stems from the fact that I've never been 'in love' before. What's more, I've never even *been* loved by anyone at all. My parents certainly didn't love me. The truth is, Emmeline, I-I don't know what love looks like."

Xavier pressed his gloved fist against his chest. "Believe me, I wish I could trust what's in here. But I don't. I worry that my heart is not quite right. That it's like a watch or clock that doesn't have all its moving parts intact. That it's fundamentally broken. Or worse, that I'm like Gareth's tin soldier—the abandoned one you found on the roof. That I'm dented and scraped and virtually hollow and don't have much of a heart at all."

Emmeline lifted her chin. There was a spark of challenge in her eyes as she said, "Of course you have a heart that's flesh and blood, that feels and functions perfectly well, Your Grace. And I think you care very much about your wards. You show care and consideration for your staff. You've told me you have a good friend, someone you've known since your days at Eton. And you also have boundless affection for Horatio. But..." She drew a breath. "But I do understand how difficult all of this is, navigating this... this uncharted territory between me and you. We've both been to places we should never have gone to. Crossed lines we never should have crossed."

Xavier clutched his hands behind his back to stop himself reaching for Emmeline. To stop the gulf between them widening with each passing moment. "Difficult. That's the operative word, isn't it? I've... I've not been fair, Emmeline. I never meant to make things difficult for you. But I have."

Emmeline's blue eyes softened and were filled with a wistful kind of mistiness tinged with sadness. "You and I have shared intimate moments that I will always cherish. I'll never regret any of it for as long as I live. Even so, we both know that someone like you, a duke—even if you *did* love me—could never offer me anything more than an invitation to become your mistress. I'm from Cheapside, not Belgravia or Mayfair."

What? Horror lanced through Xavier at such a thought. "I'm not in the market for a mistress. I never have been. And I would never insult you with such a demeaning proposition. To be perfectly honest, I'm not even sure I'm in the market for a wife." *That was still true, wasn't it?*

"Perhaps not now," said Emmeline softly. "But one day, you may decide to marry and whoever that woman is, she'll need to be someone from your own class. Someone of noble birth, who's genteel in nature, and accomplished. Someone who could give you children. An heir."

Xavier frowned as the import of Emmeline's words sunk in. She'd mentioned to him before that she might not be able to conceive a child, but really that wasn't, and would never be, a consideration in his choice of a bride. *If you ever marry*, he reminded himself.

Nevertheless, he had to make it clear to Emmeline where he

stood on the matter. "I have my wards. *They* are my family now. And I would *never* choose a bride simply because I need a... a brood mare. If I never have a child of my own, so be it. So you must not think that would have any bearing on any future decisions I would make in that regard."

"Be that as it may, I would never suit." The expression in Emmeline's eyes was resolute. "Not someone like me. Dukes don't wed their nannies. If you did, then everyone *would* call you mad. I won't harm your reputation like that. I won't give your uncle, Lord Peregrine, even more ammunition to use against you. Or men like Sir Randolph Redvers who wish to harm your reputation as an esteemed horologist. You and I... we cannot be together. It's simply not possible. It's something I must accept."

"I know. I must accept it too," said Xavier, even though every fiber of his being was screaming no. Emmeline spoke perfect sense. She was being logical. Practical. All the things he didn't want to be when it came to her. He drew a shaky breath. Firmed his voice. "So here it ends," he said. "Only..." Behind his back, Xavier's right hand twitched as temptation urged him to reach out and touch her. But then he didn't. He curled his fingers into a tight fist. "Never mind."

Emmeline blew out a breath as though she'd come to a decision. "Right. I'll begin making preparations to leave. I take it you would like us to all depart as soon as possible?"

"Yes," said Xavier just as matter-of-factly. He could do this. Make plans to send her away. "Early tomorrow morning at nine, there's a train that departs from London Bridge Station. I'll secure a private railcar. And I'll send Bertie and another footman with you all rather than Ollie. I think it would be best if Fanny stayed here too. I'll ask Mrs. Lambton to reassign her to regular household duties."

Emmeline frowned. "Do you suspect that either of them had something to do with Gareth's kidnapping today?"

Xavier kept his voice low. "I'd hate for that to be the case, but for now, I'd rather err on the side of caution. Do you think you can manage without Fanny for a while? At least until you get to Kingscliff? There are other housemaids on staff at the castle who can assist you when required."

"Of course," said Emmeline.

Xavier nodded. "I'm glad my wards have you," he said softly. "One thing I do know to be true is that you're the closest thing to a maternal figure they have. It's abundantly clear that they care about you too. I would certainly never take you away from them."

Even though I must give you up . . .

Emmeline offered him a smile. "I'm grateful, Your Grace. Truly. I care about Harry, Bartholomew, and Gareth very much too." Then she smiled a smile that seemed as brittle as spun sugar. "I suppose I should get back to the nursery and check on them."

"And I should get back to my study."

Neither of them moved.

Selfish man that he was, Xavier had wanted to conduct this difficult meeting in the drawing room, a room he rarely used. Every single recollection he had of Emmeline Chase's visits to his study, his sanctuary, had brought him nothing but joy, and he didn't want to taint that room with the ghost of a bad memory.

Then he realized, he didn't want this particular encounter to end with an image of her with a forced smile on her lips and sadness welling in her eyes.

Surely they could share one last intimate moment before shutting the door on what could-never-be? What harm could it do after all they'd shared? At least they'd both have another memory to treasure. A bittersweet memory perhaps, but it would be better than living with regret.

Oh yes, he was a selfish, selfish man.

At last, Xavier unclasped his hands from behind his back. "Emmeline," he murmured. He reached out and gently touched the unbruised side of her face with the back of his gloved fingers. "I have no right at all to ask this of you—and you have every right to say no—but might I kiss you farewell? On the cheek. As friends do?"

She took a step closer. Placed a hand flat on his chest; whether it was to ward him off or to draw him closer, he wasn't quite sure. "No," she whispered, and his heart fell. "Not as friends... As lovers do."

Xavier's pulse leapt then bolted clean away like a runaway horse. "Are you certain? Your lip is sore, and I don't want to hurt you."

Her eyes glowed. "Then you'll just need to be gentle. All I ask is that you take off your gloves. I want to feel your bare hands on me."

Xavier swallowed then did as she asked, tugging off his gloves quickly then tossing them unheeded onto a nearby chair. Desire licked at him, but he would curb his impatience and take his time. Stretch these stolen moments out for as long as he could. "Emmeline," he whispered thickly. He couldn't seem to stop saying her name.

He swept his bare fingers lightly down her cheek again, then traced the sweet cupid's bow of her top lip with a fingertip. Brushed his thumb over the plush curve of her lower lip, taking care to avoid the barely knit cut.

He felt silk and velvet. The soft caress of her warm breath. The heavenly scent of her floral perfume wrapped around him, and he inhaled so deeply, his head spun.

She needed to be closer. His other hand slid behind Emmeline's slender back, his palm coming to rest between her shoulder blades. Curse her uniform and corset and whatever else lay between him and her satin-smooth skin.

His eyes traced over her face, lingering on the light dusting of freckles on her nose and cheeks. He already knew the intricate patterns—the tiny cinnamon-hued constellations—by heart.

When his gaze touched her bruised jaw, he had to crush down a hot surge of anger.

"My poor Emmeline," he said gruffly, gently cradling her pert chin. He turned her head slightly toward the light filtering through the chiffon curtain at the window. If he ever got close to the brute that did this...

"I'm well enough," she murmured. Then the corner of her mouth curved into a smile. "Apart from the fact that you haven't kissed me yet."

"Hush," Xavier admonished, "you impatient minx. I'm learning you. How you feel in my arms. I want to take note of every little detail. Commit them all to memory. Make annotations of you in my mind." He loosened one of her burnished copper locks and wound it around his index finger before watching it unravel and slip away to curl sweetly against the hollow beneath her jaw. "There'll be one for your hair." He pressed his nose to her temple and feathered a kiss near the place her pulse fluttered. "Your scent." His mouth brushed across her cheek, now flushed pink. "Your freckles. The little sounds of frustration you make when I tease you." His lips drifted lower. "How you taste..."

Emmeline's fingers clasped his nape and he couldn't resist the temptation her mouth presented any longer. Leaning down, he carefully pressed his lips to hers and drank his fill as delicately as he could.

His kiss was light, as gentle as a man of his limited experience could manage. A series of whisper-soft caresses and glides, his tongue tip barely slipping between her parted lips before retreating. When she whimpered and tightened her grip on his neck, he swept his tongue in again, delving a little farther, savoring the soft velvet stroke of her tongue in return.

It was exquisite torture, yet pure bliss at the same time. If it weren't for the wild thudding of his heart and the hot thrum of desire racing through his veins, he'd describe this goodbye kiss as almost chaste.

He really shouldn't have started this, because ending it was proving to be more of a challenge with each and every passing second.

But end it he must, for both their sakes. Before passion took over and there was no turning back.

"Oh, Emmeline," he whispered as he drew back. He gathered her hands in his and gently kissed her bruised knuckles. "I will miss moments like this with you."

"As will I," she murmured. Then her gold-tipped eyelashes swept down and she moved half a step back. "I must go. There's a lot to organize before tomorrow."

Xavier dropped his chin in a barely there nod. "I know. I'll stop by the nursery a bit later to speak with Harry, Bartholomew, and Gareth. And I'm sure whoever Scotland Yard sends will want to speak with you too."

"I'll come as soon as I'm summoned," she said, taking another step back. Then she curtsied with due deference. Nanny Chase had returned. "Your Grace."

As the door shut behind her, Xavier realized Emmeline— *No, Mrs. Chase*, he reminded himself—had never once addressed him by his first name.

Of course, he understood why. It was a way for her to maintain a modicum of distance, even while they were sharing one last moment of intimacy.

Strange how the idea that he would never hear her say "Xavier" again hurt more than he could say.

Chapter 24

In Which There Is a Celebration Involving Drunken Signs and Sour Wine, Penny-Gaff Plays, and Fan Dances; And an Unexpected Disclosure...

Xavier placed his fountain pen into its stand and then folded his gloved hands on his desk's leather blotter. At long last, after a whole year of painstaking work—sometimes in the most trying of circumstances—his Westminster Palace clock design was complete.

"Huzzah and hallelujah," he murmured to himself. He was quietly proud of what he'd created on paper. He'd actually invented a unique, perhaps even revolutionary clock mechanism—a complex arrangement of levers, gears, and weights and a new kind of pendulum—that would maintain unprecedented accuracy. By linking the "King of Clocks" by telegraph wires to the Greenwich Observatory, the first stroke of each hour would also be accurate to within one second. How could the Astronomer Royal not be impressed?

Of course, Xavier still needed to review every detail—checking all his calculations and pages and pages of impossibly intricate schematic diagrams—ensuring everything was absolutely perfect before he submitted his proposal to George Airy for consideration. But for now, a celebratory brandy was in order.

Although, as Xavier poured himself a sizable nip from the decanter he kept in his study, his mouth twisted with a wry smile. While he *was* pleased with his accomplishment, something was missing. He should be wallowing in the soft golden glow of satisfaction that was left in the wake of achieving a hard-fought-for goal. He should be rejoicing that in the not-too-distant future his name might be associated with something wonderful for once. But he didn't feel that way. Even after a few sips of brandy, he wasn't abuzz with any emotion resembling genuine triumph.

And deep down he knew exactly why. He wanted to share his achievement with someone... with Emmeline. (He'd given up trying to call her Mrs. Chase in his head.) He didn't want to celebrate alone, but she was far away—eighty miles to be exact—in Kent. Which wasn't all that far by train but still felt a world away all the same.

The truth was, Xavier missed her. *Ached* for her in fact. He felt thoroughly empty and deflated like a ship without sails or a "puff balloon" that had lost its air and could no longer fly.

If he were truly being honest with himself, he'd also acknowledge that he missed Harry, Bartholomew, and little Gareth, too. Not only their laughter and their bright voices and incessant questions, but even their amusing shenanigans. Even Horatio seemed in a doleful mood of late. Yes, the house was far too quiet and empty without his wards. And they'd only been gone a fortnight.

Xavier replenished his brandy then moved back to the casement window and pushed it open to let in some fresh air. It was a chill day for May. Somber gray clouds were clustered over the roofs of Belgravia and even though dusk was a few hours off, it was already growing dark in his study. Shadows clustered in corners and only added to his despondent mood.

He idly wondered if the odd and exceedingly vexing household "incidents" that still happened on a regular basis would cease altogether once his Westminster clock design was submitted. The clocks throughout the house—except for those in his Horology Room—were still constantly running fast or slow. The gaslights still flickered periodically. One of the servants—Woodley and Mrs. Lambton had yet to work out who—had "accidentally" left all the first- and second-floor windows open on one side of the house one night during a rainstorm, leading to drenched carpets and drapes and furniture; nothing that couldn't be fixed, but of course, it was another inconvenient distraction.

Yet Xavier had somehow soldiered on through it all.

If Sir Randolph Redvers, or another rival clock designer had gone to such *extreme* lengths to eliminate him from the competition, well, it had turned out to be all rather pointless in the end. He'd achieved his goal despite the disruptions. Despite the stress.

But what if the saboteur isn't Sir Randolph or another competing horologist? Xavier reminded himself. *What if my uncle is my hidden enemy, the one who's constantly trying to unsettle me and portray me as incompetent?*

Only time would tell.

While Scotland Yard hadn't turned up any leads on Gareth's kidnapper yet, Xavier's anxiety about his wards' safety had at least eased now that they were far away. Emmeline sent a telegram every single day, letting him know how everyone was faring. Even though the messages were brief and matter-of-fact, he looked forward to hearing whatever news Emmeline chose to share; whether it was to let him know her father's health was improving, or how many sea snails the children had collected to feed to Archimedes and Aristotle, or that Harry was fascinated with the tides and the weather and thought she might like to be a meteorologist one day, he wanted to know it all. Indeed, Xavier had a small stack of those telegrams from Kent sitting on his leather blotter, right beside his inkwell and fountain pen, and he suspected he knew every line by heart.

The Boulle clock on the mantel suddenly chimed five o'clock, and the longcase clock followed a few minutes later. Since Emmeline had gone, Xavier felt like all the magic had left this room, and indeed, the entire house. Yet little reminders of her were everywhere. Even the goddamn roof opposite his study reminded him of her.

Xavier sighed and rolled his now empty glass between his gloved palms. No matter how hard he tried *not* to think about Mrs. Emmeline Chase, his mind always returned to her. Just like he couldn't escape his great need for her. He might be able to push thoughts of her away during the day when he was focused on his work, but at night, she filled his dreams and he woke aching for her. Not only did he miss her kisses and intimate caresses, but her smile and laughter and infinitely entertaining conversation. When he'd sent her to Kent, he'd hoped he'd become accustomed to her absence. But it was rapidly becoming evident that that wasn't the case at all.

Was this constant longing inside him—this all-consuming passion—a sign he was in love?

He hardly knew.

It certainly wasn't nothing. It would be easier to put out the sun and the stars than extinguish this endless yearning for Mrs. Emmeline Chase.

Xavier put his empty brandy glass down beside Emmeline's telegrams and a stack of correspondence. He was in no mood to tackle anything related to his estate or other business concerns. Instead, he reached for the latest edition of the *Illustrated London News*, which he hadn't yet read, and sat back down at his desk. He made a superficial perusal of the articles about the Great Exhibition, news from overseas, but none of it could hold his interest.

He was as restless and twitchy as a cat eyeing a canary in a cage. He needed to do *something*, but he wasn't quite sure what.

Casting aside the newspaper, Xavier contemplated pouring another brandy. Perhaps he should reach out to Marcus to see what he was up to this evening—

At that moment, Horatio flew through the open window and landed on his perch. "*Guten tag, mein Großherzog,*" he crowed.

Xavier shook his head in bewilderment. Where on earth had his raven learned German? This bird was more of an enigma than Emmeline Chase sometimes. "I suppose you're trying to impress me with your superior linguistic skills in order to cadge a shortbread finger," he said. The raven was eyeing the plate of untouched biscuits on the afternoon tea tray on one side of Xavier's desk.

Horatio cocked his head to one side and bobbed up and down, his avian version of "yes."

Xavier moved the plate closer to the bird and gave a nod and a smile. "Well, go on then."

"I don't mind if I do," replied the raven, then he spread his glossy black wings out to their full span of four feet and two inches. As he landed on the desk with an elegant flutter, the resultant draft wildly ruffled the pages of the discarded broadsheet... and something caught Xavier's eye. An entry in the Classified Advertising Items section.

THE OBERON MUSIC HALL—HOLYWELL ST, SHOREDITCH

Proprietor & Manager, Mr. F. Evans presents an Extraordinary Evening of Eye-opening and Side-splitting Entertainment! See the spectacular Penny Blood inspired Pantomime, *The Blue Apron and the Cleaver; or, The Sanguinary Butcher of Cripplegate.*

Marvel at Mademoiselle Fizgig performing her exotic feather-fan dance and tightrope walk. Rousing sing-alongs and miscellaneous surprise acts are sure to thrill and delight.

Doors open half an hour before the show commences at precisely 8 o'clock.
Admission: Public Room, 1s; Balcony, 2s 6d; Supper Table Seats, 3s 6d; Private box, 5s

Xavier frowned at the advertisement. Where on earth had Freddy Evans, Emmeline's brother, found the money to promote his theater production in one of London's most popular newspapers? When he'd accosted Emmeline over a month ago, he'd claimed his music hall was in danger of shutting down and that money lenders were hounding him.

Emmeline had spied him at the opening of the Great Exhibition too. Of course, half of London had been in Hyde Park that day and the price of a single ticket wasn't exorbitant. But still, for a man supposedly watching his pennies...

Xavier drummed his fingers on the blotter. He suddenly knew how he should spend his evening. He wanted to find out more about Freddy Evans's business and how much debt the young man was *really* in.

"*This* is where we're spending our evening?" observed Marcus as he stared at the sadly dilapidated front of the Oberon. The once whitewashed brick face was stained with coal grime and the sign proclaiming the music hall's name above the main entrance was askew, giving the impression that it had imbibed one too many pints. "I must say, it's rather rough and ready and not what I was expecting when you proposed a night out at the theater to celebrate finishing your clock design." He turned and clapped Lord Kinsale on the back. "It's a good thing we brought you along, Phineas. You can stand in as bodyguard should a brawl break out."

The Irish peer grunted and rolled his enormous shoulders beneath his coat. "I'd-I'd like to say that I'm n-not familiar with barroom b-brawls, but that isn't the case. My advice is f-fight dirty. Don't adhere to any of the London Prize Ring rules. Dub-Dublin back-street fighting rules are more likely to apply."

Xavier cocked a brow and tapped his cane on the litter-strewn pavement. "I'd like to see anyone get close to me once I've unsheathed my rapier. But hopefully nothing like that will occur tonight. I've already secured us a private balcony."

"As long as there's something to drink other than gut-rotting gin, I'll be happy," said Marcus. "Although, I'm quite looking forward to Mademoiselle Fizgig's fan dance."

Xavier gave a huff of laughter. The viscount always had an eye for the ladies, no matter where they hailed from. He was an equal opportunity flirt. Because of his abundant charm and devilish good looks, it seemed the man's attentions were always welcomed by members of the opposite sex.

The interior of the music hall wasn't in any better condition than the outside. Once their party was seated at the small dining table in their private balcony, Xavier cast his gaze down to the main room below.

The stall seating one would expect in a regular theater had been dispensed with, and in its place were at least thirty dining tables of various shapes and sizes with four to six mismatched wooden chairs clustered around each. Suspended above the music hall was a massive gas chandelier that had seen better days. Half the gaslights didn't appear to be working and apart from an unappealing festoon of cobwebs (that made Xavier wince) there was a silk stocking and battered top hat hanging from two of the chandelier's branches. The proscenium arch needed repairing; chunks of ornate plasterwork had fallen away, and the paint was flaking off. The crimson velvet curtains hiding the stage appeared to be moth-eaten, and above the scuffed wainscoting on the hall's walls, the flocked wallpaper was curling at the corners.

Everything looked shabby and jaded, which was a shame, because this musical-theater-cum-restaurant experience had a great deal of potential. In fact, Xavier had never seen anything quite like it. He could certainly see the appeal of dining while watching a show. The issue was, even though it was almost eight o'clock and the entertainment was due to start at any minute, the hall wasn't even half full.

"The claret's rather sour and watered down." Marcus grimaced as he held up his wineglass. "The glassware could do with a good wash too."

"Th-The ale is acceptable," said Phinn before he took a rather large pull from his tankard.

Xavier had opted for claret as well, and after he took a sip, he was inclined to agree with Marcus. Before he could offer his opinion, their meals arrived—Xavier had chosen the beef and kidney pie, Phinn the lamb shank stew, and Marcus the oyster pie—and then the gaslighting was dimmed and a ginger-haired gentleman in a top hat and tailcoat appeared on stage in front of the curtains.

Freddy Evans.

"Ladies and gentlemen," Freddy declared in the strident tones of a ringmaster that carried clearly across the hall, commanding attention. Even the dull roar of the throng assembled in the public room began to abate. "Welcome to the Oberon. Prepare to be astounded and delighted. Shocked and awed. Tantalized and titillated. But above all else, entertained!"

"Bring out Mademoiselle Fizgig and 'er fans," called one bearded fellow, his cheeks ruddy with ale and good cheer, from the main room below. "I'm sure she'll titillate us."

Freddy laughed. "All in good time, my good man. All in good time. But first"—Emmeline's brother whipped off his hat and leaned forward in a conspiratorial fashion—"get ready to be horrified and mesmerized by our cast of talented players as they perform *The Blue Apron and the Cleaver; or, The Sanguinary Butcher of Cripplegate.*"

As the young man disappeared into the wings, the curtains

jerked apart to reveal a painted set that resembled a typical London butcher's yard—rough red brickwork, sawdust, and crates were the predominant features. A burly man in a bloodsplattered apron—blue of course—brandishing a cleaver in one hand and a hank of roughly butchered meat in the other, dominated the center of the stage. A pianist off to one side belted out a series of suitably dramatic chords to herald the butcher's opening soliloquy.

As the pantomime progressed, Xavier became very focused on his meal. As far as he was concerned, a play featuring far too much melodramatic shouting, screaming, butcher's off-cuts, and fountains of (hopefully) fake blood, wasn't to his taste.

Marcus and Phinn seemed equally nonplussed... at least until the next "eye-opening" act. Following a lengthy intermission in which presumably the blood and offal and butcher's bones were cleared away, Mademoiselle Fizgig suddenly appeared on stage as if from nowhere in a dramatic cloud of purple smoke. The attractive young woman wearing nothing but a low-cut beribboned corset, drawers, stockings, and heeled boots then proceeded to flit and prance about the boards, hips swaying, blond ringlets bouncing, and rouge lips pouting. Even though she had nothing but a pair of ostrich fans to shield her modesty, she didn't seem to mind the catcalls and whistles and ribald comments of the men at all. In fact, a good deal of her act involved little more than bottom wiggling, kiss blowing, and saucy winking. Xavier was nevertheless impressed by her next "feat," which was to saunter across a very narrow tightrope suspended over the stage. (Actually, he wouldn't have been at all surprised to learn that Emmeline could walk across a tightrope.)

The next act, a supposed sailor who danced a very poor hornpipe, was booed off. Then the pianist encouraged the audience to join him in belting out a bawdy ballad about cockles and oysters and pearls, and then another featuring unruly red cocks and warm muffs. Most of the patrons—including Phinn, who had an impressive baritone—seemed to know the words and sang along with gusto.

When another intermission ensued, Xavier took the opportunity to seek out Freddy Evans. It didn't take him long to find the young man. He was lingering in the downstairs hall leading to the public room, so perhaps he'd been waiting for Xavier to appear; he would have seen that the Duke of St Lawrence had booked a private box.

In any event, Xavier supposed it didn't matter. As he approached, Freddy said without preamble, "Why are you here, Your Grace?" His wary gaze fell to Xavier's cane. "Not going to relieve me of my hands, are you?"

"I've seen enough lopping off of body parts this evening, Mr. Evans. Your hands are safe. And to answer your question, I'm here to see what the Oberon has to offer. Your sister cares very much about you."

Freddy gave a snort, perhaps of disbelief. "How is she?"

"Well," said Xavier. "But she's no longer in London. She's at the seaside with my wards and your father."

Freddy's mouth worked for a moment, but Xavier couldn't interpret the emotion behind the young man's expression. "My father wrote to me a few weeks ago to let me know that you'd acquitted his debt," he said.

"I did," replied Xavier carefully. His grip tightened on his silver-topped cane. He sensed tension in the air.

"You didn't have to." Freddy's voice was gruff.

"I wanted to."

The young man's eyes narrowed and he hiked up his chin. Was that a spark of challenge in his gaze? Or was it stubborn pride or derisive anger? "Why?" he demanded hotly. "Why would you do something like that? Toffs like you, *Your Grace*, don't usually give a rat's arse about anyone else. You only look after your own kind."

It was a perfectly reasonable question and not an unreasonable accusation. Xavier would answer it as honestly as he could. "Sometimes certain people deserve second chances," he said, holding the young man's gaze, "no matter the circumstances of their birth. Aside from that, your sister is an excellent employee. I didn't want her to be unduly anxious about your father's difficult... situation." He paused for a heartbeat then added, "She worries about you too, Mr. Evans."

Freddy grunted by way of reply. He waved an expansive hand at the public room. "The Oberon will close within a fortnight. Despite my best efforts, I can't keep it going."

Xavier studied the young man's face; it was partly in shadow, but Xavier was inclined to believe him. "I saw your advertisement in the *Illustrated London News*," he said. "And I was curious. That's why I'm here this evening."

Freddy smirked. "Like slumming it, do you?"

Xavier ignored his question. "I think your business has potential, Mr. Evans."

Another smirk and then a snort. "Well, a fat lot of good such a pronouncement will do me now, Your Grace. That advertisement you saw was my last-ditch attempt to keep the Oberon afloat. But it's all been for naught. I'm sure you can see that this business is a sinkhole for money. I need to refurbish the entire theater. My kitchen needs a better cook. My cellar needs better wine. I'd like to put on pantomimes that have wider appeal, instead of horrendous penny-gaff plays, but I can't attract or retain the right talent because the theater is in disrepair and hasn't a good reputation. I suspect that you've already formed the opinion that my shows are piecemeal at best. And you wouldn't be wrong. I'm caught between a rock and a hard place with no way out except declaring bankruptcy, just like my father did." A muscle flickered in the young man's jaw. "You may not believe me, but it kills me to think my father fell on his sword for me. And I'm still letting him down. Emmeline too. I'm the family disgrace."

Before Xavier could respond, the music hall's pianist started to bang out a lively tune and Freddy tilted into a mock bow. "You'd best get back to your private box, Your Grace," he said. "I'm sure you don't want to miss the rest of the show." And then he turned on his heel and pushed through the door leading back to the public room.

I'm the family disgrace ...

Two things occurred to Xavier as he climbed the stairs leading him back to his friends. One: It seemed that Freddy Evans had more in common with the Duke of St Lawrence than he knew.

And two: Perhaps Emmeline's father wasn't the only one who deserved a second chance.

Chapter 25

A Seaside Sojourn, a Reunion, and Revelation...

"Nanny Chase, Nanny Chase," called Gareth as he ran toward Emmeline across the pale golden sand of Kingsgate Beach. "Look what I found!"

"More sea-glass?" asked Emmeline as the excited boy tumbled a small handful of "pebbles" into her outstretched palm. The pieces of blue, aquamarine, and green glass, polished smooth by the sea's waves, glinted in the late afternoon sunlight. "How beautiful."

Harry, who was sitting on the sand a few feet away, glanced up from her notebook where'd she'd been sketching a starfish. This week, she'd decided she wanted to become a zoologist. "You have quite a lot now, Gareth," she said. "Well done."

"Yes, indeed," said Emmeline. As she picked up an ice-blue fragment to examine it more closely, she tried very hard not to compare it to the Duke of St Lawrence's eyes. But of course, she failed. When it came to her employer, the more she tried *not* to think about him, the more her brain refused to cooperate. Oh, she really was a hopeless, lovelorn case.

She attempted to hand Gareth's treasures back, but the boy

shook his head. "No, you keep them safe in your pocket, Nanny Chase. I don't want to lose them."

"Very well," she said and closed her fingers around them. "How is Bartholomew's quest for seashells going?" Emmeline glanced over to the shoreline where Bartholomew and her father were still searching for items to add to the boy's collection. Bertie waited close by, "standing guard." Emmeline experienced a pang of sympathy for the young man; attired in his formal footman's livery, he was the epitome of awkward. Every time a wave washed up and threatened to splash over the toes of his leather shoes, he took a pronounced step backward. At one point, he'd had to fight off a seagull that kept swooping down to peck at his powdered periwig and coat's brass buttons. (Although, that incident had been laugh-inducing rather than pang-inducing.)

Gareth screwed up his nose while he contemplated Emmeline's question about his brother. "I think Bartholomew's found a few shells. He wants Harry to name them all." He brushed his sandy hands down the front of his breeches. "Are you sure Cousin Xavier won't pay a visit? I want to show him my sea-glass."

Emmeline's chest cramped with a bittersweet pain. While it was heartwarming to see how much closer the duke and his wards had become, she must acknowledge that it was partly her fault that His Grace had sent them all away. Or more to the point, she was the reason he wouldn't be joining them.

But before she could respond to Gareth's question, his sister spoke. "I want to see Cousin Xavier too," said Harry. "But remember what Nanny Chase said. He needs peace and quiet to finish his special clock plans."

"I know," said Gareth with glum resignation, kicking at a nearby rock. "When can we go back to the castle, Nanny Chase? I'm getting hungry."

Emmeline's gaze skipped back to the gray walls of Kingscliff where it sat atop a chalk-faced promontory like a giant slumbering beast. The enormous clock in the castle's central tower declared the time to be almost six o'clock. "I suppose we could return home now. It is getting on a bit."

"Oh, jolly good," declared Gareth with a bright smile. "I hope there's something smashing for tea. I'll go and get Bartholomew and Mr. Evans and Bertie."

Before Emmeline could say anything, he raced off, his small feet kicking up a surprising amount of sand that landed in his sister's lap.

"Ugh," said Harry, climbing to her feet and shaking out her skirts. "Why are boys so tiresome?"

Emmeline laughed as she slipped Gareth's sea-glass into her pocket. "They can be. Some more than others."

Harry eyed her over her glasses. "Do you have brothers or sisters, Nanny Chase?"

"Just a brother," she said. Her heart clenched with an entirely different sort of pang this time. "His name is Freddy. He's a few years older than me."

Harry nodded, her expression grave. "Well then, you must know exactly what I mean. About boys. I honestly don't know why women ever fall in love and get married to the vexing creatures. I'm glad I'm going to be some sort of scientist one day and have a career. Then I won't have to marry."

"That certainly sounds like something to aspire to," Emmeline said. "But I should point out, not *all* members of the opposite sex are vexing."

Harry sighed and tucked her notebook under her arm. "Perhaps you're right. I don't think Cousin Xavier is vexing. Our mama loved our papa." She glanced at Emmeline again. "Do you think you'll ever get married again, Mrs. Chase?"

"Oh . . . I . . . Probably not," she said, suddenly feeling flustered. Perhaps she needed to have a talk with Miss Harriet

Mason about what sorts of topics were "manners" and which were not. Just like she needed to have yet another stern talk with herself about her inappropriate obsession with the duke.

Even though they'd all been in Kent for over a fortnight, Emmeline still thought about her employer far too much. At this rate, she'd never be rid of her unrequited love for this man.

The boys, her father, and Bertie joined her and Harry, and then they all began the trek back to Kingscliff Castle. It was a good five-minute walk across the strand past the other beach-goers, and then they had to scale a steep set of stone stairs up to the shop- and hotel-lined High Street of the small village of Kingsgate. One of the duke's carriages would then ferry them back to the castle. While Emmeline would have enjoyed the walk up the steep headland—and no doubt Harry and Bertie could manage it—she was concerned that such a trek would prove too difficult for her father and young Gareth and Bartholomew. Her father, while much improved, still had nights when his cough plagued him.

As they walked, Emmeline's gaze settled on the duke's childhood home and its rather grim aspect—its dark gray bulk with its crenellated battlements and looming central tower.

She shivered as she imagined Xavier as a small boy, banished to that clock tower, all alone and afraid, high above the bustling hamlet and beach. To think she might have been down on the shore, paddling and collecting shells and sea-glass while he was imprisoned with nothing to do but watch the beach below and the inner workings of the great clock. No wonder he'd developed a passion for timekeeping.

If she had the magical ability to turn back the hands of time, she would storm that castle and rescue him.

Emmeline was helping Bertie to hand the children into the duke's carriage when someone across the street by the King's Arms Hotel called her name. "Emmeline!"

Freddy?

She swung around on the footpath and then her mouth dropped open in shocked amazement. It *was* her brother.

"Freddy!" She couldn't hide the incredulity in her voice. "What on earth are you doing here? How did you find me... and Papa?" Her gaze swung to their father, whose countenance had blanched. He looked like he'd seen a ghost.

"Son," said Edward Evans gruffly. And then he dabbed at his eyes with his sleeve. Turning to Emmeline he said, "I wrote to your brother, after I left New—" He broke off and glanced at Bertie, but the footman was still fussing about with the carriage. "And then I sent him another letter after we left London. I wanted him to know that I was out of danger. And that I didn't blame him for... for everything that happened."

"I see," said Emmeline. Perhaps that explained why she'd caught glimpses of Freddy near the park in Belgrave Square and then at the Crystal Palace. She beckoned to her brother. "Well come on then, Freddy. Don't stand there like a shag on a rock."

He gave a quick nod, then, hands stuffed deep in his coat pockets, he crossed the street. When he reached them, he chewed on his lip for a moment then said, "It's... it's good to see you both."

Edward Evans snorted. "Is that all you're going to say? Come here, Son." And then he reached out and embraced Freddy tightly. When he drew back, he wiped his eyes on his sleeve again.

Freddy eyed Emmeline sheepishly. "Might I have a hug too, Sis?"

Emmeline gave an inelegant sniff and dashed at her damp cheek with her fingertips. While part of her wanted to embrace her brother, she wasn't quite ready to forgive him for everything he'd done. All the pain he'd caused their family. She also didn't trust him. Not yet.

"I'm on duty," she said, and gestured with her chin at the carriage. "I'm taking care of my employer's wards."

Freddy nodded. "I understand, but I . . . I need to speak with you. It's important."

Even though Emmeline's curiosity was piqued, she frowned. "Very well. I suppose you'd best come back to the castle with us then. We can talk in the garden."

"I can walk and meet you there," said Freddy. "If there isn't enough room in the carriage."

"All right," said Emmeline. She wouldn't let her wards out of her sight until they were safely installed in the nursery at Kingscliff with one of the maids and Bertie watching over them. "I shall see you soon."

Freddy nodded. "I'll be there." Then he turned and strode away, shoulders hunched, his hands still in his pockets, heading for the castle on the cliff.

"It's good of you to see me, Em," said Freddy not half an hour later. They faced each other in Kingscliff's knot garden on the leeside of the castle. "I know you don't have a lot of reason to trust me, considering how things ended the last time we met."

Emmeline nodded. "You could say that. You were trying to drag me back to the Oberon and throw me on stage to do Lord knows what to keep you in business."

Freddy winced. "I'm truly sorry for that. But I was desperate and afraid that I—" He pressed his lips together.

"Afraid that you were going to end up in Newgate like our poor father?"

"Yes. I still might unless . . ."

Emmeline frowned. "Unless what?"

To her surprise, Freddy reached into the pocket of his sack coat and withdrew a silver pocket watch. And not just any ordinary sort of pocket watch.

Before he even placed the timepiece in her hand, Emmeline knew what it was. It was a priceless Markwick that bore a striking resemblance to the one she'd seen at Pembridge's all those weeks and weeks ago. The one that Mr. Howell from Howell's in Chancery Lane had outbid her for.

"Freddy," she breathed, turning it over and examining the hallmark before flipping it open and studying the watch face inside. "Where on earth did you get this? It's worth a fortune." Then her heart almost stopped. "You didn't st—" She broke off before she could complete the horribly insulting thought.

"No. I *didn't* steal it," said Freddy. "It was gifted to me by an anonymous stranger. Just yesterday. It was delivered to the Oberon with a handwritten note proclaiming that if I took it to Christie's or Sotheby's it would fetch at least five hundred pounds at auction. If not more."

"Really? That much?" whispered Emmeline. Then she cleared her throat and said, "You said that you don't know who sent this."

Freddy rubbed his stubbled chin. "There was no name on the note. But I did wonder if it might be . . . your employer."

Emmeline's eyebrows shot up. "The Duke of St Lawrence? Why would you think—" She narrowed her gaze. "Do you have the note with you?"

"I do," said Freddy. Again, he reached into his pocket and then withdrew a fine parchment envelope which he handed to Emmeline.

As soon as she saw the handwriting, she knew it was true. "Freddy, you're right. The duke is your mysterious benefactor." She lifted her eyes to her brother's. "But why?" She was truly baffled.

He shrugged. "I'm not sure, but two nights ago, he came to the Oberon with two of his friends to see a show. We had a brief, private exchange in which he said that sometimes certain people deserved a second chance. I thought he was referring to Father because he settled his debt so he could be released from prison. But maybe he meant me too."

"I don't think there's any 'maybe' about it," murmured Emmeline. Her throat suddenly felt far too tight and her gaze was so misty, she could barely see the flowers in the knot garden or the bright sea beyond.

Why, why would the duke do this? His generosity appeared to know no bounds.

He's done it for you, *Emmeline, you pigeon-wit. Despite the fact he said he doesn't think his heart functions properly.*

She handed the Markwick pocket watch and the duke's note back to her brother. "You should take the duke's advice and sell it. You'll be able to pay off all your debts. Start afresh."

Freddy nodded as he pocketed both items. "The Duke of St Lawrence clearly values you, Em. One might even venture to say that he likes, even cares for you."

Emmeline swallowed. "I . . . Perhaps he does. A little. I honestly don't know what to think."

Her brother nodded. "Toffs, eh?" Then his expression changed, his forehead furrowing. "There's something I need to tell you. Something rather unsavory. Perhaps even alarming. And it doesn't portray me in a flattering light either." He blew out a breath then said, "Sod it, I have to tell you, Em. Your duke has a powerful enemy."

Emmeline frowned in confusion. "How? Why would you know anything about that?"

Freddy wiped a hand over his brow and looked out to sea before meeting her gaze. "The day I encountered you near St Paul's, when the duke and I had words, two strange men turned up at the Oberon a few hours later. One was rather large with a distinctive scar across his face."

Emmeline sucked in a breath. "What? Did you learn his name?"

Freddy nodded. "He told me his name was West. His friend, a smaller wiry fellow, never gave his name."

"What did they want?" asked Emmeline. "They didn't threaten you, did they?"

"Not in so many words, but they were intimidating to say the least. The scar-faced man, West, said that he and his friend had observed the altercation between me and the duke. And then they offered me money to spy on him... and you. They said they were employed by a well-to-do gentleman—I never learned his name either—who, for his own reasons, wanted to unsettle and intimidate the duke by disrupting his life as much as possible."

Emmeline gasped. "What did you say? Don't tell me you agreed."

Freddy looked shamefaced. "I did. I was desperate, Em. And the money they offered allowed me to pay several outstanding bills, including the wages of my cast. I was able to place an advertisement in the *Illustrated London News* to garner more attention for my new show."

Emmeline shook her head. She was unable to hide the disappointed disapproval in her voice as she said, "I can't believe you would do something so sneaky and underhanded. At least it explains why I thought I saw you twice."

"Yes, I did spy on you, Em... and Father. And the duke," he said, remorse weighting his words. "You won't believe me, but I missed you and I was worried about you. West and his crony told me the duke had lost his marbles, so I wanted to see for myself. I wanted to make sure that you and Father weren't in any danger. So over the next two weeks, I watched you."

"I saw you in Belgrave Square and at the Great Exhibition."

Freddy's mouth curved with a ghost of a smile. "That day you were in the park in Belgrave Square, you looked so happy, Em, playing with the duke's wards. And the way you and the duke both looked at each other in the Crystal Palace, I could see you had a special rapport. I couldn't betray you. So I fed

West a load of balderdash about where I'd seen you and what you'd been doing. I think they wanted me to wheedle my way into your good graces again. To perhaps persuade you to join their cause. But in the end, my stories weren't enough."

Emmeline's skin prickled and she suddenly felt cold. "What do you mean?"

"West tried to talk me into doing other nefarious things to upset the duke. Petty criminal things such as throwing rocks at the ground floor windows of St Lawrence House late at night, and breaking into his stables in the mews to let out the horses, or tampering with deliveries left at the servants' entrance, but I refused. Spying was one thing. Breaking the law was an entirely different kettle of fish. I could sense West was starting to get annoyed with me for not doing his bidding."

"This West and his partner," said Emmeline, "are you sure they never gave you even the slightest hint about who might be employing them?"

Freddy shook his head. "No. Never. They only ever referred to the man paying them to pull the strings as the guv'nor."

The guv'nor. Hot anger fizzed and flared inside Emmeline like a firecracker about to explode. If she ever found out who it was—

"But," added Freddy before she could complete her thought, "the last time I met West in a public bar off Fleet Street late one night—the night before the Duke of St Lawrence came to the Oberon—he was farewelling another man who mentioned something about needing to get back to St Lawrence House before he was missed. He also intimated he had a sweetheart waiting for him. West used the man's name when he said goodbye."

Emmeline's pulse immediately leapt. "Who? What was his name? What did he look like?"

Freddy worried at his lower lip. "I only caught a glimpse of this chap, mind you. And I might have misheard his name. The tap room was noisy—"

"Freddy!" Emmeline gave him a light punch on the arm. "Out with it."

"All right, all right, Em. Calm down," said her brother, rubbing his bicep. "The fellow was tall, about my height, with a slender build and brown hair. About my age, too, or slightly younger. And the name I heard was Ollie."

Chapter 26

Concerning Another Teleportation Cock-up, Crabcakes, Syrup Puddles, Befuddlement, and Somersaults...

*O*llie.

Ollie was the wolf in sheep's clothing. The domestic saboteur. The betrayer.

The bastard!

Emmeline couldn't believe the duke's footman would stoop so low. Those were the thoughts that kept running through her head as she supervised the children's dinner hour in the nursery. Her smoldering anger grew hotter and brighter the more she contemplated everything the despicable blighter had done.

And to think that he might have a female accomplice as well. It was impossible to tell whom Ollie had been specifically referring to when he'd mentioned he had a "sweetheart." If the woman was one of the St Lawrence House maids, Emmeline had no idea who it might be. Ollie tended to flirt with *everyone* including Emmeline. He'd even flirted with Mrs. Lambton and Mrs. Punchbowl on occasion.

After Emmeline had farewelled Freddy—he was going to invite their father to dine with him at the King's Arms—she'd quizzed Bertie if he'd ever noticed Ollie pursuing any of the maids. But Bertie had just blushed and said he had no idea if Ollie had a ladylove.

"Do *you* like Ollie, Nanny Chase?" he'd then asked, his eyes not meeting hers.

"I... Why no, Bertie. Not like that. I'm definitely not looking for a paramour. Besides, I'm sure the duke frowns upon any fraternization between staff members."

Bertie had nodded. "I expect you're right," he'd mumbled, toeing the edge of the wainscoting with his shoe.

Poor Bertie. Emmeline suspected the footman might have a bit of a crush on her, but she'd rather hoped someone else might catch his eye. Another maid at St Lawrence House perhaps.

Someone like Fanny? Except... Emmeline frowned. After talking with Freddy, she was starting to wonder if the nurserymaid *might* be Ollie's sweetheart.

An image of Ollie and Fanny in Hyde Park, right before Gareth had disappeared popped into her mind.

Apparently the maid had been most put out after she'd been informed by the duke that she wouldn't be accompanying his wards and Emmeline to Kent. Later on in the nursery, the young woman had been in a pouty, sullen mood and had accused Emmeline of blaming her for what had happened to Gareth. That she was being punished for letting go of the boy's hand for a brief moment.

Emmeline had been quite taken aback by Fanny's attitude. She'd reassured the young woman that she didn't blame her. That it was the scar-faced stranger who'd been responsible. But what if Fanny and Ollie had been working together all along?

Emmeline had to let the duke know as soon as possible of this new, explosive intelligence that Freddy had shared, but the telegraph office at the train station would be closed by now. Aside from her own father, she didn't know if she could trust anyone to hand deliver a message. In any event, the next train to London from Kingsgate Railway Station via Dover didn't leave until nine o'clock the next morning.

As soon as the children were asleep, Emmeline would *have* to teleport to St Lawrence House. It was the only way she could warn the duke about the very real danger lurking under his own roof. She reasoned it wasn't *really* breaking the Parasol Academy Rules for her to do so. Surely it was her duty.

After Emmeline read the boys a bedtime story—Harry had her nose buried in a zoological journal—she tucked them into bed as the sun was setting. Since they'd been at the seaside, the children had worn themselves out every single day with energetic romps at the beach, and along the clifftops, and exploring the enormous castle and its grounds. Once they were asleep, they wouldn't wake until morning. Even so, Emmeline had asked one of the resident housemaids that the children had taken a liking to—a young local lass named Milly—to sleep on a pallet bed in the nursery adjacent to the children's bedchamber. Just in case one of the children had a bad dream. She'd told the maid she had a megrim and wished to take a sleeping draught, so she might not wake up if any of the children stirred. Milly, not suspecting anything was amiss, had readily agreed.

Emmeline wasn't anticipating that anyone would try to kidnap the children from their beds—Kingscliff Castle was well-staffed and the duke had sent instructions indicating that several footmen were to guard the entrances every single night. Besides, Emmeline reasoned that she would only be away for a handful of hours at most.

Once Emmeline had retired to her room, she locked the door. It had been weeks and weeks since she'd last teleported and she couldn't afford to muck this up. The logical place to teleport to was the wardrobe in her bedroom at St Lawrence House. No one would observe her arrival. And when she met with the duke, she'd simply tell him a white lie . . . that she'd traveled by train and then hired a hansom cab to convey her to

Belgrave Square. Hopefully he'd forgive her for leaving his wards behind. Such a powder keg of a secret about Ollie had to be shared.

Emmeline withdrew her leyport key from the pocket in her uniform and slid it into the keyhole of the ancient mahogany wardrobe in her castle bedchamber. It might have been her imagination, but the pewter key seemed to vibrate and tingle in her hand as she turned it in the wardrobe's lock. It was almost as though the key was thrumming with anticipation.

As soon as she'd opened the door and pushed her gowns aside, she located the leylight in the dark shadows. The tiny tongue of flame flickered, drawing her in, inviting her to make use of its power, asking her to share her destination. So Emmeline did. She focused all her thoughts on her wardrobe at St Lawrence House, drew a fortifying breath, then whispered, "*Vortexio.*"

Almost immediately, she was caught up in a great whirlpool of white light. It spun her around and around, propelling her heavenward, as though she were as weightless and insubstantial as a swirling cloud of moondust and starlight.

When the discombobulating journey stopped, Emmeline was so giddy and breathless, she reached out a hand to steady herself. Her fingers encountered something hard and smooth like polished wood—a door perhaps—but when she opened her eyes, she nearly fainted. She wasn't in her wardrobe in her bedroom.

She was in the very middle of the Duke of St Lawrence's study, her palm pressed to the back of a chair.

Only a few feet away stood the duke himself. Framed in the doorway of his Horology Room, he stared wide-eyed and gaping, because he'd just witnessed a woman materialize from nowhere right in front of him.

Crabcakes and dickens on toast with a good helping of bugger and blast.

How on earth was she going to be able to explain *this* away?

The duke's jaw closed then opened again as though he were about to speak but words failed him.

"I'm so sorry," began Emmeline just as the duke said, "Please don't tell me the wind blew you into my study. I know that's not true because the window's closed."

Emmeline screwed up her nose a little. "I could have been blown down the chimney?" she ventured hopefully.

"I don't think so," said the duke, holding her gaze. "You're not covered in soot." He drew closer until he was standing right in front of her. "There's not even a smudge on your face. Not like the first time we met." He suddenly reached up and brushed his gloved thumb across her cheek. "I don't know how or why you can do what you do, Mrs. Chase," he said in a low, velvet-smooth voice. "But what I *do* know to be true is that I've missed you."

Oh... Emmeline's heart promptly melted into a warm, golden, syrupy puddle. "I've missed you too," she whispered. "Rather a lot." *More than I should say...*

His hand dropped away but his eyes still held hers. "I've suspected for some time that you can perform magic. Unless you have some other sort of plausible explanation for what I witnessed just now?"

"I..." Emmeline swallowed. There didn't seem much point in lying about anything under the circumstances. "It's difficult to explain—and I can't really tell you exactly how I can do what I can do—other than I'm a Parasol nanny. As part of my training at the Academy, I learned to teleport between places and use incantations to clean up messes and repair broken things. I have magical pockets in my uniform from which I can withdraw items that will assist me to effectively carry out my duties. My Academy-issued umbrella and parasol can be used for protection too. I can also converse with Horatio like he's a person. We can send messages to each other's minds. It's a bit like sending mental telegrams without the wires."

The duke's eyebrows shot up. "You can? I'm not sure whether to be intrigued or horrified by the notion."

Emmeline laughed at that. "Horatio is a very entertaining conversationalist and he thinks the world of you." Then she sighed. "I'm supposed to be discreet when using magic. And I'm only meant to employ my skills while in service to my charges or carrying out official Academy business." She winced. "I'm not very good with the discreet bit considering I've told you almost everything. And I have been known to bend the rules when it comes to the last bit too."

"I see," said the duke. "I'm a horologist who's always believed in scientific principles. I analyze evidence and draw logical conclusions from what is before me. But for once—and most inexplicably—all that doesn't matter to me. While I still don't understand how your magic works, I've somehow come to accept that you can make seemingly impossible things perfectly possible. Perhaps I believe you because I trust you."

Emmeline smiled shyly. Hearing the duke had absolute faith in her meant so much. "I trust you too," she said. "Although, Mrs. Temple would be *very* miffed if she found out that I've shared so many of the Parasol Academy's secrets with you."

The duke's expression shifted into the realm of concerned. "You've taken a huge risk coming here the way you have. Which begs the question: Why? Why did you choose to teleport—is that the word?—into my study tonight? Is it something related to my wards? Are they all right?"

"Oh yes. They're fine. Perfectly fine," replied Emmeline hurriedly. "Snuggled up safely in their beds in Kent with one of the maids sleeping nearby. And there are footmen on all the doors. So you have nothing to worry about on that score."

"So why *are* you here?"

Emmeline inhaled a bracing breath. "I found out something significant early this evening. Something you'd want to know straightaway. I learned the name of the servant who's been upsetting things in St Lawrence House and who may have had a hand in Gareth's attempted kidnapping."

The duke's eyebrows shot up toward his hairline. "You did? Who is it? How did you find out?"

"My brother, Freddy, told me. He came to visit me in Kent." And then she recounted everything that her brother had disclosed to her.

"Ollie," said the duke in a voice that contained an ominous note like distant thunder. "It was Ollie all this time?" Then under his breath, "The devious dog."

"It would seem so," said Emmeline. "As I said, Freddy didn't hear the name of Ollie's sweetheart, so it's unclear whether she has been involved in all the household havoc. Perhaps he might share that information."

"Perhaps. Do *you* have an idea who she might be?"

"Fanny springs to mind."

The duke gave a decisive nod. "I agree." His mouth had compressed into a hard grim line. "With any luck, Ollie might also disclose the 'guv'nor's' actual identity." He crossed to the bellpull and gave it a tug. "I'll have Woodley summon the man himself."

"What will we tell Woodley and the other servants? About my out-of-the-blue arrival that no one witnessed?" asked Emmeline.

"We'll simply say that you arrived via the kitchen entrance when no one was about. Do you think that would suffice?"

Emmeline smiled. "It seems more plausible than telling them the wind blew me through the window or down the chimney."

The duke shook his head. "Part of me thinks I must be dreaming. The idea of you teleporting from Kent is . . . fantastical. I wouldn't have believed it if I hadn't seen it with my own eyes."

"How do you know you're *not* dreaming?" teased Emmeline.

The duke smiled. "Because in my dreams you're never wearing that horrid cap, Mrs. Chase." Leaning closer, his warm breath caressed her ear as he added, "Aside from that, no dream I've ever had smells as wonderful as you."

And then, damn it, there was a knock on the door and the duke couldn't say anything more because Woodley had arrived.

"It wasn't me, Your Grace. Honest. I don't know what you're talking about," declared a white-faced Ollie. He swallowed, his Adam's apple bobbing frantically above his collar when he noticed that Xavier was holding his silver-topped cane. It was well-known amongst the staff at St Lawrence House that there was a sword hidden inside that innocuous-looking gentleman's accessory. "I've done nothing wrong. I swear. Everyone says it's the ghost who's been upsetting things."

"What rubbish. There is no ghost," returned Xavier hotly. He gripped the top of his cane tighter to stop himself from grabbing the footman by the lapels and then pummeling him to dust. "Are you seriously going to tell me it was a ghost who tried to kidnap my young ward in the middle of Hyde Park? A five-year-old child? I should hand you over to Scotland Yard. In fact, I can ask Woodley to summon the constable outside in the square right now."

The butler, who was blocking the study door, gave a sharp nod. "I'd be happy to, Your Grace. Tom is on duty at the front entrance. Ned is waiting outside in the hall too."

Ollie's countenance turned as green as pea soup. "I-I d-didn't do anything wrong," he stammered weakly.

"Then how do you account for everything Mrs. Chase's brother heard?" demanded Xavier. He gestured at Emmeline, who was standing by the fireplace, observing the exchange. "How do you explain your association with this scar-faced man named West? The same cur who tried to abduct my ward! While you were standing close by!"

"I can't," whispered Ollie, transferring his weight nervously from one foot to the other. His gaze darted about Xavier's study, landing everywhere except on Xavier. "I can't say anything. Otherwise—"

"Otherwise, what?" snapped Xavier, his tone sharper than his rapier.

Ollie swallowed and pulled at his collar. "Otherwise West or the guv'nor might have something to say about it. You don't know what they're like."

Aha! So Freddy Evans had been telling the truth. Despite the fact Ollie seemed genuinely afraid, Xavier had not one speck of sympathy for the man. "Yet you didn't seem to have any problem taking money from this guv'nor character to create chaos in my household. For months and months. If you tell me his name, Ollie, and why he's orchestrated this whole insidious campaign against me, perhaps Scotland Yard will go easier on you. Maybe you won't be thrown in prison for the rest of your days for aiding and abetting the kidnapping of an innocent child."

Ollie shook his head. "I don't know the guv'nor's name. Only that he wanted you to be constantly disrupted and unsettled. So that's what I did. That's all I can tell you. He's the one who arranged for West to try to kidnap Gareth. I wasn't involved in that."

"Yet you were there when it happened," Xavier all but snarled. He stalked over to the window behind his desk and braced his forearm against the wall. He needed to put some distance between himself and the footman to stop himself beating the truth out of the sniveling swine.

Emmeline cleared her throat. "Ollie, *was* the goal to stop the duke from completing his work? So he wouldn't be able to meet the submission date for the Westminster clock competition?"

The footman shrugged, his expression sullen. "How should I know?"

Xavier snorted. "Well, if it was, he hasn't succeeded." He

glanced at Emmeline and managed to throw her a small smile. "I completed my design two nights ago."

Emmeline's answering smile was as bright and joyous as a sunbeam striking the sea on a summer's day. "Oh, that's absolutely wonderful, Your Grace. Congratulations. I'm so happy for you."

He inclined his head. "Thank you."

"Yes, well done, Your Grace," added Woodley. "That's quite an achievement. I know you've been working on your plan for such a long time."

"I have another question for Ollie, Your Grace," said Emmeline.

Xavier gestured with his cane. "Ask away."

The nanny faced the footman. "When you saw West at the pub off Fleet Street a few nights ago, you mentioned you had a sweetheart waiting for you. Who is she, Ollie? Is she one of the maids at St Lawrence House? Has she been involved in this plot to undermine the duke too?"

Ollie looked down his nose at her. "That's none of your business."

Undaunted, the nanny asked, "Is it Fanny?"

The footman snorted. "Hardly. She's not my type. If you must know, I've been courting a housemaid who works at one of the other nearby toffs' houses. Her name is Flora. We both sneak out at night sometimes and meet up in the mews. She's Scottish, and like you, a redhead. A right cracker of a wen—"

"Enough," snapped Xavier. "There's a lady present." He didn't want to, but he withdrew his rapier from his cane. As he moved forward, the gaslights glancing off the steel blade, Ollie stepped back a pace, his expression fearful. "I've heard quite enough. Perhaps you'll be a little more forthcoming when the police arrive to take you to Scotland Yard for questioning. Woodley?" He addressed the butler. "Ned's outside, you say? He can help you escort Ollie to—"

"I won't go!" cried Ollie. He looked wild-eyed and green again as he began to back toward the door, but Woodley—a tall, imposing man despite his middle age—was barring his way. "You can't make me."

All of a sudden, Emmeline was moving swiftly toward the panicking footman. "Ollie, you look like you're going to be ill or faint. Here"—she thrust a small, cut-crystal bottle beneath his nostrils—"my smelling salts might help."

And then she whispered something that Xavier couldn't quite hear.

A second later, a few tendrils of pale purple mist wafted out of the tiny bottle and straight into Ollie's face... or rather straight up his nose. The footman's gaze grew soft and dreamy. "Oh, hullo there. Give us a kiss then, pet."

Emmeline stepped back just out of reach. "Oh, I don't think so, Ollie. Why don't you accompany Woodley outside into the hall? He and Ned are going to make sure you're nice and safe and comfortable for a spell." She caught the butler's eye—he appeared not to have noticed anything odd taking place as Ollie's back had been facing him—and she murmured, "That lockable storage cupboard beside the servants' stairs might be a suitable place for Ollie to wait and contemplate his life choices until a certain Scottish 'you know who' arrives."

Woodley bowed. "Great minds think alike, Nanny Chase. I'll have Ned stand guard until they do."

"Does that meet with your approval, Your Grace?" asked Emmeline over her shoulder.

Xavier quirked a brow. "It does indeed." The nanny had somehow made Ollie as malleable as a warmed pat of butter, so he wasn't going to second-guess her.

Woodley summoned Ned, and then they both escorted a pleasantly bemused and still inanely grinning Ollie out of Xavier's study.

As the door closed behind them, Xavier resheathed his

sword. "Brava, Mrs. Chase. I don't know what you did exactly, but it was truly marvelous to behold." He was grinning a little inanely too, which was not like him at all.

"I cast a confusion spell. But I'm afraid it only works for a few minutes," she said. "I suspect Ollie will soon be back to his normal self and no doubt he'll try to escape from the storage cupboard. I hope the lock is sound. Ollie isn't a small man. A few well-aimed kicks and he might break free."

Xavier nodded. "Good point. I'll have a word to Woodley and have Ollie moved to the coal cellar if needed. While I'm waiting for Scotland Yard to arrive, I'll also take the opportunity to speak with Mrs. Lambton about the maids. I don't believe for a minute that Ollie was courting a Scots lass from a neighboring house. Do you?"

Mrs. Chase shook her head. "No. At this point, I'm still inclined to think it might be Fanny who's the accomplice. But I don't have any real evidence. Only a suspicion."

"I trust your suspicions. You have good instincts. Right." He sighed. "I'd best send word to the Yard before I do anything else."

The nanny nodded. "Before you do, I wanted to thank you from the bottom of my heart for what you did for Freddy. The reason he traveled to Kent was to tell me about the Markwick pocket watch he received. I know it was you who gave it to him, Your Grace, and you didn't have to do that. You've done so much already."

Xavier cleared his throat. "Think nothing of it, Emmeline. That watch should have been yours all those weeks ago. I bought it off Howell not long after you started here, with the intention of giving it to you sometime in the future. To make your life a little better. Just like you've made my life better."

Her expression softened. "You say and do the loveliest things sometimes, Your Grace. You might not wish to acknowledge it, but you do have a heart that is capable of much more than you give it credit for."

Before Xavier could respond—he was, for the moment, quite flummoxed—she continued. "Well, I suppose I should teleport back to Kingscliff—"

In a handful of strides, Xavier crossed the short stretch of carpet separating them and caught one of her hands. "Don't go, Emmeline. Not yet. I might need you again. We still haven't worked out who this blasted guv'nor is. I'm sure my wards will be safe for the time being."

Emmeline bit her bottom lip and that's all Xavier could seem to focus on. "If you're certain."

"I am." Because he couldn't help himself, he raised her bare hand to his lips and feathered a light kiss over her knuckles. Then he turned it so her palm was facing upward before pressing a soft kiss to her wrist, right where her pulse fluttered. "Will you wait for me in my Horology Room?" he murmured.

"Of course, Your Grace."

He gave a sharp nod. "Good. But you must call me Xavier when we are alone. I decree it."

When she smiled softly and said, "Very well, Xavier," his heart—the one she'd brought to life—practically performed a somersault in his chest.

He hadn't lied when he'd said he needed her.

He needed her more than words could ever express.

Chapter 27

In Which a Barrage of Questions Is Followed by Disclosures and Declarations (One of Which Features a Double Three-legged Gravity Escapement); Concluding with a Question and Irresistible Invitation...

*T*icktock, ticktock.

Emmeline paced the floor of the duke's Horology Room, her footfalls keeping time with the innumerable clocks and watches on display. The duke—Xavier—had been away for over an hour and she was literally dying of impatience to know what was going on.

Of course, she could leave the Horology Room and seek him out. But she'd promised that she'd stay here and wait. *Why* she had to stay hidden she didn't know. Unless Xavier thought Ollie might be difficult and kick up a great fuss when the police arrived... But she'd already proven time and again that she wasn't a shrinking violet. She wasn't a fair society maiden who needed protecting from anything unsavory.

She would have been happy to help Mrs. Lambton question the maids. But perhaps Xavier thought they might be more forthcoming with the housekeeper. Fanny might be mulish like the last time Emmeline had seen her. If that were the case, it was likely she wouldn't be able to coax anything useful from the young woman. Especially if it were incriminating.

Horatio would be pleasant company, but he hadn't been in his master's study and his perch in the Horology Room was vacant as well. He *might* be upstairs in the duke's private suite, but Emmeline could hardly go looking for him there.

Yes, if anyone spied Nanny Chase entering the Duke of St Lawrence's bedchamber or adjacent sitting room, her career would be as sunk as a French naval ship at the Battle of Trafalgar. That would be a surefire way of waving goodbye to her career as a licensed Parasol Academy nanny for good.

Emmeline plopped into a damask-upholstered wingchair by the Horology Room's fireplace and hugged a silk cushion to her chest. The deep velvet-blue vaulted ceiling soared above her. Even though it was filled with shadows, the gaslights picked out the silver and gold constellations along with the moon and the sun.

Her gaze lit on the inscription above the jib door: *Tempus Rerum Imperator*: *Time, the Ruler of all Things*. Except, for Emmeline it wasn't time that ruled her. It was the duke.

Xavier had her heart. He was the man she'd follow to the ends of the earth and love until her dying day.

She released a wistful sigh and hugged the cushion tighter.

If only they could be together. If only Xavier would love her and she could forget about all the barriers between them—both the Parasol Academy's rules and society's that were keeping them apart—then they might have a chance. If the rest of the world went away and it was only her and Xavier building a life together . . . creating a family with his wards, how glorious that would be.

Something *had* changed, though. Xavier had asked her to stay. His declaration that he'd missed her had been genuine. And when he'd murmured in her ear that no dream he'd ever had had smelled as wonderful as she did, her knees had virtually turned to blancmange. Hope began to flutter in her breast and for once, she didn't have the will to crush it.

The hum and buzz and soft ticking of countless seconds and minutes was a quiet counterpoint to the beating of Emmeline's own heart. She was about to abandon her seat in favor of perusing the contents of all the display cases when the jib door opened and the duke himself stepped back into the room.

At last!

Climbing to her feet, Emmeline tried to read his expression but failed. Before she could stop herself, too many questions tumbled out in a great rush. "How has everything gone? Did someone from Scotland Yard arrive? Did Ollie finally confess who the guv'nor is? Did Mrs. Lambton find out anything useful from Fanny?"

Xavier gave a short laugh. "By Jove. What a barrage. It's like I've stepped in front of a firing party."

"I'm sorry," said Emmeline. "Waiting is difficult sometimes. Especially when there's so much at stake."

"I know." The duke sighed and ran a gloved hand through his jet-black hair, ruffling it into spikes. "I apologize for taking so long. To answer your questions, I still don't know who this guv'nor character is. Ollie wasn't forthcoming, even after a detective from Scotland Yard arrived. The stubborn dog refused to admit anything, so he's been arrested on suspicion of aiding and abetting Gareth's kidnapper. He's been hauled off to spend the night in a holding cell at the Old Bailey, so perhaps he'll be more amenable come morning. One thing that is clear to me after tonight is that Fanny *is* Ollie's sweetheart."

Emmeline wasn't surprised. "Did she say something to Mrs. Lambton?"

Xavier shook his head. "No. Mrs. Lambton didn't have the opportunity to talk to her because she's gone."

"Gone?" repeated Emmeline.

"Yes. Up and left. Absconded." Then Xavier explained what had happened. "While Ned was guarding the storage cupboard, not long before Scotland Yard arrived, Fanny approached and she was crying. She asked to speak to Ollie, and Ned, not thinking it would do any harm, permitted her to do so through the door. He overhead their brief exchange."

"What did they say?"

"Apparently Ollie told Fanny not to worry. That he would be all right. Then he told her that my clock plans were complete and then his exact words were, 'You know what to do.'"

"You know what to do," repeated Emmeline, her skin prickling with apprehension. "And now Fanny has disappeared into the night."

"It would seem so. Ollie was obviously referring to my King of Clocks. But the plans are safe and sound. In fact, I keep them in a locked metallic box that's bolted to the floor in this very room in a secret cupboard. Nothing can happen to them. They can't be stolen."

"Well, that's a relief," said Emmeline. "Do you think Fanny has gone running to whoever the guv'nor is?"

"Undoubtedly," said Xavier grimly. "And now more than ever I think it must be Sir Randolph Redvers who's behind everything. No one else would care about whether my clock plans are finished or not."

Emmeline agreed. "Will you notify Scotland Yard about your suspicions?"

"I've already sent a message," said Xavier. "I imagine the police will continue to question Ollie and they'll start looking for Fanny. With any luck, they'll bring Sir Randolph in for questioning too. If he paid West to kidnap Gareth as part of his elaborate plot to upset me, I trust he'll be brought to justice."

Emmeline blew out a sigh. "I hope so. Then this nightmare will all be over and you can begin to lead a more tranquil, happier life."

Xavier's mouth kicked into an unexpected smile. "Believe me, my dear Emmeline, since I met you, that's already begun to happen." He suddenly reached out and grasped her hand. "Come. I want to show you my clock plans."

He drew Emmeline over to his enormous workbench and

bade her sit upon a tall, padded stool. Before her lay pages upon pages of intricate schematic diagrams and sketches.

"I finished this two nights ago, but this evening I've been going over it with a fine-tooth comb and fresh eyes. That's what I was doing when you arrived," he said, his blue eyes gleaming with pride. He was standing so close to Emmeline, the sleeve of his black coat kept brushing her arm and she could smell his woodsy cologne. "If everything is perfect, I'll submit my plan to the Astronomer Royal in the next few days."

"It looks magnificent," Emmeline murmured, her tone filled with awe. "I don't understand the technical calculations, but from what I can see, it's evident your vision is brilliant, Xavier."

"Thank you," he said, then dropped a light kiss on her temple. His face became wreathed with excitement as he began to describe a little of what he'd created. "My clock has an original double three-legged gravity escapement which protects the fourteen-foot-long pendulum from the elements. Which means its accuracy will be remarkable even in the most inclement weather."

"Heavens. I wish I knew what a double three-legged gravity escapement really meant," said Emmeline with a laugh. "But I'm sure it's clever beyond words. Tell me more about what your clock will look like when it's finished."

"She's going to be a beauty," said Xavier as he tugged off his gloves and tossed them onto the bench. "See here"—with one long elegant finger, he pointed to a precise rendering of a stunning clockface on the first page. "There'll be four dials—one on each side of St Stephen's Tower—and they'll be cast from iron but covered with a mosaic of opalescent glass. At night, each face will be backlit by gaslight so everyone for miles around will be able to see the time as well as hear the chimes. The Roman numerals and the hands will be painted in Prussian blue. And here"—Xavier moved behind Emmeline and leaned forward, both arms bracketing her on each side as he pointed to the edge of the clockface—"at the base of each dial, right below this ornate gilt border will be inscribed, *Domine Salvam Fac Reginam Nostram Victoriam Primam.*"

"Oh Lord, keep safe our Queen Victoria the First," said Emmeline softly. "Your design has to win, Xavier. You deserve all the accolades in the world."

The duke's bare hands slid up Emmeline's arms and came to rest lightly on her shoulders. "Any and all accolades will mean nothing at all if I don't have you," he murmured in a low voice, his breath hot against her ear.

Emmeline bit her lip as tears welled. Her fledgling hope began to beat its wings a little faster. "Do you really mean that, Xavier?" she whispered.

His arms came up to encircle her so her back was pressed against his chest. "I do," he said, brushing a kiss over her temple, then her ear.

"But . . . we said we wouldn't—" she began, but it appeared Xavier would hear none of the old arguments they'd both mounted to stop themselves crossing the lines they'd said they'd never cross.

He pulled her from the stool and gathered her close into his arms. "We were idiots," he said, capturing her chin between his fingers. "*I* was an idiot. Since I sent you away, this last fortnight has felt like purgatory to me. I didn't just miss you, Emmeline. I felt like half a man without you. A mere shadow of myself. I will readily own I've been practically mad with loneliness and longing and wishing you were here every single day."

"I didn't feel like myself either," she murmured thickly. Her fingers curled into his coat lapels seeking a way to anchor herself to this man. Come what may, she suddenly knew she could never let him go. "I think about you all the time. Dream of you too."

"It seems we are both hopeless cases." He smiled then, the precise lines and angles of his mouth settling into a soft, up-tilted curve. "I've always found you fascinating. The most intriguing distraction. Indeed, from the very start, from the day we met, I've craved your company. I find you endlessly irresistible, my love."

Endlessly irresistible? Fascinating? My love? Emmeline was so touched—so overwhelmed and flummoxed—she was momentarily lost for words.

Before she could even formulate a coherent thought beyond *Oh my, did he actually just call me "my love"?* Xavier was speaking again.

"But it's more than that, sweet Emmeline," he said huskily. Lifting her chin a fraction, he stared straight into her eyes as though he were trying to connect with her very soul. "Like the air that I breathe or even the ground beneath my feet, you are essential to me. A needed component. A vital cog. An element that makes my life worth living. You make me feel so many things that I never thought myself capable of feeling. With you, I am whole. I am at peace. I'm at home."

"Oh, my goodness." Emmeline couldn't contain her emotions now. Tears were sliding down her cheeks, even as her mouth was lifting into a smile. "What are you trying to tell me exactly, Xavier?" she whispered. "I need to hear you say the words."

The Duke of St Lawrence, the man Emmeline adored with her entire being, cradled her face between his hands. "I love you, Emmeline Chase. You've taught this man to understand his feelings. And that's the most magical, miraculous gift of all."

She clasped his wrists. Searched his light blue eyes that were as clear as a rain-washed sky at dawn. "Oh, Xavier. Are you . . . are you absolutely sure that's how you feel? Because if you're not—"

"My love." Xavier stroked her cheeks with his thumbs, brushing away her tears and any lingering doubts. "My darling, Emmeline. You make my heart smile. How could that not be love?"

Emmeline inhaled a shaky breath. Her heart was beating so fast and thrumming with so much happiness, she thought it might burst. "I love you too, Xavier," she whispered. "More than you could ever know."

"Then marry me," he said, his voice rough with emotion. "Be my wife. With Harry, Bartholomew, and Gareth in our lives, we'll be a true family in every sense of the word. I honestly don't care what anyone else thinks or says. Society and the Parasol Academy, and indeed any naysayers at all, can go and jump in the English Channel. The only thing that matters is what you and I both want. And I want you to be mine."

All at once, Xavier sank to the marble floor on bended knee and clasped her hands in his. "Emmeline Chase, will you do me the untold honor of consenting to be my wife? The woman I will love until the sun no longer rises and the stars no longer shine. You own my heart and you shall have it and everything else I have to give until the end of time."

Emmeline bit her lip as her heart swelled with the sweetest, most pure and potent joy. This man was everything she could ever want. He was more than she'd ever dreamed of. "Oh, Xavier. Yes. My answer is an unreserved and unequivocal yes. I am yours and you are mine and I will happily be your wife forevermore."

"My darling." Xavier rose and caught her in his arms. And then he kissed her, deeply, thoroughly, and with such aching tenderness that warm tendrils of delicious desire were soon unfurling inside Emmeline's body, licking along her veins and setting her aflame. Making her moan and wind her arms around Xavier's neck, unashamedly offering herself to him.

He pushed her against the bench and it was clear his desire was awakened too. Emmeline could feel the urgent press of his hips and his arousal even through her uniform's skirts and her underthings.

One of his hands curled around her nape as his hot mouth slid almost frantically along the line of her jaw. "Stay here with me tonight," he whispered roughly before he slanted his mouth over hers again, his tongue entering her, boldly stroking and teasing. "In my room." Another kiss. Hotter. Hungrier. He caught her lower lip lightly between his teeth then sucked delicately. "I want you in my arms. In my bed."

"Yes," moaned Emmeline, angling her head so he could feast upon her neck and throat. The tiny licks and sucking kisses he rained upon her fevered flesh were driving her wild. "Anything for you."

"Come with me." Xavier caught her hand and led her across the room to a towering oak longcase clock at the farthest end. He turned the gilt key in the polished cabinet below the clockface, there was a soft click and whir, and then the whole clock and the wall panel behind it slid sideways to reveal a gaslit corridor. The clock was another elaborate jib door.

"You have a secret passage leading to your suite?" asked Emmeline.

Xavier grinned. "I do. You go first. I'll close the door after us."

By the time Emmeline reached the end of the passage, she was breathless with excitement. Xavier, who was right behind her, reached past her and pressed on a metallic lever below a wall sconce. There was another click and whir, and this time when the jib door opened, the Duke of St Lawrence's opulent bedchamber was revealed. It was a breathtaking study in shades of dusky blue and rich wood with touches of gold. A low fire burned in the gray marble fireplace, and dominating the far side of the room was an enormous four-poster bed draped in sumptuous silk brocade and velvet.

"My valet, Babcock, has retired to his quarters downstairs for the night. And Horatio is asleep on his perch in my sitting room next door." Xavier tipped his chin at another oak-paneled door to the right of the fireplace. "We won't be disturbed. Wait..." He stopped and a look of horror crossed his features. "My raven can't hear your thoughts all the time, can he?"

Emmeline laughed softly. "No. He can only perceive them

if I purposefully direct them his way. Believe me, I won't be doing that tonight."

"Well, that's a relief." Xavier closed the jib door then asked softly, "Now, where were we?" His intent gaze blatantly wandered over Emmeline from the top of her head down to her toes, then back again. "Oh, that's right. You were about to take off that blasted nanny's cap for the very last time and throw it into the fire."

Emmeline could hardly object. Of course, she'd worked so hard to be a Parasol nanny. She truly loved her job and had always tried to do her very best. Giving up her Parasol Academy license also meant losing access to all the magic she had at her fingertips.

But it would be worth it because now she had something even better than magical pockets and words and parasols. Something more fulfilling that would last a lifetime. She was going to marry a man who loved her and would do anything for her and those she cared about. Just like she would do anything for him and his adorable wards. And, God willing, one day she and Xavier might be blessed with children of their own.

With a deliberately provocative smile, she removed her lacy cap and then held it out to Xavier. "Would you like to do the honors, or shall I?"

"As much as I would like to, I think you should," he said.

Emmeline moved toward the fireplace and cast the handful of lace and linen into the flames. The cap caught alight immediately, the tongues of fire consuming it until nothing but a few sparks and embers remained.

"There," she said with a saucy smile. "Is that better, Your Grace?"

"A little, but not quite," murmured Xavier. His voice was low and raspy as he added, "I think you need to take down your hair . . . and then remove your entire uniform."

Oh heavens . . . What on earth had gotten into the Duke of

St Lawrence? His eyes were heavy-lidded with lust and when Emmeline's gaze dipped to his trousers, she could see he was more than ready to make love. A heady thrill shot through her at the thought that he'd been waiting so long to be with a woman and he'd chosen her, Emmeline Chase, to be his one and only lover.

She wanted this experience—his first time—to be wonderful and utterly unforgettable.

"While I can scarcely disobey your command, Your Grace, might I trouble you to help me with all my buttons and laces and hooks and eyes?" she asked in a seemingly innocent, nonchalant sounding tone that was really meant to tease. She tugged loose the ribbons securing her pinafore then tossed it onto the floor. "There are an awful lot to contend with."

His eyes danced as he joined her by the fireside. "What, you don't have a spell for undressing at the drop of a hat pin?"

"There might be," she murmured, looking up through her eyelashes at him before she turned to present him with her back, "but where would be the fun in that?"

Chapter 28

In Which the Duke Receives a Thoroughly Educative and Memorable Lesson . . .

Xavier swallowed as he contemplated Emmeline Chase's slender back. Above the collar of her severe navy uniform, the elegant ivory column of her neck rose. Tiny curls of coppery hair that had escaped the harsh confines of her bun delicately caressed her nape and he itched to touch her there. To savor the texture of her satiny skin and to rub the soft tendrils of her hair between his fingertips. To trace a path with his tongue along her freckles and delve into her secret hollows and learn all the intimate ways that he could make her desire bloom.

In truth, Xavier yearned to touch and taste and explore Emmeline *everywhere* just like he'd done in all his libidinous fantasies. To make her arch and whimper with pleasure over and over again.

And very soon, he would.

He licked his lips. His throat was suddenly so tight with lust and longing, he had to clear it before he could speak. "You're right," he managed, his voice thick and husky. "I can think of nothing more diverting than helping you undress." Of course, he couldn't wait to see the divine Emmeline in all her naked glory, but what was the point in rushing when they had all the time in the world?

Although, a particularly male part of Xavier was urging him to hurry up and get on with it. Indeed, his member was throbbing so much, he prayed he wouldn't lose control and become completely undone even before Emmeline had the chance to remove a single hairpin or stocking.

Good God. Even the thought of seeing her bare pink toes was making him stiffer than an iron poker.

He began to slide Emmeline's hairpins free, relishing the slide of her silken hair and the occasional brush of her fingers as they worked together to loosen her magnificent locks. As soon as they tumbled down her back and over her shoulders without restraint, Xavier cast aside her pins and lifted the bright curling mass with both his hands, burying his face in it. Inhaling the heady scent of the floral soap she used.

Emmeline looked over her shoulder at him. "My buttons won't undo themselves, Your Grace."

Straightaway, Xavier gently swept her hair over her other shoulder, exposing the back of her gown again. "You make another good point, my love," he all but growled as he began to work loose the row of fiddly, tiny jet fastenings. "How the devil do you manage to get into and out of this every day?"

She shrugged. "I'm flexible," she said, and Xavier's manhood immediately jerked. Dear God, if he didn't spend in his trousers, it would be a miracle.

"You're a delectable witch," he grumbled. At last, the sides of her navy wool bodice sagged open, and he raised his hands to her shoulders to help her slide the tight sleeves down her slim but tautly muscled arms.

A lather of impatience, he quickly made short work of her acres of stiff crinoline petticoats and then she was turning to face him clad only in her corset, chemise, drawers, stockings, and boots. And of course, there was the sheathed knife that she kept strapped to her ankle.

She caught him looking at that tiny dagger and laughed. (*Bloody hell.* Even the light tinkling sound of her mirth was making him unbearably hard.) "Don't tell me that you're wondering if you can cut the rest of my garments away."

Xavier cocked a brow. "I thought you could only read my raven's thoughts." (He *had* actually been thinking that.) He studied the fastenings of her corset—it appeared to be secured by a fiendish row of metal hooks and eyes—and he scowled. "What's this godawful suit of armor constructed from anyway? Whalebone or steel?"

She propped her hands on her slender waist and jutted a hip (the damnable wench). "Steel of course. All the better for protecting one from an assailant's blade."

"Or a randy duke's sword," he muttered from between clenched teeth. He'd been wrong. This activity had rapidly moved from "fun" and "diverting" to unmitigated torture in the blink of an eye.

He raised his hands to undo the hooks and eyes, but his fingers brushed the very tops of her breasts—the plump flesh not concealed by her corset—and an involuntary groan tumbled from his throat.

"You poor man," murmured Emmeline. "Let me put you out of your misery. Close your eyes and I'll have this pesky corset gone in a jiffy."

Xavier wasn't about to argue and complied. "I thought you didn't know any disrobing spells," he said, intrigued by the sounds of fastenings popping open and the soft rustle and slide of fabric.

"I don't," she replied. "I'm just very good with my hands."

Xavier chuckled at that. "I usually am too." He could create and repair watches, manipulating impossibly minuscule parts, but present him with a woman's corset and he was all fumbling thumbs.

But this was his first time doing anything like this. And even though he was eager and more than ready to make love with

Emmeline, he was also nervous. He wanted to impress the woman he loved. Give her untold satisfaction. With her patient and expert tutelage, he had done so a month ago. But they hadn't done *everything*.

He hadn't been inside her.

At that moment his most masculine part throbbed in earnest as if to remind him, *Yes, I haven't been inside her, you great clodpole. I'm in sheer agony. What are you waiting for?*

"You can open your eyes now, Your Grace..."

Xavier did and he almost exploded on the spot. "Emmeline. My God," he breathed as his hungry gaze devoured her. "You're not just beautiful. You're exquisite."

Naked but for her cascading waves of titian hair, Emmeline was a work of art—the perfect combination of softly rounded curves and slender elegant limbs. Her alabaster skin was lightly freckled in places he'd never expected. Her plump breasts with their dusky pink tips and the soft ginger curls at the apex of her thighs made his mouth water with keen anticipation.

Holding out his shaking hands, Xavier helped Emmeline step out of the puddle of her discarded clothes. Then, because he couldn't help himself, he gathered her close, stroking his hands over almost every satin-smooth inch of her. Without her heeled boots on, she suddenly seemed so very small and delicate. Something to be cherished and handled with the greatest care. "I want you, so very much," he murmured, his voice raw and rasping.

She slid her hands up his chest and then cradled his taut jaw between her soft palms. "I know," she whispered. "And I can't wait for you to have me." Standing on her bare tiptoes, she stretched up and kissed his throat. "Make me yours, Xavier."

Xavier groaned and his resolve to take care disintegrated. Swooping down, he claimed her mouth in a hard, almost brutal kiss. His great need, his impatience was making him rough and clumsy. But Emmeline didn't seem to mind that she was crushed against him while he plundered her mouth like a starving man. She kissed him back with a fervor that matched his, her lips sliding just as urgently, her tongue tasting him just as desperately. This young woman was strong and bold and passionate with a backbone of steel. She would not break.

He needed to get her on the bed and then he needed to strip.

He tore his mouth from hers and scooped her up, conveying her across the room in a handful of strides before laying her gently on the blue silk counterpane.

"Xavier," she whispered, holding out her arms. "Come to me."

"Not quite yet." He began to throw off his clothes, almost strangling himself as he grappled with his necktie and collar. Emmeline sat up and began to help, deftly sliding off his coat before tugging the buttons of his waistcoat undone. When Xavier was down to his trousers and nothing else, Emmeline bit her lip coquettishly.

"May I do the honors?" she purred as she placed a hand upon his taut abdomen, just above his waistband. Even that light touch was the sweetest agony.

"I'm afraid that if you do, I won't last," he groaned helplessly. "I want to pleasure you first." He climbed onto the bed beside Emmeline and drew her down with him. Stroked a hand along her side and along the flat plane of her belly before he dared to cup her bare breast. "I want to make sure that you achieve satisfaction before we come together as one."

"You don't have to," she whispered, her blue eyes aglow, her smile soft. She caressed his chest and everything inside Xavier pulsed and throbbed and burned.

He caught her hand and pressed a kiss to her palm. "But I do. I've dreamed of this, Emmeline. Will you let me?"

She lay back and looked up at him through her lashes. "Do what you will with me, my husband-to-be."

So Xavier did. He kissed her long and slow and deeply until Emmeline was breathless and moaning. Then he focused all his attention on her beautiful breasts, teasing and fondling and licking for countless minutes, driving himself mad and her wild.

But he wouldn't stop there. Xavier was determined to have more of her. He wanted the taste of Emmeline's most intimate, feminine place on his tongue. He wanted to savor her very essence.

He slid down her body and his sweet Emmeline, guessing his intent, parted her thighs for him. He found that she was warm and wet and wanting.

She wanted *him*.

The mere notion was the most potent of drugs, yet humbling at the same time. Xavier swallowed. He licked his lips. His heart was almost pounding out of his chest. He had only ever read about this decadent act, and he desperately didn't want to disappoint the woman he loved.

He looked up the length of Emmeline's body and caught her gaze. "If you don't like anything that I do, you must tell me. Remember, I lack practical experience."

She reached out and feathered her fingers through his hair. "Your kisses and caresses have already made me boneless with desire, Xavier. I know you'll be wonderful. Your attention to detail is unsurpassed. Now"—her mouth curved in a sensual smile—"show me what you can do with your clever fingers and talented tongue. I've dreamed of you doing this too."

Emmeline lay back on the pillows and gave herself over to Xavier. He was an intriguing blend of raw enthusiasm and nerves. Urgent want and hesitation. Strength and vulnerability.

Everything he did inflamed her need and touched her heart. Whether it was the way he feathered kisses along her inner thighs, or how his fingers gently opened her so he could tease her with tentative flicks, then bolder licks and delicate fluttering laps . . . all of it was perfect, and it wasn't long before Emmeline was writhing and panting and arching and digging her fingers into his scalp.

When bliss at last claimed her, she shattered beneath his hot mouth with a keening cry, her body practically lifting off the bed.

This man might be a virgin, but he was a natural when it came to performing astounding feats of the lingual kind.

She felt Xavier ease himself off the bed and when she opened her eyes, she discovered that he'd at last removed the rest of his clothes. And her eyes nearly popped out of her head.

Of course, she'd already seen what the Duke of St Lawrence hid in his trousers when she'd stroked him to completion a month ago. But for some reason, seeing him completely naked and mightily aroused had her stomach flip-flopping and her desire capering. And yes, she was unashamedly ogling every perfectly proportioned inch of him. His wide shoulders, his lean corded arms, the hard planes of his chest with its scattering of black hair. The defined ridges of his taut abdomen and the sharp lines of his hip bones. His well-muscled thighs and last but not least, his impressive manhood.

As she studied him *there*, that part of him seemed to swell even more.

She suddenly couldn't wait for this man to be inside her.

It seemed Xavier was of the same mind. He joined her on the bed again, this time covering her body with his. He was hot and hard *everywhere* and the embers of Emmeline's desire burst into flames once more.

"Are you ready for me?" he asked, his usually smooth-as-velvet voice suddenly graveled with lust. He braced his weight on one forearm as he gently nudged her knees apart. With his other hand he grasped his straining member.

"Yes, with bells on," she whispered. She reached between them and curled her fingers over Xavier's. "Would you like me to guide you?"

Xavier groaned and rested his forehead against hers. "Please," he murmured. "I'm almost half-undone already and I don't know how much longer I can hold on."

Emmeline's heart clenched. Dear Lord. He was quaking, his

muscles trembling. She could feel the rise and fall of his chest and the gust of his warm breath. There were even taut lines of strain bracketing his mouth.

She opened her thighs wider to cradle him and helped him notch his hot rigid length at her entrance. "Just press forward," she urged gently. "Fill me. I can take all of you."

And he did. In one glorious surge, he slid home, all the way to the hilt, and Emmeline cried out at the exquisite sensation.

"Did I hurt you?" Xavier gasped.

When she opened her eyes, Emmeline could see that anguish had transformed Xavier's features. "No, not at all," she whispered, brushing a tangled lock of black hair away from his brow. Her eyes locked with his. "Find your own pleasure, my darling Xavier. It's time."

Find your own pleasure, my darling Xavier. It's time.

Xavier couldn't resist Emmeline's invitation. Everything inside him was urging him to move, to thrust. The way Emmeline clasped him so snugly, so greedily, he felt like he was sheathed in slick warm satin.

They were joined. United. Forever linked by this profoundly intimate experience.

Being like this, with Emmeline, was everything Xavier had ever hoped for and more.

He started up a pulsing rhythm as natural as the ebb and flow of the tide or the rise and fall of the moon. And sweet, perfect Emmeline kept pace with him, even when his hips began to pump harder and faster and the pressure inside him began to build and build, propelling him toward the precipice of a cataclysmic release. He prayed Emmeline would find her peak and hurtle headlong into ecstasy too.

He forced himself to open his eyes and found that she was watching his face with a desire-glazed gaze. Her fingers curled tightly behind his neck and her mouth curved into a smile as she whispered, "I'm almost there, Xavier. Come with me."

And that was enough to push him over the edge into pleasure, into a place where Xavier knew not where he began and where Emmeline ended. A wild and wondrous world that transcended time, where only their mutual joy and satisfaction and love existed.

As the ripples of release faded and they lay in each other's arms, spent and panting and glowing, Xavier couldn't stop smiling. Or perhaps he was grinning.

"This . . . this is what love looks like," he murmured huskily into Emmeline's disheveled hair.

She reached out and cradled his jaw, drawing his face to hers. "Love is all I see when I look at you." And then she kissed him, her lips tender and searching, and Xavier knew that whatever happened in the coming days, they would always have this perfect moment, locked away safely in their hearts.

Chapter 29

Wherein There Is a Fiery Incident Closely Followed by a Chilling One...

Emmeline wasn't sure what woke her exactly, but something definitely had.

For a moment, she struggled to recall where she was. And then she blinked sleepily and smiled. She was sated and warm in the Duke of St Lawrence's bed. Not only that, but she was engaged and in love and she'd just had the best lovemaking experience she'd ever had in her life.

And then she heard the noise again. A raucous screech.

It was Horatio. And he was squawking crazily, fit to wake the dead, in Xavier's sitting room next door.

"Fire! Fire! Fire in the hold!"

What? Fire in the hold? Hold of a ship? Emmeline bolted upright and frowned into the velvet darkness of Xavier's bedchamber. *What on earth did that mean?*

And then she smelled it. Smoke.

Oh God. "Xavier! Xavier, wake up!" Emmeline gave her sleeping fiancé a frantic shake, then she scrambled from the bed, pulling one of the satin sheets with her. Heedless of her dishabille, she flew across the bedchamber and threw open the door to the sitting room. Even though everything was cloaked in shadow, there was enough ambient light filtering through the windows to reveal that smoke was seeping into the room from underneath the door that led to the hall outside.

Nanny Chase! The raven landed on the nearby mantelpiece. *I thought you were in Kent. What are you doing—*He broke off and cocked his head, studying her sheet-shrouded form and disheveled, unbound hair. *Never mind. It's about time you and the duke got together—*

At that moment, Xavier appeared in the doorway next to Emmeline, shirtless and shoeless and his trousers only half done up.

"Fire in the hold! Intruder alert!" screeched the bird. "Half-naked nanny alert!"

Xavier pointed his finger at the raven. "That's enough from you, Horatio."

Turning to Emmeline, the duke gripped her by the shoulders. "I'll check the hall while you throw something on besides a sheet. If a fire has taken hold, we'll all have to evacuate. That includes the staff."

Emmeline nodded. "Be careful." She didn't have to give voice to the terrible thought that was uppermost in her mind. That the saboteur had struck again. And this time, the consequences could be lethal. Xavier must be thinking it too.

"I will," he said grimly. And then he gave her a swift kiss before heading for the sitting room door.

I'll help too, offered Horatio. *Let me out and I'll fly around the house to get a bird's-eye view of the fire. It will take me a minute or two at most.*

Good idea, replied Emmeline. Once she'd thrown open a casement window for the raven and he'd disappeared into the night, she raced through to the bedchamber to her discarded clothes where they still lay in a heap by the fireplace. Dropping the sheet, she threw on her dress. There was no time to don undergarments. If she were lucky, she'd have time to pull on her boots. Reaching behind her, she began to do up the buttons. Whoever designed the Parasol Academy uniform should be shot. How on earth was she to get dressed in a hurry, especially in the near dark? She was bound to get burned to a crisp before she'd even done up a few.

Then she stopped and drew a calming breath.

What if she cast the *Unsmirchify* spell?

Surely it was worth a try. It had worked before when she'd used it in an unconventional way in the duke's study after their amorous tryst.

Emmeline reached into her nanny's pocket and withdrew the small feather duster she would need to amplify the incantation. "*Unsmirchify,*" she whispered as she made a sweeping motion down her body.

A soft silver glow gently pulsed and swirled around Emmeline, and when the light faded, she was fully dressed. Even her hair was back in a neat bun. Although, her nanny's cap had not materialized. It seemed that an item of clothing, once destroyed by fire, was gone for good.

Sartorial and modesty crises at last averted, Emmeline then rushed back to the smoky sitting room to discover Xavier had returned. His eyes widened at the sight of her fully dressed. "How—" he began, then shook his head. "Never mind."

"How bad is the fire?" she asked, suddenly breathless because of the smoke and a good dose of rising panic. "I let Horatio out to make an assessment of the situation too."

Xavier's mouth compressed in a hard straight line. "It's not good." He strode past her and retrieved his shirt from the floor beside the bed. "It seems to have started somewhere on the lower floors," he added as his head emerged from the crumpled linen, "but there's a considerable amount of smoke billowing up the central staircase into the outside corridor. I could see a fierce glow emanating from the first floor and hear the crackle and pop of a fire that's becoming well established. It's not just a smoldering fire."

"Oh God. I hope the servants are all right." Even though Emmeline's room had been on the third floor near the nursery, the rest of the staff slept on the ground floor or in basement quarters.

"I trust they are." Xavier thrust his feet into leather shoes then returned to her side. "Both Babcock and Woodley were calling out from below in the entry hall and I shouted down to them that both you and I are fine and will get ourselves to safety. That they were to focus on getting the rest of the staff into the square. With any luck, an alarm has been raised to summon the fire brigade."

Emmeline nodded. "We need to get out too."

Xavier reached out and clasped her arm. "You should teleport outside. In the meantime, I need to go back to the Horology Room to retrieve my clock plans. I left them on my workbench."

Horror gripped Emmeline's lungs. "Oh no. But it's far too dangerous, Xavier."

Xavier's jaw took on a stubborn set. "I don't think the fire has reached this floor yet. There's still time. This work—my finest work—has taken me a whole year to complete. I can't let it go up in flames. Not now. I must try."

"Then I will go with you," said Emmeline firmly. "That way I can teleport us both to safety."

Xavier raised a querying brow. "You can do that?"

Emmeline gave a decided nod. "Indeed, I can."

Xavier blew out a sigh. "I don't like the idea of putting you in unnecessary danger, but very well—"

There was a sudden screech then a softer caw. *What, abandoning ship already?*

Horatio was back. Emmeline and Xavier whipped around to find him sitting on the window ledge.

"How goes it?" Emmeline asked.

The raven flapped his wings. "Fire in the hold," he crowed, then spoke to Emmeline directly in her mind. *The very center of the house on the first floor is well alight. But the servants' stairs at the end of the north and south wings look like they might be safe to use. Mrs. Punchbowl, Mrs. Lambton, and the maids and footmen appear to be gathering in the square. There's no sign of the fire brigade yet.*

Emmeline thanked Horatio and then conveyed the raven's intelligence to Xavier.

"Right, that's everyone downstairs accounted for," he said. Then he laced his fingers through Emmeline's. "Let's go. I don't fancy becoming duke toast."

Horatio cawed a goodbye from the window as Xavier and Emmeline hastened into the ducal bedchamber, heading for the door that led directly to the Horology Room.

As they sped along the secret passage, Emmeline's eyes watered and dread trickled down her spine. The acrid smell of smoke was stronger here in such an enclosed space and the gaslights were flickering madly. She prayed the second floor wasn't engulfed in flames. Or that the gas wouldn't explode. Hopefully Woodley would remember to turn it off.

When Xavier pushed aside the jib door to the Horology Room, Emmeline breathed a great sigh of relief. Even though the air was hazy with smoke, there were no other signs that the fire had reached this far. No heat or untoward sounds like crashes or explosions. Perhaps the house could be saved if the fire brigade arrived in time. It would be terrible and heartbreaking indeed if Xavier lost his entire timepiece collection.

Xavier rushed over to his workbench and swiftly rolled up his plans. "Right, my darling Emmeline," he said. "We can away—"

At that moment there was a loud crash, and a barrage of vile cursing filtered into the room. Emmeline and Xavier traded worried glances.

"Someone is in your study," she whispered.

Xavier's brows plummeted into a frown. "I need to check who it is." Tucking his clock plans beneath one arm, he started for the door concealed behind his study's bookcase. "Even though I told Woodley and Babcock not to worry about me, perhaps one of them came back."

Emmeline agreed and followed Xavier. And then she wished she hadn't, because standing behind the duke's desk was a man brandishing a pistol...

It was Sir Randolph Redvers, and his mocking smile chilled Emmeline to the very bone as he pointed the weapon straight at her and Xavier and said, "Hands up."

Chapter 30

In Which Vermin Appear; Things Get Decidedly Hot (and Not in a Good Way); And Daggers Are Shot before a Tallyho and Toodle-oo...

If he'd been asked, Xavier couldn't say he was surprised to learn that Sir Randolph Redvers was the blackguard who'd been waging an insidious war against him for months and months.

He'd also admit that, unsurprisingly, he was right royally peeved with the baronet.

Actually, that was a gross understatement. If truth be told, Xavier was gripped by a blazing white-hot anger, a fury hotter than the fire currently consuming his home. After all, Sir Randolph had a pistol trained on the woman Xavier loved and wanted to make his wife. Surely no one could blame him for wanting to gut the bastard with a blunt butter knife. *Though, that's rather difficult to do right now*, he thought as he reluctantly put his hands in the air. But he could certainly think it.

"So, it's you who's been a thorn in my side all this time," Xavier bit out from a jaw so tightly clenched, he could crush gravel between his molars.

Sir Randolph had the audacity to laugh. "I'm surprised you didn't work it out before now, old chap." He tapped his temple with a gloved finger. "But by all accounts you're a few cards short of a full deck. Isn't that right, Algie?"

Algie?

Whipping his gaze to the study door behind him, Xavier discovered his cousin Algernon Mason had stepped into the room. And he, too, was holding a pistol.

"Surprised to see me, cuz?" taunted Algernon as he approached the desk and propped a hip on the edge. "I suppose you didn't know that Randy and I are old school chums." His cold derisive gaze slid to Emmeline. "I must admit *I* was surprised to learn from your maid Fanny earlier tonight that your nanny's back in London. But then"—his mouth twisted with a predatory smile—"perhaps the rumors are true and she's more than just a nanny."

If words could physically wound, then the string of filthy curse words Xavier let fly in his head would have felled his cur of a cousin in a split second.

It seemed there'd been a two-pronged conspiracy all along and Xavier had no idea how he was going to get out of this deadly trap he'd walked straight into, let alone save the woman he wanted to spend the rest of his life with.

Guilt and despair suddenly clawed at Xavier's chest, but he would *not* be defeated. Not while love still beat in his heart. Not while he still had breath in his body and his soul possessed the will to fight for everything he held dear.

Stalling seemed like the best option at the present moment. Perhaps Woodley or Babcock would come looking for him after all. Or someone from the fire brigade.

He wouldn't do anything foolhardy and risk Emmeline's life. He also wouldn't show one iota of fear.

"Algernon," he said, his voice dripping with all the frosty ducal disdain he could muster, "I suppose you got tired of waiting for me to appear mad enough for you to haul before the Chancery Court for a lunacy investigation trial. So instead you're going to take matters into your own hands and make me die in a fire à la Mrs. Bertha Rochester. I assume that's your insane plan."

His cousin smirked. "Something like that. Although I'd call it brilliant rather than insane. Dearest Papa kept dithering about whether or not he wanted to have you declared non compos mentis. Even after I'd amassed ample evidence that you're as nutty as a fruitcake."

"He's not mad at all," retorted Emmeline heatedly, her blue eyes flashing. "You've both been paying off his servants, Ollie and Fanny, to disrupt His Grace's household to make him look bad. You"—she glared at Algernon—"so you could steal his dukedom away. And you"—her gaze shot to Sir Randolph—"to stop him submitting his Westminster clock design. You're both despicable and pathetic."

"Well, aren't we clever?" taunted Algernon. "If you think you've got it all worked out, what do you think will happen next, Nanny Chase?"

Emmeline blanched and bit her lip. Xavier knew she couldn't give voice to the terrible truth. Algernon and Sir Randolph were undoubtedly going to attempt to kill them both. Not only did Xavier and Emmeline know too much about the sabotage plot, killing the Duke of St Lawrence would also mean that Algernon and Sir Randolph would get exactly what they wanted a lot quicker.

Algernon would inherit the dukedom after his father, Peregrine, passed. And Sir Randolph's main rival for the Westminster Palace clock commission would be eliminated once and for all.

Sir Randolph gave a dramatic sigh. "Look, it doesn't matter whether or not you two know why dear old Algie and I hatched this plan almost a year ago. The simple fact is, it's time for you to die. Actually"—his dark eyes narrowed—"before we tie you up to let the fire finish you off, what's that you've got tucked beneath your arm there, Mad Mason? That wouldn't happen to be your King of Clocks design, would it?"

Xavier cocked a brow. "Why would you want the horological plans of a lunatic?"

The baronet shrugged. "Call it curiosity. And perhaps I can incorporate some of your ideas into my own design. When Algie and I set the fire, I *had* thought to let your plans burn along with you. But then I changed my mind."

Emmeline glared at the baronet. "I'm surprised you two didn't get one of your henchmen like West or one of your other hirelings to do your dirty work for you."

"Couldn't afford for anyone to make a hash of the final act, my dear." Sir Randolph pointed his weapon straight at Xavier. "Now hand those plans over, Your Grace, before I decide to put a bullet through your brain instead. You've wasted enough of my time with all this talking."

Even though every fiber within him was vibrating with burning anger, Xavier tossed his plans at the baronet. Sir Randolph grinned and slid them into the breast pocket of his greatcoat.

Algernon straightened and gestured toward the jib door with his pistol. "Right, now into the Horology Room with you two. And yes, cuz," he added in a withering tone, "I know all about your special little secret room. A total waste of money, collecting something as useless as a pile of old watches and clocks, if you ask me."

"Useless?" muttered Emmeline, her narrowed eyes shooting daggers at Algernon as they complied with his directions. "I can think of someone, or rather a pair of someones, who are utterly useless."

Once they were all in the Horology Room, Xavier and Emmeline were ordered to stand in the center of the chamber where the painted night sky soared above the quartet of fluted marble columns. Sir Randolph waggled his brows at Emmeline as he tucked his pistol into his coat, then withdrew a sizeable length of rope. "Such a shame I'm having to tie you up for the sole purpose of doing away with you, Nanny Chase," he said as he lashed her wrists together about one of the slender columns.

"You're just afraid that I might knock your block off after seeing me take down your hired thug in the middle of Hyde Park," she retorted. "You too, *Algie.*" The fiery glare she shot at Xavier's cousin should have been enough to singe the prat's eyebrows off.

The baronet snorted. "Hardly," he snapped back as he ruthlessly tightened the rope, pulling a muttered curse from Emmeline. He patted her cheek. "Now, be a good girl and die quickly and quietly."

Undaunted, she tossed her head. "Oh, sod off."

"You won't get away with this," growled Xavier as Sir Randolph tied him up in a similar fashion to the pillar opposite Emmeline's. The air was getting smokier by the minute, and he was having trouble suppressing the urge to cough.

"Mmmm, I think we will," remarked Algernon with a smug grin. He pocketed his own pistol in his coat and rubbed his hands together. "Right-o, pip-pip and tallyho, Randy my old friend. I think it's time for us to beat a hasty retreat before we're trapped in this burning house with this sorry pair."

"Toodle-oo, my loves," called Sir Randolph, blowing them a kiss before the jib door to the study swung shut with a dull thud.

Chapter 31

In Which Vermin Disappear; Knives and Dust Are Deployed; a Troglodyte Takes Action; And Dawn Makes an Appearance . . .

Curse Sir Randolph and Algernon Mason to Hades.

That was the thought running through Emmeline's mind as she watched the jib door close behind the lowest and vilest gutter-dwelling vermin she'd ever encountered. And that was an insult to all vermin.

"I'm sorry we're in this frightful pickle, Xavier," she called into the smoky darkness as she tested the strength of her bonds. "Believe me, I wanted to pull a pistol from my nanny's pocket, but when Sir Randolph ordered us to put up our hands, I thought it was too risky to try. Especially with Algernon pointing a weapon at us too."

"You are not to blame yourself for any of this. It was far too dangerous a prospect to take on two armed and ruthless men," returned Xavier, his deep voice a soothing and welcome balm to Emmeline's tauter-than-piano-wire nerves. "And I'm sure everything will be all right. Hopefully, I can loosen the knots on this rope. Failing that, I trust someone will mount a search."

"I don't wish to sound cynical, but I wouldn't be surprised if Sir Bottom and Algie tell everyone that they've seen both you and me outside in the square," said Emmeline as she tested the knots around her wrists. Her eyes and the back of her throat were stinging from all the smoke in the room and in the distance, she could detect the sound of something rather large—some substantial structural part of the house—cracking and splintering and crashing. Had the chandelier in the entry hall come down? The gaslights guttered ominously and then they were plunged into suffocating darkness.

Damn. She wished she could catch Xavier's gaze—he was only a handful of yards away—but she would attempt to reassure him anyway. "I'm going to get us out of here, my darling Xavier," she stated with a firmness that belied her racing pulse. "Remember, I'm a Parasol nanny. I have skills . . . and a knife."

"By Jove. I forgot about that," said Xavier, hope flickering in his voice. "Do you think you can reach it?"

"I'm sure I can." Emmeline had already shimmied the rope down the marble pillar toward her feet. She slid to her bottom, pulled her knees up, then twisted her body so she could grasp the dagger strapped to her right ankle. It was rather awkward (and she might have sworn in an unladylike fashion a few times when her blasted skirts got in the way and her fingers slipped) but after a minute, her wickedly sharp little knife was firmly in her hand, and she was slicing her wrists free.

As soon as they were, she scrambled to her feet then rushed over to Xavier. Her eyes had adjusted to the dark and there was enough pale gray light falling through the casement windows for her to see what she was doing as she swiftly severed Xavier's bonds.

"You're amazing, did you know that?" Xavier murmured as he dropped a kiss on her forehead.

"Thank you." Emmeline's cheeks grew warm and it had nothing to do with the encroaching fire. She quickly resheathed her knife and then reached into her pocket and wrapped her fingers around her leyport key. "You're going to be even more amazed when I teleport us both to safety. Like you, I have no desire to be turned into toast."

Somewhere close by, something made of glass exploded, and Emmeline swore she could hear the crackle of flames. It was definitely getting hotter and smokier by the moment. There was no time to lose.

Except... what if she could nip this entire disaster in the bud, right here, right now?

Xavier must have sensed her indecision as he murmured, "My love, is something wrong?"

"I've changed my mind. I don't think we should teleport outside yet," she said. "I have a better idea."

"You have a better idea than whisking us away from this flaming death trap?"

She gave a decided nod. "I do. What if I told you that I might be able to put out the fire and restore everything to how it was?"

Xavier scratched his jaw. "I would say that would be brilliant. But how?" He frowned down at her, his features half cast in shadow, half cast in veiled moonlight. "Don't tell me that you can turn back the hands of time."

"Of course not. But I do have a trick up my sleeve." Emmeline tried to smile reassuringly even though her pulse was racing like quicksilver. "Or rather, in my pocket."

She held her breath as she did just that, reached into her nanny's pocket for the only thing that could reverse this impending catastrophe: *decalamitifying* dust. Though, by employing such a powerful magical tool, she would be breaking one of the Parasol Academy's most important rules yet again. By rights, she really shouldn't be performing another Fae spell in front of Xavier. And of course, the children were not in the immediate vicinity of St Lawrence House, but miles away in Kent. So strictly speaking, she wasn't really going to use the dust in direct service to them.

Then again, this was their home. And surely the Fae wouldn't grant her the use of the dust if it wasn't all right to do so. She *had* to try. It was an emergency after all.

Closing her eyes, her heart in her mouth, Emmeline prayed to the Fae and Good Queen Maeve herself to grant her the use of the magical dust to save St Lawrence House and everything in it. For a heartbeat, nothing happened, and ice-cold dread shivered through Emmeline. Perhaps the Fae *wouldn't* bestow this gift . . . Perhaps they didn't believe this was a worthy cause?

And then she felt a familiar tingling sensation in her fingertips and all at once her whole hand was filled with powder; it was clearly a much larger amount than she'd been gifted to repair the library after the ginger beer explosion. *Thank the Fae.*

Withdrawing her hand, Emmeline showed Xavier the *decalamitifying* dust. It glimmered like silver in the pale moonlight. "I'm going to use *this* to put everything to rights."

Xavier's frown grew deeper. "Dust?"

"It's not just *any* old dust. It's decalamitifying dust. It's how I cleaned up the mess after the ginger beer explosion. Actually, I could have decalamitified the whole library, including the broken glass, but then I thought you might think that odd."

Xavier shook his head. "Good God. I had no idea. If you're not a witch, you must be some sort of goddess. Venus perhaps?"

Emmeline laughed. "I assure you I'm not. Even though we've established that I cannot manipulate time and I cannot fly, let's see if I can put out a house fire. The only problem is, I might need to be in view of the flames for this to work."

Xavier dragged a hand down his face. "Very well. We can check the hall outside my study. You can glimpse the main staircase from there. That seems to be where the fire is centered."

Emmeline nodded. "That should do the trick."

In no time at all, they were back in Xavier's study. Sir Randolph and Algernon had left the main door wide open, and a thick pall of smoke had enveloped everything. Although perhaps the roar of the fire was the most awful part—the crackle and spit of hungry flames and the distressing sound of random crashes and shatters sent icy chills racing down Emmeline's spine.

Coughing and gasping, she covered her nose and mouth with her pinafore as she dashed along the hallway with Xavier. The central staircase ahead now resembled a giant furnace. Heat blasted her cheeks, and she could barely see a thing beyond the roiling miasma of smoke. Well, nothing except for a fierce orange glow.

She needed to be quick before she and Xavier were both suffocated or worse...

Holding out her hand toward the raging, ravening blaze like she was about to feed it, Emmeline uncurled her fingers to reveal the magical dust in her palm. "*Decalamitify* fire," she whispered on a barely there breath, then blew.

The silvery dust immediately took flight, sparkling and twinkling and billowing upwards and outwards until it melded with the existing plumes of thick smoke. In a matter of moments, the whole interior of the townhouse was engulfed by swirling clouds of brilliant starlight. Indeed, Emmeline was completely dazzled. It felt like tiny glittering sequins had been thrown into her eyes.

When the shimmering brightness dissipated, the chandelier above the entry hall and wall sconces flickered back on, revealing that the fire had been completely extinguished. Everything was sparkling and gleaming and in perfect order. There wasn't even a wisp of smoke or a floating ember, or a trace of ash or soot.

It was as though the fire that had threatened to destroy St Lawrence House had never been lit.

"Well, skewer me with a toasting fork and call me a crumpet," murmured Xavier, his expression the epitome of awestruck as he wandered over to the railing and his gaze swept over the staircase and hall below. "It worked. Your dust worked!" He strode back to Emmeline and enveloped her in a huge hug. "I'll never be able to thank you enough."

Satisfaction and happiness hummed through Emmeline. "No thanks are required. Your smile is all I need. Now"—she withdrew her leyport key—"while we *could* walk out the front door, or even one of the servants' entrances, I rather think we should teleport into Belgrave Square as we'd planned. My instincts tell me that Algie and Sir Bottom might still be lurking about, waiting to make sure we've met a fiery end. No doubt there's considerable consternation and confusion now the fire has gone out. We might be able to take the pair by surprise and apprehend them."

"I would like nothing more," returned Xavier with a lopsided grin that had more than a dash of devil-may-care roguishness about it. Then his smile turned teasing. "Just promise me that we won't end up on the roof."

Emmeline grimaced. "I suppose now is *not* the time to tell you that I once ended up in the Thames."

"Oh, good Lord," muttered Xavier. "You know I can't stand the feel of wet clothing." Nevertheless, he kept pace with Emmeline as they sped back along the second-floor hallway hand in hand. She needed a door to open up a leyline portal and she had the perfect room in mind—the nearby library.

Once she'd tumbled the library door's lock with the leyport key, she quickly detected the glimmer of the leylight in the fireplace; it beckoned her into the darkened room like an old friend.

"Are you ready?" she asked Xavier, wrapping him in a tight embrace.

Even though his face was veiled by shadow, she heard the smile in his voice. "As I'll ever be. I trust you completely, my love."

Emmeline's heart squeezed with fierce joy. Then she drew a

fortifying breath and focused her entire attention on the leylight.

"*Vortexio*," she whispered while she created a vivid picture of the park in the center of Belgrave Square in her mind. Before she even had time to blink, there was an enormous breath-stealing whoosh of wind and a swirling flash of blinding white light and then in the next instant, she and Xavier were both outside in the cool night air.

A great wave of relief washed over Emmeline. They weren't in the Thames or on the roof of St Lawrence House. She and Xavier were safe and whole and in each other's arms and standing on the very edge of Belgrave Square beneath the branches of the cherry trees.

It seemed a London pea-souper had rolled in. Even so, Emmeline could see that the fire brigade had arrived, and a sizable crowd had gathered in the square—no doubt to watch the spectacle of St Lawrence House burning. As she'd predicted, there seemed to be quite a lot of head-scratching and a general air of bamboozlement now that the fire had apparently been extinguished. She quickly whispered to Xavier that they should put out a story suggesting that all the chimneys had simply been blocked, and the house had filled with smoke, so there really hadn't been a fire. Or something like that. She'd worry about the finer details when the time came to speak with Mrs. Temple about what had transpired.

As Emmeline scanned the silhouettes milling about in the fog, she detected Woodley and Babcock and Mrs. Lambton and Mrs. Punchbowl in their night things. A knot of maids and footmen too. Even the resident bobby, Constable Thurstwhistle, was "sticky-beaking," as Horatio would say.

At that moment, the raven lit on the park fence near his master. He gave a soft caw then spoke directly to Emmeline. *I say, Nanny Chase, I was beginning to worry that you'd both perished in the fire.*

It was a close call, admitted Emmeline. *Have you by any chance seen Lord Nevergrin's son, Algernon, hanging about?*

Why, yes, I have, replied the raven. *The berk is just over there, at the back of the crowd. And he's with another smarmy-looking fellow. The one who insulted you in Hyde Park and His Grace called worm's meat.*

Emmeline's pulse leapt as she looked in the direction Horatio had indicated. Sure enough, only a few yards away, were two men in greatcoats. Or rather, a pair of despicable rodents in greatcoats.

Sir Randolph and Algernon Mason.

She tugged on Xavier's sleeve, but he'd already noticed the scoundrels. In the light from a nearby gas lamp, she could see that a muscle ticked in his lean cheek.

"I have an idea about how we can apprehend Sir Bottom and Algie without coming to blows," she murmured to Xavier. "We have the advantage because their backs are to us and they don't know we're here." She slid her hand into her pocket to retrieve her befuddling potion, but Xavier shook his head.

"A reasonable man would agree with you, my darling. But considering the heinous acts they've committed tonight, and over the course of Lord knows how many months, I'm feeling anything *but* reasonable." He drew her close and pressed a swift kiss to her temple. "Forgive me for behaving like a troglodyte. I rather think blows are very much in order."

Then before Emmeline could draw breath to say she couldn't blame him for feeling that way, Xavier crossed the cobblestones and cracked Sir Randolph's and Algernon's heads together like a pair of conkers. Almost immediately, the two men crumpled to the cobblestones, but no one seemed to notice.

Xavier knelt on the ground, flipped open Sir Randolph's coat, and retrieved his stolen clock plans. "As soon as I've relieved these curs of their pistols, I'll summon Constable Thurstwhistle," he said as he thrust Sir Randolph's weapon into the back of his trousers. "I'd like these two locked up in the stone police box before they come to."

"A capital idea," said Emmeline before she added, "You know, I'm sure there's a paragraph in the *Parasol Academy Handbook* that mentions it's perfectly acceptable to behave like a troglodyte on certain occasions."

"You're joking," said Xavier. He retrieved Algernon's pistol, passed it to Emmeline, then got to his feet.

"Well, our Academy motto is, 'We're prim, proper, and prepared for anything,'" she said as she pocketed the gun. "So I rather think that last part covers any incidents requiring troglodytism. One must defend one's charges, and by extension, their guardian, by whatever means necessary."

Xavier grinned. "And you have done so ably. What would I do without you, Emmeline Chase?"

Emmeline stood on tiptoes and gave him a swift kiss. "With any luck, you'll never have to find out."

After Xavier summoned Constable Thurstwhistle and explained Sir Randolph and Algernon had been the scoundrels behind the attempted kidnapping of Master Gareth Mason, the somewhat groggy and pleasantly befuddled pair were locked up in the stone police box to await the arrival of Scotland Yard. (Emmeline couldn't resist using the befuddling potion to "revive" Randy and Algie to ensure they were compliant when being arrested.) Xavier then dismissed the fire brigade too.

"A false alarm, I'm afraid," he declared to the head fireman. He exchanged a speaking glance with Emmeline. "It was nothing but a lot of hot smoke. I must get my chimneys professionally cleaned."

Of course, the firemen all looked skeptical, and the staff of St Lawrence House all looked suspicious of their master's account of the "fire-that-never-was" too. But it was cold and foggy and everyone was weary and grateful that the whole ordeal was all over ... and quite obviously, one does not argue with a duke.

By the time everyone had drifted away, and Belgrave Square was empty except for Emmeline and Xavier, dawn was beginning to lighten the sky. Above the gray veil of fog, the clouds were streaked with pink and amethyst and soft lavender. Perhaps they even shimmered a little with a haze of silvery dust.

Xavier gathered Emmeline into his arms in front of St Lawrence House. His light blue eyes were as clear as the sea-glass Gareth had collected on the shore of Kingsgate Beach. "Shall we go inside, my darling duchess-to-be? I think we should snatch a few hours' rest before we head to Kent to collect Harry, Bartholomew, and Gareth. I can't wait to share our news that we are to be married."

"That sounds utterly perfect," murmured Emmeline. She was entirely exhausted, but her heart was brimming with so much love and elation, it didn't matter.

For once, everything was right with the world and she was certain that the future she'd share with Xavier and his darling wards would be brighter than the rising sun.

Chapter 32

Concerning the Nanny's Resignation; Jellification, Censure, Outrage, and Crusts; And the Unexpected Consequences of True Love . . .

"So, His Grace has confirmed the rumors are true. You *are* going to be the next Duchess of St Lawrence, Mrs. Chase." Mrs. Temple placed her copy of the *Parasol Academy Handbook* to one side of her desk in her Sloane Square office, then looked at Emmeline over the top of her blue-lensed ley-spectacles.

Emmeline swallowed nervously. It was difficult to tell what sort of mood the headmistress was in. Xavier had just spoken with her in private to indicate that Emmeline's services as a nanny would no longer be required because she was going to become his wife in a few days' time. And the fact he would need to hire a new Parasol Academy nanny in the not-too-distant future.

It had been less than a week since the mysterious "fire-that-never-was" incident at St Lawrence House and the sensational, if not outright shocking, arrest of Sir Randolph Redvers and Algernon Mason. Several other persons—a Mr. Walter West, a Mr. Ollie Dixon, and a Miss Fanny Sparrow—had also been charged with aiding and abetting the kidnapping of the duke's ward, young Master Gareth Mason. The newspapers had been filled with various (and for the most part, altogether inaccurate) accounts.

The social columns had also been abuzz with the even more scandalous story of the Duke of St Lawrence's engagement—that he intended to wed his wards' Parasol Academy nanny, a widowed nobody from Cheapside.

It was outrageous! It was unheard of! Were the shades of the "upper crust" to be thus polluted?

So, as Emmeline stood before Mrs. Temple's desk, knees jellified and quivering, she attempted to read the headmistress's expression. Was she upset with Emmeline? Indifferent? What would Queen Victoria say to Mrs. Temple about a Parasol nanny joining the ranks of the nobility, if anything? And what had Mrs. Temple to say about the mysterious St Lawrence House fire? But the headmistress's silvery-gray gaze was inscrutable.

Emmeline could at least respond to Mrs. Temple's simple enough remark instead of staring at her like a ninny-poop. "Yes. I am going to marry the duke," she said. "We are . . . we are very much in love. And because of that, I'm here to resign as a Parasol Academy nanny. Here . . . here is my license." She reached into her new reticule (it matched her brand-new sky-blue silk-taffeta day gown perfectly), retrieved the gilt-edged card that proclaimed she was an accredited Parasol Academy graduate, then pushed it across the desk with a gloved fingertip.

Mrs. Temple took the license and slipped it into one of her desk's drawers. Then she folded her small yet elegant hands on top of her desk's blotter. "Before I offer you my heartfelt congratulations on your engagement, I do need to clear up a few matters with you. They're related to your—shall we say?—application of the Academy's rules while working for the Duke of St Lawrence."

Emmeline knew this "talk" had been coming. It had been inevitable that she would receive some sort of censure for bending (and outright breaking) the rules. While she'd already surrendered her license, she was not looking forward to any sort of reprimand. It was sure to sting. Nevertheless, she bowed her head and said, "I understand."

Mrs. Temple removed her ley-spectacles and placed them on top of the Academy handbook beside her silver looking-glass. Her clear gray eyes met Emmeline's. "First of all, it goes without saying that you've served the duke's wards, and the duke himself, most admirably. Scotland Yard has recently apprised me of the situation, and from what I understand, you vanquished the duke's enemies and helped bring them to justice."

"Thank you, but I cannot take all the credit," said Emmeline. "His Grace was also involved in the apprehension of the men who orchestrated the kidnapping of his ward." *So far, so good...*

Mrs. Temple nodded, but then her expression changed, her mouth flattening into a disapproving line. "But..."

Emmeline winced inwardly. Why was there always a "but"? Here came the dressing-down part. Although, if she admitted her failings *first*, it might not be quite so bad.

"*But* you need to address my creative interpretation and fast and loose application of the Academy's rules?" she said. "In my defense, I *did* try very hard to use magic judiciously and discreetly. For instance, in the case of the mysteriously extinguished house fire, there *was* actually a fire. A terrible one. It wasn't merely a case of blocked chimneys as the papers reported."

Mrs. Temple arched a fine blond brow. "I suspected as much. Would you care to elaborate?"

I may as well be hanged for a sheep as a lamb, thought Emmeline, and forged on ahead. "While the duke's wards weren't in London at the time Sir Randolph and Mr. Mason set the fire," she continued, "the blaze *would* have destroyed St Lawrence House entirely if I hadn't used decalamitifying dust. And it *is* the children's primary residence. Many of their belongings—their clothes and toys and books and treasured reminders of their parents, like photographs and letters and other special keepsakes—are there. And an abundance of happy memories. They are already orphans, and it would have been tragic if they'd returned home to a pile of burned timbers and crumbled brickwork and ashes. Not only that, but the duke has created a marvelous clock room containing countless horological treasures of historical significance. It didn't seem right or fair to let the fire rage out of control. Not when I could try to put a stop to it. It was very much a calamity."

Mrs. Temple tapped a finger on the blotter. "I see. And is there anything else you wish to tell me?"

Emmeline blew out a resigned sigh. "Well, the duke was present when I cast the *Decalamitifying* spell. And then I teleported him into Belgrave Square after the fire had been dealt with in order to catch the culprits who'd set the fire and orchestrated young Gareth Mason's kidnapping. Out of necessity, I also made use of the befuddling potion in His Grace's presence." Of course, she'd also used the *Cloakify* and *Unsmirchify* spells in front of the duke on various occasions. But owning up to every indiscretion would not further her cause now.

Instead she said, "I swear the duke can be trusted *not* to divulge any of the Academy's secrets. He's one of the kindest and most honorable gentlemen that I've ever met. None of the unkind rumors about him are true. He's not mad or difficult at all."

"Thank you for your honesty, Mrs. Chase," said Mrs. Temple gravely. "And I agree, the Duke of St Lawrence seems like a wonderful man and no doubt he'll make a wonderful husband. However"—she paused as she leveled her solemn gaze at Emmeline—"you've put me and the Academy in a very difficult position. One which I'd never thought I would encounter."

She drummed her fingers on her purple-leather blotter for a

moment, then continued. "By openly employing Fae magic in front of the duke, by raising the public's curiosity about the strange nature of the St Lawrence House fire, you *did* break one of our most important rules, and in doing so, endangered the Academy and our Fae Charter. You know as well as I that the Fae will end our association if their existence is ever exposed to the general public. And if we lose the ability to perform magic, the children in our care will be less protected. Indeed, there is the potential that *all* children will be placed in a degree of jeopardy if Queen Maeve's evil sister, Mab, seeks to take advantage of such a situation. The rate of kidnappings has been very low to nonexistent for many, many years now. Ninety years to be exact. Ever since the Parasol Academy's inception. I would hate for that to change. As I'm sure you would too."

Emmeline swallowed as a sharp sliver of guilt penetrated her chest. "I . . . I would hate for that to happen too. Of course I would. But the fire was so huge, it really was turning into a life-and-death situation. If I hadn't asked the Fae for the decalamitifying dust—which they *did* bestow—if I'd let the fire run its course, both the duke and I might have perished. If I *hadn't* made these choices, Harriet, Bartholomew, and Gareth Mason might have lost their guardian. They'd have no family left at all. And if faced with the same situation again"—she lifted her chin even though her insides trembled—"I wouldn't have acted differently. I broke the Academy's rules and I took risks, yes, but I believed then, just as I believe now, that using my magic in front of the duke was the right thing—indeed the only reasonable thing—to do."

Mrs. Temple regarded her for a long moment, as though weighing Emmeline's words. "You make very good points, Mrs. Chase," she said at last, her expression stern. "And I *will* take into account that the Fae gifted you the decalamitifying dust when you asked for it. They wouldn't have done so if it wasn't deemed a worthy cause. That being said, it is a complex situation. So complex in fact, and so unique, that before our interview—after I'd spoken with your duke and he admitted he knew about your magical abilities—I communicated with the Fae Realm." Her fingers lightly touched the edge of her silver and crystal mirror, and for a moment, the glass shimmered brightly as though a moonbeam had glanced across it. "I spoke with Queen Maeve to be exact, to ask for guidance. In particular, should there be any other sort of consequence for your actions, beyond surrendering your Parasol Academy license."

"And . . . ?" Emmeline whispered as apprehension slid over her, making her chest tighten. She had no idea what those consequences might be. She'd never come across anything in the *Parasol Academy Handbook* that talked about such things.

Would she be fined in some way? Paraded in front of her former Academy peers and presented as an example of how not to behave? Would her name be engraved on a plaque in the Academy proclaiming her to be the very-worst-Parasol-Academy-nanny-who-ever-existed? Or what if . . . what if she were whisked away to the Fae Realm and incarcerated, never to see Xavier and darling Harry, Bartholomew, Gareth, or her own father and brother, ever again? Or worse, cursed in some way?

Oh God! What if she ended up with a donkey's head like Bottom from *A Midsummer Night's Dream?*

As Emmeline's mind began to careen down all sorts of panic-paved paths, Mrs. Temple spoke and put her out of her misery. "It seems the Fae, and indeed Good Queen Maeve, *have* decided to be gracious on this occasion. So . . ."

Emmeline clasped her hands to her chest, as hope sparked. "Yes, Mrs. Temple?"

The headmistress's expression, although still grave, was far kinder. "Because there were extenuating circumstances, combined with the fact that the duke has sworn upon his honor that he will never reveal our secrets, surrendering your license, which is the usual consequence, is sufficient. No other action of a censuring nature will be taken."

Emmeline almost sagged to the floor as relief washed over her. "Thank you, Mrs. Temple," she whispered. "And please convey my heartfelt thanks to the Fae and Her Highness Queen Maeve for their understanding and consideration."

"I will," she said with a regal incline of her head. "Now, with regards to the matter of fraternization..."

Emmeline felt the blood rush from her cheeks. *Oh no.* She *wasn't* out of the woods? "You-You warned me about your concerns in regard to the duke before I was sent to Kent, I know," she stammered. "And I tried so very hard to stifle my feelings. I really did, but I fell in love and so did the duke—"

Mrs. Temple put up her hand. "I haven't quite finished, Mrs. Chase," she said. The bright smile that suddenly curved her mouth was so unexpected, a feather could have knocked Emmeline over. "What I was *about* to say is that, there *is* actually an exception to the 'no fraternization' policy in the *Handbook*."

"There is?"

"Yes. It's the *True Love Clause*." Mrs. Temple put her ley-spectacles back on, then opened the *Parasol Academy Handbook* and flipped to a page toward the end. She scanned the text, pointed to a spot halfway down the page, then pushed the book toward Emmeline along with a spare ley-lens quizzing glass. "You see, it's written right here. In Chapter 26, Paragraph 30, Section 7. It says..."

Emmeline picked up the quizzing glass then read aloud, "*If True Love blooms between a Parasol Academy nanny or governess and her employer, any and all rules forbidding fraternization are forthwith null and void. Because True Love is rare and magical and should never be impeded or condemned. By the order of Good Queen Maeve.*"

She raised her wondering gaze to Mrs. Temple. "How is it that I've never seen this rule before?"

The headmistress smiled. "I don't make the rules, my dear Mrs. Chase. *The Parasol Academy Handbook*, which was created by Good Queen Maeve, does. And sometimes, certain sections, as well as spells, do not become apparent until they become relevant for a particular graduate. Think of it as a 'bespoke' handbook. But you haven't finished reading that section. There's an additional sub-clause."

Emmeline returned her attention to the book. "*Any Parasol Academy nanny or governess who resigns from her commission because of True Love must surrender her license.* However, *she does not necessarily need to give up all Fae magical tools that support the care of children, if she has gone above and beyond in the line of duty. The Headmistress of the Parasol Academy may choose to gift said nanny or governess a spool of Fae thread so that she may sew her own magical pockets for her gowns. While magical items such as leyport keys or befuddling potions or leylenses or decalamitifying dust will no longer be available, regular items such as sweets and plasters and marbles and cough medicine will always be in ready supply when required.*"

When Emmeline looked up, Mrs. Temple was still smiling at her.

"My dear Mrs. Chase, despite the fact you bent, and on occasion broke, the Parasol Academy's strict rules, I do believe you *have* gone above and beyond while serving as one of our nannies. And as a result"—the headmistress withdrew an ornate silver box from another drawer in her desk—"I would very much like to give you this so that you might continue to weave metaphorical magic into the lives of children." She inclined her head. "Discreetly, of course."

With trembling fingers, Emmeline picked up the silver box and opened the lid. And her breath caught. Inside lay a spool of fine silver thread that sparkled and twinkled like it was made of starlight. "I . . . I don't know what to say," she said, raising her eyes to meet Mrs. Temple's, "except thank you. From the bottom of my heart."

Mrs. Temple's smile was as warm as a summer's day as she

rose and rounded her desk. "You're very welcome, Mrs. Chase." And then to Emmeline's surprise, the headmistress embraced her. "I wish you and your duke well," she said as she drew back. "And if you should happen to invite me to your wedding"—she squeezed Emmeline's hands—"I would be more than a little thrilled."

"His Grace and I would both love to have you there," said Emmeline with a heartfelt smile. "We're planning on a small ceremony at St Paul's in Knightsbridge followed by a wedding breakfast at St Lawrence House. We're then going to honeymoon at Kingscliff Castle in Kent."

And then she recalled what Mrs. Temple had told her before she'd attended her interview with the Duke of St Lawrence: *I know you will be brilliant and simply perfect for this position.*

Had the Parasol Academy headmistress known how this would all turn out, even then?

Surely not.

But as Emmeline took her leave, she was convinced more than ever that Mrs. Felicity Temple actually *did* have a little Fae blood running through her veins. It wasn't beyond the realm of possibility. At least not the Fae Realm . . .

Xavier's town coach was waiting in Sloane Square for Emmeline when she emerged from the Academy into the bright spring day. A catcall and a saucy wink from Horatio, who sat upon the top of the carriage, had her smiling.

Are you coming to our picnic in Greenwich Park? she asked her avian friend. *The children would love to see you there.* She was so relieved she could still converse with the loquacious raven, that even though she was no longer a Parasol nanny, her animal whispering abilities were still intact.

Of course, the raven returned, flapping his enormous wings before taking off and soaring over the roofs and spires of London. *I'll see you there . . .*

Emmeline's smile widened when her gaze fell upon Xavier,

who'd just stepped from the coach. How handsome he looked in his superbly cut black frock coat, azure silk vest, and matching paisley necktie. Beneath his top hat, his hair was artfully tousled, several black locks tumbling rakishly over his brow. In his gloved hands he held his silver-topped cane and his eyes wore an expression of frank admiration as his gaze traveled over Emmeline.

At moments like this, Emmeline was tempted to pinch the soft flesh on the underside of her wrist in order to remind herself that she wasn't dreaming and she really *was* going to wed this beautiful, generous, exceptional man.

When she reached Xavier's side, he kissed her cheek. "How did it all go, my love?" he asked as he handed her into his coach.

Emmeline beamed as he climbed in to sit beside her on the velvet upholstered seat. "It went well, I think." Perhaps that was a bit of an overstatement, so she added with a small laugh, "Well, better than I expected. Considering all the rules I've broken, I'm counting it as a blessing that the Fae haven't cursed me with a donkey's head."

Xavier's eyebrows shot up. "Good God, I should bloody well hope not," he said. "But, you can tell me all about it on our way to Greenwich." Once the door was closed, he knocked on the carriage roof with his cane to indicate the driver should move off. On the seat opposite them lay a leather portfolio which contained his finalized plans for the Westminster Palace clock. Today was the day he would submit them to the Astronomer Royal.

Emmeline was nothing but thrilled for him and she told him so.

"I couldn't have done it without you, my darling," he said in a low voice. He reached for her hand and laced their fingers together. "I made that plain to Mrs. Temple too. In fact, during our chat, I gained the impression that she isn't quite the stickler you feared her to be. I truly think she does understand the exceptional and challenging circumstances you were thrust into."

"You're right. Mrs. Temple was more than understanding." And then Emmeline filled her fiancé in on all the details of her interview with the Academy's headmistress, including the unexpected gift she'd been given for going "above and beyond."

"That's simply wonderful," said Xavier. "Although, it's a pity you don't have a magical pocket in this particular gown." He ran a finger along the line of pearl buttons securing the front of her bodice. "Because I rather think you might need to use your *Unsmirchify* spell at some point this afternoon."

Emmeline knew exactly what Xavier meant, but she couldn't resist teasing him. "Whatever do you mean, Your Grace?" she said with exaggerated innocence. "I know Harry, Bartholomew, and Gareth are joining us for our picnic after your meeting with George Airy, but surely they aren't that messy anymore. Besides, I'm certain Mrs. Punchbowl won't pack any ginger beer."

Xavier's eyelids lowered to half-mast as he pulled off his gloves and tossed them on the opposite seat. This was followed by his topper. "You know exactly what I mean, my darling Emmeline," he said as he gathered her close, then pulled her across his lap. His bare fingers flirted with the lace collar of her gown. "The traffic is horrendous, so I rather think it's going to take us well over an hour to get to the Royal Observatory."

"It will?" Emmeline slid her hands around Xavier's neck and looked up at him through her eyelashes. "Goodness. Whatever shall we do to pass the time?"

Xavier removed her new bonnet—a lovely short-brimmed affair lavishly trimmed with lace and feathers and gentian-blue violets—and it landed beside his top hat. "I can think of a few things," he murmured huskily. Then he cradled Emmeline's cheek within the palm of his large hand. "I adore you, do you know that? Even if I'd lost my clock design and my entire horological collection and even St Lawrence House, I'd still have this." His mouth curved in a beautiful smile. "Time spent with you is more precious than anything else in the world."

As Emmeline smiled into her husband-to-be's warm and clear blue eyes, her heart swelled with infinite joy. How mistaken she'd been to ever think of them as cold. "When I'm with you," she whispered, "all I can see is forever. I love you."

"I love you too, Emmeline. Always." And then Xavier slanted his mouth over hers and neither of them cared what the time was for quite a while.

Epilogue

Concerning Seagull Tag, Rockpool Feasts, Ice Cream Cake and Puff Balloons, Family Affairs, and Things of Boundless Blue...

Kingsgate Beach
Summer 1851

Emmeline laughed as she watched Bartholomew and Horatio chasing seagulls along the shoreline of Kingsgate Beach.

Xavier, who was strolling beside her with Gareth on his shoulders, called, "Watch out, you'll get wet," as the boy, light brown hair flying in the light sea breeze, pelted past his sister, straight into the path of an approaching foam-laced wave.

Too late... Bartholomew squealed as the water—icy-cold even in late August—splashed his bare feet and ankles, soaking the bottoms of his rolled-up trouser legs to the knees. Harry, who'd been a few yards ahead of them all, studying the horizon through a pair of field glasses, turned back and rolled her eyes in apparent disgust at her boisterous brother.

Grinning impishly and clearly unrepentant, Bartholomew raced back toward his younger brother, Xavier, and Emmeline. "I love the seaside," he cried, seizing Emmeline's hand. "I wish we could live here all the time."

I second that, remarked Horatio as he swooped past Emmeline. *There's nothing like fresh sea air and playing tag with seagulls! Oh, and how could I forget rock-pool feasts of sea snails and minnows and crabs? Delish!*

"Can we, Cousin Xavier?" asked Gareth, leaning down to hug his guardian about the neck. "I love the seaside too."

Xavier gave a light chuckle. "As it's your sixth birthday today, Gareth, I'll promise you this: I'll do my level best to make sure we visit Kingscliff Castle and the beach as much as possible. At least for six months every year."

"Huzzah!" crowed Gareth.

It was, indeed, young Gareth's birthday and Xavier had proposed that they all take a late morning stroll together as a family along the beach. Emmeline and the children had all readily agreed. Their destination—a small private cove that was part of the Kingscliff estate—lay hidden beyond the rocky point below the castle.

Bartholomew wrinkled his nose—now lightly freckled from spending so many hours in the summer sun—as he looked up at Xavier. "I suppose half of the year will do."

"I should think so," returned Emmeline, squeezing the boy's hand. "Besides, we wouldn't want to miss out on all the exciting things happening back in London. Remember, we're going to see *Jack and the Beanstalk* at your Uncle Freddy's theater, the Oberon, next month."

After Freddy had sold the Markwick pocket watch for a tidy sum at Christie's, he'd cleared all his outstanding debt and, with the help of their father (whose health was much restored), had been busily refurbishing the music hall to its former glory. It warmed Emmeline's heart to see her brother and father reconciled and so content with life. Without Xavier's generous intervention, she was certain the Oberon would have closed. Instead, the business was turning into a raging success. Indeed, Freddy had mentioned in his last letter that it was packed to the gunwales every single night. He was even thinking of introducing a matinee session on Saturdays.

Harry, who'd joined them, agreed with Emmeline. "And we don't want to miss out on seeing Cousin Xavier's grand clock being built at Westminster Palace."

"Exactly," said Emmeline, smiling up at her handsome, clever husband, who grinned back at her. "It's going to be glorious."

The official announcement that Xavier Mason, the Duke of St Lawrence, was the designer who'd been awarded the commission for the St Stephen's "King of Clocks" had been made just one month after the contest had closed. Apart from their wedding day, it had been one of the happiest days of Emmeline's life. To witness her wonderful husband receiving word from the Astronomer Royal that he'd at last achieved his long-fought-for goal—to see Xavier's whole face light up and tears of joy brim in his eyes as he'd read George Airy's missive—was a memory she would treasure forever.

Xavier deserved every accolade and honor that came his way. In time, she hoped that the horrid rumors questioning his soundness of mind would fade away, and instead he would only be revered for his brilliance.

Of course, there had been a good deal of scandal generated by the criminal trials of Sir Randolph Redvers and Algernon Mason. The two men, having been found guilty of masterminding the attempted kidnapping of the Duke of St Lawrence's ward, were currently incarcerated in Newgate Prison. West—the hired thug who'd done Sir Randolph's and Algernon's wicked bidding that day in Hyde Park—was also serving time in Newgate, along with Xavier's disloyal footman, Ollie, and the disgraced nurserymaid, Fanny. It was Fanny's betrayal that stung the most. Emmeline had liked and trusted the young woman, and the children had been fond of her too. But what she'd done—joining in the contemptible plot to disrupt her employer's life by participating in Gareth's abduction—was beyond the pale. She'd been served her just deserts, just like her other despicable counterparts, and Emmeline couldn't say she didn't deserve them.

When their small party of five arrived at the end of the beach, Xavier lowered Gareth to the sand so they could pick their way along a narrow, rocky path that skirted the base of the white-chalk cliff. Above them towered Kingscliff Castle.

Emmeline had to raise the hem of her periwinkle-blue skirts, lest she trip. "What on earth have you planned for Gareth's birthday?" she whispered to Xavier as he held out a gloved hand to help her over a particularly uneven section of ground. "It must be some sort of spectacular surprise for you to go to all this trouble."

"You'll soon see," returned her husband with a mysterious smile. "And yes, it is spectacular."

Not as spectacular as you, thought Emmeline. The light breeze was pushing Xavier's unruly black locks away from his lightly tanned face, and Emmeline had never seen him look so handsome or carefree. How she loved him and their little family. She couldn't wait to share her own surprise with him too.

They made good time—their progress around the point was only slightly hampered by one stubbed toe (Bartholomew's, which Emmeline tended to with ointment and plaster procured from her gown's magical Fae pocket)—and within the space of ten minutes, they'd reached the halfway mark. Indeed, it was Gareth's squeal of delight that heralded the fact that one could see around the chalk cliff face into the neighboring cove.

"A puff balloon?" the boy cried, pointing at the enormous rainbow-hued hot-air balloon waiting for them on the sand. The balloonist and his pair of attendants waved at them all across the sand. "Cousin Xavier, are we really going on a puff balloon ride for my birthday?"

"It's a *hot-air* balloon, you ninny-poop," said Harry, but she was grinning from ear to ear.

"Why yes, we are," returned Xavier, smiling broadly at Gareth. "And when we return, we'll have a picnic lunch and an ice cream cake."

"Hooray!" cheered Bartholomew, sore toe forgotten as he led the way through the tumble of rocks toward the beach. Horatio, who'd been following them, was already perched upon a precipice on the very edge of the cove.

"My goodness," breathed Emmeline. "I'm . . . I'm speechless."

"I trust in a good way," murmured Xavier, smiling down at her.

"Oh yes," she returned warmly. Then she bit her lip as the secret she was simply bursting to reveal fizzed like champagne bubbles on the tip of her tongue. Was now the time to share it with Xavier, here, on the edge of the dazzling blue sea in the bright summer sunshine?

She glanced toward the children to check on them before turning back to her husband. "Actually, I've been waiting for the right moment to tell you about a surprise of my own," she murmured huskily as her vision misted.

Xavier's black brows inched into a slight frown. "A good one too, I hope."

Oh no, he'd mistaken the reason for her tears. "I like to think so," said Emmeline, wanting to reassure him. She took one of Xavier's large hands and placed it against the skirts hiding her belly.

Xavier's brow dipped even further as his gaze followed their hands. "Whatever do you mean?"

"I mean, my darling husband," said Emmeline softly, "that I think I might be with child."

"Good God!" cried Xavier, his eyebrows shooting up toward his hairline as his eyes met hers. "Really?"

"Really," whispered Emmeline. "I'm late. By two months."

Xavier released a wild whoop as he picked her up and swung

her around on the path. Then he seized her mouth in a fervent kiss that had Emmeline's head spinning with joy. "I can't believe it," he declared exultantly when they at last drew apart, both breathless and giddy and smiling like ninnies. "I never dreamed I'd be a father at all, let alone four times over. I'm gobsmacked, Emmeline, my love. And overwhelmed and overjoyed and—" His expression changed and something like concern shadowed his eyes. "Are you well? Are-Are you sure you're up to this balloon ride? I would understand completely if you weren't."

Emmeline laughed. "Of course, I am. Here"—she gave his shoulder a playful poke—"don't go turning into an anxious mother hen on me. I'm as well as well can be."

Xavier gave a huff of laughter. "Mother hen? I feel more like a proudly strutting cock right at this moment."

"You look like one too, what with your chest all puffed out," teased Emmeline. As Xavier took her arm and they continued to make their way toward the sand, she added, "You know, our lives will be even more chaotic from now on."

Xavier cast her a wide grin. "In only the best possible way. In fact, I've come to embrace the chaos."

Emmeline leaned her head against his shoulder and squeezed his arm. "I think we'll probably need to ask Mrs. Temple to recommend a nanny, or even a governess, after all." As they'd decided to sojourn in Kent for an extended summer holiday, they'd delayed employing someone else from the Parasol Academy to help look after the children.

Xavier nodded. "Agreed. We will make it so when we return to London."

When they reached the children, who were clustered about the wicker basket of the hot-air balloon—Harry was busily interrogating the balloonist about how the balloon inflated and what was its average velocity—Gareth rushed over to Xavier and threw his arms around his middle. "I love you so much, Cousin Xavier." When the boy tipped his head back and stared up at his guardian, he added, "Because it's my birthday, can I call you Papa? And Cousin Emmeline, Mama?"

Emmeline's heart swelled. Since she'd wed Xavier, and she was no longer officially a nanny but a duchess, the children had decided to call her Cousin Emmeline. She'd never expected any of them to call her "mama," but in her heart of hearts, she'd rather hoped that they might one day.

And it seemed that day was today. Xavier's throat bobbed in a swallow as he caught Emmeline's gaze. "Of course you can, Gareth," he said thickly, ruffling the boy's hair. "You can call me 'Papa' every day."

"I, too, would be honored, if you called me 'Mama,'" said Emmeline, her voice catching with emotion as well.

"Can we . . . can we call you 'Papa' and 'Mama,' too?" asked Harry, almost shyly. She and Bartholomew had wandered closer and had clearly overheard the whole exchange. "We"— she nodded at her brothers—"have been talking about it for a while now, but we didn't quite know how to ask."

Xavier's smile lit his whole face. "I would love that," he said to Harry. As his gaze met Emmeline's—his eyes, like hers, shining with happy tears—he added, "It seems we're officially a family now, in every sense that matters."

"Indeed," murmured Emmeline, kneeling down to gather both Harry and Bartholomew into her arms for a hug. "Indeed."

A short time later, after they'd all bundled into the hot-air balloon's basket, and the attendants had let loose the moorings tethering the balloon to the beach, Xavier drew Emmeline into the circle of his arms, her back to his front. In the distance, Horatio swooped and soared, riding the warm air currents before circling back to follow them.

"Do you know how much I love you and our family?" Xavier murmured against her ear as they rose into the cloudless summer sky.

Emmeline sank into him, drinking in his warmth and adoration, just as she drank in the sunshine, and the brilliant view of the English Channel, stretching out before them like a rippling length of royal-blue satin scattered with diamonds of dancing light. "If it's as much as I love you and our children and our baby-on-the-way"—threading her fingers through Xavier's, she drew one of his hands down to her middle—"then it's boundless."

When Xavier tipped her face up and pressed a lingering kiss to her mouth, Emmeline heard a disgruntled groan.

"Ugh, they're kissing again," grumbled Bartholomew.

"Oh, leave them alone." That was Harry. "It's what husbands and wives who love each other do."

"Yes, it means our mama and papa are happy," added Gareth. "Look at the view instead."

A wolf-whistle from Horatio had Emmeline laughing. As mirth bubbled up inside her, she reluctantly pulled away from Xavier and looked up into his handsome face. His light blue eyes, glowing with happiness and love, clearly proclaimed everything he felt for her without words.

She might not be able to teleport or perform spells like she used to when she was a Parasol nanny, but Emmeline would own that she'd never been more content, and that her life had never felt more magical.

Yes, life was full of endless joy and bright promise. For all of them.

Afterword

Dearest Reader,

Throughout *The Nanny's Handbook to Magic and Managing Difficult Dukes,* Xavier Mason, the Duke of St Lawrence, is frequently, and unfairly, labeled by Victorian-era society as "mad" and other equally unkind and inaccurate terms when, in fact, by modern day standards, it is clear he is neurodivergent or on the autism spectrum. Xavier, particularly at the start of the book, even regards himself as "difficult." As the story progresses, I hope it's clear that his self-perception has been negatively impacted by his upbringing and experiences throughout his schooling and participation in society in general, and that he really isn't "difficult" or "mad" at all.

In writing *The Nanny's Handbook to Magic and Managing Difficult Dukes,* I endeavored to create a cinnamon-roll of a neurodivergent hero who is accepted and loved for who he is, because, like everyone, Xavier deserves the very best that life has to offer. Young Harriet (Harry) Mason, Xavier's ward, is also on the autism spectrum.

So, why have I chosen to write about neurodivergent characters, you might ask? In my own life, I have beloved close family members who are neurodiverse, i.e., on the autism spectrum or have ADHD (attention deficit hyperactivity disorder). During my twenty-year-plus speech pathology career, I also worked extensively with neurodiverse clients and their families. I hope my experiences, both personal and professional, have resulted in a sensitive portrayal of autistic characters on the page, whom everyone will love just as much as I do.

Author's Note

In writing *The Nanny's Handbook to Magic and Managing Difficult Dukes*, I just wanted to touch upon a few points of interest.

The St Stephen's Tower clock design contest that my book's horologist hero, Xavier, the Duke of St Lawrence, enters and aspires to win, was, in actual fact, a real competition... although, of course, in the telling of my "alternate history fantasy" story, I have employed some artistic license. History tells us that the contest was announced in 1846 and George Airy, the Astronomer Royal was the referee. However, the winning design wasn't selected until February 1852, the year after my story takes place, and the real clock that stands today at the New Palace of Westminster—known affectionately as Big Ben—was actually designed by Edmund Beckett Denison. I hope readers are happy to indulge my flights of fancy in the telling of this tale.

I will also admit to playing a bit fast and loose with a few other bits of history to make *The Nanny's Handbook to Magic and Managing Difficult Dukes* come to life. The Royal Horological Society that Xavier is a member of is my own invention. So are Kingscliff Castle and Kingsgate in Kent where Xavier hails from. While the Great Exhibition—housed in the Crystal Palace in Hyde Park—did indeed open on May 1, 1851, the "Dinosaur Court" wasn't located there at the time. The dinosaur sculptures were commissioned in 1852 and weren't unveiled until 1854 at the Crystal Palace Park in Sydenham in South London. But the whole idea of dinosaur sculptures was irresistible to me, and I had to write them into my story. Likewise, while stone "Watchman" sentry boxes did exist in Britain at the time my story is set, they weren't all that common. Metropolitan Police boxes only began appearing in London in the 1920s, but I couldn't resist the idea of my exceptional nannies and governesses being able to make use of a "police box" when te-ley-porting in the line of duty.

I will freely admit to deliberately using anachronistic words and phrases on the odd occasion ("gobsmacked," "stickybeak," "berk," and "bellend" spring to mind) simply for the amusement factor. *The Nanny's Handbook to Magic and Managing Difficult Dukes* is essentially an historical romance with light fantasy and comedic elements—my nanny heroine can teleport and telepathically talk to a raven—so I thought, why not? I hope readers will forgive me for choosing such words for laughs (or at the very least a smile or titter).

Last of all, "puff balloons"—scones fried in lard and slathered in golden syrup—were a treat my dearly departed mother-in-law used to make. Our Aussie family actually calls them "puff balloonies," but I believe they're related to puftaloons, an early Australian "bush kitchen" fried quick bread or scone.

Acknowledgments

Thank you to my beautiful, wonderful family for always being there for me, through thick and thin. You mean the world to me and I couldn't do this without you.

To my wonderful agent, Jessica Alvarez, for your brilliant insight and for being a steadfast champion of my ideas, I sincerely thank you.

To my fabulous editors... venturing into a new genre is both exciting and terrifying, so thank you for your wisdom and support during my journey into the realm of romantic fantasy. I'm loving every minute of it, and you are a huge part of that.

To all my readers, thank you for joining me on this ride. I'm eternally grateful to you all, because without you, I wouldn't be able to do what I do.

Visit our website at
KensingtonBooks.com
to sign up for our newsletters, read more from your favorite authors, see books by series, view reading group guides, and more!

BOOK CLUB
BETWEEN THE CHAPTERS

Become a Part of Our
Between the Chapters Book Club
Community and Join the Conversation

Betweenthechapters.net

Submit your book review for a chance to win exclusive Between the Chapters swag you can't get anywhere else!
https://www.kensingtonbooks.com/pages/review/